THE FOUR GUARDIANS

Volumne one

Rachel Harwood

self published

Copyright © 2023 Rachel Harwood

All rights reserved

The characters and events portrayed in this book are fictitious. Any similarity to real persons, living or dead, is coincidental and not intended by the author.

No part of this book may be reproduced, or stored in a retrieval system, or transmitted in any form or by any means, electronic, mechanical, photocopying, recording, or otherwise, without express written permission of the publisher.

ISBN-13: 9798387300301
ISBN-10: 1477123456

Cover design by: Art Painter
Library of Congress Control Number: 2018675309
Printed in the United States of America

*this book is dedicated to my mom and my son
who never stopped believing In me*

there are always two choices. two paths to take. one is easy and its only reward is that it is easy

GREAT EXPECTATIONS

CONTENTS

Title Page
Copyright
Dedication
Epigraph
The Four Guardians   1
Prologue   2
Chapter one   5
Chapter two   8
Chapter three   14
Chapter four   23
Chapter five   32
Chapter six   37
Chapter seven   47
Chapter eight   51
Chapter nine   57
Chapter ten   66
Chapter Eleven   68
Chapter Twelve   72
Chapter thirteen   76
Chapter Fourteen   82
Chapter fifteen   97

Chapter seventeen	103
Chapter eighteen	106
Chapter nineteen	110
Chapter twenty	118
Book two	122
Chapter two	127
Chapter three	131
Chapter four	133
Chapter five	138
Chapter six	144
Chapter seven	150
Chapter eight	156
Chapter nine	163
Chapter ten	170
Chapter eleven	178
Chapter twelve	183
Chapter thirteen	190
Chapter fourteen	193
Chapter fifteen	195
Chapter sixteen	199
Chapter seventeen	201
Chapter eighteen	206
Chapter twenty	213
Chapter twenty one	220
Chapter twenty two	223
Chapter twenty three	226
Chapter twenty three	228
Chapter twenty four	234

Book three	242
Chapter two	249
Chapter three	253
Chapter four	260
Chapter five	265
Chapter six	269
Chapter seven	273
Chapter eight	281
Chapter nine	288
Chapter ten	291
Chapter eleven	296
Chapter twelve	298
Chapter thirteen	304
Chapter fourteen	313
Chapter fifteen	317
Chapter sixteen	324
book four	327
Chapter two	330
Chapter three	334
Chapter four	339
Chapter five	343
Chapter seven	347
Chapter eight	353
Chapter nine	356
Chapter ten	360
About The Author	367

THE FOUR GUARDIANS

Volume one
The beginnings of the Guardians
By Rachel Harwood

PROLOGUE

In the beginning, and at an ending there was nothing, and then a light burst upon the emptiness. One universe had ended, and another was beginning. This cycle had been in existence since before time, and it would continue for forever.

The light hovered in the darkness and thought about the death of the last universe. It had been destroyed by an imbalance of good and evil. Evil had risen and destroyed the balance and thus the universe had ended. This was something that bothered the light. Was there a way to keep the balance in check, and thus preserve the lives of those who lived within her?

As she hovered in the nothingness, she thought long and hard about this problem, and her light pulsed. She sent out pieces of herself, and began to create stars and galaxies, and then planets could come into existence. And with the planets would come the gods and the races that would fill the planets with life.

All of this took time, and the light watched as her children began to grow beyond primitives and to found civilizations, following the edicts of the gods of their worlds. Some worlds developed quickly, and their societies flourished. But then the gods began to fight, and so their followers did the same.

She tried to stop this, but her power was so great that she would destroy the very worlds she was trying to save. But she knew that if this continued, she would die, and all life would die with her. She had to find a way to save her children, and herself.

Then a thought occurred to her. What if she could create

some beings that could keep the balance for her? What if she could put some of her power into these beings and use them to help her children?

As she watched the worlds, she found a being of great power, and put a thought into his head. He had been looking for a female to help in his greatest creation. The light influenced him and made him think of a planet. And she put some of her power into the being he had planted on this world.

With the success of this, the light began to reach out to certain of her children and influenced them. She began to gather followers, and to make her presence known to the gods and the mortals. She touched the lives of mortals and helped them to right the balance on their worlds.

As she gained more followers, she found that though they were obedient, they did not have any central priesthood, as other religions did. But she knew that it would be only a matter of time before she could organize them under the beings that she would create to act in her stead.

She watched over the one she had given her power to and contacted her when she was ready. Now, events were in motion, to create more of these beings who would carry a part of her inside them, so that they could help her find a way to keep the balance and not get destroyed like the others.

She told the first guardian of the others that she would create, to help maintain the balance. Each of these beings would be infused with one fourth of the universe's power, and since the universe was without limits, these four would be more powerful than anyone else.

The light would put into place rules that would be strictly adhered to, to prevent her chosen ones from abusing the power that they were given, and so they would not go to war with each other. War between the guardians would end everything.

The rules were thus,
1 obedience to Ultimate Mother was required above all else
2 put others before yourself.
3 restrict yourself when it comes to your power.

4 family is important.
5 do not start a war.
6 guide others and help those who need it.
7 help each other.
8 do not raise the dead.
9 mourn the loss of any life.
10 pray for the souls of those who die.

With these rules in place, she put the consequences of defying them as death, of body and soul, meaning if you broke the rules, you would be wiped out of existence, and no one would remember you. You would cease to be.

For the second being, she found a race of special unicorns and planted in one of them some of her power, in an infant. After some more time, she found another being and planted some of her power in that child, and finally she found a bloodline of great power and planted some of her power within that child as well. Now she had four beings that could help her.

These four beings would help keep the balance of light and dark, of good and evil, and they would be called the Four Guardians of the Universe. From these beings, more would come to help keep the balance, and help maintain the universe and all its different dimensions.

CHAPTER ONE

The room was dimly lit with red candles. A feast was laid on the table and the chairs numbered ten in all. The food was untouched, and plates of gold and jeweled cups full of wine sat upon the black wood of the table. The chairs were made of black metal, bent, and twisted into grotesque caricatures of faces, and twisted bodies, in an attitude of torture and fear.

Smells of food and smoke filled the air, with a hint of a flower. The flower smell was very faint now, though it had been strong a few moments ago. The smoke came from the candles, lending an air of mystery to the room. And in the background, screams could be heard, a cacophony of painfilled sounds that were always there.

Only one chair was occupied now. Kai sat in silence gazing at the black gemstone on the table in front of him. There had been others at the table, but they were gone. They had been conspiring against him. And they had paid the price for thinking him ignorant of their plans. Now he was the last of his kind. For he was a Mahceen, a mix between a god and a demon lord.

Such unions were forbidden for a reason. The offspring of such unions were stronger than both of their parents and could be unstable. That is why there were only ten. And now there was only one. He was the strongest of the Mahceen, the first of them. And now he was the last. A sneer touched his lips. The others had been fools to think that they could beat him, and now would spend an eternity knowing that he had won. They could now howl in the emptiness of the soul gem, for all time.

Kai was tall, with black hair, red eyes, and pale skin. He was well built, strong features, and an arrogant stance. His eyes were shaped as almonds, and his ears were pointed. His chin was firm, and his hands smooth. There was a golden metallic hint to his skin. He knew what he wanted and did not care if anyone got hurt, in the process. He was determined to rule many worlds and prove that he was the strongest.

The door behind Kai opened and Shadow entered. Shadow was a special type of dragon, and he served as Kai's chief servant. He made sure that the trivial things were taken care of, so that Kai could focus on the important things. Such as laying the trap that had ended the threat of the other Mahceen. Shadow was completely loyal to Kai, for good reason. Kai had saved Shadow, as some of the other Mahceen had tried to kill him.

Shadow was a lava dragon. He and his kind had to live close to lava that flowed out of the ground. They could not be long from the heat of the flowing rock, as they needed that heat to survive. But they had discovered that they could live longer away from the melted rock, in human form. In dragon form, they all had black wrinkled skin, and glowing claws. They were strong, if they stayed in the heated earth.

Shadow had defied the other mahceen, when they had wanted him to kill others of his kind for defying them. Kai had stepped in and stopped them. As Kai had seen in Shadow a chance to make a completely loyal servant and believed that he could be useful for Kai's purposes and had stepped in and saved Shadow and his kin. And so now Shadow was completely loyal to Kai.

"I see that the black lotus worked. A rare flower, the black lotus, and most effective. You set the trap well, as I knew you would, oh, Clever One." Shadow said, his voice soft. The black lotus was rare as most of the immortals destroy it. The black lotus could, when mixed properly with other herbs, and burnt, could function as an inhibitor, making it impossible to use magic. By using the black lotus, and luring the other Mahceen here, Kai had eliminated the threat to Shadow and his kind.

Kai leaned back in his chair and tossed the gem to Shadow. Take the soul gem to my treasure room. I am the clever one, and they were all fools, to think that they could hid their traitorous thoughts and plans. Give it a place of honor. And now I will search for the perfect female to help in the creation of my greatest treasure. A Mahceen that I will create that will be loyal to me and be my number one general as I take over the worlds of this galaxy. A Mahceen that I will control and will know her place."

Shadow nodded. He took the black soul gem to the treasure room and put it on a pedestal in the center of the room. Enchantments and monsters would guard the stone from theft. Though few people would be foolish enough to try and steal from Kai. The only beings who came here were the demons that cleaned the treasure and none of them would ever try to steal anything of the master's or they would find themselves being tortured and Kai knew many forms of torture. He was the Master after all.

Shadow, in his human form, was pale, with red hair and deep green eyes. He was slender, and tall. His nose was hooked at the end and his lips were thin. His brows were slightly bent over his piercing eyes. He was intelligent and believed that Kai was destined to succeed. He served Kai and made sure that those who conspired against him paid the price. For Shadow would always be loyal to Kai, and Kai knew that of all the creatures that served him, Shadow would never betray him. There was no reason for him to do so. So, Kai knew that as he searched for the one who would help him bring his perfect creation, his realm would be well cared for.

CHAPTER TWO

Kai's search was extensive. There were goddesses, mortals, and others but none of them could pass Kai's requirements for his perfect creation. His standards were exceedingly high as this would be his greatest creation. He was determined to make sure that the mother of his child would be perfect. A thought occurred to him suddenly. What about a planet? A planet was a living being although in a unique way than other females.

Kai searched for a young planet, one where life was just beginning. Pristine and untouched by mortals or gods. He found the perfect one after a long search. The plants were just beginning to evolve, long grasses and ferns rippling in the fresh breezes that kissed the surface. Nothing else stirred on the planet, for life was still primitive, underdeveloped fish and crabs.

Kai nodded as he gazed out at the vale. This was the perfect place for his perfect creation to begin life. He would leave the early years of the child's life in the hands of Shadow. He had other things to concentrate on rather than the raising of a child.

"Here I will create my greatest creation, and here will she dwell, until she is old enough not to be a nuisance. She will grow under the tutelage of Shadow, and he will teach her to be obedient to me and carry out my will. And no one will be able to stop us."

The first thing that was needed was a suitable dwelling place. A tower of black stone of the vale. Slowly, the top of a tower rose and grew until it dominated the vale. A tall black tower, complete with gargoyle statues and twisted windows, reared up in the center of the vale, casting a shadow up on the ground.

Kai nodded in satisfaction. It was a proper place for the child to grow up and Shadow could teach her in her early years. He wanted her to grow slowly and develop at a pace that would allow her to be trained properly as his general.

He had settled on a female as he believed a female would be easier to control than a male. Now that the tower was ready, he knelt on the ground and concentrated on the image of what he wanted. It would take some time for the child to develop but he had the time. He was immortal after all, so what was time to him? Now that the seed was planted, he returned to his realm of darkness and told Shadow what was expected of him when the child was ready to be born.

Nine months later, at dawn, Shadow watched as the patch of earth that held the infant stirred and then burst like a bubble. The most perfect infant lay crying in the dirt, and Shadow knelt and picked her up. He cleaned her off with magic and gazed at her. Deep blue eyes, the color of sapphires, gazed at him, soft dark red lips parted, and he produced a bottle for her.

"Welcome to the universe, little one. Your name is to be Debarra, or Fireheart, in your father's language, but I will call you Rose. I believe that you will be more than your father thinks. A flower is what you are, grown in the ground and I know you will have thorns amidst your petals. Perhaps you will prove to be stronger than your father thinks you will."

The infant drank the milk and gazed at him. Shadow, still carrying her, turned, and walked to the tower. Imps would take care of the cleaning and care of the tower, and Shadow took care of Rose. He bathed her, fed her, and watched as she grew.

Rose was a special child, and unbelievably beautiful. Her blue eyes were inquisitive, and she was highly intelligent. She was walking by a year and talking by 18 months. Her magic, her inheritance, would come more slowly. Shadow taught her how to act like a queen, how to walk with confidence, and how talk like a leader.

Her skin, a light brown, had a golden metallic tint, and her hair, as it grew, was a light chestnut brown, with streaks of deep sunset red running through it. She was strong willed and beautiful, and grew slowly, as she was an immortal, so she did not need to grow quickly.

Rose gazed at Shadow one day, and asked him if he was her father, and Shadow responded.

"No, I'm not. I serve your father, and he has placed you in my care, until he believes you are ready to join him. He will come for you when he thinks you are ready." Rose looked thoughtful, and then she asked.

"Why does my father not raise me himself?"

"Your father is a particularly important and busy man, and believes that you will be safer here, until you are old enough to protect yourself from the dangers of being his daughter. You will face many dangers in your life, and I am to prepare you as best as I can. He is also very powerful, and he can teach you many things that I can not."

Rose thought about this and then said.

"I hope I will not disappoint you or my father. I will try my best to learn from you and be as good as I can for my father when he comes to get me. I do not entirely understand why he would not want to raise me, but I will learn what you can teach me and try to be a good daughter."

Shadow nodded and studied her. She did not belong in the dark realm of her father, but Shadow would train her, and teach her what she needed to know. It was her god blood that dominated, though he was not sure why. Her father's demon blood dominated him, so it was strange that it would be the opposite for her.

She was very different from her father, and there was something more to her, though Shadow did not understand fully what, or even why. She was not dark or twisted, but perhaps that was because she was born under the sun, and not in the darkness of her father's realm.

Primitive elves began to dance among the slowly growing, developing trees. Shadow kept an eye on them, as Kai did not want Rose mixing with lesser races, as she was meant to eventually conquer them. She was meant to become her father's general and conquer worlds for him. Shadow knew this, and taught her about her people, and her father.

As Rose grew, the world also grew, beyond the primitive stages. Trees grew taller and animals began to move about. Insects began to hum, and birds began to sing. Flowers began to grow and bloom, bringing sweet smells into the air.

Shadow watched her and knew that she was indeed different from her father. Though she was arrogant, she was not cruel, and though she was demanding she was not spoiled. Shadow did not spoil her, though he did let her play with toys, and taught her how to read in many languages. Her god half dominated, not her demon half. And Shadow knew that this would create some problems later in her lie.

He did not mean to come to love her as his child, as he knew her father would not be happy about this. But in watching her, he could see everything that she could be, and everything she was not. She was different, and that would make her dangerous to her father, if he believed that she was stronger than he thought.

Rose would sometimes leave the tower, to explore the world, though she would not go far from the tower. Shadow had told her not to wander too far from the tower, as the world could be dangerous. Shadow taught her what she needed to know, and as she grew, she became more arrogant, and demanded more freedom, though Shadow made sure that she paid attention in her lessons.

He taught little magic to her, as her father wanted to teach her all she needed to know. Shadow did teach her how to direct troops, and how to command the lesser races. But he also taught her to play the game of politics, as she would need to know this when she joined her father. He taught her how to be a lady, and how to act like she was always in control.

Shadow taught Rose also about demons and demon lords, and politics. Politics among demons and demon lords were a lot more vicious than among the other races, as demon frequently lied and cheated if they could. They also would kill without remorse, as they sought to take what others had. They were always trying to advance themselves at the expense of others.

Shadow also taught Rose about the different races, humans, elves, dwarves, and even gods. He taught her about the races of centaurs, fairies, nymphs, minotaur, leprechauns, and others. He was truly knowledgeable about these races, as he needed to be, as he spent time among the lesser races so he could manipulate them for Kai.

Shadow watched as Rose grew, and he watched the elves as they grew as a race, and as a people. Humans also began to grow beyond the primitive stages, coming out of the caves, and learning about the world. Rose was approaching her five hundredth birthday, an important date, as her father believed she was finally ready to join him in his realm.

Five hundred years was a brief time for an immortal. Rose looked around at her room, full of light, and warmth, and sighed. "I hope my room in my father's palace is nice. Shadow says that he lives underground in a huge cavern. I wonder what it will be like, underground. I will just have to get used to it." The imp that had taken care of her room, nodded. The imp never spoke to her, as she was its superior, and it was afraid of her father.

The imps were black skinned, with yellow eyes, and bat like ears, with a whip like tail that was tipped with a poisonous barb. Their clawed hands were delicate, and they were skilled as house keepers. They were small, only reaching Rose's knees.

Shadow entered her room. She looked over at him, and he could tell that she was uncertain about going to her father's house. He smiled and spoke.

"Do not be afraid, for you can manage whatever comes your way. I have taught you all you need to know, so just remember all I have told you and you will be fine." Rose nodded and followed him to the portal that would take her to begin the next chapter in her life.

CHAPTER THREE

She noticed the screams first. It was hard not to notice them. Shadow had told her about the noise and told her to just ignore it. She would get used to them in time. The torches that lined the hallways alternated red and blue flames, casting dancing shadows along the way. Grotesque skulls and twisted bones made up the walls as she followed Shadow down the hallway to meet her father for the first time.

Before they entered the room, Shadow turned to her, and said firmly.

"Do not show any emotions on your face. You are superior to everyone except your father. Do not look at anyone except him. Do not falter or slow down, just walk to him at a steady pace, and ignore everyone else." She nodded, and Shadow opened the door.

Demons and demonesses filled her father's throne room, all determined to gain the favor of Kai, through his daughter. She was an unknown factor in their quest for the favor of her father, and they hoped that by gaining favor with her they could gain it with her father.

Rose glanced at all the twisted faces, and she steeled herself. Shadow had told her to be careful in her dealings with her father's followers, as they would try to use her for their own gain. Demons were not to be trusted. She knew how to use them, as Shadow had taught her how to the play the game of politics. She would turn them against each other and use them for her own ends. She was just not sure what her ends were.

Kai gazed at the young woman who entered the room. She was extraordinarily beautiful. Perfect in every way. Deep sapphire eyes the shape of almonds, pointed ears, like an elf's, full red lips up turned at the corners, light brown skin, with a faint golden metallic tint, and light chestnut hair, with streaks of fiery red running through it. She walked with a light step, confident and in control.

The assembled demons and demoness gazed at her, and she faced them with her chin lifted and her face impassive. She did not reveal how grotesque she found their faces, or how suggestively the demonesses were dressed. An odor filled the room, as several types of demons oozed different types of slime and some of them had pustules on their bodies. She suppressed a shudder at the sight and smell of these creatures and knew that she did not fit in with them. But she turned her eyes to the throne on a raised dais in the center of this dark room.

She gazed for the first time on her father, and could see similarities in them, in the shape of his eyes, and nose. He was strong in features and demeanor. He was sitting on a throne of blackened skulls, of different races, though death was the great equalizer. He leaned back, studied her, and nodded. He stood up and turned to the gathered crowds. She did not bow to him, as this would lessen her in the eyes of the demons, so she remained standing, facing him squarely. He addressed the assembled demons.

"This is my daughter, Debarra, and I acknowledge her as my second. Her orders will be taken as if they come from me. Any disrespect towards her will result in immediate retaliation and I will enjoy that. You will address her as you do me, and I will know if anyone tries to use her."

Rose was not sure what that last meant but showed none of her trepidation. Shadow had taught her well, and her training paid off, as she faced her father and his minions, and she nodded in acknowledgement of her father's words. The demons and others bowed to her and acknowledged her as her father's daughter, and as his second. A demoness then stepped forward, and bowed to her, and spoke.

"I will take you to your room now, so you can clean up

and get ready for the feast to celebrate your arrival oh Perfect One. I have prepared a bath for you and will help you get ready." Rose nodded and after inclining her head towards her father, she followed the demoness down several hallways, and found herself in a room of luxury.

Rich tapestries and velvet furniture adorned the room. Fur rugs and carpets of velvet festooned the floor. Gold filigree gleamed on the dark wood of the chairs and couches. Gold and jewels decorated the frames of the pictures. The pictures themselves were exquisite, incredibly detailed, and depicted scenes of glory and battle, of corruption and pleasure. Incense filled the air with pungent odors.

The demoness led Rose through a black door to a bathing room, where a warm bath was already prepared. Rose shed her clothes and sank into the warm water. The demoness, and a few others, washed her, rubbing sweet smelling oils into her skin. They washed her hair, which was exceptionally long, and brushed it out. The clothes they put on her were revealing and seemed designed to emphasize her female figure.

The black material was silky, and soft, with gold thread worked into it. It left her stomach bare, and the slits in the skirt seemed designed to reveal her legs, and the shoes were little more than light slippers. Her arms were decorated with golden bands and wrapped around her legs were golden straps.

A golden band with jewels was placed in her hair. And earrings of rubies were placed in her ears. Rings decorated her fingers, and ribbons of gold were woven into her hair. The clothes were adorned with jewels that were each worth a fortune. The jewels glittered in the light of the torches, casting sparks of light around her.

Rose shifted, unsure of the clothes, or the fact that so much skin showed. She took a breath, and the demoness spoke in an oily voice.

"You look perfect, and your father will be pleased, Glorious One. Follow me and I will take you the feasting hall."

Rose nodded and followed her down the hallway to the

feasting hall. All her father's followers were there, and they stood up as she entered, and watched as she walked around the tables to reach her father, who was watching her intently.

Rose walked with her head up, her movements were confident and graceful. She did not look at anyone as she walked up to her father and took her place at his side. Kai nodded and motioned for her to take her seat. She did so, and Kai turned to the others, and clapped his hands, bringing the servants out with the food to be placed on the tables.

The food was not what Rose was used to, as she had never been to a demon feast before. Demons did not eat normal food, as they eat things that most others would not eat. Rose could not identify most of what was put in front of her, but she also did not want to disappoint her father, so she ate things that she could not name, nor did she particularly like, but she did not say anything, she simply ate.

After the feast, entertainment was provided, and what passed for entertainment by demons was not something Rose was prepared for. The cavorting demons twisted and moved in grotesque motions, and their shadows painted the walls with twisting images. The demonesses danced suggestively; their bodies revealed in the strange light of the torches. Rose was disturbed but did not let it show. This was for her father, and she did not want to disappoint him. So, she watched, and listened.

How long she sat there, she did not know, but she did start to get tired, and stifled a yawn. Her father noticed this and stopped the festivities. Rose was then taken back to her room, and she fell asleep on her new bed.

Rose woke with a start, as something startled her. A demoness was standing over her, with a tray of food. She frowned at the demoness and told her not to stand over her like that. Then, Rose sat up and accepted the food. As soon as she was done, the tray was taken and another demoness appeared, with clothes for her.

She was not allowed to dress herself, as she was an

important person. She could hear the screams and wondered if there was a way to make it so she could not hear the screams in her room, at least. No one else seemed bothered by the screams, they were just background noise.

After she was dressed, the demoness took her to her father, who was in the middle of torturing souls that he had collected. Shadow had told Rose that her father engaged in such activities, but she had not expected the true nature of this torture.

Kai looked over at her, and she gazed back at him. He nodded at her and turned back to his victim. The screams were coming from others around the vast room. She looked around and could see others being tortured.

There were many different forms of torture, and all of them were painful. Some souls were placed in fire, and others into what looked like acid. Because these were souls, they could not die, but they could feel pain. And everything you could imagine, and many things you would not want to think about were being done in this room.

Kai turned to her, and said, "I will be teaching you this, and many other things, so you should watch and learn. As my second, it will be up to you to disperse my punishments. I will expect nothing but your best effort. I will let you know who to punish, and how long they will be punished. And if they are to be killed. You may not be able to kill a soul, but you can kill a demon."

Rose did not know how to respond, but she nodded. He then held out the hot poker, and told her to take it, and apply it to the man on the table in front of him. Rose stared at him for a moment, and then took the poker, and laid it on the man. He screamed, and she pulled away, but her father grabbed her hand and forced it back on the man.

"Do not pull back just because he starts screaming, he needs to feel the pain. He is being punished for murder, so he needs to feel the pain, so he can know how his victims felt before they died." Rose swallowed hard and nodded.

"These people are here, all of them, to be punished, for in life they were murderers, dictators, assassins, thieves, tyrants, and all manner of foul beings. I gather their souls at their deaths and bring them here to be punished." He gestured. "I also punish demons that get in my way, or defy me, for I am the Master, and I will be obeyed."

Rose gazed at him, and something seemed to shift in her, and suddenly she found herself hating her father, and she did not want to be like him. But she also knew that for the time being she had to play along and do as she was told.

So, Rose's education into the arts of torture and magic began, though she hated every minute. The screams even began to echo through her dreams, and she came to hate the time she spent with her father. She struggled to keep her feelings hidden, knowing she would get in trouble if he found out how she really felt.

But then something happened that would change everything. Rose sat in her room, in a rare moment she was alone, and was drawing a picture. The picture was of a valley, with three lakes. In the space between the lakes, she drew a forest full of red trees, and people whose skin was patched green and brown. She drew some dunes and large plains. She also added a swamp along the edge of one lake and put some mines in the mountains that surrounded the valley.

She gazed at the detailed drawing of the valley and did something that would change her relationship with her father, as she willed the valley, she had drawn to become real. This was the first time she attempted something like this. But she wanted this valley to be real, even though it was not attached to any world.

She felt suddenly tired, as her magic, her power worked to make the valley real. She would learn later that what she had done would change the lives of a powerful race, and her own. For in making the valley real she had made this valley a place where her father could not go, but she could. For she was thinking of running away.

She did not want to stay in this place of darkness, with the never-ending screams. She felt like she was just an object to her father, something to be used for his own ends, with no consideration about what she wanted. He treated her as if she had no will of her own, that all she existed for was to serve him. She wanted different things for herself and right now what she wanted was to get away.

Suddenly her door flew open, and her father stood framed in the doorway. Rose turned to faced him, startled, as he had never come into her room before. He stood there, his face twisted in anger and then he growled.

"What do you think you are doing?! I did not give you permission to create anything. I did not tell you could do this. You little fool, I will teach you not to do things without my say so." She felt a pressure building around her, holding her in place.

Anger flared inside of her, and she retaliated fiercely. All her pent-up anger at all the things that he made her do came out all at once and she managed to catch her father off guard. Kai found himself flattened against the wall opposite her door and as he looked at Rose, he saw her change.

Her skin paled, her eyes turned red, and her lips turned blue. The demon blood in her was roused, and it was stronger than he had anticipated. She was stronger than he had thought her. Anger burned in her eyes, and she growled.

"You do not get to tell me what to do any more. I will do what I want whether you like it or not. If I want to do something I will, for you cannot control me anymore. I do not want to see you in my room again!"

Kai found the door shut in his face. He glowered at the door and shouted.

"Stay in there then and don't come out until you can behave, and you will receive no food or water until I say so!" He stalked off, angry and humiliated, glad that no one had seen him.

Kai had never been caught off guard like that. He was furious that she done so, but there was some pride as well.

She was growing up, and now he just needed a different way of handling her. He had an idea, but it would take some time to get ready. So, Kai moved off down the hall to begin his preparations.

Shadow had seen the whole thing, though he would never say that he did. He stood in the shadows, and nodded, knowing that Rose was indeed unlike her father, and was quite possibly stronger than Kai. He knew that Rose would be fine in her room for a while, as she could conjure up food and water if she wanted, and she had put up a barrier around her room so that the screams could not be heard within it.

Shadow knew what her father would be planning now. He would find a way to control the girl, and the Rose that Shadow had raised would disappear. The dragon found himself thinking about how to help her get out of this place and save her from her father. This was the first time Shadow had ever thought about betraying Kai. But he could not let Rose be destroyed by her father.

Inside the room, Rose stood, shaking with anger. She had never felt this kind of rage before. She wanted to hurt someone, preferably her father. She did not want to stay here, but knew that for her to leave, she had to have her father's permission, or Shadow's help. Rose blinked slowly as the thought occurred to her that Shadow knew how to get out of here. He would need to, so he could take messages, and bring in the souls that her father tormented.

The one thing her father had never taught her was how to make portals that would take her away from here. He had not wanted her to know how to do this. So, she would need to find a way to convince Shadow to help.

She knew that getting Shadow to help her would be difficult, as he was loyal to her father, but she could convince him to help her. He had raised her for the first part of her life, and she trusted him. She would need to do this carefully but believed that she could get him to help her get out of this place.

Her eyes fell upon the drawing, and using what magic

she knew, she placed around the valley that she had created protections against her father, so he could not follow her there, and then she began to plan her escape.

CHAPTER FOUR

Corwin glowered at his brother, as he did not believe what he was hearing. How could they retreat from mortals when they were High Fairies? They were stronger, more powerful, and better than these humans, and believed his brother, the King of the High Fairies, was a coward for not staying and fighting.

Darwin, Corwin's brother, King of the High Fairies, did not want to continue this war. Causalities had been high on both sides. Many lives had been lost and he wanted to avoid more conflict. The High Fairies were in the process of preparing to leave this world and seek a new home. As the High Fairies were advanced in technology and magic, they were creating ships that could take the survivors to a new place.

A new star had appeared in the sky, and Darwin and his scientists had determined that a new world, hopefully without humans, had been created. Darwin knew that although his brother did not believe in this course of action, most of their people did. They did not want to continue this war either.

Darwin thought of the Shoulai dragons that they had found. This small family were the only survivors of some of the most powerful dragons that had ever existed. Humans were violent, and jealous of anyone that was stronger than they were, and always seemed to find a way to destroy them. That was why he wanted to leave and find a place where his people could live in peace.

The seven tribes of the High Fairies were tired of fighting, even the Horse folk who were known for their fierceness. They all wanted to leave and find a place where they could pursue their own lives, and not have to worry. This was something Corwin did not understand, as he was the younger brother and had been spoiled by their mother, who had recently been killed in a raid by humans. This was the reason Corwin wanted to stay and fight, not understanding that though Darwin had loved his mother, he had to think of all the people, not just himself.

Darwin was responsible for all seven tribes of his people and could not let personal feelings get in the way of taking care of his people. His brother did not understand this and was angry with Darwin for perceived cowardice. But work on the ships had already begun, and the High Fairies mixed magic with science to accelerate the work and make sure that they could accommodate all the animals and other things that they would be bringing.

There would be seven ships, one for each tribe, and each tribe would have unique needs. The Shadow tribe needed their ship to be darker than the others, and the Swamp folk would need space for their plants. The Horse folk had vast herds of cattle and horses that would need accommodation, and Desert folk would need proper places for their camels.

The Artisan tribe would need space for the herds of sheep, llamas, and alpacas that they used for their work in weaving and yarn making. And the Craftsman tribe would need space for the equipment for their work. And of course, the farmers would need space for their crops and seeds, for while the High Fairies were powerful in magic, they still liked to do somethings without it.

The organization of doing this and making sure that no one got left behind was complicated and difficult enough without his brother making trouble. There were many things that would need to be done to make sure that everything was accounted for.

The High Fairies were intelligent and knew how to get things done. They did not want to stay here any longer than necessary and they all knew what they needed to do.

The tribes, though each different got along well and they all respected the differences in each tribe, though there was some trouble with the Shadow folk, as they were different from the other tribes, as they lived and existed in the shadows and this caused some trouble, especially among the younger ones who thought that the Shadow folk were evil because they lived in the shadows.

It did take a while and there were more attacks by the humans, but finally all the ships were ready, and all the High Fairies gathered in their tribes on their separate ships with all their belongings. The course was set, and the people were ready to find a new home, ready to be able to pursue the life they wanted. Away from conflict and away from the humans. Darwin gave the signal, and all the ships took off, leaving the humans behind to kill themselves off if they wanted to.

Corwin glowered out the porthole, gazing out at the world that had cost him his mother, and cursed his brother, vowing to gain the throne one day and go back to that world, and take his vengeance out on the humans. He would not let this stand. But to get throne he would have to get the support of the royal council and the people, and he knew that would not happen anytime soon. And his brother had two children, a son named David, and a daughter name Dophina.

The Shoulai dragon family, the only ones of their kind left numbered five. The father, Frank, was a blacksmith, as were both of his sons, Zach, and Ox. The mother, Shalia, was a seamstress, and their daughter, Laura, was not right in the head, as she had lost her husband and child to the humans, and the grief had changed her.

She had to be taken care of, as she would not eat unless someone helped her, and would not bathe without help or even change her clothes. So, Shalia spent much of her time caring for her daughter. The Shoulai dragons could shapeshift and had hoped that by taking the shapes of humans, they could avoid conflict with them. But this had not worked out so well, as they were vulnerable in human form.

The High fairies had found Frank and his family, and recognizing them for what they were, the High fairies had offered them sanctuary. Frank and his family were grateful for the help. The Shoulai dragons had been peaceful, but humans had forced them to learn how to fight. The war between the Shoulai dragons and the humans had not lasted long, and the humans had learned to fear the dragons.

But some humans had learned of a weakness in the dragons and had begun to hunt them down and kill them. The dragons had taken on the shape of humans to hide, so that they could survive, but the humans still hunted them. The dragons did not understand why the humans would not just leave them alone.

But the last family of the Shoulai dragons had found sanctuary with the High Fairies and had hope that they would be able to save their race. They would be able to find some peace and just live their lives as they wanted. They would be able to continue their people's culture and keep their people's memories alive.

When the ships arrived at their destination, they found an asteroid with an atmosphere, a large asteroid. It looked like a valley nestled in a range of massive mountains. Three lakes gleamed like blue jewels against green grass. In the space between the lakes a red wood forest grew. Along the edge of one lake, a swamp existed, and there was even a large desert.

The ships landed, and the High fairies got out. The mountains were thickly forested, and soft grass covered the ground. Flowers provided a soft scent, and butterflies hovered over the pale petals. A sense of peace and warmth filled the air. Here there was a feeling of new life and new beginnings.

Darwin looked around and knew that no humans existed here. There was no sign of anything but butterflies and flowers. Here his people could begin over and find a place of peace. Here was a start of a new chapter in his people's lives. He sent out scouting parties, to see what could be seen. And his people began to set up an encampment.

The herds of cattle were brought out of the ships and began to graze on the fresh grass. The horses, and sheep and other animals were also brought out of the ships and were allowed to begin grazing. Tents were set up in neat rows, with space for the vehicles to move. The vehicles did not run-on fossil fuels but instead on special crystals that prevented pollution.

The High Fairies were highly organized, and careful. They did not want to damage the land, though they knew that when they started to build their city and villages, they would do some damage. They wanted to take care of this place and keep it as unharmed as possible.

The desert tribe sent some of their people into the desert land that had been noticed, to explore, and see if there were any oasis in the desert. The asteroid was very spacious and had plenty of room for all the High Fairies. The desert looked like it would be perfect for the desert tribe and seemed to have plenty of space for them.

The swamp tribe, led by the ones called the Elders, sent their own scouts to the swamp that had been seen on the approach. They wanted to know what kind of swamp it was and if there was a place big enough for the tribe to settle in. Swamps could be treacherous, and sometimes solid ground was hard to find.

The horse folk were pleased to find that there was plenty of space for their herds of cows and horses. The grasslands were spacious, and the grass was excellent quality. The lakes would provide water, and their herds could be moved around to prevent overgrazing.

The shadow tribe, of course, did not need the same things as the other tribes. They lived and existed in the shadows, and the mountain forests provided them with plenty of shadows. Though their numbers were smaller than the other tribes they liked plenty of space and the mountains were perfect.

The farmers found some good land for setting up their farms and began to construct the buildings that they would need, such as barns and houses. Their cattle were for milking, and they needed to make sure that they had shelter for they did not know if this place had seasons. As the asteroid had an atmosphere it would have weather, but they did not know what kind of weather, or how severe the weather would be.

The craftsman tribe found a place with some caves and found that there was minerals and metals in the caves, and began to construct a city around the caves, and began to mine the jewels and metals. Their voices filled the air as the architects drew up the blueprints for the city and started with the sewers which were particularly important.

They discovered that the mines renewed the resources every night. They could mine all day in one spot and when they came back the next day, there was no sign that they had done anything, other than the equipment that they had left behind. As they realized this, they decided to use the gemstones and metals to build their city. If they were going to have bottomless mines, they would need to do something with all the gems and metal.

On the other side of the valley the city of the artisans was beginning as well. When they were informed of the nature of the mines, they grew excited and decided to use this resource to build their city as well. They would construct a city unlike any that had ever been seen and would call it Jewel City.

The craftsman tribe would build a city for function rather than aesthetics. They would build factories and workshops. They would be able to build a central power unit, with their crystals to power it, so that they could power the lights and factories.

Some of the farmers would set up near the craftsman tribe city so that they could provide food for the city. The nearby lake would provide the water necessary for their needs, and the ground was soft and easy to plow. For now, they would live in tents, until the houses were built. Temporary enclosures would house the animals, and canvas shelters were made to keep the animals sheltered.

The rest of the farmers set up near Jewel City, or what would become Jewel City. They would plant some crops, and make sure that the season was still good to plant, before they planted more. The herds of alpacas, sheep and llamas would be cared for in places with plenty of grass and water.

Frank and his family would set up a farm and forge. The tents were set up next to where they would build the house, and Frank and his sons would retrieve stone for the house from a quarry that was found nearby. Others were using the quarry as well, for it was convenient to the area.

They also dug a well, and laid plans for a sewage tank, for they would have flushing toilets when they were done with the house. Frank and his sons were particularly good builders and knew what was needed for the house. They were also extraordinarily strong and could use magic for some the work. They began by digging out the basement and preparing a hole for the sewage tank.

The tank was made of cement as was the foundation of the house. The tank would need to hook up to the well, so that water could go into it. They then put a pump on the well, that would be connected to the house, so that they would have water for the kitchen and the bathrooms. They would need to lay the piping and make sure that there would be no leaks.

They would also need to run a pipe to the forge, and near the animal corral. The forge would need the water to help cool the metal they would use to make different things. You would think that forges were obsolete, but they were still useful, as some of the High Fairies liked to do things that could be considered old-fashioned. And some of the High Fairies still liked to use swords, for keeping in shape.

Though the High Fairies were strong in magic, there were somethings that they still needed to work towards, like staying healthy, and exercising. They found that sword play and things like that could keep them in shape, and so many of them practiced it. And those that did like hand-made swords from an old-fashioned forge. And they would explore different worlds and some of the worlds were still medieval, and they would need such things as hand forged weapons to make sure that no one suspected them of not being human.

After they laid the foundation and the sewage tank, they began work on the walls and floors of the house, including the wiring of the power unit. The crystal that would provide energy for the house, was of medium size, and would provide the energy for the lights, running water, and heater. They would need to make sure that all the wires that would connect to the different rooms and appliances were well laid and did not fray.

The pump for the water would, of course, have its own crystal, as would the forge. It did not matter if the crystals got wet, so the pump would never run out of power. As they placed the wood for the walls, they made sure everything was well insulated, and laid out properly.

Soon the house was done, and the forge was well underway. The corral held a few horses, and cows, and the crops were growing. They all worked hard to make sure that the house was furnished and that everything was in its place. They made beds, a refrigerator, a stove, and a fireplace, along with, of course, bathtubs, and sinks and toilets.

The city was well underway as well. The High Fairies were very efficient and organized. The foundations for the palace were already laid, and the walls were going up. Because they were using jewels to construct the city, they made bricks with the gemstones, and placed a mortar of ground-up diamonds and cement.

To make a brick with jewels, you first ground up the gemstone, and then poured it into a mold, which was placed in the sun, and they used magic to harden the gemstones in the molds, so that the brick would be solid and without blemish.

This process was easy, and the bricks were made swiftly. The palace would have four wings in it each one made of a different gemstone. One wing, where the living quarters of the royal family would be made from emeralds, the living quarters for the servants along with the kitchen and storerooms would be made from sapphires. The quarters for visitors, and the royal council and their families would be made from rubies, and the final wing which would house the gardens and the royal stables would be made from amethyst.

The city would be divided the same way, with four districts. One would be for the weavers, one would be for the sculptors and painters, one would for the actors and the last would be for all the others. Here and there would be restaurants and clothing stores and other types of stores, though the High Fairies did not use money or anything like that.

As powerful beings, they could conjure anything they wanted, so wealth did not matter to them. The only thing that mattered to them was gaining knowledge. So, in their stores, to obtain something, you needed to answer a question, or trade something they wanted.

As they did not have money, there was no greed, and with that came the opportunity to learn and grow in knowledge. When you could have anything, you wanted with a just a thought, you found that learning new things was more important. And when you were immortal, learning kept you out of trouble, and gave you something to do.

As the building of the city progressed, someone arrived that would change everything for the High Fairies, and her name was Rose.

CHAPTER FIVE

Rose had finally convinced Shadow to help her get away from her father. Shadow cared for her, and he believed that Rose's destiny was to live beyond her father's control. So, when her father left on an errand, Shadow went her room and told her that her father was gone. And then he took her to her father's stable. In the stable was an incredibly special horse. This horse was a black unicorn. Her mane, tail and hooves were gold, and a golden horn spiraled upward. Her coat was as black as the shadows that filled the stable.

Rose had been in her father's dark world for about four hundred years. Though time passed differently on different planets, Rose counted her years by how time passed on her mother planet.

Rose gazed at the black unicorn, and Shadow looked over at her.

"This was meant to be your present at your coming-of-age party, which you will not be attending, since you are leaving. Her name is Midnight. We must hurry, though, so just mount up and let us go before the stable demons show up." Rose nodded and approached the black unicorn.

Midnight studied her and nickered softly. Rose found that she could understand what the unicorn was saying and responded.

"I want to leave here too, so let's do it together." The unicorn nodded, and Rose climbed up on her back. Midnight pawed the ground, and Shadow nodded. These two were meant to be together. He took a breath and opened a portal.

He went through the portal first, and then Rose and

Midnight did. She was a surprised to see a city being constructed, in her valley, but Shadow seemed to know what was going on and led her down into the city. He had come here just a little while before this, so he could see that the valley was safe for her. They made their way through the streets that were not finished and went to the palace that was being built in the center.

Many of the people stopped to watch them. The people were different from many of the races she had learned about, and asked Shadow about them.

"These are the High Fairies, a powerful magical race, and I had heard that they had left their old home. I am glad that they found their way here, as it will be safe for you among them."

"Why" Rose asked, "is it a good thing they are here, in my valley."

"Because they can help keep you safe, and they know a lot of things that you can learn. They are a good people and will be willing to help you out. Let me do the talking, when we face their king."

Rose sighed but nodded. She looked around, and watch the buildings being made. She noticed that the stones that were being used were unusual. They were unusual colors. Some were blue, some were red, and some were green. The stones also glittered in the sunlight. Just like gemstones would.

They arrived at the palace, and she dismounted. A groom came over and took Midnight into the completed stables. Rose moved closer to Shadow, and whispered, "I think they are using gemstones to build this city." He nodded, and they were greeted by a stuffy looking man.

"Who are you, and why are you here?" He asked.

"My name is Shadow, and this is Rose. We need to speak with your king, on a matter of some importance." Shadow answered. The man studied them and shrugged.

"The king is holding court right now. We were not expecting any visitors. I am sure he will be willing to speak with you, however. Please follow me." he gestured, and Rose and Shadow followed him into the palace. Some parts of the palace were done, though many were not.

They had to walk through a mess, as there were building tools and people everywhere. Rose looked around and could see that everyone seemed to be doing their own thing, which put together was like organized chaos. But no one got in each other's way and things were getting done. No one seemed to be in charge, but everyone knew what needed to be done, and they did communicate about what each other was doing. They did it this way, so that everything was done together, and everything flowed smoothly.

The throne room was just as messy as everywhere else, but the king sat on his throne and looked up as Rose and Shadow were introduced. Shadow stepped forward and bowed to the king and then requested a private audience with him. The king looked thoughtful for a moment and then nodded. He told everyone to continue without him, and then took Shadow through a side door.

Rose stood aloof from the people in the room, watching them. She was uncomfortable but hoped this would pass. As she stood there, a small delicate girl approached her. Her eyes were a deep amethyst, her skin pale, and was older than she appeared.

She smiled at Rose and spoke.

"Hello, my name is Dophina. You must be incredibly special to have a lava dragon as an escort. I am studying to be a healer, though my mother disapproves. My brother is around here somewhere, no doubt flirting with some of the girls." Rose blinked, as Dophina said this very fast.

Rose did not know how to respond, but years of practice had her smile and nod in response. Dophina continued talking, and taking Rose's hand, led her around and introduce her to some of Dophina's friends. The young girls smiled and told Rose that they had to introduce her to their dress maker, as blue satin would bring out her eyes.

Rose was uncomfortably aware of how she was dressed. Her

clothes were revealing, and she felt like a great many of the men were staring at her. She had spent many years in a place where her clothes were designed by demonesses. She did try to be friendly, but the girls seemed to understand that she was uncomfortable and led her over to some of the columns that were being decorated, out of the spotlight.

Finally, after what seemed an eternity, Shadow and the king returned. They sought her out, and the king smiled at her, and spoke.

"I see that you have met my daughter, Dophina. Shadow has told me much, and he has asked that we help you. I am glad to have learned that you are the one who made this valley. My people and myself are grateful to have found this place, as we were trying to get away from war on our home planet. I think a way to thank you for helping us, is to take you into my family."

Rose blinked in surprise, and responded,

"That is very gracious of you, but you do not have to do that, your majesty. I am grateful for the gesture, but it is unnecessary."

"Please call me Darwin, and I believe it is necessary, to thank you for making this place, though I am sure you did not expect anyone to be here when you arrived. We needed a place to have peace, and you have given us one. In a way you have saved us. And so, I take you into my family, and will see to it that you are cared for."

Dophina smiled and hugged Rose, excited to have a sister. Rose looked over at Shadow, who shrugged. Rose did not know about this, but it seemed too late to do anything about it. The announcement had already been made, and everyone cheered.

Shadow took Rose over to a corner and told her that he had go. She did not like it, as she knew that her father was likely to punished Shadow, though he was unlikely to kill him. Her father could not come to the valley. This was her place, and she had made sure he could not come here.

But she knew that Shadow was too valuable for her father to kill. But the punishment would be severe. Shadow knew that but was prepared for it. Rose was not meant to be her father's tool; she was meant for greater things than that. Her father might not like it, but that did not matter. Rose was special, and she needed to find her place in the universe.

So, Rose found herself by herself in a strange place, with a feast being prepared to celebrate her acceptance into the household of king Darwin. She agreed to follow all the laws of the High Fairies, and all the rules for the royal house. Corwin, Darwin's younger brother, really did not like this, but his brother was king.

No one could have known that this girl would show the High Fairies that one person could change everything.

CHAPTER SIX

The day after the feast, Rose made her way to the stable, to visit Midnight. She could not have known that her destiny was about to change again. For in the stable was someone who would show her what it meant to be a part of something greater than yourself.

As Rose entered the stable, she noticed someone in the stall of her unicorn, though right now Midnight looked like an ordinary horse. He was tall, even bent over, as he studied Midnight's hooves.

"Who are you and what do you think you are doing to my horse?" Rose demanded. The man stood up, and she blinked. He was about seven feet tall. He turned around and studied her.

"My name is Zach Dragoon, and I was checking your horse's hooves, to see if she needed new shoes. The king likes to keep all the horses in good condition, so I come and check on them once a week. And I could ask you who you are, but I saw the news last night."

She frowned at him and nodded. Just because she was a mahceen, did not mean she was ignorant of science, and she had learned about their news network last night. She did not like that the whole valley now knew who she was, but there was nothing that she could do about it.

"If my horse needs new shoes, I will take care of making new ones for her. I can take care of her myself." Rose said. This was not entirely true, as she had no idea how to care for a horse. She had not learned to how do things like that. Zach just smiled, and then said.

"How about I take you fishing tomorrow? They put some fish in the lake. I enjoy fishing, and my mother is a particularly good cook. Dawn is the best time for fishing, as the fish are waking up and they are hungry. I will pick you up an hour before dawn." Before she could reply, he stepped around her and left.

Rose stood there for a moment, staring after him. She frowned. No one had ever been that brusque with her before, and if he thought that she was going fishing, he was mistaken. If she wanted a fish, she would just conjure one. She went over to Midnight and stroked her nose.

"That was a very strange man. I think I will go for a walk, and then go to the library. I need to learn about these people. They are different than any I have encountered before." she sighed and then turned away from Midnight and left.

Throughout that day, Rose worked on getting to know this race of powerful beings. They had an interesting history, and she noted that while they did have great powerful magic, they still did things with their hands. They used machines to do somethings, but magic for others. They did not rely entirely on science or magic but had found a way to combine these two forces, and make a society based not on greed, but respect and knowledge.

She learned that they did have knights, and a regular army, but they preferred peace. That was why they had come to the valley. They had grown tired of constant war with the humans and had come here to find peace. She found that she admired these people for their choice to leave behind a world of war and death, to find a place where they could live in peace.

That was the main reason she had come here too. She did not belong in her father's realm of darkness and pain. She did not want to be used by her father, to conquer worlds, or make the innocent suffer just to please her father. She did not know yet what she wanted to do, but she would not be used by anyone.

Why was she so different from her father? Rose was

uncertain. His blood was in her veins, but she did not delight in causing pain. She had felt her demon half, the day her father had come storming in, but she did not indulge it like he did.

Maybe it was because of her mother. Rose knew that her mother was a planet, so maybe there was something special in her because of that. Maybe because of what her mother was, Rose was not like her father. All Rose knew at this point, was that she was not like her father, and had no intention of going anywhere near him ever again.

The next morning, in the hour before dawn, Rose heard a noise outside her bedroom door. Someone was arguing. She sighed and got up to see what was going on. As she opened her door, she saw Zach and a maid.

"What is going on out here? I am trying to sleep." She said, and Zach looked over at her and smiled.

"Don't you remember what I said yesterday? I am taking you fishing today, and I brought you one of my mother's old dresses, so you do not ruin any of yours. Put it on quickly and let us go." He tossed her the dress, and she caught it.

Rose did not want to go fishing, but as she gazed at the strange man, she found herself curious about him. So, she sighed and slipped inside her room and pulled the dress on. Zach's mother was a large woman, so Rose did have to modify it a little so that it would fit.

After she was dressed, Rose stepped out of her room and found Zach waiting for her. He smiled and nodded and led the way down the hallway out of the palace, and to the stables. Midnight was ready to go, along with a massive horse who was reddish. This horse was obviously Zach's, who was large himself.

They mounted up and Zach led the way through the sleepy, partially built city. They left the city behind and rode over the grass to the nearby lake. A boat was resting on the shore of the lake, along with fishing gear. As Rose dismounted, she looked over at Zach and informed him that she did not know how to fish.

He smiled and told her that he would teach her and helped her into the boat. He rowed out a distance from the shore and dropped the anchor. He then proceeded to teach Rose how to fish. He showed her how to put bait on the hook, and cast.

Rose studied Zach as they waited for a fish to bite.

"You are not a High Fairy, are you?" She asked, and Zach shook his head.

"My family and I are Shoulai dragons, the last of our kind. We were on the same planet as the High Fairies and managed to join them. The High Fairies took us in and have helped us. I am the oldest son, then there is my brother Ox, and my sister Laura is the oldest child. She did have a mate, and a daughter, but the humans killed them.

When we heard of a rumor that the High Fairies were building ships to leave the planet, we jumped at the chance to get away from the humans and find a place where we could use our talents with blacksmithing and in coming with the High Fairies, there is a possibility that we could save our race."

Rose was silent, as she thought back to her lessons, before she went to her father's realm. Shadow had mentioned the Shoulai dragons, but had told that they were in hiding, being hunted by the humans. She had not actually met any humans; other than the ones her father had taught her to torture. Overall, she did not like the sound of humans.

"I have never met any humans, but they seem brutish and violent. They seem to revel in death and enjoy the suffering of others, including their own kind. Maybe the universe would be better off without them." Zach studied her and spoke.

"Even though they have hunted my kind until only my family is left, it is not my place to judge them. I hate them for what they have done to my people, but they are still sentient beings, and are capable of change. What they need is to have someone help them see that just because someone is different, it does not mean that they should destroy them.

Humans are like children, and like children they do not seem to think anything through. But not all humans are bad. I came to know a few that helped us. They warned us of others who were coming to kill us. There are some out there that are worth protecting. The children for example should not be blamed for the sins of their parents.

We should help the humans and the other races learn that acceptance and tolerance are needed if we are to have peace, and they need us to help them find a better way. There is talk about going out to the surrounding worlds and seeing if we could help the humans and other races that exist out here, but carefully, and not without consideration to the risks involved."

Rose gazed out at the rising sun, watching it as the light danced upon the water. All her life she had been told she was superior to everyone, that she was better than everyone. She did not believe as her father did, that the lesser races existed to serve the greater power, which her father believed was him.

The sounds of birds filled the air, and the smells of the fresh morning surrounded her, as she sat on the gently rocking boat. Her sapphire eyes gazed at the dancing waves that caught and reflected the sunlight. The waking world seemed to be fresh and new as she thought about what she knew, and what she had just been told.

As she thought about what Zach had said, she wondered if she should try to see the humans and other races not as objects to be used but living beings who had hopes and dreams of their own. She should get out of the valley and see for herself what the lesser races were really like.

Just then her rod bent, and she grab it, and with Zach's help she reeled in her first fish. For few more hours, they caught several fish, then Zach took the boat back to land. There he taught her how to clean the fish which she found gross, and took her to his family's farm, which was nearby. She was not certain that she wanted to meet them so soon, but she did want to learn how to cook.

Zach took her into the kitchen and told her to wait, so he could get his mother. Only a few moments after he left his brother, Ox, came in. He stopped, and stared at her for a moment, and then backed out slowly, his face a little red. Like his brother, Ox was big. Not just tall, but broad too.

Rose looked down at herself and could see what had embarrassed him. Her legs were exposed, up to the knee. And her hands were red and raw from cleaning the fish, and her shoulders were bare. She had not considered her clothes, as she had not worn very much for the years she was with her father. She readjusted her dress and looked around at the kitchen. It was all skillfully done. The fridge, stove and sink were of stainless steel, and the cupboards and drawers were painted a light blue.

The handles on the drawers and cupboards were made of silver and carved to look like dragons. They were very finely wrought, and skillfully placed. She examined one and was startled to see that she could make out individual scales.

Zach came in then with his mother, trailed by his sister. Rose gazed at them both, and could tell that they were related to Zach, by the fact that they were also tall, and his mother had the same-colored eyes. His sister's hair was gray and lank, which was startling, as she was not much older than Zach.

Shalia smiled at Rose, and shooed Zach out of the kitchen. She then turned to her daughter and got her to sit down in a chair. Rose was uncertain about this, but Shalia put her at ease. She showed Rose how to cook the fish and make sure that they did not stick to the pan. Zach smiled at Rose and Ox sat as far from her as he could. Frank sniffed at the fish and smiled.

"These look good and smell great. I hope they taste like they smell. But no one has introduced me to our guest yet." Rose smiled back at him and told him her name was Rose, and Zach had taken her fishing for the first time and then she asked about how he had gotten so skilled as to make the incredibly detailed handles on his cupboards.

Frank laughed and told her that Ox had made them. Ox was a very skilled smith and would get better as he practiced. Zach was skilled as well, and usually made exceptionally fine weapons. Frank was proud of his two sons and was glad to see that they were making friends, especially such pretty ones.

Rose flushed then smiled and thanked him for the compliment. After they were done eating, Zach said that he should get Rose back to the palace, and Sarah told her not to worry about the mess, they would take care of it. Rose had never eaten anything like the fish and other food, but she had enjoyed it, as she had eaten nothing but demon food for a long time.

Later, after Zach had left, Rose stood in an unfinished garden. She thought about the things she had learned that day and wondered about it. The universe was larger than she had thought, and many things were different, but for first time she felt a part of the events, not just an observer.

But Rose did have a stubborn streak, and a temper, as Dophina would learn when she told Rose of her mother's decision to arrange a marriage with a much older duke.

Rose had just finished breakfast and had left her room to go to one of the gardens that was finished. Upon entering the garden, she heard what sounded like someone crying. She walked over to the sound and found Dophina crying. Rose sat down next to her and asked what was wrong. Dophina took a deep breath and responded.

"My mother wants to arrange a union between me and Duke Anadi. He is much older than I am. My mother thinks a union between us will be politically beneficial for her. But I do not want to marry him. I want..." Dophina paused for a second and looked at Rose. "I want to be with Jack Hunter. He is a baron, but my mother sees no benefit to my union with Jack. I do not even know if Jack likes me, as my mother keeps us apart."

Rose gazed at Dophina. Even though Rose had only been here for a few days, she did like Dophina, and understood what it was like to have a parent try to control you. Rose stood up and asked where Jack normally was at this hour, and Dophina told her that he was on the practice grounds. Rose nodded and stood up. Dophina watched her leave, wondering what she was doing. Rose asked a servant how to find the practice grounds, and when she got there, she asked around and was directed to Jack Hunter. He was practicing archery, though he preferred swords.

Jack Hunter was tall, with vivid red hair and deep green eyes. He looked up as she approached him and when she was close enough, he spoke.

"How can I help you, my lady?" He asked, and she looked at him, and asked if he knew Dophina, and if he liked her. Rose had learned to be very direct as demons sometimes did not understand subtlety. Jack blinked and thought about it.

"I had heard that Dophina and Duke Anadi were to be married, as soon as Dophina comes of age. You know that, and yet," he studied her, "You ask me how I feel about her. That is very direct, and I do not know how to respond. Why would you ask this?"

Rose shrugged and responded.

"I do not believe that anyone should decide the fate of another. My father was very controlling, and I did not like it so why should someone else go through that? Just answer the question, would you?" Jack studied her and took a breath.

"I do like her, I find her beautiful, but I do not know how to approach her, especially if her mother has already made an arrangement." Rose shook her head and looked at him.

"Why don't you ask her anyway? She likes you too, so take a chance. All you need to do is be careful not to let anyone find out, just yet. No one should have the right to tell another what to do." Jack looked down and thought about Dophina. He smiled and nodded. If he was going to take a chance, he wanted to do it. He wanted to know if he and Dophina would have a chance. He told her thanks and hurried off. Rose turned around and found Zach watching her.

"What are you doing here?" She asked him. He smiled and replied.

"I like to check on the equipment, to see if it needs to be repaired. I saw you and wanted to say hi. So, do you know how to fight with a sword or anything?" Rose shook her head and spoke.

"My father did not want me to know how to fight, just how to direct troops. I was supposed to conquer worlds for him, so I needed to know battle strategy and things. Sword play did not come into my education." Zach nodded and then asked her if she wanted to learn. She thought about it and then shrugged. She felt like maybe this was a good thing for her know.

Zach led her over to where they had the practice swords and other weapons. All the practice swords were made of wood, padded with some wool. She picked one out, but Zach shook his head and made her put it back. He then looked through the practice swords and pick one out for her.

This sword could be used both one handed and two handed, as needed. Double edged, if it was made of metal, a very versatile weapon. Zach handed it to her and showed her the correct way to hold it. He then began to teach her how to use the sword. There were practice dummies set up for people to use so he took her over to one and began to teach her how to use a sword.

He did not coddle her. Zach was a good teacher, but he did make it hard on her. When she complained about it, he smiled and told her that an enemy would not take it easy on her, so he would not. She grew frustrated and threw down the practice sword. As she started to turn away, though, Zach caught her arm.

"Learning new things is never easy, but if you give up, then you prove to others that you can be used and manipulated easily. If you want to prove yourself to the High Fairies, then pick up the sword, and keep going." Rose gazed at him, then lowered her eyes.

All her life she had been taught that she was superior to everyone else. She stood above them all, her father had repeatedly told her. She was so far beyond everyone that she would never belong to anywhere. As she looked around her, at these people, she wondered about them. So much power, so superior to the lesser races, but they did not act like it.

But Rose was not one to be manipulated. She had just spent time in a place that if you did not do the controlling, you were controlled. And the games that the demons played were far worse than any that these fairies could play. Rose had not let the demons control her, and she would not let these people do it either. She was far more capable than these people might think. If they wanted to play games, she could too.

Rose bent down and picked up the fallen practice sword. As she faced Zach, he smiled and nodded, and began again. For the space of two hours, he taught her, and though she fell many times, and got tired, she would always get back up.

Dophina gazed uncertainly at Jack as he walked up to her. He smiled and handed her some flowers. He then asked her if she would like to take a walk with him. She smiled shyly and agreed. He smiled and took her around the city to look at some the buildings that would be the settings for movies and other works of art.

CHAPTER SEVEN

As Rose spent time with these people, the more she came to like them. They knew what they were doing and could work together very well. She would watch as they built the city, as they were very skilled architects, and they made sure that each building was built with skill and made to last. The city would need sewage treatment plants, water storage, electricity, which was made using the crystals.

They also needed waste management. They reused everything. The High Fairies had made garbage cans that would teleport any trash thrown into it to a facility that would break it down and create different things out of the garbage.

Most food waste was turned into fertilizer for the farmers. Plastics were turned into different plastic items, and paper was reused. They worked hard to make sure that there was no waste, to protect their newfound home, and made sure that everything was taken care of.

They did not limit their buildings to squares, but incorporated towers, and round buildings and even triangles. They also made sure that there were plenty of parks and gardens. Trees lined the streets which were broad with plenty of space for the clean vehicles and walking.

They also made gyms, and practice areas for weapon practice, shooting ranges for their blasters, and places for children to come and have fun exploring. They made sure that there were places for relaxation, such as spas and massage houses.

Every need and want was considered, and everything were built with skill and precision. They even put sculptures and statues into the parks and gardens and in front of buildings. They also made museums and places of learning. They made schools for the children and for grown-ups. There were libraries as well.

They did not rush anything though. They were careful about planning out the buildings and making sure that everything was in readiness before they began. They were also careful about how to place the streets and sewer lines. They did not want to make any mistakes with their new city. They wanted to make sure that this city lasted forever, since they were immortal, if they did not get killed.

Rose learned a lot about buildings and safety as she walked around with Zach and on occasion his brother. Zach loved his brother, and enjoyed doing things with him, and teaching them both. Ox fought with a battle axe, and a big one at that. It would take three normal men to lift Ox's battle axe. Zach liked to train them together.

Rose and Ox did not always get along, as Ox struggled with jealousy. He was used to having his brother to himself. He did not know if he liked sharing him. And secretly, Ox was attracted to Rose, but he would not say anything. Zach and Rose were drawing closer, and Ox would not interfere with his brother's affairs.

Darwin watched her from a distance, at first. He knew that Rose was helping Dophina get close to Jack, but he did not mind. He did not approve of his wife's decision concerning Dophina and the duke Anadi. He knew that if Dophina defied her mother in this affair, then a breach in his family would likely occur. But he wanted Dophina to be happy, which was why he had stepped in when his wife tried to stop Dophina from studying to be a healer.

The more Darwin watched her, and the more he heard about her, seemed to justify his decision, to take her into his family. He believed that it was the right decision, as he did not want Rose as an enemy. She was stronger in magic than he was and could destroy him if she wanted to. But Rose seemed content to spend time with Zach and his brother and learn things she had not been able to before.

Now that the High Fairies had a place to stay, some of them wanted to explore the surrounding worlds. They wanted to see if there were any threats to their peace. Rose, Zach, and Ox, when they heard about this wanted to be the first ones to look around. So, Rose went to Darwin and asked him if she, along with Zach and Ox could be the first scouts.

Darwin thought about it and then agreed, and told her to get ready, as the scout ships were almost done being prepared. She smiled and hurried off, to go tell Zach and Ox. If the world they scouted posed a threat, they were to report immediately, but if not, they should explore it and see what there was to see. Rose knew that she was taking a risk in leaving the valley, but she refused to live in fear of her father.

Zach smiled at her as she told them the news. Ox was not certain about this, but he was not going to back out, as he did not want to appear to be a coward, so he nodded, and began to get ready. Zach studied his brother and sighed softly. He was aware of Ox's feelings for Rose but knew that the time was not right for this.

Zach had not intended to develop feelings for Rose, certainly not the romantic type. He was confused by his feelings, and knew that he was not right for her, but could not stop how he felt for her. He did not know what to do about it but hoped that time would sort things out. For now, he would just enjoy what he had and have some fun with Rose and Ox.

The ship would land briefly, to drop them off, so as not to attract attention, as they did not know what was on the planet. They would be able to communicate telepathically so they would not need anything that would give them away. The planet chosen for this first foray, was a desert planet, with truly little in the way of cover, but they could possibly find some interesting artifacts, or life forms. The scans that had been done showed little in the way of life, but there could still be something, deep below the surface.

The Desert tribe gave them some clothing suitable for the desert and made sure that they had some salt. Salt was particularly important for desert travel. If they ran low on water, they could conjure some more. They would have provisions for ten days, after that they would either leave the planet or make some more. They were all extremely excited to be doing this and made sure that they had everything that they would need.

CHAPTER EIGHT

The pilot watched them as they sat down and strapped in. He nodded and closed the hatch. Rose paid attention to his movements and watched as he prepared to take off. It would not take them long to reach the planet, as it was sharing a sun with the valley.

In fact, if anyone lived on the planet and looked up at the sky, a new moon would have appeared in the sky. It would only take a few hours to reach it. As they traveled, Rose asked the pilot questions, about how to pilot the ship. The pilot, whose name was Robert, was extremely happy to answer her questions, and enjoyed talking to her.

When they arrived, Robert took them down behind some dunes. They grabbed their packs and left the ship. Rose blinked in the bright sun, which reflected off the sand. The sand itself was red, and the dunes looked like they were bleeding.

Zach stretched, and looked over at his brother, as behind them the ship took off. Ox sniffed lightly and looked around.

"There is a lot of iron rust here, almost like the entire planet is nothing but rust. Look at the sand, how it is all red, and if you look over at the cliffs they look like their bleeding." Rose nodded and looked around.

"We could set up camp by the cliffs, for now, and see if the scanners can pick anything up, but I do not think there is anything alive here. Unless it is all underground. I feel something though..." She trailed off, as she looked over her shoulder.

Something beneath them shook the ground, and the sand on the dunes seemed to collapse in on themselves. They took off running as the sand began to sink. Both Zach and Ox unfurled their wings, and Zach grabbed Rose as they took to the sky. Rose gasped as beneath them a giant maw of some primordial beast opened in the desert sand.

The roar that sounded through the air was earth shattering, and all three companions winced as the sound seemed to be coming from all directions at once. But the three companions were already out of reach, and the creature, whatever it was, vanished form view.

Ox and Zach made their way to the rocky crags that jutted out of the dunes. They landed, and Rose straightened her shirt. They all looked back at the now flat sand and wondered what the creature was.

"I have never seen or heard of anything like that before. I wonder what it was." Rose said. Zach shook his head and Ox shrugged.

"I want to know why it waited for the ship to take off before it showed up, and what triggered it afterwards." Zach said, and Ox nodded. Rose did not know, but whatever it was, they all hoped to not see it again. They found some shelter to wait out the rest of the day and set up camp. Rose gazed out at the sand and wondered what else was out there, but knew that traveling during the day, in a desert was not always smart, but she was grateful that they could all see in the dark.

After the sun had set, Zach got out the sensers, and set them up, to see if they could find any other form of life, other than the monster that had tried to eat them earlier. Rose scouted around to see if she could find a cave or anything like that, so that they would know if anyone had ever lived here. Caves could be good places to find artifacts, as most primitive humanoids found caves to be safe.

Ox kept an eye out for any creatures that might come out at night. Desert nights were easier to travel in, but could be dangerous, as many desert creatures came out at night. As each of them set about their tasks, they stayed close to each other as they did not want to become separated. That could be dangerous too.

The sensors in place, Zach looked out at the sand, and wondered if anyone had ever lived here. They would take samples of the sand and rocks back to be studied, and some of the plants too. They would try to not leave any trace of their presence and try find out what they could about this planet.

Then he heard Rose calling to them and hurried over to her. She had found a cave, but what was in it was not what he expected to find. What they found was bones. Humanoid bones filled the cave, with evidence of violence. Some were holding stone knives, and others were locked together in battle, strangling each other. It seemed as if they were fighting to not to go outside, for the entrance to the cave was clear.

Zach knelt and studied some the bones, wondering what was so frightening that they did not want to leave. The dry air of the desert had preserved some the clothing of the people and the cloth was still soft to the touch, but it was not made of animal skin. It was plant fiber. As he picked up a piece, to study it closer, Ox came over, and spoke.

"We have company coming. I saw a dust trail rising in the desert, coming our way. But I cannot tell what they are from this distance." Zach nodded, and stood up, and they all went to see if they could tell what was coming. They used special binoculars to see into the distance.

It looked like birds. Big birds running across the sand. They wondered if the creature in the sand would make an appearance. Zach checked the sensors and looked over at his companions.

"It looks like a flock of big birds, bigger than ostriches. I do not know if anyone is riding them, but they are big." Rose looked out and studied the approaching flock. As she looked closer, she could almost see something. She was not sure about what it was, but there was something off about the birds.

As the flock drew closer, Rose blinked, and spoke up.

"I do not think those are birds, but reptiles. I cannot see any feathers, and if you look carefully, you can see that they have ridges on their backs. And they do not have wings but folded up arms. And they look like they are running from something."

Zach nodded and looked over at his brother, who nodded as well. They both looked out and Ox shed his human form, taking on the form of the dragon that he was. Rose had never seen either of them change before and gazed in awe at the huge beast that suddenly shared the cliffs with them.

The huge primitive dragon, bigger than any dragon she had ever heard of, took off from the cliffs, and flew in the direction of the running creatures, to see what he could see. He flew with care and looked carefully at his targets.

As he came up, the creatures bleated, and turned to the side, and he could see what was following them. Humans, on the backs of other lizards that had been trained to herd their own kind, and they were herding the lizards, like sheep.

He turned around and returned to the camp. He shook himself, and turned back into a human, and looked over at his companions.

"There are humans out there, big ones, they look like they are herding the lizard things. And they are coming in this direction. I do not know if they were heading here originally or if they are following me, but they are coming."

Rose looked out at the creatures that had indeed turned in the direction of the cliffs. She looked over at Zach, and he took a breath, and spoke.

"Let us get ready for them but be cautious. We can disguise the sensors, and try to look like ordinary travelers, if they have them here." Rose went over to the sensors and with a wave of her hand made them look like some of the plants in the area.

Zach and Ox sat on some rocks, and Rose made a small fire. When the riders arrived, they sent someone up to see who the strangers were and where the beast was. They found three strangers, sipping some soup. Two matched the size of the riders, but the third was smaller. They gazed at the smaller stranger, as they had never seen anyone so small.

Rose gazed back at them, no fear or uncertainty in her eyes.

She was not afraid of these riders, though Zach and Ox had something to do with this. The riders then spoke in a language that Rose recognized from Shadow's lessons when she was small. Zach and Ox could enact a spell that would let them communicate, but Rose did not need too.

She responded to the riders, to their astonishment, in their own language, and told them that she and her companions were just travelers and meant no harm to the riders. The riders spoke softly together, and then told Rose and her companions to come with them to the encampment at the bottom of the cliffs.

By now Zach and Ox had made it so they could speak and understand this language as well, so they talked softly with Rose and agreed to go with the riders. Their mission after all was to explore this planet and discover what was here. These riders were something, and so they would study them, and bring back as much information as possible.

The riders led the way back down the cliffs, and to their own encampment. Rose did not show any uncertainty, as she was confident that she and her companions could manage anything that happened.

They arrived down at the encampment and took note of the way these riders set up camp, and how the lizard creatures were settled in for the rest of the night. They were taken to the biggest tent and introduced to the leader of the band of riders.

The leader was a woman, and she was dressed in clothing suitable for a harem, not traveling in the desert. Gold chains wrapped around her waist, and golden bracelets tingled on her wrists. Her skin was brown from exposure to the sun, and her dark eyes appraised the strangers.

"My name is Thera, daughter of Thuna and Thut. We are taking the Chuduk to their nesting grounds. We are surprised to find travelers, dressed strangely, in this part of the desert at this time of year, and we are curious as to what you may doing here. And did you see the strange beast, that startled the Chuduk?" Rose responded.

"We did not know that we were in your territory, and we did see the beast, but it flew over us, and disappeared into the deep desert. We were merely curious about this area and came to explore it. We did find some things of interest, but by far you are more interesting. And we seem to have forgotten our manners, for my name is Rose, daughter of none, and these are Zach and Ox, sons of Frank the smith."

Thera studied both Ox and Zach who were watching her guards. They remained close to their small companion, protective of her. This seemed appropriate considering her small size. But despite her smallness she spoke with authority, and confidence. Rose did not seem to be intimidated by the fact that she was the smallest one here.

Thera nodded in acknowledgement of Rose, and stood up, towering over the smaller woman, then gestured to her attendants. She told them to bring refreshment for their guests and told them to make sure that the guests had shelter for the night. Her attendants nodded and moved off to conduct her orders.

Refreshments, of course, included Chuduk meat, some strange but sweet fruits, and some sliced cactus. The drink that was offered was light in taste, and very refreshing after the hot sun. After they had eaten, they were escorted to a tent that had been set up for them.

As they entered, and were left alone, Zach looked over at Rose, and asked.

"How do you know about these people's language, and culture? I have never even heard of them before. You, though, seem know all about them." Rose looked up at him, shrugged and responded.

"I did not know anything, until I heard them speak. Shadow, the one who brought me to the valley, taught me a lot of things before I went to my father's realm of darkness. These people talk in a language that he taught me, he called it Ginatha, and told me that the people who spoke it had all died out centuries ago.

CHAPTER NINE

The Ginathias were a desert dwelling people, but they had been wiped out when their home planet was hit by an asteroid that had destroyed it. They were not space travelers, so how some of them obviously got here, I do not know. Maybe, some space travelers found out about the asteroid and were able to get some the Ginathias off their planet and bring them here.

Their society is based on merit, not inheritance. If you can prove yourself, then you can become a leader, but even if your parents are famous, you still must prove that you are capable. So, even if your parents are the tribe leaders, it does not mean that you will become leader. You must prove that you are capable of being leader." Zach studied her and asked.

"What do you think they will do with us, especially you, as you are smaller than they are. And our clothes though similar is different. I do not want to get to their city or whatever just to be sacrificed because we are different."

Rose shook her head and responded.

"If these are Ginathias they do not practice sacrifice, but they might make us, or at least me, go through what is called the Gauntlet, which is a series of trials. They would make me do it because I am smaller than you, so they would want to see if I could do it. But I do not know if these ones will do that. Their society could be different than what I was told about. We will just have to see. If they do prove to be true Ginathias, then we should not worry too much as they will be honorable. For now, let us just get some sleep, it has been a long day."

With that, Rose stretched out on the piles of cushions and fell asleep. Her companions, though, stayed up a little later and talked about somethings before they too went to sleep.

In the morning, they ate breakfast in their tent, and then stepped out to watch as camp was broken, and preparations made to continue. Thera made sure that her guests had rides and then they left, herding the Chuduks. Rose found the experience to be fun, though both Zach and Ox stayed close to her. Being smaller than the Ginathias was not a detriment to staying on her Chuduk, but she did have some trouble steering.

Luckily the Chuduk she was riding was well trained and stayed with the others. Thera watched her and nodded. She did not know where these strangers were from, but there was something special about all three of them, but she was more interested in the woman. Who was she, and why was she so small?

To have these men as an escort she must be someone of importance. A princess or a shaman in training. Thera was determined to find out. After they arrived at the feeding grounds, she would find out more about this woman.

For next two days Rose and her companions rode with the Ginathias, and she grew to like Thera, and hoped that they could be friends. But it all depended on what they would find at these feeding grounds. But as they approached, a layer of smoke filled the air with haze, and the smell of burning flesh hung in the air. The Chuduks shied away from the smell and the smoke.

Thera immediately sent out her people to round up the Chuduks, and the rest went over the rise, and looked down at what was left of the Chuduks' feeding grounds. The buildings that had been set up were all made of stone, but they were still blackened. The grass and trees around the oasis were smoking, all black with a few small fires still going.

Burned and blackened bodies were scattered here and there, the origin of the burning flesh smell. Thera jumped off her own Chuduk and went over to two of the bodies, a heart-rending wail bursting from her lips. Rose went over to her, knowing that the bodies were Thera's parents, who had been waiting for their daughter.

"Who could have done this, and why?" Zach asked, looking around in sorrow. Ox shook his head, saddened at the sight of some smaller bodies, children who had been caught in the flames. More wails filled the air, as the Ginathias found loved ones among the dead.

Rose studied Thera. The Ginathia knelt beside her parents and wept. The Chuduks stood together, huddled as they gazed out across the land that had once fed them. The people seemed not to hear Zach's question, but they had, and Thera slowly stood up and looked over at him.

"This is the work of the Rogues. They are murderers and thieves. They were once among our people, but they did not like our laws. They rebelled against our elders and were banished. They should have been killed. They raid our caravans and destroy our homes. And now they have attacked our feeding grounds. We need this land to feed the chuduks. If they cannot eat, then they will not produce eggs and they will starve to death.

The elders will need to hear about this. The Rogues have crossed a line. They will pay for what they have done here. I will not rest until every Rogue is fed to the desert sands." The other Ginathias nodded and agreed with her. She detailed some of her people to repair the stone corrals for the chuduks and see if they could salvage anything.

The rest of the people made ready to ride back to their city and tell of what had happened. Rose stood in silence, watching the Ginathias, and wondering what to do. She had never seen war, though she knew about it. But she had seen other things, in her father's realm. She gazed out at the burnt land and knew something had to be done.

Zach studied her, knowing something of what was going on in her head. He knew that she was thinking of what she could do for these people. He watched, as she closed her eyes and then he felt a shifting in her. She knelt and put her hand upon the ground and healed it. She could not bring back the dead, but she could make sure the chuduks had something to eat.

The Ginathias blinked and turned to look at her. Rose faced them and spoke softly.

"I cannot bring back the dead, but to thank you for your generosity and for allowing us to come with you, I could not help but make sure that the chuduks had food. I am not like you, but I want to help. I will help you if you let me." Thera gazed at this small but powerful woman. She had known that there was something special about this woman, and now she knew that Rose was indeed much more than what she seemed.

The Ginathias thanked Rose and asked her to come with them to their city. She looked over at Zach and Ox who nodded. If they could help, then they should help. The journey was only a few days, as they pushed the chuduks as fast as they could. They rested only a few times, for only a few hours.

The chuduks were staggering with weariness when they reached the city, which stood on a small plateau. On three sides, the cliffs and walls protected the city, the front wall was accessible by a ramp. The gate was closed, though it swung open as they approached.

Thera and her companions immediately became wary as they entered the city. All was quiet, there was no sound, not even whispers. At this time of day, the city should have been filled with sounds of talking, shouting, and children laughing. But there was nothing, not even a dog barking. Thera looked over at the newcomers and could see that they too could feel that something was wrong.

Then a soft gasp escaped the lips of one of the Ginathias. As they entered the marketplace, they could see the people, but they were all frozen. No one was moving. Rose dismounted and walked over to one of people. The person's eyes moved, but the rest of them could not. They were alive, just unable to move. Rose frowned and looked over at Zach, who shrugged.

"They are alive, but they cannot move. I do not know how this happened, but it would take a powerful magic to freeze all these people. I wonder what has happened, here."

Maybe it was you." One of the Ginathias said, pointing at Rose. Zach and Ox immediately went over to her. They stood, towering over her, glaring at the one that had spoken up. Rose frowned and gazed at the Ginathia.

"Why would I restore your feeding grounds and then freeze your people? That would make no sense. I have never been to this city, and I certainly would not freeze people, which is something..." She trailed off, and then turned to the grandest building in the city. The palace stood above everything in the city.

Rose frowned and then began walking towards the palace, with the others following. She felt something remarkably familiar about all this and wanted to confirm her suspicions. When they arrived at the palace, they found the doors opened, and Rose led the way in, her steps echoing in the still air.

When they arrived in the throne room, they found a man sitting on the throne, watching them. Rose stiffened and glared at him.

"I knew there was something familiar in this. What do you think you are doing here, father?" The man sneered and responded.

"I am taking over this planet, silly child. And I have come to take you home, and teach you that no one defies me, as Shadow learned. He can no longer turn into a dragon. I have taken that from him as punishment for helping you be foolish. No one escapes me, and this time there will be no one to help you get away."

Rose faced her father, anger burning in her eyes. She was not going back with him, and he was going to learn that Rose was stronger now than when she had been with him. She had learned things, beyond his influence, and she would not give up what she had found.

"I am not going anywhere with you, and you are not taking this planet. I am not who I was, and I will never submit to you. I will stop you, and free these people, just watch. I may be your daughter, but I am not your slave." Kai glowered at her and spoke.

"You are a silly little girl, who needs to learn respect for her father, and obedience. You are my creation, and you will learn to obey me without question. Now stop this nonsense and, I will spare the people of this world. Otherwise, I will make sure no one lives upon this world, except the dead."

Rose growled, and stepped forward, gathering her magic. She would not go anywhere without a fight, and she fully intended to fight. Kai felt her gathering her magic and attacked first. Rose managed to catch herself before she hit the wall. Vaguely she heard Zach ordering everyone back, but she was focused on her father, and as before, she felt a power growing inside her.

She was not just her father's child. There was more to Rose than even her father knew, and this is what made her stronger than her father. She was the daughter of a planet, and the power that a planet held was greater than even the Gods that governed it. A power existed that even the Gods could not defy. That power came from the universe, and that power was a part of Rose.

The ensuing fight was incredible. Blast after blast of sheer energy flowed between these two immensely powerful beings. Cracks formed in the ceiling and the columns that held up the palace. Zach could see a danger to everyone and began to use his own magic to pull all the frozen people out of the building, Ox helping. Thera and her people began to move back and watched from afar the battle that would determine the fate of their world.

Finally, though they were forced to flee the palace, and gathered in the courtyard. As they watched, the building came crashing down. Zach stared at it, and then ran toward it, shouting out Rose's name, calling to her. As he shifted some of the stone, he could feel her heartbeat, and went towards it. Suddenly what felt like a powerful wind exploded out. Zach staggered, and then he saw her hand, amidst the fallen stones. He grabbed the stone and threw it, and then knelt at her side.

He could hear others approaching as he brushed her hair away from her face.

She stirred at his touch, and slowly opened her eyes.

"I won, he has left this world, and will not come back. The curse on the people will start to fade, and everything will be ok, but I am very tired. I think I will sleep for a while if you watch over me."

Zach nodded, and told her he would watch while she slept, and she smiled shifted slightly and closed her eyes. Her breathing deepened, and her lips parted slightly, as she fell asleep amidst the rubble of the palace. Zach picked her up gently and carried her away from the broken building.

The Ginathias did begin to wake up, and they all seemed to know that Rose, who Zach held cradled against him, had been the one to break the curse. They gathered around the ruined palace and began to clear the rubble. They would rebuild, and make it better, and they would also make a statue of Rose, and place it in the main square. This they would do, to honor the one who had saved them.

Zach and Ox went back to the cliffs and waited for the ship to come and pick them up. Rose was quiet as the ship took off, and she looked out across the stars. Zach studied her and wondered what he could say to comfort her.

Rose wondered if she would have to fight her father every time, she left the Valley. Would she be doomed to fight him for an eternity? Would she never be free of him, and find her own way in the universe? How long could she keep fighting, before he won? And she also thought of poor Shadow, a dragon who was trapped in the form of a human.

She did not know what to do, but she did not really want to kill her father, or keep fighting him, but she was determined to never lose. She would not give in to him, and she would not stop fighting for her freedom, even if it meant fighting her father forever.

When they landed, they went to the king to give their report. Rose had difficulty speaking about her fight with her father but managed to get through it. Zach and Ox also helped describe the events of their adventure on the desert planet, which they decided to call Ginathia. The king was extremely impressed, and happy to know that Rose was ok.

A few other teams had gone out to explore the nearby planets but had not found as much excitement as Rose and her companions. The planets that they had explored had been devoid of life or had very primitive life upon them. The High Fairy king was impressed with all of them and was glad that no real threats existed too close to his people.

As Darwin leaned back in his chair, he gazed at Rose, who still appeared tired after her trip. He dismissed her and told her get some rest. She nodded in gratitude, and strode off, her entire being radiating weariness. Zach watched her go, concern on his face. Rose's fight with her father had taken a toll on her, in many ways.

Zach and his brother also left, going back to their family's farm, to rest and recover. Zach was aware of how his brother felt for Rose but could not deny his own feelings. When he had seen the building fall, Zach had to admit that his heart had skipped a beat, afraid for Rose, and he could not deny it.

Zach sat at the end of his bed, thinking of what had happened, and wondering what to do. He did not want to hurt his brother, but his feelings for Rose were growing, and he did not know what to do about it. The dream he had had before he had even met Rose had told him to teach her how to fight, and how to manage different situations, and how be prepared for anything that might happen, not to fall in love with her.

But as he thought about how he had felt when the building had fallen in on her, and he could not deny that his heart had stopped when he thought of her buried in the rubble. He could not deny how he had thought that his world had ended when she had vanished in the building.

Zach lowered his eyes and thought about his brother. Ox was the one that Rose should be with. Ox was steady and clever, and gentle. He was strong and was a warrior. Zach did not want to hurt his brother; he loved Ox and wanted him to be happy. That was why Zach had always tried to bring Ox with them when they did things together. He was trying to get Rose to notice Ox, and get with him, not Zach.

Zach sighed and tried to find a way out of this situation. But he could not, as thoughts of Rose filled his mind, and he could not help but think of how much he loved her.

CHAPTER TEN

Rose could not sleep, as she thought about what had happened. She did not understand what she was feeling towards Zach, but it was something new. She had never learned about love, as her father thought that emotion to be a weakness. But as she lay on her bed, she could not forget how it had felt to be in Zach's arms, and to see the concern in his eyes, when he had found her in the rubble.

She had never encountered anyone like Zach. He had not cared about her status or what she was, he had only cared to see her as someone that she could be. He had shown her how much she had been missing in her life before he had come into it. She had lived an isolated life, first in the tower with Shadow and then in her father's palace.

Her world had always been structured and ordered. Everything that she had learned had been ordered by her father. She had not had any friends, even the demonesses. They had just seen her as a way to get close to her father. They had not cared about her, as they had not been capable of it.

Here in this place, though, there were people who cared about her, as a person, and the first one had been Zach. He had not seen a spoiled, willful child, but someone who was special. As Rose thought about all the things that Zach had taught her, and done with her, and for her, she felt something growing inside, something she did not understand.

But as she slowly drifted off into slumber, she could not help but think of Zach Dragoon, and how it had felt to be held in his arms.

Ox too was thinking of Rose, and how he felt about her, but

he knew that he did not stand a chance against his brother and would not get in between them. He had seen the fear in Zach's eyes, as the building had come down. He had felt that too, watching Rose and her father fight. It had taken every ounce of will power, for him not to run forward and put himself between her and her father.

Ox sat at the end of his bed, and thought about his brother, and Rose, and knew that he would not try to stop what was happening. He loved them both, and wanted them to be happy, even if he was not. Whatever happened, he would not interfere. He would just be happy for them both.

CHAPTER ELEVEN

Darwin was talking to Cogiere, the head of the royal council, when his brother came into the room. Corwin had heard a rumor, that he wanted his brother to confirm it. The rumor was that Darwin wanted Rose to be put on the council. Corwin believed that everyone was being foolish about this girl and did not approve of his brother's actions concerning her.

As Corwin came up to his brother, and Cogiere, he heard Darwin saying that Rose could be on the council, in a junior position, as she was proving to be an asset to their people. Before Cogiere could respond, Corwin spoke up.

"Why would you put someone who is not even a member of our race on our council? She has been on one mission for you, so how has she proven herself worthy of this honor?! You are rushing into this, and you need to stop and think about what you are doing! She does not belong with us, and she should not be honored in this way!"

Darwin frowned at his brother and responded.

"She has proven herself in other ways, besides just going on this mission. She has been working hard on understanding our laws and learning our customs. I have heard nothing but good things about her ever since she came here. She has done nothing against us and has done many things for us. So, I have decided to put her on the council, as a junior member, and that is final!!"

Cogiere took a breath and told Darwin that he would see to it that Rose's name was added to the list of the council members and that she would be informed of her new title. The king nodded, glowered at his brother, and walked off, as he had other things to take care of. Corwin frowned after his brother and glared at Cogiere. Cogiere merely nodded his head and turned to walk off when Corwin grabbed his arm.

"You know that he is being foolish, Cogiere, and yet you and the others indulge him. Just because she created this valley, does not mean we should bow down to her. She is not a member of our race and has not endured what we have. She should not be honored in this way."

Cogiere studied him and shrugged and replied.

"Your brother is king, and I will follow him always. He is a good man and has a lot of pressure on him. He is doing what he believes is right for the people. He has always done what he believes is right for the people, regardless of any personal feelings. That is difference between you and him. He thinks only of others, you think only of yourself." Cogiere then turned and walked away, leaving Corwin fuming.

Dophina burst into Rose's room, startling her awake, and started talking about Jack. Rose smiled and asked her if it could have waited. Dophina blushed, and smiled, and then laughed, a bit sheepishly. Rose stretched, and yawned, her sapphire eyes dancing with amusement. Dophina told her to stay in bed, she would get Rose something to eat.

As she waited, a knock came on the door. Rose stood up and wrapped a robe around herself and answered it. It was Cogiere, the Head of the Royal Council. Rose blinked in surprise, and then invited him in. He turned to her and bowed slightly, she nodded her head, and then asked.

"To what do I owe the pleasure of your company, so early, my Lord?" Cogiere took a breath and began.

"I have come here to inform you that you have been chosen to join the council, as a junior, or advisory member. In this role, you will be able to attend our meetings, and give your opinion. You will not be allowed to vote, yet, but if you continue to prove yourself, you will eventually have that right. We, the council, may send you out on missions, in the name of the king. We will also allow you to choose your missions, so if you find that you do not like a mission that we have chosen, you can decline.

This decision was made by the king and accepted by the council. We appreciate all that you have done for our people and hope to continue having a good relationship in the future. We are glad that the king has chosen you for this role and will appreciate any help you can give us in this capacity."

Rose blinked and stared at him. She did not entirely believe him, but she could not disbelieve either. This was completely unexpected and had completely thrown her off. As she stood there, staring at Cogiere, Dophina entered, with some breakfast, and blinked as she saw Cogiere standing there, and asked what was going on.

"I have just informed Rose that she has been accepted by the council, in a junior role. Your father asked it of the council, and I presented it to them this morning, and they voted to accept her. She cannot vote, yet, but will earn that right. Now, if you ladies will excuse me, I do have things that I need to do. Good morning to you Princess Dophina, and I will see you both later."

As he left, Dophina looked over at Rose, who still seemed to be in shock. The princess sighed and went over to Rose and shook her a little. Rose blinked, and then sank into a nearby chair. Rose did not know how to respond to this. She had not been among these people long only about a year, but they seemed intent on including her in their society. It was astonishing to her that they would honor her so much, even though she was not really one of them.

Rose was not sure about this, but did not want to disappoint anyone, so she sighed, and ate breakfast. Dophina told her about the present that Jack had given her, a bracelet, with Amethyst flowers. Rose smiled and said that the bracelet was beautiful. She listened for a time to Dophina, but then a knock came on the door. It was Zach, with a picnic basket, and a smile.

"I know that you are supposed to be resting, but I wanted

to take you on a picnic, to the lake. It is a beautiful day, and I wanted to spend it with you." Rose smiled and nodded, and Dophina smiled too. So, Rose got dressed and went with Zach to the lake shore, where they spent the rest of the day just relaxing and talking.

Rose told him about the council, and her new position on it. He was startled but believed that she deserved it. She shook her head, and said,

"I have only been here for about a year. I do not know that I have proven myself to be worthy of the honors they are giving me. I am still young, and inexperienced. I want to see unusual places and meet new people. I do not want to be trapped anywhere. I was trapped by my father and will not do that again." Zach smiled and replied.

"I do not think that they want to trap you. They want to include you. The High Fairies are a highly advanced race, in many ways, and they are good people. I believe that when they look at you, they see potential, and they do not like to waste potential. You may be young, as I am, but you are brave, and experience will come in time. As we are both members of immortal races, we have time to learn a great deal."

She nodded and sighed. He reached out and took her hand, and just held it. She let him for a minute, and then pulled her hand away. As he watched her, he understood what she was feeling. She was confused, but she was, at heart, a good person, though he wondered why she was so different from her father.

CHAPTER TWELVE

Kai leaned back in his throne, watching the demons cavorting around him, and thought about Rose. Maybe, having a planet as her mother had not been a clever idea, though it had seemed that way at first. It seemed to have affected her in unexpected ways. She was not what he had had in mind when he had created her.

She was strong, and determined, but she was not as obedient as she was supposed to have been. He had seen the demon in her, coming out when she had faced him in her room, and on the planet. But her god blood seemed to dominate, and he did not understand why. He had monitored her, watching, and listening in as Shadow had taught her.

Everything seemed to have been going well. Shadow had taught her as Kai had told him, making sure that she understood her roll in her father's plans. She had been arrogant, but compliant. She had wanted to please her father, and he did not understand what had changed. What had happened to change her so drastically?

As Kai watched the demons dance, he knew that there were some who had heard of his defeat, at his daughter's hand. He knew that there would be some that would think of him as getting weak, and he would make an example out those fools, but for now, he would watch her, and wait. He would get back at her, and he would make sure she knew who the stronger of them was. For now, his plans to conquer worlds would go ahead, and he would lead his armies, and do whatever he wanted.

Rose did not understand what she was feeling towards Zach,

but she liked it. She liked being with him and watching him. She spent time on the farm, learning how to cook and do other things, and still practicing with the sword.

She also spent time at the council and learned about how it worked. The council oversaw things like judgements and made sure that everything was going smoothly. The king would attend the meetings and would listen to the concerns that would crop up and pass judgement if he believed he was needed.

The people would bring their concerns to the council, and the council would make sure that everyone was heard, and that things were managed fairly. They made sure that the people knew that they were being heard and cared about.

Most of what was coming before the council, now, were disputes between the different guilds, and land allotment for their work. Each Guild had unique needs, and different tastes. Such as the actors guild needed buildings for various aspects of their work. They needed a building for costumes, make-up, hair, and other preparations, and then a building for practicing, and a building for their final productions, and a building for editing.

The weaver's guild needing a building for processing wool and dying wool and a building for the weaving machines. They also wanted a building to store the material until it could be sent to the factory to be made into different things, like clothing and blankets. They also needed a building for the silkworms, and a building to process silk. They also needed a building to process cotton from the farms.

The baker's guild needed a building for making their products, and for storing their products until they could put them into the stores, and bakeries around the cities. The farmers guild needed buildings to store their products until they could be put into the stores. Then you had the light makers guild, the wood carver's guild, the glass makers guild, the sculpture making guild, and all the artistic guilds, each with their own needs.

The other city would take some of the products of the artisans and make other things for them. Such as furniture, clothing, and other products. The city of the craftsmen would take some of the things of the artisans and mass produce them or create unique items. The craftsmen would refine some the things that they got, and make sure that everyone would have furnishings and other valuable items.

They also made things like refrigerators, microwaves, and stoves, and things like that. But unlike humans, they built these things to last. They did not make things for profit, but just to make them. So, another problem was what to do with the ones that they did not really need.

Rose thought about this and knew that what they needed was a way to trade with humans, without the humans knowing that the people they were trading with had magic, or anything like that. They needed to find some planets that were at the proper stage of development, though the artisans and craftsmen could also make things for underdeveloped planets, which had not reached the level of technology that they had.

Medieval planets did exist, and so did planets of industrial ages. And planets of advanced science. All they needed to do was find these planets, and make sure that the people did not learn about the fact that they were trading with High Fairies, who could pass themselves off as human, if they were careful, so Rose was put in charge of finding planets with which they could trade.

If they were careful, they could do this, and make sure that they did not have an excess of products, as that would cause a whole lot of different problems. So Rose, with Zach and Ox, set out to find planets that they could, with caution, trade with.

Traveling was fun, with Zach, as they flew through the cosmos, in search of planets with intelligent life. Rose knew that there were some that did not agree with this decision and knew that the leader of those people would be Corwin. Corwin was like her father, in that he thought of himself as superior to others. He did not know his people, or care to know them.

Rose studied the stars, outside the ship's windows. She had learned of some planets, with potential, and was making her way to one. Zach and Ox were in the rec room, wrestling. She smiled at the thought of Zach and wondered if they would get some time alone together.

The ship did not take long to get anywhere, as the ship could travel faster than light. They could get anywhere they wanted in a matter of hours, or a few days. The target planet was several days away from the valley, so they would have time to relax before they arrived and spend some time together.

Zach smiled at her, as they sat alone together in the mess hall. No one else was there, as everyone else was in bed or doing their duties. He liked spending time alone with her, and she liked spending time with him. They talked about things, such as what he liked to do when he was not busy, and what she had liked to do when she found time to be alone. He also told her about his people, and their culture, and how he missed the ones he had known, before the Hunters had gotten them.

She did not understand, why the humans, such a versatile race, were so destructive. If they had worked with Zach's people, or the High Fairies, they could have had an easy life, but they just wanted to kill and destroy anyone who was not like them.

She did not understand why a race who lived such short lives only seemed to be intent on finding better ways to kill each other, and anyone who was not like them. If they could find people to trade with, they could help guide them, carefully, to find better ways to live, and improve the standard of living, teach them how to get along with others, and not to simply destroy everyone.

CHAPTER THIRTEEN

They would have to teleport to the planet's surface, as the ship could not land, without giving the whole thing away. That was okay, as they would then have a chance to check out the clothes and customs of the people, as they could also render themselves invisible, if needed.

This planet was in the industrial age. Electricity had been discovered, and industries had been started. They were just getting into the technology revolution.

As the three companions walked down the street, invisible, they caught sight of some of the people, and what they were wearing. The woman was wearing a skirt, with a white shirt, and the man she was with was wearing a white shirt, and jeans. In fact, as they continued to watch, they noticed that everyone was wearing white shirts. And all the women wore skirts of assorted colors, but the men were all wearing jeans.

Rose and her companions modified their clothing to match the clothes of the natives, and were glad that though they did draw looks, it was just because of the size of Zach and Ox. They were noticeably big after all, and that was unusual anywhere.

As they walked down the street, Rose did notice that she was being looked at as well. Though she was extraordinarily beautiful, she did not care about her appearance, though she did take care of herself. So, when people stared at her she became uncomfortable, and finally, as one man stopped to stare at her, she spun and spoke.

"Did your mother ever tell you that it was rude to stare." The man flushed and looked away. Rose shook her head, and they continued to walk down the street. Zach hid a smile, and Ox looked around, and then he noticed a poster, and pointed it out to the others.

They all went over and looked at it. It depicted a trio of people, all dressed in white shirts, and all holding signs that announced a dance that night, at the Rock n Roll café. The address was given, and all were advised to bring their dancing shoes.

Rose looked at her companions, and noted,

"It might be a good idea to go, as it would be an effective way to get to know a culture. Dancing and music can be a good indication about the culture and political environment. We need to know this if we are going to start bringing our products here." Zach nodded and Ox agreed. So, they made note of the address and began to make their way there.

When they arrived, they noted that there were already a lot of people at the café. They did gain entrance and looked around. All the tables had been pushed over to the wall, and the floor cleared. Servers moved around with trays of drinks, and snacks. People were talking about many things, including who was running for president of the world.

At least, Rose thought, the world was united. It was different to see humans that did not have conflict on their world, though she wondered how it had come about. As they moved around the room, they paid attention to what everyone was saying, so they could scope out the political environment.

Soon the trio that had been on the poster came out on to the stage, and everyone turned to face them. Rose and her companions watched as the trio stepped forward and welcomed everyone to the party and asked if everyone was ready to have some fun.

Rose watched the people carefully, as they all responded that they were ready. So, the trio struck up their instruments and began to play. It was a lively tune, and Rose like it, but she noticed that no one moved. She glanced at Zach who shrugged. And Ox looked around, confused, as all three of them wondered why no one was moving. The song ended and the trio thanked everyone, and then they changed their music.

This song was different from the first one and everyone began to move, just a little. Swaying in time with the song, the crowd closed their eyes and just swayed. Rose shrugged at her companions, and they shrugged and began to sway.

The trio played for quite a while, and with each song a different movement moved through the crowd. Rose and her companions followed the movements of the others and wondered what was going on. After the trio was done, everyone commented on how fun the dance had been, and how they were now all tired.

A line of vehicles was waiting outside, for everyone. Rose and the others climbed into one and were asked where they wanted to go. Rose looked at Zach, and then asked if they could be taken to the nearest hotel.

The driver nodded and took off. Rose sighed, and wondered what was wrong with these people, but knew that they need more information. The sun was setting, and everyone was heading home.

The driver pulled up to a building and told them good night, and before Rose could asked how much they owed for the ride, took off. Rose sighed. This planet was weird. They went in and got rooms for the night. Again no one mentioned payment. She wondered about this and decided to do some nighttime investigation to find out.

She showered and washed her hair. It took a while to wash her hair, as it was incredibly long. It did reach her knees. After she had climbed out of the shower, and dried her hair, she began to brush it. This also took a while, but she was used to it. Then she laid down on the bed and wondered about this planet. She shrugged, as she could do astral projection, so her body could rest, and she could look around.

Being in her spirit form did have some drawbacks. She had to be careful about where she went as some people were sensitive to astral forms and they would feel her. She did not like it when someone noticed her. It took her only minutes to float down through the rooms and found Zach waiting for her. She blinked, and looked around, and asked.

"Where is Ox?" Zach smiled and responded.

"He stayed behind, to watch over our bodies, to make sure we are still there in the morning. I did not think it was smart to leave our bodies unguarded in a strange place." Rose thought about it and agreed that it was best that their bodies were not left alone.

So, the two of them set out to see what they could find and learn about this strange land that they were in, and how to set up a business, and everything they would need to know, so that they could begin a trade with these people.

They also discovered why no one had mentioned payment for the taxi or the motel. These were services provided by the government and were funded by taxes, so no one was left out on the streets or driving drunk. So, in essence there were no homeless people, as no one was allowed to be outside after a certain time.

What they found was a society governed by rules that were different than what they were expecting. They found that everyone went to bed at the same time, 9:00 o'clock sharp, and that everyone got up at the same time, 7:00 o'clock sharp. Dancing was only allowed at certain places, and they could only dance to certain songs and in a certain way.

Businesses all closed at 7:00 in the evening, and everyone headed home. If you were out of your house after 9:00 you were fined. The only ones out after 9:00 were the police officers, who made sure that no one else was out. To start a business, you needed to have a license, which could take a few weeks to get.

You also had to have a building, and inventory. This world did have microwaves, and refrigerators, and things like that, so they could modify the appearance of the appliances, to match the ones that were made here, and so make sure that no one could guess that the appliances were not made on their planet.

The history of this planet was not war free. They had had

many wars, but about twenty years ago, they had discovered the nuclear bomb. One had gone off and caused widespread death and disaster. After that, all the countries had gotten together and decided to not have any more wars. It was too dangerous to have the power to destroy all life, so the countries agreed to destroy their weapons and joined as a united world.

Now everyone followed the same rules, but there was not any stifling of advancements. Instead of weapons, they had begun to focus on other areas of technology, like microwaves and other appliances to make things easier for everyone, and advancements were being made in other areas of study like medicine and even space flight, though they were years away from managing that.

And this also not to say that distinct cultures did not exist. The world was a big place and there were many places where things like clothes and languages were different. History was taught, and museums were built to celebrate the past, and learn from it.

There was room for improvement in many areas, though they were doing well. With a business here, the High Fairies might be able to help these people. They could work within the rules, to help these people with advancements and guiding them towards a bright future, but they did need to learn how to dance properly.

In the morning, as Rose and Zach returned to their bodies, Ox was waiting with breakfast, for his brother, as Rose had her own room. After they had eaten, they went to investigate how to find a building and getting all the necessary licenses and things they would need.

They went to the offices of the business bureau, so they could get started. They produced all the necessary paperwork, as they had learned that night about identity papers and everything they needed to do to make this legal. They made sure that everything was in order, and then started the process.

Over the next few weeks, they managed to get the license, a

building, and a warehouse, to store what would not fit in the store. They made sure that everything was set up, and then began to get the products in. Just a few at first, but when the factories in the valley were all up and running, they would get more. Rose and Zach Ox did not stay, now that the store was set up, but they would watch it, and stop by when they could.

When they got back, Rose went to give her report to Darwin. He listened, as she told him about what they had found, and how they had set up the store, and what she wanted to do, behind the scenes, for these people who had put aside the differences of the different areas of their world and had chosen to find a better way.

He told her that he would think about the behind-the-scenes aspect and congratulated her for her excellent work. She was glad that everything had been quiet. She did not want to repeat the fight with her father so soon. She would rest a few days, and then make her way to the next world.

CHAPTER FOURTEEN

The next world, preliminary reports stated, was more of a medieval world, one that had more magic, than the last one. Here on this world, she would find a market for the artisans, for their tapestries and sculptures. Here also she would find a market for some more magical items that were made by the healers, and weapons made by the craftsmen who still practiced blacksmithing.

So, she and Zach, along with Ox, went to this world. She did not know that in time this world, would be the scene of her greatest triumph, and her greatest tragedy. She dressed, not in a dress, but in leggings made of leather, with a white shirt, and a leather vest. Soft boots reached halfway up her calves, and on her hip went a sword.

Zach dressed in leggings, a vest without a shirt, and boots that reached his knees. Ox dressed in a comparable manner and carried his battle axe. Zach took his massive sword, which he placed on his back. They knew that this world might be more dangerous than the last and made sure they were prepared.

They did not know that the world they were going to would be significant to them, otherwise perhaps they would not have gone. But the strands of fate were tightening around them, and they could not escape. So, they made their way to the world of magic, known to its inhabitants as Joran.

Rose gazed around at the people, some of them elves, and some dwarves. They moved carefully, each race staying with their own kind. She did not know what the situation here was, but she would find out. So, she and her companions walked through the marketplace, looking for a merchant who might be able to distribute the High Fairies products.

As they moved through the crowd, they heard shouting, and all looked over at a commotion near one of the stalls. Soldiers appeared, making their way through the crowd. As Rose and the others watched, a young man was being accused of stealing, and he was protesting, saying that he had only picked the apple up, and had intended to put it back with the others.

Rose shook her head and started to turn away when something caught her eye. A shiny glint on the young man's shirt, stood out. As he was hauled past her, she saw a pin on his shirt, of gold. It looked like four golden stars around a fifth. She did not know what that symbol meant, but she wanted to find out.

"I want to talk to that young man, because I think he is innocent, and I am curious about that pin I saw on his shirt." Rose told her companions. The two large men looked at her and then at each other and shrugged. So, they followed the soldiers, who were taking the young man to prison. They waited for a while before going into the prison and asking about him.

The warden frowned at them and told them that the young man could get out of prison, if they paid the debt he owed. Rose really wanted to roll her eyes but managed not too. She asked how much, and he told her a gold mark. She had seen such coins and reached a pouch at her belt. The pouch was empty, but he did not know that, as she pulled out a gold mark.

The warden took it, went into the cells, and returned with the young man. He frowned at them, but did not say anything, as they took him outside.

"I am grateful for your help, but I could have managed that myself. I know how to take care of myself. And my name is Gordyl." He said this extremely fast, but as he tried to leave, Rose caught his arm, and asked.

"Where did you get that golden pin? And by the way, my name is Rose, and these two are Zach and his brother Ox."

Gordyl studied her and then looked down at his chest, at the pin that rested there.

"I have had this pin for years. My mother gave it to me. She told me that it would bring me luck, but I have not noticed any. I am always in trouble, even though I never start it. I was just picking up the apple that had fallen, so I could put it back. I have money and do not need to steal. I do need to get back home and, thank you for helping me."

Rose watched him go, wondering if there was more to the pin, then Zach touched her arm, and she looked over at him.

"It is getting late, and the merchants are going home. We need to get back to the inn. We can find a merchant in the morning and find Gordyl as well. But in the morning." Rose nodded and the three companions made their way back to the inn, that they had taken rooms in earlier.

Rose thought about many things, as she lay on her bed. Most of all she thought about Zach, and if they could have a future together. She smiled, as she thought about it. But how would any children they might have turn out? If they could have children.

Zach lay on his bed, which, like his brother's, was too small for his big frame. He was thinking of Rose, and if they could be together. He was sure that he loved her, and he wanted to be with her. As he drifted off into sleep, he knew that he wanted to take the chance.

As they woke in the morning, they noticed a commotion outside, and hurried out to see what was happening. A crowd was gathering in the main square, it seemed as if all the people of the city were gathered here, elves, humans, dwarves, all watching the stage that had been set up in the square.

Rose could not see what was happening, thinking it was a hanging or something, but then a ripple passed through the crowd, as a shadow swept over them. A large dragon landed in front of the governor's palace, and a man dismounted, climbing the stairs to the stage, and stepping forward, he began to speak, his voice carrying over the crowd.

"I am come to tell you that the king has fallen. Assassins in the night crept up through the castle and killed him. He fought fiercely but was brought low by a poisoned knife. We know who sent these assassins, and we are even now preparing to seek revenge on our beloved king's death, as it was foul elves that killed him. So, we will march upon the elven lands and rid ourselves of their scourge," as he spoke, all the elves in the crowd stared at him, and placed their hands on their weapons, looking around, on their guard for hostile actions.

The dwarves also frowned and looked around, studying the humans. They did not believe that the elves had anything to do with the death of the king, but humans were not always known to be rational. Rose returned her attention to the speaker, as he continued.

"We call upon on all loyal citizens to help us, as we prepare ourselves for war. We will do whatever it takes to avenge our king's death and end the threat of the elves. We will face them down and finally be rid of their threat, and we will be free of the elves, who think of themselves as superior to us, and who will stop at nothing to take what is ours. We will show them that we are not weak, not foolish, and we will show them that humans are strong, and they will regret killing our beloved monarch, as we wipe them from the face of our world."

Zach looked around and could see that there was going to be trouble, but as he turned to speak with Rose and Ox, he heard Rose speak up, over the crowd, and this is what she said.

"You should not condemn an entire race just because of the actions of a few. And you can say that elves did it, but you have not proven anything. All we have is the word of one man, and I chose to believe that not all elves should be punished because of a few who, if they are assassins, hold no allegiance to anyone. I do not believe that the elves should be wiped out just because you say so."

Zach closed his eyes, as all the people, human and not human turned to face them. Rose stood straight, and as tall as she could, her hand resting on the hilt of the sword she wore on her hip. Zach assumed a position behind her, and Ox standing to the side. Each of the big men gripped their weapons and faced the crowd.

The man who had been speaking, gazed at her, frowning. He did not know her, but there was something about her that was almost familiar. She stood her ground, her chin raised in defiance of the soldiers that were making their way through the crowd.

"War is not always the answer and should be used only if there is no other recourse. I did not see the elves attack your king, and all we have is your word and how do we know that we can trust your word. How do we know you are the type of man to know what honesty and honor mean? You would condemn an entire race to extinction, without considering the consequences of that action."

"Enough," the man shouted, "I will listen no more to your words, woman, as you are obviously a lover of elves. You do not understand our ways, and we will avenge our king's death, and you will be arrested as traitors." Rose shook her head and drew her sword.

Zach did the same, and Ox gripped his battle axe. All three of them stood their ground and got ready to fight. But just as the soldiers reached them, the dragon suddenly bellowed, and everyone looked up. The soldiers stopped and looked over at the dragon. The sky was suddenly filled with other dragons, white, gold, and silver.

Rose blinked, as the red dragon that the man had arrived on arched its neck and it roared. Then it spread its wings and took off, leaving the man behind. The red dragon took to the skies and faced the other dragons. It roared, and flapped its wings, as it sought to intimidate the other dragons. It was not working.

"Let's get out of here, while everyone is distracted." Zach whispered to Rose softly. She looked over at him, and then studied the crowd, as the soldiers were looking at the dragons too. She did not want to leave, but Zach was right, the situation was volatile. She nodded and they slowly began to back away from the soldiers.

It was hard for Zach and his brother to be unnoticed. They were larger than most people. But by moving slowly, and ducking a little, they did manage to get far from the soldiers, but as the soldiers turned back to them, they all heard a shriek of pain, so loud that it flattened everyone.

The red dragon fell from the sky, surrounded by a halo of lightening, ice, and fire. The people in the square screamed as it fell, and ran from it, trying not to get crushed. The other dragons, hovering over the city, roared as they watched him fall.

But suddenly there were more red dragons, coming to aid of their companion, for even as the one fell from the sky, the red dragons fell upon the other dragons from the side.

Rose had never seen a fight between dragons but wished she did not have to watch it. The dragons attacked with such ferocity that their blood rained from the sky, to drop on the people below. The hot blood ignited fires and caused widespread destruction.

The screams of dying people and dragons filled her ears, and the smell of burning flesh clogged her nose. Smoke filled the air from the many fires that had been started. Zach grabbed her, and pulled her out of the main square, into an alley where they could be safe. He watched for few moments, and then shook his head. It was not right that dragons should fight, and he knew that he could do something to help. He looked over at Ox and told him to stay with Rose.

Ox nodded and moved closer to Rose, who frowned at Zach and asked him what he was going to do. Zach took a breath and told her that he was to go to take on his dragon form and stop the fight. It was dangerous, but he needed to stop the dragons from fighting, and he knew that he had a better chance to do it in his dragon form, which was bigger than the dragons here.

Rose nodded and Zach stepped out, and spread his wings, taking on his dragon form as he flew upward. The other dragons did not notice him at first, but with a roar that shattered glass, he dove at the dragons, forcing them to break apart. They all recognized him for what he was and hovered as they faced him. No dragon would harm one of his kind, and in the language of the dragons, he demanded to know why they were fighting each other.

"We fight because we are compelled too by the humans and elves. We do not wish to fight each other, but their magic binds us and forces us to do this. We would that they would just leave us alone." Zach contemplated this, and then reached out with his mind towards Rose, and told her what the dragons had said. She did not like the thought of the dragons being enslaved to anyone, and so she tapped into her own magic, and undid the spells that bound the dragons to their masters.

Her power was so much stronger than the elves and humans, that it reached out to touch every dragon on the planet and unbound them from their masters. But as she reached out to the dragons, she asked that they try not to do too much damage, as there were those who were innocent. She asked the dragons to just do a little damage and then leave.

The dragons were all free, and found themselves in control of themselves, so they began to take revenge upon those who had enslaved them and to break down the buildings that they had been kept in and gathered their eggs, and then they flew off, after doing some damage to those who had forced them to do their bidding.

Rose staggered slightly, and Ox caught her. Zach landed and watched as the dragons roared their elation and took off, leaving the city to burn. They did not care about the city or those within it, for they were free, and wanted only to return to their ancestral homes in the mountains.

"Come on, we should be getting out of here." Zach said, looking over at his companions. Rose nodded, and she shook off Ox's hand, and tried to walk forward, but did not get far. This time Zach caught her, and he picked her up, and cradled her in his arms.

She sighed, and let him, knowing that she would need some

time to recover from her use of her magic. She knew that one of the reasons that she tired when she used her magic, was because she tried not to. Magic cost energy, and if you did not use it as often as you should, it could make you tired. Like your muscles, magic needed to be exercised if you did not want to tire easily when using it.

Though she tried to deny it, magic was a part of her, and she might need it in future, so she determined to use it more, so she would not get tired so easily. If she needed to face her father, she wanted to be strong enough to fight him.

They managed to get out of the city, as many others were able to as well. They found themselves surrounded by what could now be called refugees. Zach and Ox parted the crowd easily and walked for quite a while before they stopped. Zach put Rose down, and they all looked back at the burning city.

"I hope that the dragons will be ok, and that I did the right thing." Rose said softly, as they watched the city. The people were no longer concerned about any war. They looked back at their city, and cursed the dragons and the elves, and nobles, and just life in general. Zach studied her, and wondered what she was thinking, and thinking that the fire light made her even more beautiful.

"I believe that you did do the right thing, in setting the dragons free, and I believe that they should not be forced into anything. No one should have their right to choose taken from them. We are all born free, and that is how we should stay." Rose looked at him and smiled. She finally admitted to herself that she loved this man, and that she wanted to be with him.

As they sat around the fire, a figure approached them. As he stepped into the light, they were astonished to see Gordyl. He looked weary, and dirty. But on his tunic the pin stilled gleamed. Before he could ask if he could share their fire, he fell over.

Rose reached him first and saw an arrow sticking out of his shoulder. She pulled him over to the others, and with her magic, removed the arrow, and healed the wound. Then she turned him over and shook him until he woke up.

"How did you end up with an arrow in your shoulder?" Rose asked, as she helped him into a sitting position. He shuddered slightly and took a breath.

"Some soldiers tried to ambush me. I was forewarned where they were, but they still managed to hit me. I was looking for you when they struck. They did not follow me, as it was getting dark, and they did not want to be ambushed themselves. I am glad that I found you. I was told to tell you something important.

It is important for you to know that you have been chosen for a great purpose. You will learn about this purpose in time when you are truly ready for the task. The power that chose you is greater than the gods, demons and even planets. She truly is the ultimate power that exists everywhere, and she has caused all things to exist. She will reveal herself in time. You still have a while to go before you are ready. Now I must go, but I wish you luck and may the stars guide you home."

Gordyl stood up and bowed to her, and before she could ask any questions he was gone. Disappearing into the night, leaving her with more questions than before. She thought about trying to follow him but did not want to get lost in the dark.

Zach shook his head, and investigated the darkness, thinking. Ox stirred the fire and sighed. Rose shook her head and wondered what Gordyl was talking about. She sighed, and then announced that she was going to sleep. She wrapped herself in her blanket and laid down. Zach looked over at his brother, and said that they should set a watch, and Ox volunteered to go first.

Zach nodded and laid down, watching the stars, as they glittered overhead. He wondered how he was going to propose to Rose, because he knew that he wanted to. No matter what, he wanted to be with her if he could.

Ox woke Zach up at midnight and went to sleep. There was movement in the dark, but no one bothered them, as Zach was formidable in the best of times. And with the woman he loved nearby, no one would try anything.

In the morning, as they prepared to move out, Rose gazed back at the city, and wondered what would happen now. She knew that a war between the humans and elves would not be a good thing, and even without the dragons they would still fight. But she did not know what would happen.

They traveled to the next city, finding chaos, as no one knew why the dragons had left. And no one wanted to know what kind of being was powerful enough to release the dragons from the spells that had bound them. And no one knew if the dragons would return to get revenge for their enslavement.

Rose shook her head. She and her two companions knew that the dragons just wanted to be left alone. They did not care about what the humans and elves and dwarves did, as they just want to find places for themselves where no one could reach them.

In this turmoil, no one would really be interested in tapestries. But Rose and her companions talked to several merchants and found one that was willing to look at the tapestry that they brought with them. The quality was excellent, but he was not so sure about the theme. It was a scene of a field of flowers, with a winding river running through it. A few trees were visible and some birds, along with a deer drinking from the river.

He thought about it for a few moments, and then decided to buy it. He asked if they would be coming again, and Rose nodded, and told him what kind of tapestry themes were popular, and what were people looking for in their tapestries and rugs.

He told them that the current popular theme was fights, like knight jousting and battle scenes. Rose nodded and told him that they would have some of those when they came by again. He nodded and paid them a good deal of money for the tapestry they had given him.

They left the merchant and headed back to the inn, when

they saw a woman being dragged off by some men. Rose immediately went over and kneed one of men, forcing him to let go of the woman. The other turned to her and told her to mind her own business, and Zach reached over and pick the man up, and told him to leave, before he made Zach mad.

Looking at the size of Ox and Zach the men decided that it was not worth it and left. Rose shook her head and turned to the woman, who was attempting to fix her dress, which had gotten torn in the scuffle.

"Are you alright?" Rose asked, looking at the woman with concern. The woman looked up at her and nodded.

"I am fine, just a little rattled is all. I have no idea what just happened, or why those men grabbed me. Thank you for helping me, my name is Milly. What is yours?"

"I am called Rose, and this is Zach and his brother Ox. We are traveling merchants, looking for places to sell our tapestries and rugs, along with other things. We were just heading back to our inn. You should get home, before those men come back." Milly nodded, and after looking around, she started off, being careful of where she walked.

"Maybe we should follow her, to make sure she stays safe." Rose said, and her companions nodded, and so they followed Milly back to her home, near the governor's house. After they were sure that Milly was safe, they returned to their inn. They ate supper, and then Rose took a bath. They retired to their rooms and went to sleep.

Rose was awoken in the predawn hours, by Zach's hand over her mouth. He studied her carefully, and then whispered.

"Get dressed, we have trouble brewing. Ox already has our bags packed. Be as quiet as you can." Rose looked at him, a question in her eyes, but he shook his head and mouthed "later." she nodded in acknowledgement, and he turned around. She slipped off the bed and noticed the smell of smoke in the air. The fireplace was empty, the fire having gone out, so it was not coming from that.

She pulled on her clothes and follow Zach out of the room.

Ox was waiting for them in the hallway. As they descended the stairs, they all could tell that something was going on. All the other guests at the inn were down in the common room, demanding to know what was going on. The innkeeper, looking worried, told them that an unknown army had come upon the city, and had launched an attack.

This had no connection to the dragons, as they had already left, but no one had been forewarned about this army. In the confusion the dragons had left behind, no one had expected something like this to happen.

Rose looked over at Zach and Ox. The last thing any of them had wanted was to get caught up in a war. Even as they wondered how they would get out of the besieged city, a soldier entered, and told all the men to get ready to go to the wall to help defend the city.

There was an immediate outcry of protests at this news, but the soldier was not in the mood for arguments. He stepped aside, and more soldiers entered, and began to round them up. Rose moved closer to Zach, refusing to be separated from him, and the soldiers studied her. She looked at them defiantly and spoke.

"Where he goes, I go. I know how to fight, and I can help. Just try to stop to me." With that she started towards the door. Upon reaching it she looked back and asked.

"What are you waiting for, an invitation? Let us go." Zach smiled and looked over at his brother, who shrugged, and then they followed Rose outside, and to the wall. She had never been in a battle, but she had grown up in a place where screams were so common that she put them out of her mind and focused on the task at hand. She did as her training had taught her.

She surveyed the enemy lines, looking for weaknesses and ways to exploit them. She took note of the siege engines, and their placement, watching them. She calculated the time it took the men staffing them to load and fire them, and the angle of their descent.

Then as she watched the boulder coming down, she reached

out with her magic, and caught it. She held it for a moment, and then threw it back at the catapult that had fired it. The catapult exploded under the impact of the boulder and killed and injured those who had been around it. She did this to every single catapult.

With the siege engines out of commission, it became easier for the defenders to repel the attack. Rose took up a bow, and fired arrow after arrow, never missing her target. She was magnificent, in Zach and Ox's eyes. The fires that had been started in the town, and the fires of the enemy encampment, seemed to exist solely to illuminate her as she fought in her first battle.

Finally, the enemy fell back, unable to continue the assault. The light of the rising sun fell upon the city, and they could all see a young woman, lowering her bow, the sunlight illuminating her as if on purpose, to show the attackers the one that had turned the tide of battle.

Zach went over to her, picked her up, and kissed her. At first, she squirmed but then she relaxed and enjoyed her first kiss. As Zach pulled back, he flushed slightly, and smiled at her. She smiled back, and then kissed him.

Ox looked away, wishing that things had been different, and Rose would have fallen for him, but he had to admit, that his brother was much more impressive than he was. As he looked out at the enemy encampment, he noticed something. And he touched his brother's arm. Zach frowned and looked over at him, and then to where he was pointing.

A massive battering ram was being brought through the encampment. A massive rams head had been carved into it, and the long dark wood had been soaked in water, to prevent it from being burned. Rose stared it. She had never seen anything like this. Zach put her down and looked over at his brother. Ox nodded and took a breath.

The two brothers jumped down from the wall, their own magic protecting them, and then they waited, for the battering ram to come closer. Both the big men ready their weapons and made ready for their attack.

Rose guessed what they were doing and took up her bow. The other archers did the same. The commander, shouted, and told them to hold their fire until the ram was closer. As Rose watched the ram, Zach and Ox got ready. Before the ram came within bowshot range, the two big men charged. With bellows that could be heard from the walls, the two brothers, each wielding massive weapons, charged at the battering ram.

Even as those on the wall looked on, the two brothers wreaked havoc among the attackers, each wielding their weapons with great skill, and strength. Even the great battering ram did not stand a chance against the ferocity of these two brothers. The attackers fled, not wanting to face the wrath of Zach and Ox.

Rose and the defenders cheered as the two fighters chopped the battering ram into pieces. After they were done, they made their way through the carnage back to the city. The city commander looked over at Rose and said softly.

"It was a good day for our city when the three of you decided to come here. I have never met any warriors like you. Thank you for helping us. I will see to it that the gate is opened for your friends." He turned away and hurried to the gate, which was opened just enough to let Zach and Ox back in.

They were given a warm welcome, as they returned to the city. Rose pushed her way through the crowd to join them, smiling at them. She had felt a slight tremor of fear when both jumped down from the wall but had trusted them. Zach beamed down at her, and she stood on her tippy toes to reach his mouth.

They were escorted to the governor's house, where the city governor received them himself, and given many rewards, though they protested them. They did not need rewards, as they had just been helping. But the city people would not hear of them not taking the gifts. They had run off the attackers.

The commander of the attackers was unhappy with how

things had turned out. He had not expected such resistance here. But his army was scattered, and his siege engines destroyed. He did not want to return to his lord, with such a defeat. So, he drank some poison, knowing that this was the only way to avoid the torment his master had planned for those who could not achieve what he wanted them too.

Rose, Zach, and Ox were embarrassed, to say the least. They had just been doing what they believed was necessary for the defense of the city. They did not want to be honored, for just doing their duty. But the people of the city were most insistent.

By the time they were able to get away from the citizens of the city, sunset was approaching. They had been fighting most of the night and part of the day. They were all tired and found their rooms in the governor's house to be most inviting. Rose stretched out on her bed, thinking about kissing Zach, and how good it had felt.

Zach was thinking about what he could do to propose to Rose. He knew that he needed some incredibly extraordinary gifts, to give her. As he thought about it, an image came to him, of a sword wrapped in fire, a ring with a sapphire rose placed upon it, and a saddle worthy of her horse. He nodded and determined to start on those things as soon as they got home.

Ox knew that he would be attending his brother's wedding, as it was only a matter of time now, before Zach proposed to her. His heart was heavy, for his love of Rose had only grown. But he knew that he would stand there, and not say a word, watching the woman he loved marry his brother. What he could not have known was that something was going to happen that would change everything.

CHAPTER FIFTEEN

In the morning, the people greeted them warmly, and the three companions enjoyed some breakfast. The soldiers of the city had cleared the field of the remains of the attackers and had made sure that no other enemy army was nearby.

Though the townspeople did not want them to go, Rose and her companions did have business elsewhere. So, burdened down with gifts, the companions left the city behind, wondering if any more armies would attack. They did not know, so they decided to be careful, and make their way to another city, to find more markets for their tapestries and rugs.

They passed through several villages over the next month, but no sign of any trouble. Finally, they came to the capital city of the kingdom that they were in. It was large, with three gates, each facing a different direction. Behind the city rose cliffs, forming a barrier to attack from that direction. The walls were in a half circle around the city, and there were three tiers.

The topmost tier was the palace of the king. Its many towers rose above the city with gay pennants blowing from them. The wall that formed the barrier between the palace and the second tier was thick and strong, with only one gate. The second tier was the houses of the nobles and merchants. Here and there gardens could be seen.

The bottom tier was where everyone else lived, and had the markets, and inns, along with taverns. Rose gazed it and thought that it looked like every other human city she had seen. Humans did not have much imagination when it came to construction. But, in time, they would find diverse ways to build things.

By this time, the human king, Thero, had heard of the heroes of Tamberling, the city that they had saved, and had gotten descriptions of them. They were recognizable, as Zach and his brother were huge, and Rose was beautiful, so as they came to the gate, they found themselves looking at a welcoming committee. The soldiers bowed them through, and then formed up around them to escort them to the king, so he could thank them personally for saving Tamberling.

Rose did not like all this attention. She had not come here to be a hero, just to help find a market for the weaver's guild. She had not started this journey wanting to be recognized by anyone, except the merchants who would sell the carpets and tapestries of the weaver's guild. Now she found herself facing a human king, the son of the king that had been killed by elves.

The young king greeted them warmly and thanked them for protecting the city of Tamberling. He told them how grateful he and his people were to know that they did not fight alone, against the invaders, but that they had allies in this fight. Rose did not know about any invaders, but she told him that they were glad to have been of service to the city. They were not soldiers, but merchants, seeking a market for their home's tapestries and carpets, and other woven goods.

The young king was taken aback by this announcement, but he knew that even merchants needed to know how to fight, to protect themselves from bandits. He asked where they were from, and Rose responded that they were from a distant land, which was called simply the Valley, as it was a valley, hidden in the mountains.

They did not know about this Valley, but if it had soldiers like these merchants, they might prove to be good allies, in the coming war. He asked if he could speak with her in private. Rose hesitated, but then nodded, and told Zach and Ox to wait for her. Zach did not like the idea of her being alone with anyone, but he trusted her, and agreed.

So, the king took her to his private study, and shut the door.

He waited for her to sit, before he did. This indicated respect, and he wanted every advantage he could get, because what he was going to ask her was not an easy thing.

"This attack on Tamberling, was not the first, nor will it be the last. A dark sorcerer has been gathering his forces, not just of humans, but of orcs and goblins. Trolls and ogres, and even giants have joined him. He gathers at the edge of my kingdom, and even with our allies, the elves, and dwarves, we are outnumbered. The army he has gathered is massive, and it begins to look bleak for us. And without the dragons, we must travel slowly. We do not know how the dragons broke free of our spells, but we fear they will join our enemies. Without the dragons we are outnumbered, and if they join with our enemies than we are in great peril.

I have no reason to think that you and your people might help us. We are gathering our own forces, but we have little hope. I know that some people are trying to get us to attack the elves, but right now we need them. We have little experience with war, as it has been centuries since the last. We need help from those that know how to fight. And you do. Will you be able to appeal to your people, for help? We need all the help we can get."

Rose leaned back in the chair. This is what had driven the High Fairies from their former home. They had fled their home world because of war. She could tell that the human king was telling the truth. He was desperate. He was pleading with a stranger for help. And he did not know it, but Rose was the one that had released the dragons.

"I cannot speak for my people, but your cause is just. I will go and speak to my people on your behalf, but I cannot make any promises. And as for the dragons, they just want to be left alone. I do not think they will join anyone. I have seen the signs of mobilization in your lands, and I have seen the elves and dwarves going to join their own kindred, to prepare for war. You must hold onto hope, and I will do what I can."

He thanked her profusely and asked her if she needed

anything for the journey back to the Valley, but she shook her head. He took her back to the throne room and she went over to Zach and Ox and spoke to them about what the king had said. Both brothers did not know how the request for aid for the humans, elves, and dwarves would be answered in the valley.

They left the next day, making their way to a place where they could contact the ship and get back to the valley. The ship's captain, as they teleported onto the ship, asked them about the time, as they were not due to come back for another few weeks. Rose told him about the plight of the humans, and their plea for help. He did not think it was such a good idea, but he got them back to the Valley quickly.

Rose spent a day in preparation for going before the council and the king to place the plea of humans at their feet. During that day, Zach went in search of something special. An incredibly special type of metal that could only be found in the heart of a star.

Being a dragon, he was immune to fire, but to go into the heart of a star was dangerous. His magic would protect him, but it would cost a great deal. But he knew that it would be worth it to get the right kind of metal for her new sword. So, he found the closest star, and willed himself into it. It was intense, the heat and light, but he could see what he wanted.

He reached out and grabbed a lump of metal. It was warm in his hands, and he could feel the fire of the star burning in it. It was the fire that he wanted, as he could keep it, with certain spells, so the fire would never go out. After he had obtained the metal, he went to the forge, and began his work.

Soon the only sound that could be heard, was the pounding of his hammer. The only thing he was aware of was the smell of metal, the sound of his hammer and feel of the heat of the forge. The only thing he did not do, was cool the metal in the water barrel. To do so might kill the fire he wanted to burn forever in the sword.

His arm swung the hammer, pounding the metal, capturing the flame of the star. He shaped the sword bending and folding the metal until it finally took on the shape he wanted. He smoothed the metal, sanding it down a little, to make the metal gleam. The fire wreathed the blade, dancing and shifting. The flame took on the color of her eyes, a deep blue, to dance and flicker along the blade, to reflect the eternal fire she had ignited in him.

Once the blade was done, he turned his hand to the hilt. Carving it of gold and gemstones, he made it in the shape of dragon its wings forming the crosspiece. It was long enough that she could use both hands, if necessary, or just one. He carved each individual scale, giving the hilt grace and beauty.

For the eyes of the dragon, he inserted sapphires, diamonds for its teeth and claws, and placed tiny rubies along the edges of the scales. No mortal, even a dwarf, could have matched the skill of a Shoulai dragon, when it came to such things. They had spent much of their time in study of blacksmithing, silversmithing and jewelry making. They were unequaled in skill of such things. And Zach made something that there would never be an equal sword to.

The Burning Blade, holding within it the fire of the stars, rested upon the anvil. From the tip of the blade, to end of the hilt, there was no equal. It would never dull, never fade, and the flames would forever wreath it, to represent the eternal nature of his love for her. He gazed at it and knew that he would live to see her wield it in battle.

Going into a star had taken a toll on him. His magic was weaker, perhaps because of the very act of going into the heart of a burning star had cost him some of his magic forever. He did not know. But now that the sword was done, there were two other things to make.

He made the ring first, enchanting it to help keep her safe, and then came the saddle. He made it so it would never wear out and would prevent her from falling off. Gold lined the edges of the saddle, in the design of vines. Gemstones rested upon it, sparkling in the dim light of the forge.

It did not take him as long to make the ring and the saddle, as it had to make the sword. But now he had everything he need to propose to Rose. He went to his mother and told her of his plans. His mother smiled and told him she was happy that he had found Rose. Zach's mother then went and told her daughter, who did not respond other than a slight nod.

Frank was excited, and with Sarah went to town to begin to gather the things they would need for the wedding. Rose had not said yes yet, as Zach had not yet asked her, but there seemed to be no doubt his parents' minds that she would say yes.

Ox did not know what to do, but he knew that he would not stop his brother, and would lie through his teeth, and tell him he was happy for him and Rose. None of them knew that something was going to happen, that would change everything.

CHAPTER SEVENTEEN

Rose spoke her piece before the council, asking for help for the mortals on Joran. Maybe if they could help these people, a peace treaty could be signed, and they could find a way to help them more and have influence in the lives of the good people of Joran, maybe they could help them become better. She told them that if they had the power to help then they had the responsibility to help.

Corwin could not believe that anyone would listen to what he considered rubbish. They had come to this valley to get away from war, and this girl wanted to drag them into one that was not even their business. Who cared if this Joran planet was overrun by orcs and goblins, who cared if they killed or enslaved other lesser beings? Who cared if the world of mortals was destroyed?

He did not count on Rose being so eloquent. She spoke with passion, about responsibility, obligations, and the rights of all. She spoke against slavery, against injustice, against turning their backs on people who needed them. She spoke for helping those who needed help, for those who did not have the strength to protect themselves, and for those who were innocent.

Caught up in her passion, the council voted to help the people of Joran. They turned to a man called Lord Um, who oversaw the knights of the High Fairies, and his twin brother, Lord Im, who was in charge of the archers, and charged them with going to Joran to help the people.

Corwin jumped to his feet and declared.

"You are all fools. Why should we help these people? What

benefit can come from helping them, and why should we care if they are killed, or enslaved? They are not of our people, but are mortals, like those that chased us out of our home world. Why should we do anything for mortals, who if they learned of who and what we are would just turn on us!? And why should we listen to this girl, who is not even of our kind?"

Darwin climbed to his feet and faced his brother.

"We are of a race that is both powerful and good. We did leave our home world to get away from war, but if we turn away from this situation, we make ourselves no better than those we left behind. We are of a superior race, and this is an opportunity to prove that. And need I remind you that I adopted this girl into my family, which makes her one of us. We will do what we can for the good people of Joran, and I will not have you call anyone names."

Corwin glowered at his brother. He looked over at Rose and said to her.

"Just because you are the creator of this Valley does not mean that I will bow to you, nor will I ever accept you as part of this family or people." With that he turned and stormed from the room. Silence filled the room, but everyone agreed with their king. They would help the people of Joran because they wanted too, and because they were better than what Corwin thought of them.

Lord Um faced Rose and said softly.

"I agree with you. We need to do this, because if we do not, then we are condemning the innocent to death, torment, and slavery. We are better than that, and we will prove it. I will go and begin at once, to prepare the knights for the journey to Joran. And I would like to accept you into the lowest order of knights, which means that you can advance in rank, all the way to the highest order. As there are seven orders and you will be able to go through each."

Rose was taken aback, by the offer. She had not intended to join the knighthood, just get them to help the people of Joran. Lord Um smiled at her and told her that they could go through the ceremony of acceptance later, as he was sure that she had things to do right now as well. She nodded and watched as he left. These people kept surprising her at every turn.

She shrugged then, and went to the stables, mounted Midnight, and rode out to the farm. When she got there, she found Zach, looking a little nervous, waiting for her. She dismounted and went over to him. It had been over a year and a half since she had come here to the valley. She had known Zach for much of that time, and she felt safe with him.

As she approached, Zach could only wonder what the future held, though he knew that something was coming, he did not know what it was. He intended to spend what time he could with her and watched her as she came over to him.

"How did the meeting go? Did you manage to convince them to help Joran?"

"Yes, the knights are preparing even now. Lord Um, the head of the knight's council has taken me into the lowest order of the knights and is preparing for the acceptance ceremony. His brother, Im, is making sure that the rest of the army is getting ready, though it will take some time to organize them. I hope to be able to leave for Joran within the week."

Zach nodded, and studied her, noting that she looked tired. He took her hand and led her into the kitchen, where he got her some tea. She sighed. Zach watched her and knew that she was glad that she had been able to get the High Fairies to help. She was tired because she had expended a lot of energy into her speech, and a lot of emotions had come into play.

"Maybe you should get some sleep. You can take a nap on the couch, if you like, and later, I will take you on a picnic, just the two of us." Rose smiled, and then went into the living room, and laid down on the couch. Zach watched her for a moment, and then when he was sure she was asleep, he got everything together.

CHAPTER EIGHTEEN

After about two hours, Rose woke up, feeling much better. Zach stood in the doorway, and smiled at her, she smiled back, and stood up. She followed him to the horses, and climbed up onto Midnight, and followed Zach as he led her down to their favorite picnic spot.

The sun was warm, as they dismounted, and Rose stretched in the warm light. Wildflowers bloomed, and their scent lingered in the air. Some bumblebees hovered over the sweet-smelling flowers, humming contentedly. It seemed as if everything was happy and perfect.

Zach watched her for a moment and stood up and fetched some items from his saddle bag. One was long, and wrapped in cloth, one was in a small box, and the last was covered by a blanket. Rose studied him, curious, and he took a breath.

"Among our people, it is a tradition to give someone you love three gifts, and I have spent the last few days making these three things for you, and before you accept them, I will ask you something. Now the first thing is this." He pulled the blanket off the first item, revealing the gold embossed saddle. It was perfect for her, and beautiful. Then he opened the box revealing the ring, and finally, he unwrapped the last item, revealing the sword.

Rose stared at him, as she realized what he was going to ask her. He stepped forward, and knelt before her, and asked softly.

"Rose Debarra, will you accept these gifts, and me? Will you marry me?" Rose's heart sang, and she smiled and told him yes. Zach leapt up and grabbed her and kissed her. She laughed and kissed him back. He swung her around and scared off the bees.

They then enjoyed the picnic, both happy and content, but over Zach's heart hung a cloud of uncertainty, as he wondered if he would live long enough to marry her. He knew that he was dying, for in going into the star, and pouring so much of his magic into the sword, and the ring, and the saddle, he had drained himself, and could no longer feel connected to his magic, but he would go with her and fight with her, and he wondered how she would react when she found out, but was determined that for now, he would say nothing.

Ox professed his happiness for their engagement, when they told him, but Rose thought she heard something in his voice, but then Shalia hugged her, and Frank congratulated his son. As a seamstress, Shalia would be making the dress. She had already been to the weaver's guild and gotten the fabric that she needed. Now she measured Rose and pinned the dress to the right measurements.

Darwin was happy for her as well when she told him later. Dophina was ecstatic, and immediately began to plan the dinner, and everything else. Rose smiled and told her that Shalia was making the dress. And she wanted to have the wedding down by the lake, at the same spot that Zach had taken her to, when he had taken her fishing for the first time.

Dophina nodded, and she began to count things off, on her fingers, about what needed to be done. When asked if she and Zach had picked a time for the wedding, Rose responded that they were going to have it after they had helped the people of Joran. Dophina nodded again, and after she had eaten, she dashed off, to get a hold of the flower growers, and the chefs, and everyone that was needed to make sure that everything was prepared for the wedding.

Rose smiled and shook her head. She wanted a quiet ceremony but knew that as a member of the royal family, she was not likely to get that. Soon everyone in the Valley would know and be getting ready for her wedding.

After dinner, Rose went to the incomplete headquarters for the knights, and went through the acceptance ceremony.

Unlike some races, the High Fairies did not discriminate between the genders. If a woman wanted to join the Knighthood, then she was welcome to do so.

Rose took the oaths of the knighthood, which were to uphold the honor of the knights, to stand for truth, and justice, to defend others and to protect the innocent. To act with honor in her dealings with others, to trust the other knights and to stand with honor in all things.

As the ceremony wound to an end, she shuddered, and watched in astonishment, as the armor of the knighthood of the stars wound its way around her. It was like cloth, not metal, and allowed her to move freely. It shimmered like metal, and felt hard, but it moved with her. Um looked at her and spoke.

"The armor will change color with each advancement. The knights of the stars are the lowest level of the knighthood, with the knights of the moon next, and after that the knights of the sun, and then the knights of the earth, and then the knights of the sky, and after that the knights of the dragons, and then the knights of the phoenix, and finally the knights of Battle. The Battle knights are charge with the protection of the royal family and are the ones that lead the others into battle, and to victory.

Your advancement in the ranks of the knights depends on how you manage yourself in battle, how you treat others, and above all your actions, which should reflect the honor of the knights. You are taking the first steps into the world of adventure and honor, and we are glad that you have joined our ranks. We will fight with you whenever and wherever you need us."

Rose nodded and inclined her head. Um smiled and nodded back. He had heard many things about this extraordinary girl, and he knew now why everyone liked her. There was something special about her, a kind of presence to her that was different than any he had known.

The next day, Rose went to the farm, and noticed that Ox

was avoiding her. She liked him, but she was in love with Zach. She did not understand why Ox was avoiding her, for it had never occurred to her that Ox was in love with her. She sought out Zach and spent some time with him. Sarah did some more measurements for the dress and showed Rose a picture of what it would look like when it was finished.

It would be fit for a queen, layers of silk and tulle. Silver roses would be added around the hems, and golden vines would wind between them. It would have a train of silk, which would need two people to hold it up. The veil would soften her face and would be held up by a diadem of silver with pale jewels.

Frank was making the diadem. He was happy that his family would be growing, and he was intent on making her diadem to be the envy of all the high-born ladies. He had procured some aquamarines for it, as well as some diamonds.

Rose was happier than she could ever remember being. She was no longer who she had been when she had arrived at the valley. She had grown up and learned things that she had not thought possible. Her world had grown to include so many people, and various places. She wanted to see more, to learn more, and she believed that Zach would always be there, and he would never hold her back.

The next few days went be fast, but finally all was in readiness for the trip to Joran, Rose only hoped that they were not too late. Now that they had been to Joran, they did not need the ships to take them. Those that had been there could now teleport to the place that they had seen. So, Rose took a deep breath and gathered her magic, and took them all to the planet Joran.

CHAPTER NINETEEN

She took them to a place that would hide their arrival, so that their allies would not be afraid. They marched to the capital of the kingdom that she had been at, to find it surrounded. They did not hesitate, but charged down towards the city, taking the invaders completely by surprise.

As the invaders tried to flee, the gates opened, and the defenders of the city charged. The invaders found themselves trapped between the two forces. They were crushed. As they were orcs and goblins, they did not surrender, but some did escape.

When the two forces met, the leader of the defenders, who recognized Rose, greeted them warmly, and spoke.

"You arrived just in time, we were almost out of supplies, and hope. But the main armies have already left. They went to the mountain pass of Thekos. They are hoping to stop the main force of the invaders there. All our allies are going to join them there."

Rose nodded, and asked for a map, so they knew where to go. A map was brought, and she studied, along with the other leaders of the High Fairy forces. Because they were not mortal, and because of their magic, they could march for days straight without rest, and reach the pass faster than normal people could.

They had brought some of the Horse tribe with them. Even though the horse folk were not very bright, they were fierce warriors, and they were highly effective calvary. But once unleashed they could not be reined in. The knights had their own horses, each trained in the art of war. The regular troops would walk, but they could move faster than mortals.

Three days forced march and they arrived at the pass. Thankfully, no attack had been made, and Rose, with the leaders of the High Fairy forces, went to the leaders of the defenders. They learned that they had arrived a day ahead of the enemy forces, and they could deploy their troops where they thought they could do the best.

Rose looked over the strategy that the defenders had put in place, looked over at her companions and shook her head. She spread a map of the pass out on the table and began to explain her own plan for the defense of the pass.

She would have archers cover the entrance, high on the sides, and lay traps along the front. Bulwarks could be built at the narrowest parts of the pass. Pits could be dug to slow the charge of their enemies. Rockslides could be rigged. And they could prepare the calvary for sweeping the sides and back of their enemies, by hiding them in various places outside the pass.

Work began on her plans, and improvements and alterations were made. All the humans, elves and dwarves went to work preparing the defense of the pass, though they had already put up some defenses of their own. The Horse folk found hiding places among the hills and small groups of trees around the pass. There were also rock piles in which they could hide.

All the rest of that day, and into the night the preparations were made, and in the morning, news came that the enemy army had been seen. Everyone hurried into their positions, and made ready, knowing that they could not let the enemy get passed them, or their homes would be lost.

The leader of the enemy army, a powerful sorcerer, could sense something waiting in the pass. If was as if a hidden power was lying in wait for him. He would be at the back of the army, pushing his creatures to crush the defenders, and believed that this battle would over quickly.

He did not know that the High Fairies were here, and they

knew how to fight, and how to win. They had centuries of experience backing their movements, and they did not mean to let this man and his hordes of goblins and orcs to run roughshod over the people on the other side of the pass.

The advancing orcs and goblins noticed that the ground in front of them was wet. They did not know why, but they kept going, until a single flaming arrow arched through the sky, and landed on the wet ground, which had been soaked with oil. The fiery arrow landed on target and set the oil on fire, incinerating the first few ranks.

The creatures caught in the inferno screamed in pain, as their flesh was consumed by the flames. The smell of burning flesh filled the air, and smoke choked the attackers, as the wind blew the smoke back over them. The ranks following them fell back, only to be confronted by the Horse folk, who came out of their hiding places and swept along the sides, their sabers striking fast and fiercely. When the horse folk disappeared, the flames died down, and the sorcerer saw what had been done, he withdrew, to ponder what had happened, and to rethink his strategy.

His forces set up camp, building defenses around it, and watching for trouble. Sentries were put out, and the orcs and goblins, along with their allies, watched the pass. They did not know that at that moment, in the pass, a young woman was planning something. She did not want to sit idle and knew that a preemptive strike would prove to be a clever idea.

She gathered the leaders of the defenders and told them of her plan. It was bold, and she was confident. So, they agreed and gathered a small force. Stealth was important on this mission. Three groups were formed and set off in slightly different directions.

Zach went with Rose, and crouched with her, in sight of the sentries, though they could not see even Zach. The night was dark, and the fires hindered their sight. Rose gripped the hilt of her new sword and took a deep breath. The signal was given, and she drew her burning sword, and charged.

Caught completely off guard, the sentries were delayed in calling the alarm. Some trolls leapt up, and found themselves facing a young girl, holding a burning blade. Trolls did not like fire, as they were vulnerable to it, but they did not think that a young girl would be much of a threat, so they charged anyway, and Rose put them down.

The smell of burning flesh filled the air again, as Rose's sword cut through her enemies. But the defenders did not stay long, withdrawing as suddenly as they had come. Pulling back into the night, the defenders slipped away, leaving the enemy encampment in chaos.

In the morning, the horde came again, with the giants leading this time. But Rose had a plan for these, and she put it into action. Beneath the giants the ground gave way, up to the giants' knees. Then came the arrows, a nuisance to the giants, but the arrows were only part of the plan.

As the giants struggled out of the trenches, Rose drew her own bow, and aimed at the lead giant. He bellowed in rage and came on towards the defenders. As he and the other giants made it to the edge of the pass, Rose fired her arrow, and it hit, not the giants themselves, but a single rock, that started an avalanche of rocks that slammed into the giants and took them down. The defenders rushed forward to finish off the survivors.

Behind the giants came the trolls, which were fired upon by fire arrows, and they broke and ran. The dark sorcerer roared in frustration, and then unleashed his magic. But the High Fairies blocked him from doing so, and suddenly, from the sides, again came the Horse folk, their shrill war cries filling the air.

Rose looked over at her companions, and smiled, and called to the people, and told them to charge. As one the defenders charged forward and met their enemies on the field of battle.

The noise of steel clashing against steel, the smell of hot blood, the surge of adrenaline, surrounded her. She fought fiercely, her sword swinging, as she blocked and struck out at those that stood against her. She did not stop, as she saw the leader of the enemies unleashing his power against the defenders. She fought her way forwards, unaware that Zach was staying close to her.

She believed that if she could take down the sorcerer, then maybe his troops would lose heart for the battle and be easier to defeat. And she would be able to show that she was worthy to be Zach's wife. She did not know that what was about to happen would change everything for her.

The dark sorcerer saw her and turned to face her. He did not know who she was, nor why she was so intent on reaching him, but he was not about to let a girl stop him from his plans of conquest. As she reached him, the fight began.

Rose was still new at swordplay, but what she lacked in skill, she made up for in courage. Rose was not one to back down. She fought well, but suddenly, she tripped. A fallen warrior behind her, had tripped her, and her helmet fell off, her long hair breaking free, to fall in a cascade of chestnut strands around her.

The dark sorcerer raised his enchanted mace, and began to swing it at her unprotected head, but it never reached her.

Zach appeared out of nowhere, and the mace hit him full on in the chest. As he went down, Rose's sword, which had fallen from her appeared in her hand, and with a scream of rage, she thrust it through the armor of her enemy, piercing his heart, and going all the way through him. The dark sorcerer stared at her, and then at the burning sword, which should never have even been able to dent his enchanted armor.

The burning sword was not an ordinary blade, as it contained the heart of a still burning star. The power of the metal, and the magic woven into it had shattered the enchantments the sorcerer had wound around him. The burning blade was the most powerful weapon in the universe.

As the sorcerer fell, the magic he had used to bind his army together fell apart. The different tribes of orcs and goblins fell upon their rival tribes, and the humans, elves and dwarves watched in amazement as their enemies fell upon each other, and ignored the allied peoples, who began to fall back.

But the one who had killed the sorcerer did not care about what was happening around her, for she was losing the man she loved, and did not understand why.

She knelt next to Zach and pulled his helm off. Ox came running up but stopped at the sight of his brother's wound.

Zach looked up at her and gazed with love at her tear-filled face. He reached up and touched her cheek and spoke softly.

"Do not be sad, little one. You do not need to be sad for me. I have done what I needed to in this life, and that was to help you. You are strong, and beautiful, and alive. I love you and know that you will find the one you are truly destined to find."

"I do not want anyone else; I want you. Please, Zach, do not leave me. I need you." She plead with him, her heart in her eyes, as she watched him grow weaker. She did not know enough to heal him but did not understand why his own magic was not healing the wound. He smiled at her and said softly.

"You do not need me anymore. I have given you what you need, and now I go to rest. I have given all my magic, to your sword, and the ring, and the saddle. I walked into the heart of a burning star, to get the metal for your blade, I poured all my love into the ring, and put all my skill into the saddle. All these things will help you in the days ahead.

Ox, my brother, will you watch over her? Will you promise me, now and forever, to stand with her, and help her?" Ox choked back tears, and made the promise, knowing that a death promise would bind him forever. But he did not care, for he was losing his brother, and would have said anything to give him comfort.

Zach shuddered and looked back at Rose, whose tears ran down her cheeks, to fall like tiny stars from her face. He took a shuddering breath and spoke his final words.

"I will always be with you, little Rose, and I will always love you...." His eyes closed and he shuddered once more. A soft exhale of breath, his soul leaving, escaped his lips, as he went still. And thus ended the life of Zach Dragoon, the eldest son of the last of Shoulai dragons, he who had given his life for the one he loved.

A cry of aching pain broke through the sudden silence, as Rose gave vent to her grief. In this moment, all light went out. The sun was covered by clouds, and winds began to blow whipping everything around. Lightening flashed across the sky; thunder boomed overhead. Rain began to fall, hard and fast. It seemed as if all the universe mourned the loss of this one man.

Rose cradled Zach's head, her own bowed. Ox wept; his heart broken as he gazed at his brother's still form. He knew that his parents would know of Zach's death, and his sister too. They would all have felt Zach's passing. It did not matter, that Zach had died a hero, only that he was gone.

The leaders of the allies found her, still holding on to Zach, in the middle of the storm. She wept freely, her broken heart plainly visible in her eyes. She was hurt beyond any words of comfort. She had never even considered what it would be like to lose Zach, and now that it had happened, she did not want to be around anyone. She only wanted to be left alone with her pain.

Ox came over, and gently composed his brother's limbs. Lord Um and his brother looked at each other, knowing the sorrow of loss. They had lost comrades in arms before, but this was Rose's first time. She pushed Ox away and refused to let anyone near her.

She did not care that the battle had been won, she did not care that victory was hers. For her victory was tainted by this loss. Her grief and pain would not allow comfort to be given. She would not leave, would not let anyone touch him, as she clung to him, her heart seemed to wither within her. Finally, unable to look at him anymore, she stood up and gazed at the others for a moment, and then turned and vanished into the rain.

She could hear them, calling to her, but she did not heed them. She wanted to get away, and closed her eyes, willing herself anywhere but where she was. A flash was seen in the dark, a flash of blue light, and she was gone.

Ox called her name, but there was no answer. Rose had fled, and she was gone. He bowed his head and wondered how he could keep his promise to his brother, if he could not even find her. Ox looked at his brother and felt the tears filling his eyes again. How could his family continue without his brother? What would happen now?

With heavy hearts, the High Fairies gathered Zach's fallen form and carried it back to the valley. They told the king what had happened, and that Rose could not be found. Ox stood with his parents and his sister, as they laid Zach into his grave. The wound in his chest had been repaired, but he was still gone.

Zach was the first to die in the valley, and everyone felt a heaviness in their hearts. There were some though, like Corwin, who used Zach's death as a reason that they should not have sent any help to Joran. Though they did not understand, they also used Rose's disappearance as a reason she should not have been taken into the royal family. They did not understand the depths of Rose's anguish, and they would find that when Rose returned, she would not be the same child that she had been.

CHAPTER TWENTY

Several years passed, and there was still no sign of Rose, and Ox was now alone. His sister, mother and father had all followed Zach to the grave. They had given up hope, and so had perished. Ox lived because of his promise. The death promise he had made to his brother had kept him alive and found him taking care of his family farm by himself.

He did not know where Rose was, only that she was alive. He wondered how she was doing, and if she would ever come back. He did not know that she would be quite different when she returned.

Rose stood at edge of the cliff, looking out at the world that she had been on for the last several years. She had learned many things, and now faced a challenge, one that would test her. A presence stood before her, such a presence that she had never felt before. It was vast, filling her mind with its power. And as she faced it, a voice sounded through her mind, talking to her.

"I am the ultimate mother, the awareness of the universe itself, and I have come to you this day, for a purpose. I have been guiding you for all your life, helping you when you needed it. You know who and what I am, as I have spoken to you often. Now you face a choice. Will you join my cause, and serve me? Or do you want what you lost? If you choose the easier path, Zach will be alive, and you will marry him. But if you choose the harder path, you will save countless lives.

I chose you and caused you to be born. I have watched all my children fighting, destroying each other just because they thought they could. I have tried to help them, but I cannot take away their right to choose. I have need of you and others to help maintain the balance of light and dark, of good and evil, or all inside of me will perish. And I will end. And all will end with me. There are things that I cannot do, without disrupting things. I need someone who will be able to do the things I cannot, to be a guardian of my children in ways that I cannot.

I am all-powerful, and I am a part of all things. I feel everything that all my creations do. I feel their pain, and their joy. But my power is such that if I try to take a personal hand in things, I can cause more harm than good. I know where help is needed, but I need someone whose power will not end up destroying everything, to go and help. But the choice is yours. Which path will you choose, the easy one or the hard one?"

Rose closed her eyes and thought about Zach. She wanted to be with him so much. She had been trying to find a way to end her own life, so she could join him. But then she thought about Ox and Zach's family. She was not the only one who had lost someone. She was not the only one in the universe to have suffered loss.

She thought about a village she had recently been to. A wedding had been taking place, and the children had filled the air with their laughter. They had danced and played games and everywhere the feeling of joy and happiness existed. She thought about what would happen if someone came to that village, to destroy it, for no better reason than they thought they could.

How selfish she would have to be to turn away from those she could help. How like her father she would be, if she chose the easier way. She knew that Zach would choose the harder path. Zach had never been selfish; he had always found a way to help others. She would never have been able to live with herself, knowing she had turned away from those in need, where Zach never had.

So, as she stood there, Rose went to her knees, and said, in a steady voice.

"I will pledge myself to you, and I will choose the harder

path, if you can take my depression away. I cannot live like this anymore. I do not want to feel like this, like there is no meaning in life. Help me, and I will help you."

"Done!" The voice of the ultimate mother said, and Rose shuddered, as she felt a great burden rest upon her shoulders, and a lightening of her load at the same time. She threw her head back and for the first time in ten years she laughed.

Ox did not understand why he was in court. He had not done anything wrong, but a friend of Corwin's was accusing him of stealing water from his pond. Ox would never have done such a thing, as he did not need to. But Corwin was determined to get Ox out of the valley, since Ox was not a member of the High Fairy race. Corwin had been getting worse, ever since Rose had left.

As Ox prepared to speak in his behalf, the door to the courtroom opened, and a voice, clear and beautiful sounded through the room.

"That is enough of this foolishness. No one stole anything, and everyone in this court knows it. Ox is not going anywhere, and that is final."

Ox and everyone else turned to face Rose. She was dressed in leather clothing, a white shirt, and had her sword buckled at her side. Her long hair was done in a braid and draped over one shoulder. She walked with a newfound confidence and gazed at the one that was accusing Ox.

"We all know that Corwin put you up to this. And in case you have forgotten, I made this valley, and you are here only because I allow you to be here. If you want to continue being here, I suggest you drop this case and leave Ox alone. Especially since he is the last of his kind." The man lowered his eyes, and the judge dismissed the case. He would have ruled in Ox's favor anyway, but this gave him a better way out of it. Rose looked around, and then turned to Ox.

"I am sorry about your family. I did not know that they had all died until recently. They were good people, and I know that they have found rest from their cares. You should go back to the farm, and I will meet you there later. I need to see a few people first." Ox wanted to ask her how she was doing, and where she had been, but he knew that she would tell him when she was ready. So, he nodded and told her that he would see her later.

Emotions filled Rose, as she watched Ox leave. She felt bad that he had been through so much, but she knew that he would fine. She took a breath and mounted her horse and went through the now finished streets of Jewel City, the glittering buildings surrounding her, and made her way to the palace.

The grooms, who took care of the horses, stared at her as she rode up. She dismounted and handed the reins of Midnight to one of the grooms. Without a word, she left, going up the stairs into the building. She looked around, and noted that it was beautiful, now that it was finished.

The servants, and house cleaners all stopped to star at her as she walked past them. She had a particular place to be and did not have time for idle chitchat. She was ready to do this. She was no longer the spoiled arrogant child that she had been. Zach's death had changed her.

Rose made her way to the council chambers, as she knew that is where everyone was. She did not stop to talk to anyone as she walked down the hallway. She had a purpose, and she would not back down for anyone. She finally reached her destination and without waiting to knock or be announced, she opened the doors, and faced the startled people within.

"I am back." She announced.

BOOK TWO

Chapter one

Quicksilver

The Undarai existed, and they were beautiful. Undarai meant Children of the Stars, and they were just that. In the night they glowed with a pale light, their fur as pale as the moon. They resembled unicorns but were far more. Their spiral horns were of pearl and silver, reaching upwards for the stars. Their manes and tails, and hooves were all of silver, and the soft fur was white, and glowed in the moonlight.

Many considered them to be holy creatures, healers of mind and body. They were glorious, and they shared what they knew with the elves, and humans, and dwarves. They were teachers, guides, and creatures of peace. They used a form of runes, drawing the runes with their horns.

They healed and taught, and lived and loved, until a jealous human did something unspeakable. He killed an Undarai. He took the horn, and tried to do magic with it, but only found a curse upon all he did. He could not heal, he could not teach, he could only undo what had been done. All he did with the horn ended in darkness.

In the death of this one Undarai, the others broke a promise to the Universe, and they abandoned the people they had been teaching, and fled. They had promised to always help others, but with this death, they stopped, and so, their deaths became the punishment for the breaking of this promise

Some blamed the Undarai, and began to hunt them, killing

them and taking their horns. The Undarai pled with the humans, telling them that they did not know that the curse had existed, but the humans did not want to hear. For a time, the elves sheltered the Undarai, but they could not stop the humans.

The oldest of the Undarai finally gathered what was left of his people and took them into the highest mountains to get away from those who hunted them. They hid in the high valleys, where snow never really melted. They did what they could to keep their people safe but knew that the humans would eventually find them.

A thousand Undarai had lived upon this world. Now only twenty survived. And one of them was to give birth to the one who would be the last of her kind. For the humans had tracked the Undarai even here.

The labor was hard, but soon a foal was born. She was born just as the morning star entered the sky, beaming down upon this valley in hope and warmth. As her mother licked her clean, the herd gathered and asked what name was to be given to this creature of wonder.

"Umdari, is her name, for it means hope in our tongue. And she is the hope of her people." The eldest of the Undarai smiled and nodded. It was a good name for her, this bringer of hope. Hope that they were going to survive.

But a darkness lay upon the horizon, a darkness in the form of human hunters who had found the Undarai. A day had passed since the birth of Umdari, a day of light and joy to her people. But as she reached the edge of the trees, she heard a noise, and smelled something in the air. Her mother smelled it too, and quickly put Umdari into a pile of snow, and told her to stay put, and not to move, no matter what.

The herd ran into the woods, seeking places to hide, but they walked right into the traps and snares of the hunters. None survived, except one little Undarai hidden in the snow. She could hear her people, and the hunters, and she shivered, until finally all sound ceased.

After a while, footsteps, crunching in the snow could be heard. Soft steps, which came closer and closer, until a figure could be seen. Chestnut hair, reaching her knees, done in a braid, was draped over her shoulders. She was dressed for the weather, in furs and boots. She looked around, as if searching for something, and then she turned to the snow pile.

The small Undarai climbed out of the snow, and gazed at this strange woman, who looked at her with sorrow.

"I am sorry I could not get here in time to save the others, little one. But I do know that you cannot stay here, alone, and I do not think that you would be safe anywhere on this planet. If you will trust me, little one, I will take you to a place where there are no humans to hurt you, and you will safe."

Umdari gazed at the strange woman and felt something inside her stir. She went on trembling legs to the woman, and the woman picked her up.

"My name is Rose Debarra. And I am glad to meet you, little one." Light surrounded them and Umdari found a strange sensation running through her. Rose changed her shape into that of a squirrel, for where she was taking the last of the Undarai was indeed a world where humans did not exist, and the animals had evolved to speak and act like humans, except that they did not know about Undarai and would not want to hurt her.

Rose had been to this world before and had contacted a creature that would take the small squirrel into his care. She knew him as William Wolverine, and he was the leader of a large community that thrived near the sea. The Undarai would be safe here, until Rose came for her. For Rose did not intend to leave Umdari here, for her destiny was beyond the boundaries of any world. She could become if she chose, the second guardian of the universe, if she wanted to.

Rose had chosen to become the first guardian, which was the Guardian of Destiny. She was a high priestess of the Stars, and served the Ultimate Mother, who was the universe. Rose had been sent to get Umdari, but had not expected to find the child alone, with all her family gone. It was sad, but necessary.

As Rose emerged from the light, she found herself in the form of a red furred mouse. She always changed her appearance here, for humans did not exist, and she did not want to stand out. Rose looked down at the small squirrel she held in her paws. The squirrel's fur was a glittering silver in color, and it reflected the light of the sun, casting dots of rainbow light around her.

Rose walked along the cliffs and found her way to the cliff caves of William and his creatures. She was known here, so she walked right in. She wound her way through the caves, and tunnels, to the home cave of William Wolverine.

He looked up as she entered and smiled. Then his eyes fell upon the bundle that she carried. He rose to his feet, and went over to her, and peered at the small creature that she held in her arms. He studied the small squirrel, who looked up at him, with wide crystal blue eyes.

"Her family is no more. She is the last of her tribe. I arrived too late to save the others, but I managed to get her out. I cannot take her with me, as I travel a lot, and that is no life for one as small as she. I thought that you and yours would be able to take her in and care for her."

William took the small squirrel, who shivered at his touch. He studied her and looked up at Rose.

"Of course, we will take her in. She needs us. I think I will call her Quicksilver, for her fur. She will be taken care of here. We will teach her our ways. And she will be safe here." Rose nodded. Then she spoke softly.

"When she is old enough, I will come back for her. Her destiny is great, and she will be needed elsewhere. I know that you will teach her what she needs to know, and that she will be loved here. I will come for her when she is ready."

William nodded. He could tell that this squirrel was special, beside her fur. She was small and delicate in appearance, but there was a strength in her. When William looked up, Rose was gone. He was not surprised, as she did this type of thing often.

William took Quicksilver to the nursery. She would grow up here, with other small creatures, and she would be loved and cared for. The old mouse who oversaw the nursery took the small squirrel, and fed her, and placed her in a crib.

The other babes in the nursery crowded around her, and a black furred squirrel, small himself, peered at her. Her blue eyes looked at them, and then she pulled the blanket over her face. The old mouse shooed them away and told them to leave the new one alone.

The black furred squirrel, known as Kit Nightstalker, stayed close to the crib, and played quietly near her. She pulled herself up and watched him. Neither of them knew what the future held, but a friendship began that day that would help them both through the troubles ahead.

CHAPTER TWO

William watched as the small squirrel grew, and when she was old enough to leave the nursery, she was placed with the healers. Kit went into training as a fighter. Quicksilver was a gentle soul, sweet and kind. But she was also taught how to fight, as they never knew when that training would be needed. The seaside cliffs could get attacked by sea rats, and everyone would be needed to fight.

The Seaside Fortress was a sprawling complex. There were many caves, dug out by the moles. The tunnels were extensive throughout the cliffs, but they were made in such a way that there would not be a collapse. The lower caves along the bottom of the cliffs were covered by netting designed to look like rock.

The caves were home to many creatures, along with squirrels, there were mice and moles, shrews, and hares, and even otters. Sea otters were the fishers of the caves, and they would go out to catch fish and shrimp. They were also scouts, to keep an eye out for Sea rats and those creatures that traveled with them. Along the top of the cliffs, the creatures planted crops of grains and there was even an orchard.

Quicksilver was a good archer. She was very skilled in healing as well. She did spend time with her closest friend, Kit. At times they were inseparable. They would go on picnics and walked along the beach. They would play games together, and they would play with other youngsters.

Quicksilver did not remember her real family. She had only been a day old when they had killed, so she could not even remember that her name was not Quicksilver. Kit was her best friend, and she cared for him. He loved her but did not say anything.

A day was coming soon though, when Quicksilver would leave, and Kit would go with her. As the seasons turned, and the small squirrel grew into a beautiful young creature, her silver fur gleamed in the sunlight. Kit was bigger, his fur black as night. His eyes were green and fierce. His preferred weapon was the hammer, and he was always near Quicksilver.

Her clear blue eyes were usually as warm as the summer sky. But when she was upset, they would cloud over. No one wanted to make her upset, as no one could stand the sight of tears in her eyes. She was as sweet as candied apples, and as gentle as summer rain.

Kit was stern and unyielding unless it came to her. He always gave in to her, and he kept her safe, no matter what. He could feel it, though, something changing. A change in the wind perhaps or something deeper. He did not know what it was, but he could tell that something was bothering Quicksilver.

Quicksilver was having nightmares. She kept dreaming of the same thing repeatedly. She did not understand what it meant, but at the end of every dream, she would see a red furred mouse standing at the base of some mountains and waiting. It was as if the mouse was waiting for her. She did not understand. But something inside of her told her she needed to find the mouse, and soon.

But even as she began to prepare for a journey, an attack came. A fleet of sea rat ships was spotted by the sea otters, and the alarm went off. The bells sent a tremor through the caves, and everyone began to get ready for a fight. All the entrances were shut, and all the fighters went to their designated areas. And all the babes were placed in special caves where they would safe and not underfoot.

Quicksilver did not like fighting, but she knew that her home was worth defending. She knew that the sea rats wanted the cliff caves, and they would try every so often to get them.

They never succeeded though. For the creatures here were willing to fight for their home, and they were all trained to fight.

Even as Quicksilver prepared her bow, she was joined by Kit, who had his own bow. They would fire arrows for a while, and hopefully drive the sea rats back out to sea. No one could have guessed that something would happen this day that would change everything.

Something inside Quicksilver was growing, and she did not know what it was. She did not know that she was something more than a squirrel, and that her heritage was a type of magic never seen on this world. Her magic was growing inside of her, and it was waiting to come out.

She watched as the sea rats came ashore, and got ready to start firing, but then she noticed something. A group of creatures, bound together by chains, was pushed into the front. No one moved inside the caves.

"Those bloody cowards," Kit hissed. "They are using the galley slaves as a cover. They are hoping that we will not fire because we do not want to hit them. But if they get close enough, we should be able to fire over the galley slaves." Quicksilver gazed out at the shuffling creatures. Her heart went out to the poor slaves.

The galley slaves were thin and worn. The heavy chains that bound them chafed at their wrists and ankles. They were sick, and tired. And something awoke inside Quicksilver, something that had been growing inside of her, and now needed to be released.

In the dark cave, a glow began to surround her, as she gazed at the plight of the slaves. The power of her people came alive within her, and it reached out to the slaves, surrounding them in light. In this illumination, the slaves found their chains falling off, and their wounds healed. A sense of peace and rest touched them, and they found that even their souls were healed.

Kit stared at the glowing Quicksilver, uncertain as to what

was happening. She did not understand it either or wondered what was happening. The magic that had been unleashed did not stop at freeing and healing the slaves. The light reached out and touched the sea rats and they could not stand the touch of this pure light. They screamed in pain and agony, as the holy light of the Undarai awoke and touched them.

Creatures filled with such hate and greed could not stand before the light of the Undarai. It was a pure light, filled with love and peace, and creatures who had given in to hate and war could not stand it. Most of the sea rats simply died, unable to bear what they felt. The others went insane, and attacked each other, unable to deal with what they saw. For they saw the truth of what they were.

As the rising sun filled the sky, Quicksilver's light faded. It left behind a memory of joy and love in the minds of the good creatures it had touched, and a memory of agony for the evil creatures, who could not stand the revealing light.

The ships bobbed on the water, their anchors holding them fast. There were no survivors. The shore of the sea in the morning light was red with the blood of the fallen vermin. The seabirds wheeled overhead, calling in their shrill voices as they looked down upon the slaughter on the beach.

CHAPTER THREE

William walked up behind Quicksilver, who did not know what to do or say. She did not understand what had happened, or how it had happened. William took a breath and placed a big paw on the young squirrel maid's shoulder.

"Come with me, little one, we need to talk." She nodded, and followed William to his study, wondering what he knew. Kit followed but kept his distance. He did not want to leave Quicksilver alone if there was something wrong. As she sat down, and William gazed out at the shore, he took a breath, and spoke softly.

"I am sure that you have a lot of questions, about what happened this night, but I do not have the answers. When you were just a day old, a mouse called Rose brought you here, and placed you in my care. She told me that you were alone in the world, and that you needed a home. I took you in, as I take so many in.

She told me that she would come for you, when you were older, but I think after last night, you need to look for her. I do not know where she is, but she always comes from the east. Perhaps if you went east, you would find her. There are mountains there, and maybe she comes from them. She will know what is happening to you, and she can help you."

He looked over at the silver furred squirrel maid. He loved her, as his own, though he was a wolverine. He was a good leader for the creatures that lived here, and he cared about them all. He did not want to send her away, but he knew that she would unhappy, without the answers that Rose could give her.

Quicksilver looked down at her paws, thinking. She did not want to leave here. It was her home, but she needed answers, and if this mouse called Rose had them, then she would go and look for her. She took a steadying breath and nodded.

"I will go and prepare for this journey. I hope I can find her and get some answers." She looked up at William, and hesitated. She loved him, and did not want to leave, but she would go, and hope that she could come back some day. When she opened the door, she found Kit waiting for. He looked at her and said firmly.

"You are not going anywhere without me. I will follow you, no matter what and help you find this mouse." William studied the big black squirrel, and somehow felt that it was only right that he went with her. Quicksilver was glad for the company.

As they left William, they found that many of the creatures could only stare at the silver furred squirrel. The light she had unleashed had filled the caves and touched all the good creatures within them. No creature would ever look at her the same way again, and this made her glad she was leaving, so she would not have to face those stares.

They packed for the journey, placing clothes, food, tents, and blankets into their packs, along of course with herbs for healing. Quicksilver made sure that she had plenty of herbs and medicines for the journey, placing them in pouches on a belt that hung at her waist. She gripped a staff, and placed her bow and quiver on her back, with the pack.

Kit carried more than she did. He was bigger, and stronger, and determined to take care of her. His hammer rested on his back, within easy reach of his paw. He studied her, and she smiled at him, glad to have him with her. Everyone watched as the two squirrels began their journey to the east in search of a red furred mouse, with blue eyes.

Neither of them had ever been away from the caves. They had never journeyed far from their homes. But they were together, and they would do this together.

CHAPTER FOUR

Rose did not understand why the council kept sending her to put out fires that kept cropping up in the Valley. Darwin was sick, with an illness that could not be cured. It was called the Fading. Slowly, his mind and eventually even his body would fade away, leaving only memories in the minds of those around him.

As a member of the council, she had been there, when he had announced his illness, and the fact that he did not believe his son to be a worthy successor of the throne. He had given the council a list of names of possibilities, but she had the feeling that they were keeping something from her. It had been sixteen years since she had taken the last of the Undarai to the world of animals, and it was about time to get her.

For the last several years, she had been all over the valley, even finding the Tree folk, who called her Shakera, or great mother in their tongue. They had caused a little trouble when some of the Horse tribe had tried cutting down some of the red trees.

She had been sent out to stop a war, which she had, and learned that the Tree folk could get the wood that was needed without cutting the trees down. They cared for the trees and could take wood from them without hurting the trees. Most of the wood that was being used came from the mountains surrounding the valley, it was only out of need that the Horse folk had tried cutting down the red trees.

Rose had convinced both sides to not go war, and learned about the Tree folk, so she could find a solution for both sides. She had also had to talk down the Swamp folk from causing trouble for the farmers on the edge of the swamp. The farmers had wanted to the drain some of the swamp, and the Swamp folk had not liked that idea. There was plenty of space in the valley for the farmers without them draining the swamp.

She had spent some time with the Swamp folk, learning about them, and learning about the Elders. The Elders were the oldest members of the High Fairy race. They had been together for so long that they now functioned as one entity. Even though they were three, two women, and one male. They moved, spoke, and functioned as one.

The Elders were approaching an age that few beings reached, which was a million years. They were extraordinary, but they did not remember their individual names. They were simply the Elders. Everyone respected them and honored them. Many people sought their advice, and always made sure to listen.

Rose had found them fascinating and had spent time talking with them and getting to know them. She had spent about a year with their tribe, which consisted of many of their children. She had found their tribe to be good at tending to the wildlife in the swamp and taking care of each other.

Rose now turned to other things, though, as she had many responsibilities, one of which called her back to the planet where she had left the last of the Undarai, where she would go to find the Undarai, and bring her to the valley. She did not know yet, that Quicksilver had set out to find her, but she would learn this, when she went to the planet to find her.

Rose was also facing a problem of a personal nature, in the face of Ox's confession of his feelings for her, and she was not ready to face her feelings, and so told him not to mention it again, and then she went to the planet where she had left the Undarai, only to find that Quicksilver had set out to find her. William told Rose what had happened, and that Quicksilver, with a young male squirrel by the name of Kit had set out to find Rose.

Rose closed her eyes and took a breath.

"When did they set out?" She asked, and William told her that they had set out about a week ago. Rose nodded and left to find Quicksilver. She knew that the young male squirrel might be a problem but decided to deal with that when the time came.

Quicksilver did not know what to do, as she and Kit faced a marsh. They could go around it, but that could take a while. Going through might be faster, but they risked getting lost. They had left the coast behind a few days ago. So, far their journey had been quiet. They had filled their water bottles at a fresh stream the day before.

The two young squirrels did not know what to do but decided that going around seemed safer. They were not in any real hurry. So, they set out around the edges of the marsh, watching carefully for dangerous land, and sudden quicksand.

Kit watched Quicksilver as they traveled. She was uncertain about this journey, as she did not know how long it would take to find this mouse. The world was bigger than she had thought and could be more dangerous as well. She was also uncertain about having brought Kit, not wanting him to get hurt.

Kit was fine, but he was concerned for her. Neither of them had ever been this far from home, and he wanted to keep her safe. He was trained as a fighter, but he stilled worried about her. Her nature was such that she might put herself in danger to help someone else.

As the day went by, they could not see an end to the marsh, so they found a fallen tree to make camp in. Everything was wet so they could not have a fire, but that was okay, as they did have blankets, and each other. They did not know that they were in trouble or would have been if not for the fact that a fog came up, and the soft ground had not let any of their track's show.

A small band of weasels had been following them for a while. But as the fog came up, they lost the trail. The tracks were gone, and the fog covered everything. It was as if the earth itself did not want them to find the two squirrels. They wandered around until one of them noticed that they had wandered into the marsh, for he screamed as he was pulled under.

Quicksilver and Kit looked up, as they heard the scream, and other voices calling frantically to each other as they sank into the marshy water and disappeared. Quicksilver shuddered, as she thought of the poor creatures sinking into the dark water. Kit put a paw on her shoulder and drew her close. She fell asleep against him and wondered who the creatures had been that had been caught by the marsh.

They moved on in the morning, careful of the soft ground, and found firmer ground as they walked away from the marsh. They did not know how close they had come to trouble, but they were cautious as they moved farther and farther from the familiar lands they had left behind.

Rose found their trail at the edge of the marsh. She was not looking for tracks or anything like that. She was looking for something that could not be seen only felt. For the ground would remember the feeling of the Undarai as she walked on it, and there would be other signs of the passing of such a being as the Undarai.

She followed them as they walked east, and followed hard, as she did not want to lose them. She would try to get ahead of them after a while and try to get to the eastern mountains before them, and make sure they found her there.

With this plan in mind, Rose took a short cut, determined to get ahead of the Undarai and her companion. Rose knew this world well, and knew that the way east was not easy, but she was confident that she could manage the difficulties along the way.

Quicksilver gazed at the dark trees of the forest. They were huge and had a sense of age about them. There was a watchfulness in the air, and a quiet hush filled the trees. The two squirrels did not falter though, and they climbed into the branches of the trees and began to move swiftly through them.

The shadows were long underneath the dark trees, and the

squirrels looked for a spot for camp, and maybe some fruits or nuts to scavenge. Their supplies were beginning to get low. As they moved swiftly, they suddenly heard a commotion ahead.

CHAPTER FIVE

As they drew closer to the sounds, they peered downed and saw a family of hedgehogs being harassed by some evil looking foxes. The two squirrels looked at each other and knew that they needed to help. So, Quicksilver drew her bow, and Kit, his fur blending into the shadows, slipped close.

The leader of the foxes was a big male, and he held a rusty sword in his paw, menacing the hedgehogs, who were all curled up. The other foxes surrounded the hedgehogs and were being careful with their spikes. Not one of the foxes was watching the trees, where two squirrels were getting ready to help the hedgehogs.

Kit came out of nowhere, with a roar, swinging his hammer, and Quicksilver shot off two arrows in rapid secession, hitting two foxes and Kit took down a third. The foxes, caught by surprise, were quickly chased off by the two squirrels.

Quicksilver dropped out of her tree and looked at the two foxes she had killed. Tears welled up in her eyes, as she thought of killing living creatures. Kit went over to her, and calmed her, assuring her that everything was all right, and that she done only what was necessary.

The hedgehogs unrolled and looked at the two newcomers. The oldest one came over and patted Quicksilver's paw.

"You came just in time. We could not keep rolled up forever, and those foxes were close to getting us. But I know those foxes will be back, so we better move on. Come with us, and we will take you somewhere safe, we will." The two squirrels nodded and followed the hedgehogs down to the river, and then across it.

On the other side, the forest seemed to change, becoming more open and lighter. The trees became birches and aspens, instead of spruces and pines. A light wind rustled through the branches of the slender trees, and the sound of birds filled the air.

"If you don't mind me asking, why were you in those darker woods, when it seems brighter over here?" Quicksilver asked. The leader of the hedgehogs looked over at her and responded.

"We were looking for one of our own. He wandered over there and has not come back. He and I got into a fight, and he left. We tracked him as far as we could, but then we were ambushed. We fear he is either a slave now, or dead. Those murdering foxes have a stronghold in those woods and any who get too close are captured or killed. It has been that way for long seasons."

Kit shook his head. He did not like the sound of these foxes, and he knew that Quicksilver did not either.

"Has no one tried to get rid of them?" Kit asked, and the hedgehogs all looked sad.

"A long time ago, when I was a little one, there were those who went and tried to fight the foxes. But they were defeated in the battle, and no one survived. The leader of the foxes declared himself king of these lands and demanded that tribute be paid. Twice a year they come to gather food and take tribute. Some are wanting to fight, but others are scared. No one who goes over there ever comes back." Kit nodded, but he did not stop thinking about it, and neither did Quicksilver.

Quicksilver did not like to kill others. She did not like hurting any beast. But she knew that she could not just leave without trying to help. She could not bear the thought of just walking away, without trying to help. But she did not know what to do. Maybe some rest would help her think of something.

The hedgehogs lived in a community with other creatures, including squirrels, otters, mice, and others. They greeted the newcomers warmly and welcomed them. Some of the male squirrels looked with admiration at Quicksilver, as she was very pretty, and some of the other females looked at Kit with thoughtful expressions. But it was clear to anyone that these two were not for anyone else.

The day was warm and bright, and the hedgehogs had come home safely. Every beast lent a paw to help prepare a celebration. But as the evening fell, a warning bell was heard. Foxes were coming. All the mothers grabbed their babies and ran into the shelters, closing the doors. All the males gathered to protect their families.

As the foxes came up, their eyes dark with anger, they pinpointed the two newcomers. The two squirrels stood out, by reason of their fur, and the fact that they were armed with real weapons. All the other creatures here were farmers and all they had were pitchforks and shovels.

"Give us the two squirrels, and we will leave. For they must pay for killing the foxes in the woods. They have broken the law and must face the consequences of that. Ignorance is not an excuse." Nobody moved. No sound was made, except the rustling in the trees. The leader of the foxes opened his mouth to speak again, but he was cut off by Kit.

"Even if we did go with you, you could give us no assurance that you would leave these creatures alone. You have terrorized these innocent creatures and stolen that for which they work. You are nothing but bullies and cowards, and I would not trust your word as far as I could throw you." The foxes tensed, and those that had bows raised them.

Quicksilver was not going to let these foxes kill any of these creatures, but she did not want to surrender either. She wished that she understood how to use whatever her gift was, as she believed that it could help them, but she did not. The land, though, was stirred by her presence, and something happened.

The foxes did not understand how they were suddenly upside down, their weapons on the ground. The trees now held the foxes, and none of the beasts knew how it had happened. But a red furred mouse, who just happened to have found her way here understood. Rose was hidden right now, but she smiled and nodded to herself.

The land itself was responding to the danger that the last Undarai was in. The land was protecting her, in a way that no one could have predicted. Quicksilver was growing, and her magic was growing with her. Her people had been protectors of the natural world, and this world was responding her growing power.

The foxes struggled, trying to break free. But the trees would not release them. They were a threat to Quicksilver, and so, the trees would hold on until they were no longer a threat. The weapons that the foxes had dropped sank into the ground, where the foxes could not get them. Only after their weapons disappeared were the foxes dropped by the trees.

Shaking in fear and humiliation the foxes glowered at the creatures, and the leader, a big fox who was called Blackfur, growled.

"This is not over, you will all pay for this, and I will enjoy putting you out of my misery." He swept his cloak around him, and with the other foxes, he left. Quicksilver lowered her eyes, as she knew that he was telling the truth.

A rustling sound came from over to the right, and Rose stepped out. She held up her paws, indicating that she was a friend, and everyone relaxed, as they saw she was only a mouse. Her fur was not a usual color, but mice were good creatures.

Kit frowned as he studied this newcomer, and he realized that this could only be the one that he and Quicksilver had come to find. She smiled at him and spoke softly.

"My name is Rose, and I have been looking for you, just as you have looking for me. Before we get into all the questions that you have, we need to do something about the foxes, who are all holed up in the dark fortress a few days aways. I cannot go anywhere, knowing that there are creatures who need some help."

"And what do you think we can do, against the foxes? Their

fortress cannot be overcome, as we do not have the numbers to do anything. We are in more trouble now, then before." One of the creatures, an otter, asked.

"Numbers are not always what are needed to win." Rose answered.

"They are helpful though." Kit noted. Rose smiled, and turned to him, and spoke.

"Have you already forgotten what happened with the sea rats? Quicksilver does not need an army, as her power will suffice for what is needed. There is also the fact that the very land will fight for her if she needs it too. For Quicksilver is far more special than you know. She is all you need to take down the foxes."

Quicksilver thought about what had happened on the beach. She was not sure if she wanted to see that happen again, but she also did not want these good creatures to continue to suffer. Kit was not sure that she should try, as it could put her in danger, but he had just seen the trees stop the group of foxes that had been here. He knew that it would be up to Quicksilver, as she was the one who would be doing whatever it was, she did.

Quicksilver studied the creatures around her, looking for the first time at their clothes, and their demeanors. They were not as healthy as they should be, and their clothes were patched and frayed. They were suffering a lot under the rule of the foxes, and she looked at the little ones, who should have been playing and laughing, and she could not see them doing so. This was not a good place to be, but it was their home. And she and Kit had brought more trouble to them. She knew that she needed to help them if she could.

Quicksilver looked over at Rose and took a deep breath.

"I do not know how I do the things I do, or even how they happened. But I could not leave here knowing that I did not at least try to help. If I can help these good creatures, then I will." Rose nodded. She knew how Quicksilver felt and knew that this was a good indication of her character. So, with some others who did not want to serve the foxes anymore, Quicksilver, Kit and Rose set out to go to the fortress of the foxes and face them down.

CHAPTER SIX

Blackfur fled from the throne room. His leader, King Redeye, was not happy. Redeye was not a fox to cross, and he did not like being denied anything. He wanted the two squirrels that had killed his foxes, so that the creatures nearby would not get brave enough to stand up to them. The foxes were not as numerous as they had once been. The fortress was not as strong, as time and weather were taking a toll. Even the slaves could not keep the fortress in as good of condition as it had once been.

Redeye did not like the thought of his soft life being disrupted. He liked the way things were. He did not want to hear about a squirrel that could command the trees. He did not want anything to destroy what he had made here. He wanted everything to continue being the way he wanted it. And he was not going to let any beast get in his way. He ordered the foxes to prepare to march on the creatures and enslave them all. This would take a few days, but he would not let that stop him.

He could not have known that his reign of terror was going to end, and a single silver furred squirrel was going to do it.

At dawn of the third day, they came to the fortress, and look upon it. It was a dark and brooding thing, made of dark stone, and it looked like it had seen better days. Sounds came from it, as inside the final preparations were being made. Rose recognized the sounds and whispered softly.

"I think they are getting ready to march." The others looked over at her and then at the fortress. The rising sun had yet to touch it if it ever truly did. Rose knew that Quicksilver would need the night in which to unleash her light, as it would only be visible at night. They needed to delay the foxes from leaving. Her blue eyes went to the drawbridge, and she took a breath.

"I am going to jam the drawbridge, so they cannot leave. We need to keep them here, until nightfall. Then Quicksilver will be able to use her light." Quicksilver did not know how to turn on the light, but she hoped that Rose was right.

As the drawbridge began to fall forward, it suddenly came to a stop. Rose had thrown a sword, into the chain, and as it was a special sword, it would not break no matter what. She had not thrown her burning blade, but another enchanted sword from the valley. The chain was stuck, and the drawbridge would not open enough for the foxes to leave. On the top of the wall, one fox noticed the mouse who had stopped the bridge and called out to the others down below.

Blackfur climbed up and looked down at the mouse who stood on the road. She looked up at them and smiled.

"I do not think you are going anywhere today. And by tonight, you will no longer threaten the creatures in the area. Enjoy your last day." With that she vanished into the trees. The foxes trapped inside of the fortress had no idea what was going to happen, as they tried to reach the sword that was stopping the drawbridge from opening but it was not possible for them to touch it. The flames of the sword prevented them from touching it.

Quicksilver was not sure if she could do this. She had never tried to control the light before, as she had not known she could. Rose talked with her and told her to just breath and try to think about how she felt when she first used the light.

Quicksilver thought about that moment. She had seen the galley slaves being pushed out in front of the sea rats, and she had felt angry, and scared, and had wanted to help the galley slaves. She had wanted to heal them and set them free. She had felt a sense of light inside of her and thought about what it would have been like to be a galley slave, or any kind of slave.

Quicksilver did not like slavery, and the thought of any beast being beaten or abused for no reason made her angry. She wanted it to stop. She wanted all creatures to be free to choose their own way. She wanted the suffering of others to stop.

Just as the sun was beginning to go down, the foxes finally succeeded in removing the sword from the drawbridge and began to get ready to march on the forest creatures, but they did not get far. At the edge of the trees, Quicksilver stood, with Rose and Kit. The woodland creatures were nearby, ready to fight if they were needed.

As she stood there, Quicksilver took a breath and closed her eyes. And as it had the night on the beach, so it did now. The light came forth, shining brightly in the dying light of the sun. And as the light reached out, it touched the foxes and they fell back. Quicksilver's light brightened with every moment as the sun faded, and it filled the dark fortress with its pale luminosity.

Every fox that the light touched trembled and shook. As with the sea rats, the light forced them to confront the truth of who they were. It showed them the pain and fear that they had inflicted upon others, and it forced them to confront who they were. And like the sea rats, they could not manage it.

Redeye, on his throne, looked up as the light entered the room. He screamed as the light touched him, and he died, with a look of terror on his face. The foxes that saw how this pale light affected the others fled before the light and ran from the truth of who they were.

The woodlanders felt only peace as the light touch them, for they were not cruel. The truth only confronted those of a dark demeanor. For those of goodly heart it healed them of pain and injury and gave them a sense of peace. The slaves that had been inside of the fortress came out and found their family and friends waiting for them. Quicksilver looked over at Rose and asked softly.

"What does this light mean, and how do I make it?" Rose smiled and responded.

"It is a holy light, and it comes from your desire to help

others and to heal them. You are a what is called an Undarai, which means a Child of the Stars. Your people are, or were, a special race that held within them a light of healing for those of good hearts and a light of revealing for those of a dark disposition. This light is part of your heritage. Only one of your kind can do this, and it can only be seen at night. Just as the moon and stars are only seen at night. It can be felt during the day, not seen." Kit frowned and asked.

"What do you mean were? What happened to them? She looks like a squirrel, like me." Rose looked over at him and sighed.

"No, but I will not go into details here. It is not knowledge that every beast needs to know. Why don't we go to the eastern mountains, and I will tell you more when we get there." She looked around, at the woodland creatures who were greeting their family members who had been taken by the foxes. Then her eyes went to the dark fortress.

It was crumbling now, more rapidly than it should have been. Already signs of age were showing. The walls were falling in, and the windows sat empty and dark. Just as the light had affected its inhabitants, the light had affected this place of darkness and sorrow. Rose shook her head.

"Let us leave here. It is not a pleasant place to stay." The others agreed and they left the moldering ruins to crumble. They traveled a distance into the forest before setting up camp, and making sure that the former slaves were fed.

Quicksilver sat alone, wondering about what it was that she had done, and how she managed to do it. She did not understand what she was, or even who she was. Her pale blue eyes went over to the red furred mouse who had all the answers. She did not know who Rose was, but she seemed familiar, as if Quicksilver had met her before, but she could not think of where or when they had met.

For her part, Rose did intend to teach Quicksilver what she could about Quicksilver's people, and what they could do. Rose did know their language and would be able to teach that to

Quicksilver, but as for the magic of her people, Rose did not know very much about it. But she knew where to go to find out.

Kit felt like a barrier had been placed between him and Quicksilver. He had always known that she was special, but he had never imagined that she was not a squirrel. He wondered if he could still be a part of Quicksilver's life, if she was so different, and powerful. Would she even want him around, if he could not do anything special, like she could? He took a breath and was ashamed of himself for such a thought. Quicksilver was not petty, and she would not want him out of her life just because of this. He knew that she cared for him, and she was his friend no matter what.

After they had seen that the woodland creatures got home safely, and the news spread that the foxes were no more, Rose took Quicksilver and Kit in the direction of the eastern mountains. As they traveled, Rose told Quicksilver what she knew about Quicksilver's people. Quicksilver felt like a barrier had been built between her and Kit. She wanted him in her life, but how could they be together if they were not the same species.

Rose told Quicksilver of the day that they had first met, the day that Quicksilver had become the last of her people. Quicksilver wept softly, sad that she would never meet her family, or her people. She had always sort of hoped that she would be able to find someone like her, but Rose's words ended that hope.

Kit did not understand much of what was said, but he felt as if he were losing Quicksilver and he could not bear that thought. He loved her and did not want to be without her. But would she be able to stay, and where would she go if she could not?

Rose could see that Kit cared for Quicksilver greatly. She thought about what could be done, though none of the solutions would be easy. Quicksilver was alone, but she was also a female. If she were compatible with Kit, perhaps her race could be saved. But that question would have to be answered later. Right now, they needed to get to the mountains, where Rose had set up a portal to the Valley, and which would change Quicksilver to a young woman, instead of a squirrel.

CHAPTER SEVEN

The last night, before they reached their destination, Rose looked over at Kit. She studied him intently, and then spoke.

"Tomorrow Quicksilver will be leaving this place, and it is unlikely that she will come back. You present a problem. To cross the boundary, you will need to be changed. The only way for you to follow Quicksilver, will be to drink some of her blood, which will protect you from the forces that will be directed towards you. I do not know what other changes may occur, if you do this, but it is the only way for you to follow her. I have already spoken to her, about this, and she has agreed to go through with it, if you genuinely want to come with us."

The thought of drinking blood was repugnant, but as he looked over at Quicksilver, he could not imagine being anywhere without her. In her paws, she held a small cup, filled with what looked like liquid moonbeams. He gazed at her, with her silver fur, and pale blue eyes. She did not want to be parted from him, and she held the cup up.

Without hesitation, Kit took the cup, and drank. It was like ice, as it spread throughout him. A thousand sensations swept through him, and he was more aware of things around him, and as the cold receded, he realized that he could feel Quicksilver.

It was as if, by drinking her blood, he could read her thoughts, and feelings. She cared a great deal about him but was hesitant to admit it. She felt that a barrier had been placed between them, with the discovery that she was not a squirrel. Kit did not care if she was a squirrel or not, he loved her anyway. Rose blinked and then studied him and shook her head.

"Well, that is that. Tomorrow we will head through a portal to a different place, and both of you will change. The magic inside Quicksilver's blood will protect Kit, and he will be able to come. Now we should get some sleep, as tomorrow will be busy."

Uncertainty filled Quicksilver. She could feel Kit, just as he could feel her. His love for her seemed to permeate his every thought. She was uncertain about her own feelings, but she did care for him. She hoped that things would work out in the end.

The next day, as they traveled to the portal, Rose would look back at the two squirrels. She knew what was going on and she knew that they would both need time to get used to what was happening. They would find that time in the valley.

Finally, they reached the portal, and Rose activated it. A door of swirling colors filled the air and stood on its own in the clearing. Quicksilver and Kit gazed at it uncertainly, but Rose gestured them through. Kit squeezed Quicksilver's paw and stepped through. Quicksilver took a breath and followed him, and Rose stepped through, closing the portal as she did. It would not do to have a hapless creature step through and be destroyed.

On the other side, she found both of her companions in panic mode. Neither of them had ever been anything other than squirrels, and suddenly they found themselves without fur and tails. Rose sighed and managed to get them to calm down. Kit stared at his hands, without fur, and with five fingers. The fingers were long and slender, and smooth.

Quicksilver seemed to be having trouble balancing without her tail. She would take a few steps and then almost fall. Her blue eyes were filled with fear, and uncertainty. Rose took her hand and straightened her up.

Rose smiled and handed clothes to them. She took quicksilver over to some trees away form Kit, and she helped her get into her dress. Then she went over to Kit and helped him get dressed. She was glad that she was not self-conscience so she could help him, as he was married, and she had been raised by demons.

"Do not think about your tail. Just stand still for a moment, all right. And breathe, everything is all right. You just need to focus and calm down. Do not think about what just happened, and just breathe." Quicksilver nodded, and stood still, her eyes closed, and focused on her breathing.

Kit leaned against a tree, his own eyes closed, as he took a few steadying breaths. He shook a little and stood still. Rose watched them for a moment and nodded. She was glad that they had listened to her and calmed down. After a few minutes, Quicksilver opened her eyes and looked around.

They were in a forest of red trees. The sounds were familiar, as she could hear birds singing, and the sound of a brook, bubbling nearby. A rustling sound caught her ears, and she looked over a red furred squirrel leaping through the branches of the trees. This squirrel, however, did not speak, but make squeaking sounds. Quicksilver looked over at Rose, who smiled, and said softly.

"The place you grew up is a place where humans never existed. The animals took an advanced state, learning to speak and do things that animals elsewhere cannot do. The ones here are nothing but animals, no thoughts other than of food and mating. But I know that the world you grew up on was special, and I hope to keep it that way. But come, we need to go. I have a carriage waiting for us, to take us to Jewel City."

Quicksilver nodded and Kit stepped away from the tree. They took a few moments to learn how to balance without a tail and managed to get to the waiting carriage. Rose did not want to overwhelm them all at once, so the carriage was drawn by horses. They climbed in and the carriage driver led the horses through the trees, and onto the road that would take them to Jewel City.

Rose talked with them as they traveled, telling them about the place they were going. She explained that the race that existed here was not human, though they did look human.

THE FOUR GUARDIANS

They were High Fairies, an extraordinary race that had come to the valley, looking for peace. They had found it, and more. This was their home, and they took care of it.

The High Fairies welcomed nature into their lives. They admired its beauty and grace. They had added gardens to their city, and trees lined the streets. Because of their magic, they could make anything they wanted to grow. Even apartment buildings had gardens, on their rooftops. On the balconies of the apartments, flowers would grow, and green things could be seen.

Rose also told them that there was different technology here than what they understood too. There were things that they would see that they would not understand at first. Like torches were not use to light rooms, and there were vehicles, like the carriage, but also different ones. She told them that it would take some time for them to adjust to all the different things that they would see, but they would get used to all the technology.

It would take them a few days to reach the city, so on the first day, they made camp on the edge of a swamp. Fireflies danced in evening light, and Quicksilver gave off a pale light. Kit studied her and decided that it did not matter what form Quicksilver took, she was beautiful no matter what.

In this form, Quicksilver had pale skin, as pale as the moon. Her pale blue eyes were warm, and bright. Her face was heart-shaped, and her lips were light pink. Silver hair framed her face, shimmering in the light. She smiled at the dancing fireflies, as they seemed to be attracted to her and they danced around her, in a halo of light.

Rose studied Quicksilver and wondered how she would teach this girl what she needed to know, about her people and her heritage. Rose knew only a little about the Undarai and had already told Quicksilver what she did know.

Rose leaned back and looked up at the stars that shined in the night sky. There was a place she could go to get more information, but she did not know when she could find the time. She was going to be busy, teaching these two about the new world they had stepped into. They would need time to adjust to the changes that had been made to their bodies. Rose studied Kit, knowing that he was going to need to be taught by someone who knew how to fight with a big weapon.

Ox was the first name that popped into her head. He fought with an axe, which was like a hammer, so he would know how to teach Kit. She nodded. Ox would be a good teacher for Kit. Rose knew that Quicksilver was a healer, so she would be able to go the healer's school to learn there. And Rose would teach her the language of her people, so she would know something of them.

Rose hoped that these two would be able to adjust to the changes to their bodies, and their environment. But Quicksilver would need to learn how to read and write in her language, and Rose knew only a little about that. But what Rose knew she would teach Quicksilver, so there was a basis for her to learn the rest.

The next day, as they traveled, Rose told them about what she had thought about the night before. Kit did not want to be separated from Quicksilver, but he knew that he needed to learn, and he would be able to feel Quicksilver, no matter how far apart they were.

Quicksilver did want to learn how to be a better healer, but she also wanted to learn about her people. When she voiced this concern, Rose smiled, and responded.

"I will teach you what I can, and I know where to get a book about your people. I will teach you what little I know about your people's written language, so you will be able to learn the rest. You are incredibly special, and the people here will treat you both well. You do not need to be afraid, and I will help you as much as I can."

Quicksilver nodded, and then asked about the people in the valley. Rose smiled and began to tell them about the High Fairies.

"The High Fairies are good people. They value knowledge

above greed. They do not have money, but there are diverse ways to get what you need. They will ask questions, and they will listen to you. They will be very curious about where you are from, so do not be afraid to tell them. They like innovative ideas, and new knowledge.

They care for each other like no other race that I have been around. They believe that everyone deserves to live as they choose, without judgement. They consider life to be sacred, and value it. There are fighters among them, but they do not take joy in killing others. They are willing to do whatever they believe is necessary to protect the innocent, and they always take care of those who cannot care for themselves.

The High Fairies believe that every life is connected to all others, and the loss of life is seen to diminish all life. They will take life if it is the only choice they have, but they try not to kill if possible. Even in the heat of battle, they will always accept surrender. They would rather talk than fight, and they try to keep things peaceful if possible.

They are a people that sees the value of all, and they try to show this value in all that they do. This is not to say that they do not get into arguments, for they do, but they try to see the issue from both sides. The High Fairies just want to live as they want, and find peace, and knowledge. And they would like all races to be able to learn how to do this but know that it will take a while for the other races, of humans, elves, and dwarves to find a way to live in harmony."

CHAPTER EIGHT

On the day of their arrival to Jewel City, the carriage stopped so they could get out and see it before they entered it. Both Quicksilver and Kit had to blink as they looked at a city that was a work of art.

Trees lined all the streets, and gardens and parks were placed everywhere it seemed. The city welcomed nature, for there were no walls. The buildings, built of different gemstones, gleamed in the light of the sun overhead. Each building was different, in size and shape, but they blended to create a seamless whole.

No other city that Kit and Quicksilver would ever see would ever come close to the beauty and grace of Jewel City. The High Fairies had the time, and the power to form what they wanted, and a city unlike any other had been created by these patient and remarkable people. Each building was a work of art unto itself, but it left Kit and Quicksilver speechless.

Rose smiled at them. They had never seen a city before anyway, and to see this one, so beautiful and serene, was overwhelming. The focus point of the city was the royal palace, and all the city was designed to bring your attention to that one building.

The royal palace sat in the center of the city, and it dominated the scene. Tall towers, graceful and proud, rose out of the building. A dome, done in gold and rubies, sat in the center, and all around it the buildings seemed to spiral. All the streets led here, where the royal family lived. Lawns of dark green grass surrounded it, with patches of flowers that were laid out in a spiral pattern to cover it. Tall trees, swaying in the breeze, gave shade to the grass and flowers below. Rose touched her companions, bringing them back to reality. She smiled at them and said with pride.

"Welcome to Jewel City, home of the High Fairies, and me. You will learn many things here and find many wonders. And there is no other city like this one. You will find no trash, no waste, no pollution, and everyone is doing exactly what they want to be doing. Everyone here can do what they want, though there are laws, which everyone follows. The laws are not put into place to restrict, but to protect.

We will go first to the school of healers and enroll Quicksilver. She can stay at the palace with me, and Kit, the one called Ox will come tomorrow to take you to his farm, so he can teach you there. Now, let us get back into the carriage and we will go into the city." Quicksilver nodded, and followed by Kit, she climbed back into the carriage. Rose followed them, and the driver urged the horse forward, to the city.

The school of healers was near the palace, and they greeted Rose warmly as she entered, followed by Quicksilver and Kit. She went to the front desk and talked to the woman there. The woman smiled at Quicksilver and blinked slowly. She then looked over at Rose, who nodded.

"Welcome to the school of healers, lady Quicksilver. We have some openings, and we will gladly enroll you. Just give me a minute to get your information, and I will print out a class schedule for you. Now I will ask you some questions, and we will begin."

Quicksilver nodded, and as the woman asked her the questions, she answered, sometimes with help from Rose. The woman typed the information into her computer and printed out a class schedule for Quicksilver. She told Quicksilver not to worry about being behind or not understanding some things, the teachers would help her.

Quicksilver accepted the schedule and nodded. Rose smiled and touched her arm. Quicksilver looked over at her, and smiled, a little uncertainly. Quicksilver did not know what the computer was, as she had never seen one, but she would learn.

Rose led them out, and back to the carriage. From there, they made their way to the palace. At the palace, they climbed out, and gazed in awe at the building, for it was more beautiful up close. Rose led them up to the door, and into the palace. Quicksilver and Kit were in awe inside too. The furniture was carved with care, and diligence. Flowerpots were everywhere, sending sweet perfumes into the air. Tapestries hung upon the walls, exquisite in detail.

Some tapestries depicted gardens, other forests, and still others scenes of battle. Vases of blown glass rested in recesses in the walls, with plants of many kinds sitting in them. Gold held the windows, which looked like they were made of stained glass. The light from the sun would shine through the colored windows and splash colors everywhere.

Rugs covered the floors, soft and plush. The rugs too were works of art, their multiple colors adding warmth to the atmosphere of the palace. Even the wealthiest of human monarchs would never be able to display so much wealth. But these were not humans, and the price of the gems that had gone into the construction of the palace and the city were without measure.

Wealth meant nothing to the High Fairies. They could conjure anything they wanted, so material wealth had no meaning to them. No one had been paid to make all the things that adorned the palace. They had done it because they had wanted to, not for any gain. For if you could have anything you wanted with a thought, only the creation mattered.

To do things with their hands was special. They could have just conjured all these things up, but instead they took the time to do it by hand. They liked to do things without magic, so they could have a sense of accomplishment. To master something without magic was a goal that many of them enjoyed.

Rose led her companions through the halls to a place where they could bathe and get a change of clothes. She directed Kit through one door and went with Quicksilver through another.

The High Fairies had a sense of propriety, and men did not bath with the women.

There were servants to help Kit, as he had not bathed since his change. It was different to bathe without fur, except a spot on his head. He used the soap that rested along the edge of the pool. After he had washed himself, he soaked for a while, feeling Quicksilver through their connection. She was having fun with Rose and relaxing in the warm water.

After they had both finished, Rose took them to the kitchen for a late lunch, as it was still daytime. She made sure that there was no meat, as she knew that her companions would not touch it, for several reasons. Quicksilver would not eat meat, as a matter of principle, for she was not one to hurt another just for an extra food. Kit would not eat it because Quicksilver would not. So, Rose put soft bread, cheese, butter, and some vegetables on the two plates.

Then she led them out into a garden so they could eat. She got some food for herself and sat with them. They began to ply her with questions about some of the things they had seen, and she answered them as best she could. Television was difficult to explain, as she had a tough time finding the right words to explain it.

Computers were a little easier, as she told them that computers were just machines designed for recording information. They were like portable scholars. They stored information and if you knew how, you could find that information.

She told them about some other things and tried to explain things using simple words. They had both come from a world without all this, so they were confused, but Rose knew that they would adjust in time. As the day wore on, she talked to them about cars, and buses, and the fact that none of these hurt the environment. The High Fairies were exceptionally good at preventing pollution, as they cared for the home that they had found here.

When they were done eating, Rose took them back to the

kitchen to put their dirty plates into one of the dishwashers. She told them that the dishwashers took care of cleaning the dishes, to save time, for the cooks. Quicksilver could see the advantages of this, and so could Kit. Quicksilver noticed some of meat dishes and shuddered slightly. She did not understand why anyone would kill a living thing and eat it.

Rose then took them to their rooms. Quicksilver looked around at the luxurious surroundings and wondered if she could be comfortable here. There were so many new things to see and learn. She sat down in one of the chairs and looked out the window. Trees and lights greeted her. Flowers bloomed, and the wind bent them. But Quicksilver knew that she would never truly feel at home here. She wanted to go back to the simple world she had left behind.

Kit stood at the window of his room, looking out at the strange sights that he could see. In the back of his mind, he was aware of Quicksilver, and her desire to go home. He felt the same but knew that both would never be able to go back to their world, and they would need to adjust to this one.

Food was brought to their rooms later, and Quicksilver was glad that there was no meat on her plate. She ate by the window, watching the trees and plants, and sighed. She was homesick, but like Kit she knew that they would never return to the world that they had known.

They both slept uneasily, but they were ready for the next day, as they found clothes had been set out for them. Quicksilver gazed at the dress and wondered if they had anything not quite so fancy. It was a pale blue dress, with lace around the sleeves and along the bottom of it. The shoes that had been left out fit her perfectly and matched the dress. She went to the mirror to look at herself, and saw a young woman, who looked scared and uncertain, standing in a dress fit for a queen. She had not really looked at herself since the change had occurred.

A knock came on the door, and Quicksilver answered it, tripping a few times before she got there. Rose studied her, and noticed the dress was very long, and Quicksilver looked down.

"I am not used to wearing so much lace, especially around my feet. Is there a plainer dress I could wear?" Rose smiled and then bent down. She touched the lace around the bottom of the dress, and it came off.

"I do not know what they were thinking, dressing you like this on your first day of healer's school. You are going to need something a little less fancy and a little more practical. Come over to your wardrobe, and we will see if we can find something better."

The wardrobe was filled with dresses, all of them like the one she was already wearing. Rose shook her head and turned to Quicksilver.

"I think I will need to talk to the royal dressmakers. They like to dress women up like dolls. Let me see about I can do right now to fix this." Rose studied the dress, and then touched the lace around the sleeves, and it too came off.

Rose used her magic to modify the dress, making it more practical in appearance, and a little shorter, so Quicksilver did not trip on it. When she was done, she nodded and told Quicksilver to look in the mirror.

Quicksilver blinked. The dress was plain now, and simple. It was not so long that she would trip on it, and there were no extra decorations to detract from the simple beauty of the dress. And Rose had taken the heels off the shoes, making it so they were not likely to trip Quicksilver, who was not used to wearing heels.

"I like this so much better, thank you, Rose." Quicksilver told her. Rose nodded and said that they should get down to the dining room for breakfast, and Rose would see that Quicksilver got to the school. As they left Quicksilver's room, Kit greeted them, and could not help but stare at Quicksilver, until she blushed.

"Come on you two, let us get to breakfast. And Kit, close your mouth." Kit flushed and remembered that his thoughts were not private anymore. He followed the two women to the dining hall and introduced them to the royal family.

Dophina smiled at Quicksilver and greeted her warmly. Dophina's mother nodded in acknowledgement, and Darwin smiled at her. Dophina's brother nodded absently and kept eating. Corwin was not there. He did not like to eat with anyone. Kit stood off to the side awkwardly for a moment, but Rose took his arm, and led him over to a seat.

Dophina told Quicksilver that she had been a student of healing though she had graduated from the school a year ago. She would be willing to help Quicksilver if she needed it. Quicksilver thanked her for the offer.

None of food that was offered had meat in it. Quicksilver and Kit were grateful for that. Breakfast was porridge, sweetened with berries, with toast and butter, and to drink there was apple juice, and orange juice, with milk as well.

CHAPTER NINE

After breakfast, Rose took the two of them out to the front of the palace, where Ox was waiting. Kit blinked as he looked up at the big man. Ox smiled and held out his big hand. Kit accepted it, and Ox looked over at Rose.

"I will train him for four days, and then give him two days off. I do not want to overwhelm him, after all. On those two days off, he can come here, and spend time in the city, learning about how things work here. I will call you before I send him here, so you can make sure that he has an escort, and so he can spend time with Quicksilver." Rose nodded. She watched as Kit climbed into the vehicle with Ox and left.

Quicksilver felt very alone, but she could feel Kit in her mind, and knew that she was not alone. He was uncertain too. That made her feel better. Rose took her over to the end of the drive where a big vehicle was waiting, with more people on it. Rose climbed up into it, and Quicksilver followed. They sat down together, and Quicksilver looked around at the other people. The bus began to move, and Quicksilver gripped her seat hard. Rose smiled and took her hand.

"You do not need to be afraid. This bus is very safe. I have ridden on it many times. I know that all of this is a lot to take in, but I know that you can do this. You are special, and very smart. I know that you will do well." Quicksilver took a breath and nodded and tried to relax.

They arrived at the school for healers, and Rose walked with her into the building and made sure that she got to right room. All the supplies that she would need were provided for her, and though she was incredibly nervous, she would try her best. She was surprised to learn that she would be in classes for four days with two days off. The same days off that Kit had.

Quicksilver was nervous, as she collected the materials that they had set aside for her and was glad that she could read the books. She went into her first class and sat down. She sat in the back of the class and did not look at anyone.

The teacher did introduce her, and everyone greeted her. She smiled and looked down at her books. This first class was about herbs, and their uses in healing. She knew something of herblore and was surprised to see that they used some familiar herbs.

As she readied herself for the class, she noted that computers were not used in this class. They discussed the different herbs that could be used for different illnesses, and how to prepare them for use. They talked about how to grow the herbs and what times were best for picking the herbs.

The second class was about aromatherapy, and how different smells could affect the body. They talked about how the smell of lavender was vastly different from the smell of lemon. How people reacted to the different smells could help find ways to make them better with those smells.

After this class was lunch, and Quicksilver avoided the meat. She sat down with a plate of bread and cheese, along with some sliced fruit and veggies. She looked over the notes that she had taken and wondered if some herbs were common around the universe.

After lunch, the class was how to heal the mind, and deal with trauma. Emotional healing was different then physical healing. Emotional injuries had no physical wound but could be more harmful to the person. Trauma could be anything that someone was having a challenging time dealing with. Such as grief, or abuse.

The last class of the day was dealt with physical trauma, such as broken bones, and cuts. Quicksilver was not as behind in these types of healing, as she had learned some from the animals that had helped raise her. Overall, Quicksilver found that she was good at this.

Kit did have structure in his training. Ox was a good teacher and started the day with explaining how this training was going to work. Kit knew something about how to fight with his hammer, and Ox would focus on getting Kit used to his new form, and teaching him about blacksmithing, and other weapons. He would also teach Kit about farming, and how to take care of animals.

Kit looked at the farm and wondered how he was going to take care of Quicksilver if they were so far apart. He could feel her, in the back of his mind, and he knew that she was uncertain about this separation as well. But they both knew that it was for only a few days.

Ox showed Kit the room where he would be staying when he was there. Most of the rooms were much the same as they had been when Ox's family had been alive. But when Rose had contacted him about Kit, he had cleaned out his sister's room, and put all her things into the attic.

Ox would also teach Kit about the technology of the High Fairies, so that he would be able to deal with surprises, like the tv coming on or the radio. He also taught him about showers, and hygiene, like deodorant and brushing your teeth.

They worked out a routine for Kit's training. After breakfast, they would go the barn, where Ox had set up some training dummies, and Ox would help Kit refine his fighting. They would do this for a few hours, and then they would go to the forge, where Kit used a different hammer and learned to make things. The things he made were clumsy, as he did not know how to do this, but skill would come with time.

After the forge, was lunch, and then how mend fences, and take care of the many animals that were on the farm. Ox taught Kit how milk the cows, and collect eggs, and such things as that. And after the farm chores were done, they would go and shower, and Ox taught Kit how to cook, just not any meat.

For four days this is what they did and then Ox would take Kit into the city to spend some time with Quicksilver and show them around the city. Rose would come with them if she could, but the king was getting worse, and she spent a lot of time with the counsel.

Rose did keep her promise to Quicksilver, though, and found a book, written in the language of the Undarai, and had been teaching her what Rose knew so that Quicksilver would be able to read about her people. Rose made sure that she could spend a little time with Quicksilver every day.

Rose was also teaching Quicksilver how to fight. She gave Quicksilver a strange horn, that as Quicksilver took it, became a sword that looked like it was made of crystal. Quicksilver was not sure if she wanted to learn this but decided that it was probably a clever idea.

Soon a month had passed since Quicksilver and Kit had come to this place of wonder. They both missed their home, but they had each other, and Rose, and Ox. Kit liked Ox, for Ox was patient, and took his time in teaching Kit about the things that he knew.

Quicksilver liked to learn about healing, and she learned that her people had been healers and teachers. As she learned her people's language, and was able to read the book, she learned a great deal. For her people had left behind a record of their magic, the rune magic, that they had used. And Quicksilver was beginning to learn about that.

Then one day, Quicksilver, looked up at the tv in the classroom, as it showed something that had cut into the broadcast. It was Rose, who looked angrier than Quicksilver and anyone else had ever seen. She had just found out about what was happening to the Shadow Fairies. They were being attacked by some of the younger fairies and killed.

Rose, on this broadcast, announced that she had just put a curse on the Shadow Folk, so that no one who would do them harm would be able to even touch them. No one had the right to harm another out of ignorance, and nothing justified the killing of anyone just because they were different. She had learned that this behavior had been going on for a while, and no one was sure just how many of the Shadow Folk there still was.

Rose, though, in her anger, had made the curse a little stronger than she had intended. Now if someone touched a Shadow Fairy, they disintegrated and if the Shadow Fairy touched something it disintegrated. The Shadow Fairies could still touch each other, but now no one could harm them, as even a weapon would turn to ash if touched their skin. Rose had made sure that the Shadow Fairies would be safe from anyone who would do them harm and had saved a tribe of the High Fairies.

The High council studied each other and agreed that Rose was one step closer to being named King Darwin's heir. She still did not know that her name was on the list as a potential heir, as Darwin had not wanted her to know.

Corwin, the king's brother, was also on the list, but the council was leaning towards Rose. She was a remarkable woman, and the different tribes all liked her. She had spent time among the different tribes and had gotten to know them and their cultures. She had helped the tribes when trouble had come up, and all the leaders of the tribes respected her. All these things were in her favor.

Though Darwin had a son, he did not think that his son would make a good King. If Darwin had not gotten the fading illness, he would have been king for a long time, as his people were immortal. He had submitted a list of names to the council, so that they could choose an heir.

All the names had now been eliminated except for two. Rose and Corwin were the last names on the list, and the council could not choose, for both had legitimate claims. The council did not like Corwin, but he was the king's brother, and he was not unpopular among the people. But Rose, in their eyes, was better suited to the role. And she was adopted into the royal family, so her claim was legal as well.

Rose was not one to be tied down. She liked to roam, going to new planets, and meeting new friends. She would not want to be confined to the palace, but the council knew that the people would not care. After all, everyone knew the laws, and knew what would happen if the laws were broken. The High Fairies basically ruled themselves.

The council could continue to take care of the day-to-day things that would come up, and they would only need to bother Rose if it was an especially important problem. Corwin, though, wanted to go to war with the humans, and conquer them. The High Fairies did not want to do this. So, after several days, the council decided to let the people decide.

Rose was not in the valley now. She had come across a new planet that she was investigating. The king was now bedridden and getting worse. The council announced that a vote would be cast for the one who would take the throne after Darwin died. All the High Fairies gathered, in all the tribes, and cast their votes for the king's heir.

By a landslide, the votes were in Rose's favor. Corwin's closest friends voted for him, but everyone else chose Rose. Even the Elders voted for Rose. The people knew her, as she had spent time among them, and they all knew that Corwin wanted to renew the war with the humans, which they did not want to do. Rose knew that the High Fairies were happy with the way things were and she did not want to change anything. She understood them better than Corwin did, and she knew that they wanted to put conflict behind them, as much as possible, and just live as they wanted too.

So, the council began to get things ready for Rose's coronation. They went to Ox and asked if he would make a new crown for her, for this was tradition that every new monarch had their own crown. And they asked him not to tell Rose.

Kit was startled that they would ask Ox, but Ox smiled and agreed to do it. He was the best after all, and he did not want anyone else to make something for Rose. Ox began by collecting the things he would need, like gold, and jewels. He had an idea about how the crown would look, and he was skilled enough to pull it off.

The royal dressmakers also began to make a coronation gown. They decided the color would be red, with gold trim, and ribbons. They already knew Rose's size and they were determined to make a dress worthy of her.

Corwin did not know how the vote had gone, because he believed that he would win. So, he began to prepare for his own coronation, not knowing that he was not the one that the people had chosen. He was arrogant enough to believe that he would be the next king, just because he was the king's brother.

CHAPTER TEN

Quicksilver continued with her studies, learning about anatomy and how to mend the body and mind. She was not involved in the preparations for Rose's coronation, so she kept up with learning how to be a healer. She did not know that she would, in time, become the greatest healer that the universe had ever known.

When Rose returned from her journey, she noticed a lot of activity. She learned that the king had died a few days ago. She was upset that she had not been there for him. But she went to Dophina and comforted her. Dophina was very distraught, and she clung to Rose as she wept for the loss of her father.

Jack, Dophina's boyfriend, was there well, though Dophina's mother did not like it. Rose, after spending some time with Dophina, went to the council chamber. No one was there, but she just wanted some peace, to deal with her own emotions on the death of Darwin.

He had been a good man and had lived for his people. He had treated her fairly, and she had come to care for him. No heir would be announced until a week after his death. For the next week, everyone was supposed to reflect on Darwin's life and legacy and mourn his loss.

School had canceled for the week, and so Quicksilver found herself wandering the city by herself. She saw signs everywhere that Darwin had been very loved by his people, and they were all filled with sorrow at his death. She had met him only a few times, as she had become friends with Dophina. For all the knowledge of this race, there were still things that they could not heal.

THE FOUR GUARDIANS

Kit was on the farm, helping keep the farm going, as Ox worked on the crown for Rose. He was almost done, for he had been working for long hours during this week, to get it done. The dressmakers had also been working hard to get the dress ready, as they wanted to be done in time for the coronation.

The crown was of gold, of course, and Ox had put all his skill into it. Four roses, each on a side, were adorned with rubies, and the leaves, and vines that connected them were emeralds. The skill of Ox had made it so that the crown was light, but sturdy, and was perfect for Rose.

The dressmakers had lavished all their skill into the dress for her. The red gown was adorned with golden roses and vines. Gold ribbon was worked into the hems, and golden thread was used for the roses and vines. Spun gold wove around the bodice, and everything was perfect. There was not a thread out of place.

Quicksilver was not sure why no one had told Rose about her being chosen for the throne. But everyone kept it noticeably quiet. Rose, for her part, was hoping that Corwin had not been chosen. She did not want to think about what would happen if Corwin took the throne.

The week of mourning ended, and on the next day, as Rose entered the council chambers, Cogiere, the head of the council stood up and looked over at her, and Corwin. Rose noticed the floating cameras and knew that everyone in the valley was watching. Cogiere took a breath and walked over to Rose. He then knelt and proclaimed.

"All Hail Rose, empress of the High Fairies, Ruler of the Valley." Rose was stunned, as the rest of council joined in Cogiere's pronouncement. Corwin was just as startled as she was, but his expression quickly turned to one of fury.

"What do you mean, she is chosen? She is not even one of our kind?!!" Corwin yelled, but Cogiere looked over at him, and said firmly.

"Your brother put her name onto the list, he adopted her into his family, and most of the people voted for her. As for naming her empress, instead of just queen, that came from the Elders, who mentioned it to others, and we all decided to endorse the title. In the years that she has been among our people she has become immensely popular.

She made this valley, which has allowed our people to thrive. She accepted us as we accepted her. She has spent time among the different tribes, learning about them, and she saved the Shadow tribe. She has done much for us and has not asked for anything in return. Rose has proven herself to us, and she has proven herself to the people. They do not want to go to war, as you do. For we are happy here, and we have no intention of going to war, unless our mortal allies need us."

Corwin looked over at Rose who was staring at the council. She did not know what to say, for she had not been expecting something like this. She did not want this title, but according to the laws of the High Fairies, she could not abdicate. She did not want to do this, but she would, because she respected the people and their laws.

"Why would you not tell me that my name was on the list?" She asked Cogiere, who responded.

"Because King Darwin did not want you to know. He wanted to make sure that the people were cared for, and he believed that you were among the ones that would make sure that they would be cared for after his death. All these assignments that we have been giving you were to assess how well you could manage problems when they arose.

We do not want to tie you down, in court and things, as we know that you want to explore. All day-to-day tasks would handled by us, and we would only bother you if we needed to. We want you to be able to find lands for trade and find us allies among the mortals. We are grateful to have someone like you on the throne, for you lead from the front, and care about us."

Corwin could not believe what he was hearing. He did not like what the council was saying. That someone who was not even of their race cared for them. Corwin was furious and he spoke up, forgetting that this meeting was being broadcast to the whole valley.

"This is ridiculous. She is not of our race and has no claim to the throne. I will not allow this to happen, and I will make sure that she does not ascend to the throne. I will not allow my people to become weak, as she wants them too. I will lead them and show you all that they are nothing but sheep wanting to be lead wherever I want them to go." Rose frowned at him. She shook her head and responded.

"You do not know this people as well as you think. They are not sheep, and they are not weak. I have never believed any such thing. I know the laws of this people and I know that once an heir has been named, that no one can change what has been done, and I will not allow you to destroy what your brother has created. Your people do not want to go to war. They are content with the way things are now, not how they have been. They are stronger than you think, and I may not like what has been decided here, but I will not back down, and I will not allow you to drag these people in your personal vendetta war."

Corwin opened his mouth to respond, when the door to the council chamber opened, and admitted the Elders. They walked together, moving in unison, and faced Corwin. Their voices blended as they spoke as one.

"We have heard every word you have spoken, Lord Corwin. We do not like being called sheep. We will not follow you, and we will not allow you to use us as puppets. Therefore, we chose Rose. She has come to know our people as you do not. We are intelligent and capable of thinking for ourselves. Rose knows this, and she respects this. We will not allow you to sit upon the throne, for you are incapable of putting the people before yourself.

We lost many in the war with the humans on our home world. You are not the only one who suffered loss. But we wish to put this behind us and move forward. You wish for us to become like the humans and kill for no reason. We do not wish to continue in such conflict. We are happy here, and we are glad that Rose has been chosen. You will not find enough support to overthrow her. For all the valley now knows what you honestly think of us, as this entire meeting has been broadcast across the valley."

Corwin's eyes went to the cameras. He had forgotten that they were there. Everyone in the valley had heard what he had thought of the people. He growled in anger and left the room. He was not going to let this happen. He would find a way to stop this.

Rose looked over at the Elders. They smiled at her and added their voices to the announcement of her title. And the word of the Elders was respected by all the High Fairies, as the Elders were the oldest members of their race.

Rose did not want to become empress, but she knew that she would do it for the people, for she knew that they would have no one else. And she did care about these people for they had taken her in and had accepted her as one of their of own. So, she sighed, and reluctantly acknowledged their decision.

The next day was a day of preparation. Rose, with Quicksilver, and Dophina helping, got into her coronation gown. It took a while, as the dress was heavy. But it fit her, and Dophina tied it up in the back, as Quicksilver began to arrange Rose's hair. This also took a while, as Rose's hair reached her knees. Quicksilver did some elaborate braiding, weaving golden ribbons into the braids, and letting some of her hair hang in loose curls.

Rose was uncomfortable, in the hot and heavy dress. She preferred her travel clothes, which consisted of a shirt, vest, and leather leggings. They were light, and easy to move in. This dress was not. She could not breath very well, and the skirts kept tripping her up.

The coronation would take place at midnight, as a new ruler was always crowned when the old day ended, and the new day began. A feast was prepared, for after the ceremony. Decorations filled the halls of the palace. Everywhere in the valley there was an air of holiday, as the High Fairies prepared to welcome a new ruler. Everyone was celebrating this day, for they had not crowned a new ruler for a long time. They were happy that they had found someone that understood them as a race and accepted them as individuals.

At the appointed hour, the great hall in the palace was filled with all the nobles. Garlands of gold were hung around the room, and flowers filled the air with a soft fragrance. Cameras were placed so that those were not at the palace could still see what was happening. No one was asleep, not even the children. Everyone was watching the coronation.

No one had yet seen the crown. It sat upon the throne, covered in a velvet cloth. Ox had brought it in only an hour before. He and Kit stood to one side, standing with Jack Hunter, and Dophina. Cogiere, as head of the council, was standing next to the throne, as he would be the one to place the crown upon Rose's head.

Five minutes before midnight, trumpets sounded through the halls. Everyone turned towards the door and faced it. The door opened and a carpet of red velvet was unrolled. Two little girls wearing gold dresses stepped forward and scattered rose petals upon the carpet.

Then Rose entered. Ox gazed upon her and felt his heart jump in his chest. She was stunning. The red and gold gown seemed to enhance her beauty, and she walked with a grace that no one could have matched. Her hair, with the golden ribbons woven into it seemed to reflect the light from all the lanterns hung in the room.

She walked forward, steady and calm. At least on the outside. She did not like the feeling of being on display. She was not a doll, to be dressed up and viewed by others. But her eyes went to only one man. She sought out Ox and found him gazing at her with admiration. She felt a flush touch her cheeks and took a breath. She finally reached Cogiere, and he smiled at her, and faced the crowd.

"On this night, as the old day fades away and the new day begins, we have gathered to crown a new ruler. We have lost our king, and we mourn his passing, but the time has come to place another upon this throne, to lead us forward into the future. We place this burden upon her shoulders, for we know that she can bear it, and she will lead us, and we will follow.

Let us now praise her name, our new empress, Rose Debarra, for she is ours and we are hers. Let us rejoice that we have her to lead us, and we have faith that she will do so for a long time. Let us hold to the path that we have chosen and stand as one in placing her here upon this throne."

But as Cogiere turned to the crown, to remove the covering, a commotion broke out at the doors. Corwin entered, followed by a group of his friends, and faced Cogiere and Rose.

"I will not allow this to happen! You will not place a crown on her head, for I will remove her head before that happens." He stepped forward, drawing his sword, and Rose raised her hand. Corwin found himself frozen mid step.

"You still do not understand your own people. You cannot rule anyone without understanding. The people are stronger than the throne, for they outnumber the royals. I will not kill you, out of respect for your brother, but I will not allow you to harm anyone here either. So, I banish you, and all who follow you from the valley. If they will renounce you and swear allegiance to me, they can return, but you will never be allowed to return here, for this is my valley, and I will not let one such as you be here." Corwin felt her magic, her power, as he began to fade. All those who were with him did the same.

Everyone stood still as Corwin faded away. She had sent him back to the world that he hated. There was nowhere else that she could think of that would be worse. Cogiere took a breath and then turned to the people. He took the covering off the crown, and everyone gasped at the skillful creation.

Rose turned to him as he lifted the Rose Crown from the throne and placed it upon her head. It fit perfectly. The gemstones glittered in the light of the lanterns, and she faced the people, as they cheered. Rose settled down upon the throne and Cogiere bowed to her, as did everyone else.

The feast was laid in the main dining hall. Rose sat at the

head of the table, and everyone sat around her. The one topic that everyone avoided was what had happened to Corwin and his followers. The High Fairies believed that she had been fair to him. No one else would have been able to do what she had done. They all knew that she had taken a risk, but she had respected Corwin's brother, and so had spared him.

So, the talk was light and happy. The people were glad that Rose was upon the throne. Though they knew that she was not going to a typical ruler, who stayed in the palace, they were glad to know this. They were not a typical people, after all.

It was close to dawn when the revelers finally went to bed. Rose looked around her new room. She would change somethings in here when she was ready. For now, she just wanted to get some rest. She struggled a little with the dress but got it off. She placed the crown on a pillow and studied it. She still loved Zach, but he was gone. Maybe it was time to move on and admit how she felt for Ox.

Ox was quite different from his brother. Where Zach had been impetuous, Ox was steady. He was a good man, and he did care for her. She had told him, though not to mention his feelings for her. She looked out at the valley, and decided that she would speak to Ox, when she was ready.

CHAPTER ELEVEN

Corwin glowered at the fire. She had sent him back to the world that had cost him his mother, and father. She had made sure that no one would come to him. How he hated her. She had taken everything from him. Everything that had mattered was gone, because of her. He could not touch her. She had made sure that he could not teleport back to the valley. So here he was, in a barren land, surrounded by those who had chosen to follow him. Two hundred in number. That was all.

He wanted nothing more than to go back to the valley and force the people to acknowledge him. But he could not. He had already tried to return, using his own magic, but she was stronger, and her magic kept him from going back.

It seemed that after the High Fairies had left, the humans on this world had gone to war with each other. Now there were only a few left. The isolated groups were struggling to survive, for after the war, there had come a famine. For there were few men left to grow food. He hated the humans, but he hated Rose more. She had gotten in the way for his plans to get revenge.

Now he wanted revenge on her, for what she had done. She had turned his brother, and the council, and all the people against him, and he would find a way to get his revenge on her. He would make her pay for this humiliation, and he would see her beg for his forgiveness.

Something stirred on the edge of the encampment, a shimmering in the air. Everyone who had a weapon grabbed it and faced the strange phenomena. Finally, what looked like a slice in the air appeared, and a man stepped out of it.

He looked around at the group of High Fairies, and his

expression became one of disdain. He did not speak, at first, but walked over to Corwin, and studied him. Corwin looked closely at the man, and he could see a resemblance between this man and Rose. It was in the shape of the ears, and eyes. And this man had the same golden metallic tint in his skin.

"So, this is what High Fairies do when they are exiled. They sit around a fire, and mope. I thought that your race was better than the humans, but now I do not know. With your power, you could make a palace to sleep in, and instead you sleep on the ground. How pathetic."

Corwin jumped to his feet and drew his sword.

"I do not need you to tell me anything. I am Corwin, and I am the rightful ruler of the High Fairies, and I will find a way to get back, and destroy that woman."

"That woman has shown you mercy, though why I do not know. You will be able to get revenge if you want it, but you will never succeed without my help. I have heard of the many things she has done, all the heroic adventures she has had, and she is wasting her talents. She is better than you and always will be. But I want her back, as I created her, and she belongs to me. I believe that we can help each other in this endeavor. You make a lot of noise here, and I will make sure she knows what you are doing, and that I am helping you.

Knowing that you and I are working together will get her attention, and she will come here. Once she is here, I will spring a trap, and take her back to where she belongs. Once she is gone, you will be able to take the throne of the valley. This world is in turmoil anyway, and you should be able to kill or enslave the humans, as you want."

Corwin studied Rose's father. He did not trust this man, but he knew that he would need help to get her out of the valley, and only she could undo the exile. Some of his men looked at each other and began to wonder if they had made a good choice, in backing him. They had suffered at the hands of the humans, but this was not how they wanted to do things.

Finally, Corwin stuck out his hand, and Kai took it. They

shook hands, and Kai smiled. It was a cold and disdainful smile, as Kai was already planning on how to betray this fool and get him killed.

Quicksilver was just getting back from school when she noticed a lot of activity. The palace servants were rushing everywhere, making sure that everything was clean. And she noticed that many of them looked nervous. One of them noticed Quicksilver and knowing that she was close to Rose came over.

"My lady, the empress is looking for you. Would you please go to her rooms and get her to calm down? She has had some bad news." Quicksilver was curious about this bad news, so she nodded and made her way to Rose's rooms.

Rose was indeed furious. She had just had a message from Shadow, who had told her that her father had talked with Corwin. She did not know what her father could want with Corwin, nor did she care. She just knew that it was a bad idea to have those two working together. She had shown Corwin mercy, out of respect for his brother, and he turned around and allied with her father. She would make them both regret that.

When Rose was mad, she tended to break things. She also yelled a lot. As Quicksilver entered her rooms, Rose spun to face her, and blinked. Quicksilver looked around, at the broken furniture, and torn tapestries, and looked at Rose.

"What is going on? It looks like a pack of sea rats came through here." Rose shook her head and answered.

"I just got word, from a reliable source that my father has made an alliance with Corwin. Corwin was foolish enough to take my father at his word. I am sure that my father has no intention of honoring whatever agreement he made, but I also cannot just let this stand. My father does not need to get involved with my business. He has no right to do so." Quicksilver straightened a chair and sat down. She did not like where this was going.

"You intend to go to the place where you exiled Corwin and

his followers and put a stop to his alliance with your father, dragging the High Fairy army with you, pitting them against their own kind. I do not think that would be a clever idea." Rose shook her head.

"I have no intention of dragging the High Fairy army anywhere. I am going to face Corwin, and I will do so alone. I should have found a different way of dealing with him. I will not allow my father to get involved with this. I am responsible for what Corwin is doing, and I will stop him. Through any means necessary."

Quicksilver studied Rose. The silver-haired maiden was very fond of Rose, and she did not think that Rose should do this on her own. So, Quicksilver took a breath and said softly.

"You will not be going alone. I will go with you. Maybe I can find a way to help prevent something tragic from happening. Maybe we can find a way to help Corwin open his eyes to the consequences of his choice to ally himself with your father. Maybe we can find a way to help him, and bring him back, as a friend."

Rose shook her head. She did not believe that Corwin would ever get over his obsession with getting his revenge or getting the throne of the High Fairies, but she would be glad to have someone else there. She just was not sure if Quicksilver was the right one to be there with her. She was going to have to fight, and she would win, she knew that. But she did not have to enjoy it.

Rose sighed. She sat down in a chair that picked itself up. She looked around and thought about how much her life had changed since coming to the valley. She had been arrogant, and she knew that she had also been spoiled. But one man had taken the selfish and arrogant child and had helped her grow up. Zach had taken a chance, and it had paid off. Maybe she should try to talk to Corwin, for his brother's sake.

So, she began to make plans to talk to Corwin. He was making trouble on the planet. She knew that maybe sending him to that planet had not been a good idea, but she had been angry. And the knights of the valley insisted on going with her, to help the humans. She was startled by their offer. This was the world that they had left, to avoid war. But the High Fairies believed that Corwin was their responsibility just as much as hers. So, they wanted to help.

CHAPTER TWELVE

A week after she had gotten the message, she and all those who were going were ready, and they used their magic to teleport to the planet. The reason that they had not just teleported to the valley in the first place was because they had never been there before. They had to know where they were going to teleport.

This planet, though, they knew it well, and so were able to teleport to it. Quicksilver looked around, and she found this planet to be kind of dreary. A thick smog hung in the air, and you could hardly see anything. The knights stood together, and Rose waved her hand, and the smog cleared.

All around them was a dreary landscape. There were no plants, no animals, no sign of life anywhere. Everything was burnt, and the smoke rose in tendrils to caress the air. Rose shook her head. She had hoped that Corwin would have stopped to think about all that he had heard from the Elders, but he had run head long into her father, and had cause trouble enough that she had to see if she could stop him.

As they began to walk, the ground crunched under their feet. The smoldering ground was hard, and puffs of dust and ash followed their feet. Rose did not like this, and Quicksilver found herself in tears over the blackened landscape. As one of Quicksilver's tears fell from her face, it solidified, and became a crystal that landed on the ground.

That crystal, as it lay there, began to change. It became a seed and burrowed by itself into the ground. It began to grow, and sprout. Everyone was already far enough away, that they did not see it, or the other tears, which did the same thing.

All along the path they took, the tears of Quicksilver began to grow, and turn into lilies.

These were not ordinary lilies. Their petals were pure white, and they seemed to shine in the darkness. Even the leaves were white, and in the center of the flowers, the stamens were silver. These plants, these flowers were called Undarai Tears, and they held immense healing powers.

But no one was watching, as they were all intent on finding the one, they had come here to find. Rose could find him without a problem, as she could feel his presence, so could the other High Fairies. They knew him and could find him easily.

Kai was watching, but not so he could capture Rose. He had been doing some thinking and realized that having Rose doing what she was doing was far better than having to watch his back for treachery on her part. She had, after all, basically conquered one of the most powerful races in the universe.

He found that he liked having her independent. She was useful to him in this way. He had decided to make a truce with her. Some demon lords had learned this, and thought he had gone soft, but now their heads decorated his gate.

Rose and her group made camp, next to a pond. They had brought horses, and the pond was still clear, so the horses could drink. Rose looked around and sighed. She had not thought that any High Fairy would have been capable of causing so much damage. Quicksilver was not happy, as she looked around, for she did not like the way this place felt. It did not feel safe.

They set a watch that night, as they felt someone watching them. They did not know who it was, but they did not want to get caught off-guard. They were in a dangerous place, and it was wise to be careful. Rose took the first watch, and gazed out at the land, wondering why Corwin was like the way he was.

Corwin was watching the fires that had sprung up. He knew who it was, as one of his men had been watching. He smiled. It did not matter how many she had brought with her. He would take her down and claim his rightful spot on the throne. And he would have witnesses to the fact that he was stronger than she was.

The next day, as Rose climbed to the top of a hill with her group, an arrow landed in the ground in front of her. She pulled on her horse's reins and gazed down the hill. Corwin stood there, with his men. They were arrayed for war and faced her troops.

"Will you really fight your own kind?" She asked and noticed that Corwin's men did not look at her, but rather at the ground. They did not want this, not anymore. They did not like turning their weapons on their own kind. Corwin did not see this, and he sneered at her.

"Why don't you fight me alone, Corwin? A fair fight, just the two of us? If you win, I will step down as the ruler of the High Fairies, and if I win, you will stand trial for what you have done, and face the consequences of your choices."

Corwin gazed at her. He was older, and more experienced, and believed that he could win. So, he agreed to her terms. She dismounted, and a space was cleared for them. She donned her armor and gripped the hilt of her sword. This was one fight she would not lose.

The two fighters faced each other, circling. Neither of them looked away. Corwin did not think that she could win, as she was only a girl. He drew his sword and charged. Rose drew hers and blocked his blow. She knew how he fought, as she had seen him on the practice field. His fighting style was offensive, as he liked to take down his opponent quickly. She went on the defensive, at first, but she waited for him to play his hand.

As they fought, she waited, and watched him, and saw her opening. Suddenly she went on the offense and came on strong and fierce. Corwin did not realize at first that there was a possibility that he could lose. But the longer they fought, the more he realized that she was better than he was. He tried to get past her sword but could not. In a final move, she tripped him, and placed her sword against his throat.

"You might as well kill me, woman, for I will never stop

until you are destroyed. I will make sure your reign is a short one. For you seem to have forgotten who I allied myself with, and he wants you." This was supposed to be the signal that Kai had given him, but nothing happened. Corwin looked around and frowned.

"Did you really think that my father would keep his word? My father does things for his own purposes, and he does not care about anyone else. He is evil, and he only made an alliance with you to get me here, for what reason I do not know, but he is not going to help you." Corwin looked up at her and could see that he had been betrayed.

Then Corwin did something that was very foolish. He threw some dirt at her and swung his sword. She dodged the dirt, and her response was to swing her burning blade. It hit him at the neck, and his face looked astonished, as it left his body behind. Rose closed her eyes, as she felt her blade slice through his flesh and bone. But she could not stop the blow, once begun.

She had not wanted this. She had not wanted to kill him. His brother had been a good friend and she had not wanted to bring more grief on the people. But the choice had been made for her. And the smell of burnt flesh filled the air, as his head fell one way, and his body the other.

Corwin's men went to their knees and placed their weapons on the ground in front them. They bowed to her and swore that they would follow her to end of days. Rose gazed at them and sighed.

"Your exile is done. You may return to the valley." They stood up, and then they teleported away. Quicksilver went over to Rose and put a hand on her shoulder. Rose closed her eyes, and tears fell, as she thought about the waste of life. She took a breath, and patted Quicksilver's hand.

"I do not know why you would weep for someone like that." Rose's head came up, and she gripped her sword tightly. She might be a tired from the fight, but she would face her father squarely. Kai raised his hands and spoke.

"I did not come here to fight with you. I came to talk. If you want to send these others away, I will promise not to attack you or try anything underhanded." Rose frowned at him, as she did not trust his words. But something told her that for this moment, he was telling the truth. How she knew she did not know, but she nodded, and told the others to leave. They did so, but they did not actually go very far, just out of earshot.

"You would think they did not trust me," he said, "but I suppose I have not earned that. I really do not care anyway. I have done some serious thinking, all these years, and I have come to a decision. You are quite different from what I was expecting when I created you. You were supposed to be my second and carry out my will.

But I have been watching you and have decided to offer you a truce. I will stop trying to control you, and you may do as you please. I doubt that I would be able to stop you from doing what you want anyway. And I had a visit from someone even I do not cross. She was very firm about this, and I will abide by her wishes. She has given me some worlds, to conquer, and in turn I leave you alone. I have agreed to do this, and wish to offer you a truce, and as a token of my honesty in this, I will give you Shadow."

He turned and with a gesture opened the doorway to his realm. Shadow stepped out and faced her. Though he was a dragon, he could no longer shape change. That was his punishment for helping Rose run away. He smiled at her and bowed. Rose gazed at him, and then at her father. She knew just how valuable Shadow was to her father, as was evidenced by the fact he had not killed Shadow when he had helped her.

She studied her father and thought about this for a moment. She did not like him, nor care about him. She also did not trust him. He was cruel and arrogant, and he collected the souls of the wicked to torture. He believed that he was superior to everyone, except one being. He could not defy the Universe. The Ultimate Mother, who had caused all life to begin.

"I will accept a truce. I have other things to be doing, other than fighting you anyway. I have responsibilities, and as a High

Priestess of the Stars, I have many things that I must take care of. I will not get involved on the worlds that she has given you, and you will not get involved on any of the worlds that I will claim." He smiled at that but nodded.

They shook hands, and Shadow stepped over to her side. Kai stretched and stepped through the door to his realm. The door closed, and Rose looked over at Shadow.

"Why would he give me you? You are his main servant, after all."

"I have trained my son to take over. Your father has been planning this for a while. After his visitation, he told me to train my son to do my job, so he could give me to you. He knows that you are fond of me, in a way you cannot be about him. And he might have worried about me helping you take over his realm. I did raise you for a while after all." Rose nodded and sighed. She was glad she did not have to worry about her father, at least for a while.

She rejoined the others, and told them about the truce with her father, and that Shadow would be coming with them, to the valley. Shadow looked over at Quicksilver and blinked. He then looked over at Rose.

"Yes, she is an Undarai. She is, in fact, the last one. She is learning about her people and their magic, and is making progress, even though she does not have a teacher. She is staying with me in the palace, in the valley." They heard a noise and turned around.

A group of humans was coming up to them. Rose studied them, watching them as they approached. They came up and then knelt on the ground.

"We have no leaders; they were all killed by the man you killed. We need some help, and we ask you humbly to help us. We will do whatever you want us to, all we ask is that you spare us." Rose shook her head. She looked over at the knights, and asked them, in their language, so the humans would not understand, if they would be willing to help.

The Knights all agreed. This world was in a bad place. The

humans were on the brink of extinction. They were few in numbers. They would need some help to recover from all that had happened. So, Rose turned to the humans.

"We will help you, but in return, you will agree to abide by our laws, and our rules. You will become a part of our empire, and by doing so, you will be protected and aided. Some of these knights will stay here, and we will send more, to gather all the humans that remain, and help them all. I claim this world, and all who dwell here, for my Empire." The humans agreed, and some of the knights stepped over to them and lead them over to a different place.

The rest of them went back to the valley, and they found that the news of Corwin's death had spread. His body had been brought, so he could be placed with his brother. The men that had followed became the most fanatical of Rose's followers. As they were determined to prove their loyalty.

CHAPTER THIRTEEN

Shadow took over the running of the servants in the palace. They did not actually have any organization. No one was really in charge. But Shadow knew how to get things done, and he would make sure that the palace was run smoothly. Rose was grateful for this.

It was a few days after she had returned to the valley, when she found her way to Ox's farm. She had some things to talk with him about and wanted to do it right away. As she arrived, she saw Kit walking across the yard. He smiled and waved at her, and she asked him where Ox was. He nodded towards the forge, where she could hear a pounding hammer.

She entered the forge and stood there gazing at Ox. He was shirtless in the heat, though normal people would have had to wear an apron, he was fire-proof, because he was a dragon. She watched the play of his muscles under his skin and wondered if he still felt for her what he had said he did. It had been a while after all.

He looked up, and immediately flushed, and she laughed. Ox grabbed his shirt and pulled it on.

"If I had known you were coming, I would have cleaned up a little." Rose shook her head.

"I am still new to this whole empress thing. And I do not want anyone changing how they act, just because of it. And I want to talk to you about something, personal." He studied her, curious, and then followed her out of the forge and into the house.

Kit watched them and decided to avoid the house for a while. He had a feeling that they needed some privacy.

Rose sat on a chair in the kitchen. Ox poured a cup of juice, and put it front of her.

"What did you want to talk about, with me?" he asked, as he poured one for himself. She was quiet for a moment and took a breath.

"I want to talk about something that I told you to never mention again. I have been thinking about it, for a while, and I have come to a decision. I value our friendship, and I want to keep it, but I also want something more. I want to be with you, and I love you." She did not look at him, as she spoke, for she was not certain how he would react.

Ox gazed her, this woman that he loved. She was different from all the other women that he had ever known. And she meant more to him than she would ever really know. He had loved her from the first moment he had seen her, sitting at the table, dressed in one of his mother's old dresses.

Ox put his cup down and went over to her. He put one of his fingers underneath her chin and raised her face to look at him. She studied his brown eyes, and a slow blush touched her cheeks. He smiled and kissed her. She kissed him back.

A thrill passed through her, knowing that she loved this man, and he loved her. By tradition, he had to court her for at least a year, before he could propose, and they would not be allowed to be alone. The High Fairies had standards after all.

Kit walked into the kitchen, and flushed, as he could see they were occupied. He coughed, and they separated, both blushing a little. Rose smiled at him, and Ox took a sip from his cup. Kit smiled, and thought, about time, as he studied them.

Rose liked kissing Ox and decided that she was not betraying his brother's memory. She would always love Zach, but he was gone, and Ox was still here. Ox was the last of his kind, and he now belonged to her. She could not have been happier.

She would wait for the year to be over, and she would be the happiest woman in the universe, for she loved Ox Dragoon, and he loved her. Kit was happy for them, and everyone else was too. They would be a strong couple, and they seemed to be meant for each other.

Quicksilver was overjoyed when Rose told her about the situation with Ox. Quicksilver hoped that she could be as sure of her feelings for Kit, though that situation was different. Quicksilver was fond of him, but she did not know if they could be together, as they were different species.

For the next year, Rose and Ox dated, and Rose took care of her responsibilities as empress. She made sure that the planet that she had claimed was doing well, and the people of the valley were satisfied with how she did things.

CHAPTER FOURTEEN

Quicksilver continued to go to healer's school and learn about the different herbs and how they could help people with different illnesses and injuries. She also learned about how to heal people's minds and souls as well. Rose continued to teach her how to fight, and how to prepare for anything that might come up.

Quicksilver also continued to learn about her people, and their magic. She studied hard and practiced the rune magic whenever she could. She grew in power and knowledge, and she found herself wondering what had happened to the horns of her people, which had been stolen. She knew that curses had befallen those that had taken the horns, but she did not know if the curses were still in effect, or if they had ended.

Onto Kit's hammers, Quicksilver drew runes of power, and magic. She made it so that his hammers would always come back to him and gave each one a special power. To invoke the powers of his hammers, all he had to do was to touch one rune and it would activate. Each of his throwing hammers could use different elements, like fire and lightning. And his main hammer could crush anything, even enchanted armor.

As the year ended, Quicksilver found herself wanting to find the horns of her people. She wanted to have something of her people, so she began to prepare to get the horns that had been stolen from her people.

Rose insisted that she wait until after the wedding before she went. The year was over, so Rose and Ox could get married now. Ox had presented her with gifts for his proposal. He given her a metal sheath for her sword, which was fireproof. He had also given her a bracelet, and some special boots.

CHAPTER FIFTEEN

She already had a ring, the one his brother had given her, and she had a wedding dress. She went into the attic at the farm and got the dress that his mother had made for her. It was protected by magic, so she did not need to do any repairs on it.

On the wedding day, Quicksilver got up early, and went to Rose's room. There was a lot of activity, as this was a special day. Ox would be down by the lake where the wedding would take place, with all the notable men in the valley, getting everything set up, and making sure that he got plenty of advice for his wedding.

Rose would spend the day with the women of court, though the whole valley would be celebrating this day. Rose would spend the morning in the gardens, getting advice from the ladies, and then she would spend probably several hours getting ready, and then heading down to the lake.

One lady, whose name was Willow, was interested in the customs of this type of wedding. She was one of the Tree Folk, one of those that Rose had created when she had made the valley. The High Fairies had discovered them early on, in the red forest in the center of the valley. Willow was the leader of the Tree Folk, and she had never seen a wedding outside of her people's. Her green hair, which looked like moss, was braided today, and her patched skin seemed to glow.

Quicksilver enjoyed the games, and the food. She was happy, and liked this place, but she did not feel quite at home. She wanted to find a place that she could call home, but she wanted to find her people's horns first. She stood near Rose, and was helping with her hair, when Rose noticed her expression.

"What is wrong, Quicksilver? You seem unhappy." Quicksilver shook her head.

"I am not unhappy, just homesick. I love it here, but the valley is not home. I would like to find a place that I could call my own. Maybe I could find somewhere to make a home for me." Rose put her hand on Quicksilver's shoulder and smiled.

"I am sure you will find somewhere to call home, but for now just be happy for me, and I will help you when I can alright." Quicksilver nodded. And she smiled at Rose.

"You are incredibly beautiful today, even more so then usual. You are glowing." Rose smiled in turn and touched her elaborately done hair. The dress fit, and it was beautiful.

White satin, with white tulle and lace, with silver roses and vines. Across the bodice was elaborate ribbon work, with a bow in the center. Ribbons were worked into back as well. Rose looked exquisite. She needed help getting into carriage that would take her down to the lake. For this one night, she had allowed her father to be in the valley, to walk her down the aisle.

Rows and rows of chairs had been set up, but so many people were there that there were not enough chairs for them all. Tables covered in presents lined the back, and the cake, which had taken several days to complete, rested on a table all its own.

The Elders were presiding over the ceremony. They stood on the platform that had been set up, along with Ox. He wore a traditional suit and stood on the platform waiting for her to arrive. Dophina and Quicksilver climbed out of the carriage first and scattered rose petals onto the white carpet. Trumpets sounded, as Rose climbed out of the carriage. Her father was waiting next to it to walk her down the aisle.

Though she did not trust nor like her father, in the interest of peace, she had made an exception for this day. She would let him be in the Valley for only this short time. After the wedding, she would make sure he left, and did not return. She would not let him violate her sanctuary here.

All eyes went to her, as she stood for a moment, and then with her father began to walk. Everyone gazed at her, and all agreed that they had never seen such a stunning bride. She was graceful as she moved, but she had only eyes for the man who stood waiting for her. He could only see her, as she came closer with every step.

She arrived at the platform, and her father stepped up with her, to place her hand in Ox's. The two of them gazed at each other and smiled. The Elders faced the crowd and spoke.

"On this day, we witness the joining of these two souls. They have fulfilled the requirements for marriage and are here today to become one. We are witnesses to this joyous act of joining in marriage. There will be challenging times, and there be good times. We believe that these two souls are strong in their love and will stand together for all time. They will now speak their vows, before all of us, to promise to love and cherish each other." Ox gazed at Rose and took a breath. He picked up the ring from the cushion and faced her.

"I will not promise you fancy houses and clothes. I will not promise you the stars or the moon. I will promise to love you with all my heart, with all my soul, and I will promise to stand with you no matter what comes our way. I promise you that I will love you for all time, until the end of days, and I will promise you that I will always be there to listen to you and hear you. I promise you my heart and my hands and my shoulders. I promise that I will help you bear your burdens and face your trials. I promise to stand by you and always be there when you need me. Will you have me as your husband?"

She smiled and nodded, and he put the ring upon her hand. She took his ring from the cushion and held it up. Then she took a breath and spoke.

"I will not promise you that we will never fight. I will not promise you that things will always be perfect. I will not promise you endless rainbows. I will promise you that I will never turn away from you. I will promise to stand by you no matter what. I will promise that I will stay faithful to you. I will promise that I will always stand by you. I will promise to always trust you and I will promise to always love you. Will you have me for your wife?" Ox smiled and nodded. She placed the ring upon his finger, and the Elders raised their voices.

"We present to you now and forever Ox and Rose Dragoon. You may now kiss the bride." Ox smiled and removed her veil. He leaned froward and kissed her, and then they took each other by the hand and faced the cheering crowd.

The feast began, and Rose and Ox set together at the head of the table. Everyone enjoyed the food and drink, and noticed the couple vanished early on. No one really blamed them, though. They had both been waiting a long time for this night.

They were gone for a week. They did not tell anyone where they had been as it was not anyone's business. The bond they had was deeper now than when they left. They had undergone a ritual of Ox's people, and like Quicksilver and Kit they now shared each other's thoughts.

CHAPTER SIXTEEN

Quicksilver had spent the week getting ready to face her quest of collecting her people's horns. Kit had spent the week looking for a place on her home world to build her a home on. He knew that she did not consider the valley home, and as they could not return to their own planet, he wanted to build her a home somewhere. He wanted to build it on the world she had been born on.

He wanted to go with Quicksilver, but she insisted that she need to do this alone. This was her first journey by herself, and she needed to do it. Kit did not like it but understood her reasons and he knew that she could this.

Ox gave Quicksilver an old cloak of his mother's. It was big on her, but she kind of like it that way. He showed her what made it special. It had pockets sewn on the inside of it that could be used to store things, like food and even a tent. The pockets were bottomless so they could fit everything she needed, without the need for a bulky pack.

She would wear her dresses, which were simple in design. The sleeves went to her elbows, and bodice was high. She looked like a sixteen-year-old girl, with pale skin, and silver hair. She was older than that now, but she liked looking this way. Rose did not think it was a good idea for her to go alone. Quicksilver was gentle, and kind. She would face many dangers on her journey, but Rose knew that Quicksilver was not really going alone.

The Ultimate Mother would be watching over Quicksilver and help her if she needed it. But this was to be Quicksilver's trial of Faith, and she had to do this without help. She was afraid to go alone, but she would do it knowing that she was going to be ok.

So, she made everything ready, using the pockets on the cloak to store all her supplies. To get anything out of the pockets, all she needed to do was think about what she needed. She carried supplies for ten days with her, and Rose gave her some coins. The coins would be blank until she used them. Rose gave her gold and silver and copper coins, so she would have enough for anything she needed.

Rose also gave her a pale horse to ride. It was a fairy bred horse, and as such it could not be stolen or get lost. It also had greater endurance and speed than a horse bred by humans or elves. Quicksilver felt better with the horse and was glad that Rose had given her one. She finally felt ready to begin her journey to collect her people's horns.

CHAPTER SEVENTEEN

Rose took her to the world that her people had lived on. She took her to the place in the mountains where Rose had first found her. She gazed at Quicksilver and sighed.

"If you need anything, you know you can contact me telepathically. I will come if you need me." Quicksilver nodded and hugged her. Then she mounted and rode away, Rose watching her. Finally, she disappeared into the trees and Rose left.

Quicksilver rode down the mountain. She needed to collect a thousand horns. And she did not know how to find them or where to start. But she would keep faith that she would find them. It took her three days to get out of the mountains. She found at the base, the remains of a village.

It had only been close to eighteen years since the last of her kind had been killed here. But the village looked like it had been abandoned for longer. Nature was fast reclaiming the land, with trees and bushes growing in the remains of the houses.

Birds were nesting in the remains of what had once been the town inn. The walls that still stood were tall, and the windows were many. It must have been a big building. A tall elm tree stood where the common room had been.

Quicksilver looked around at the village and wondered how long it had been abandoned. Rose had told her that she would be able feel when one of her people's horns were near, but she could not feel anything right now. Just a curiosity about this village.

She stayed the night in the village, taking shelter by the

walls of the inn. The horse ate some grass and drank from the pond. It never strayed too far from her. In the morning, she found the remains of a road, and figured that was the best way to find someone who might know something about her people.

As she rode, she noticed a change in the landscape. It very swiftly changed from rolling hills to flat land, with only a few trees to break up the grass. Here and there were the remains of farms, with walls marking where the houses and barns had once stood. The road changed too, becoming more traveled on. She reached a village by the end of day, and this one had people.

She entered the village cautiously, as she was just a girl, and she was alone. A lot of the villagers gazed at her, because it was not every day someone with silver hair like Quicksilver's came into the village. And she was very beautiful, with pale skin, and pale eyes. Everyone in the village was darker than she was.

The village seemed to have been having some hard times. Some of the houses were boarded up and empty. The clothes on the people were frayed and patched, and the shoes looked like they were ready to fall apart. The demeaner of the people was one of wariness and uncertainty. It seemed as if they had been having some tough times.

She dismounted in front of the inn, and young man came out to take her horse to the stable. She took a breath and entered the inn. The innkeeper stared at her, as she came over and in her soft silvery voice asked him if he had a room for the night, along with a bath.

It took a moment for the innkeeper to find his voice, and he told her he did have a room, and could get a bath ready in the bathhouse behind the inn. She nodded and asked how much. He told her that the price would include dinner and breakfast and told her that it would be a silver half crown. She nodded and took out the coins and told him that she did not eat meat. And she wanted just water to drink. He was startled by this, but he did get some strange requests from travelers sometimes.

She found a seat, and took off her cloak, draping it on

the back of her chair. She settled down on the chair and looked around. Some of the men noticed the sword strapped to her side. She was too young and fragile seeming for a swordswoman.

Food was brought for her, just vegetables and bread with butter, with a cup of water. She ate in silence, sipping from the cup, and making sure that she ate everything on her plate. Many of the others in the inn watched her and wandered who she was and why she was alone. When she was done eating, one of the barmaids showed her to the bath house. She bathed in the warm water and soaked for a while. After that she was shone to her room.

From the looks she had been getting, she was worried that someone might try to come into her room. So, on the door, she drew, with her finger, a sealing rune. It would make sure that the door could not be opened from the outside.

The rune flared and the light spread all around the door. The door shifted and groaned as it stretched to lock itself in the frame. Quicksilver took a breath and then laid down on the bed. All the bugs seemed to flee the bed making it, so she was the only one on the bed.

She was awoken in the middle of the night by sounds outside her door. She could hear people whispering, as they tried to get into the room. It was not working. The rune was holding, and the door stayed shut.

In the morning, as she came down, she noticed a group of men watching her. She supposed that these were the men that had tried to get into her room. She ate quickly, and the stable boy brought her horse out to her. She handed him a small silver coin and mounted up. She wanted to get out of here quickly.

Her horse could sense her unease. So, he took off, galloping, as she clung to his back. She would not fall off, as the saddle was enchanted, so she just held on. Since the horse was fairy bred, he could gallop faster than an ordinary horse, and he could keep it up longer.

After a few hours, they both figured that they had

outdistanced any pursuit, so the horse slowed down. Quicksilver was glad he did. She sighed and hoped that the humans would not come after her. She had no desire to meet them at any time.

She looked around, now that they were going slower, and noticed that a change was occurring. The ground grew rockier, and uneven. Piles of stones lay here and there, as if someone had been taking the stones somewhere, and then just decided not to take them anywhere. She wondered about it, as then she felt something.

It was like a tingling sensation passing through her. She looked around, and then saw the remains of a castle. She gazed at it and urged her horse over to it. The horse did not like the feeling of the castle, and neither did Quicksilver, but something was drawing her to it.

She dismounted in what had once been the courtyard. Her horse nickered softly, and she nodded. There was something here, that did not feel right. She went up the stairs and pushed the rotting doors aside. Her skirts rustled a little as she stepped into the corridor.

She looked around and noticed the bones. They lay here and there on the floor, looking like they had been fleeing something. The skeletons looked human, and she shuddered as she gazed upon them. They seemed to warn others to leave and get away.

She walked carefully, holding her skirts up and not stepping on any of the bones, as she moved towards the place they had been fleeing from. She finally came to the main hall of the castle, and she pushed these doors open, and found a room filled with skeletons, laying where they had fallen.

Upon the throne a skeleton sat, looking bigger than the others. It sat in an attitude of pain, slouched over. The remnant of it clothes were clinging to the bones, showing in rotting splendor what the skeleton had once worn. Held in its hand was a silver and pearl horn. She moved carefully and made her way over to the skeleton on the throne. She gazed at him, with pity.

How could he have known that a curse would befall him if he took the horn of the Undarai? How could he have known that only death and pain were the rewards for murder? Quicksilver lowered her eyes and felt a tear course its way down her cheek. Then she stepped forward and placed her hand on the horn of one of her people.

At first it seemed as if the skeleton did not want to let go. Then it seemed to sigh, and the horn was free. She stepped back, holding the horn in her hands, and watched as all the skeletons seemed to sigh and then they faded into dust. As if the horn had been what had held them here, they were all set free, and the curse that had befallen them was ended.

As she turned, she could see the dim image of one of her people, and it nodded to her, and then faded. For the soul of the Undarai had been set free, by her claiming of its horn. She sighed and then left the melancholy castle.

She looked at the horn that she now carried. It was smooth, and warm. There was a magic in it, but no mortal could claim the power of the horns, only an Undarai could. She knew that each of horns would hold magic within it, and she hoped to use that magic to help people. But first she needed to claim them. And there was a thousand of them.

CHAPTER EIGHTEEN

It took a few more days to reach the next village on the road. It was different from the first one. This one seemed to be more prosperous, and lively. She did not know that the other village had been within the influence of the curse from the horn she had claimed. With the curse lifted, the village was already beginning to improve. This village was not within the influence of the curse and so had been spared any problems. She dismounted in front of the inn. A young man came out to take her horse, and she entered the inn.

This inn seemed more prosperous than the other one, and she found herself listening to music from a flute player on a stage off to one side. There was only one room left, and she took it. A bath was prepared for her, and she soaked for a while. She was feeling dirty, after having been in the castle with all the skeletons. She did not have a smell like humans did either.

The food was good, even though they were a little curious about her aversion to meat. They had some milk for her to drink, and she listened to the flute player while she ate. When she went to bed, she again used the sealing rune to make sure no one could get in.

As she sat on the edge of the bed, she pulled out the horn, and gazed at it. This was all that remained of one of her people. There was an air of melancholy about it, as if the one it had belonged to was sad over what had happened to the humans. There was no hate for what had happened, just sorrow. It seemed to shimmer in dim light of the room. She wondered about it and wished she could have spent time with her people, as it was hard to know someone if you had never even met

THE FOUR GUARDIANS

them.

As she laid down, her hand gripped the horn, and she fell asleep, holding on it. And she dreamed for the first time in her life.

The dream was like something half remembered, the colors faded, and the images blurred. But she knew that this was connected to the horn. It was a memory of the Undarai whose horn she held. It was not a happy memory, as it showed her the images of what the humans had looked like as they raised their hands against the Undarai and the fear and sorrow that he had felt as life was taken from him.

She woke with a start. And she noticed that there appeared to be some diamonds on the pillow. She picked them up and gazed at them. It was the first time she had noticed this and wondered if she had always done this. Could she be making the diamonds in her sleep? Or was it because of the horn she held?

She left some of the diamonds on the table next to the bed. They did not mean anything to her, but she knew that humans were fond of such things. She left the inn, and rode on, wondering about the dream, and what it had meant. Had it been a memory of the one the horn belonged too?

The horn was safely tucked away in one of the pockets on her cloak. She was not wearing it, as the weather was warm. Not that the cold really bothered her. She had been born on the top of a mountain after all.

Suddenly the horse stopped. She became aware of a sudden silence in the air. All sound had stopped. She looked around, her hand resting on the hilt of her crystal blade. Her pale blue eyes studied every shadow, and every movement.

Then she heard a noise to her right, and she urged the horse towards it, and found a creature that was under attack. He was not human, and was big like an ogre, but was not an ogre. She felt as if she should know what he was. He did not have any weapons, but his hands were big enough to be trouble if they caught you.

"Hey, leave him alone!" Quicksilver shouted as she urged

the horse on. The attackers turned to face her, as she drew her crystal blade. The horse jumped over the men, and landed next to the creature, and faced the humans. It pawed the air, pushing them back.

"This is none of your business, little girl, so you should leave, while you can." One of the humans told her. Her eyes flashed coldly, and she shook her head. The creature who had been under attack blinked as he gazed at her. He knew what she was, even if the humans did not. He was not going to say anything though.

She faced the humans bravely, though her hand trembled as she gripped her sword. She did not like fighting, or killing, though she had done both. The humans all gazed at her, and to her astonishment they backed away.

She watched them for a moment, curious as to why they were backing away. The sunlight glinted off her silver hair, and a thousand dots of rainbow light cascaded around her. She was beautiful, and the humans could feel that she was special, and they did not want to harm her. Finally, one of them spoke.

"This creature scared away our sheep. He came out of nowhere and they ran off." Quicksilver blinked and then looked over at the creature. He sighed, and spoke, in a deep rumbling bass.

"I did not mean to scare off the sheep, and I offered to help find them. But these humans decided to attack me instead." The humans looked down, and Quicksilver asked.

"Why did you not go after your sheep? It seems like that would have been a better use of your time. I do not know how long ago you lost your sheep, but they could be very far away by now." The humans looked at each other and had to agree that what she said made sense, so they took off, to go look for their sheep.

Quicksilver shook her head and turned to the creature.

"My name is Quicksilver, what is yours?" He smiled at her and responded.

I am called Theac. I am an agonor. We are related to ogres,

but we are smarter and not violent if we can avoid it." She smiled at him, and noticed that he had been wounded, though not seriously. She slid down from her horse and pulled out some healing things. She applied a compress to the wound and wrapped it skillfully. He thanked her, and then asked.

"What are you doing in these parts, if I may ask?" She gazed at him for a moment and then said softly.

"I am looking for somethings that have been stolen."

"By yourself? That seems a little dangerous for someone like you."

"I can take care of myself. I know how to fight if I need too. I am not made of glass." She spoke firmly. He nodded, and then asked.

"Can I travel with you for a while? I may be able to help you find the things you are looking for." She hesitated, and thought about it, and something inside her told to accept his offer. So, she nodded and told him he could come with her, for a while.

He nodded and fell in line next to her. They traveled in silence for a while, and then he asked her.

"Do you know where to look for these things you are looking for?" She shook her head.

"I do not know where they are, I only know that as I get closer, I will feel them and be able to find them. I have already found one, and there is another within a few hours of here." Theac nodded and told her that there had once been a beautiful lake nearby, but it had dried up years ago. Quicksilver frowned and asked how the lake dried up. Theac sighed and told her.

"Someone killed a very powerful being and took its horn. Then they went to the lake and bragged about it. Suddenly a windstorm began, and the water began to boil. It boiled and boiled until there was no water left in it. All the fish and creatures that had lived in the lake had been boiled to death, and lay on the ground, rotting away. No one knew how it had happened or why it happened so fast, except for the fact that the lake was fine, until that man had come with the horn."

Quicksilver shuddered at the thought of an entire lake

boiling away. But she knew why it had happened. The man had killed one of her people and a curse had fallen upon him and those around him. She wondered if the horn was still there.

"What happened to the man?" She asked softly. Theca sighed and told her that the townspeople had burned him, with the horn. But no one had touched the horn after the man had died. It was left in his ashes. Even now, years later, the horn lay in a pile of blackened bones.

So, they made their way to the dried-up lake and to the remains of the town that had once stood there. All that was left was a few walls and foundations. Old, rotted boats lay where the water had once been, their wood bleached by the sun. No rain had fallen since the curse had come about. All the land was suffering from the drought, as she could see only a few sullen birds flying overhead.

Theac took her to the place where the horn lay. It was a little blackened by the fire but was still pearl and silver. She knelt and gazed at the bones. Then she reached out and placed her hand on the horn. As she lifted it up, a shadow appeared in the sky, and she looked up.

For years, no rain had fallen here, because of the curse. Now that she had touched the horn, the curse was lifted, and the rains came. Theac threw his head back and laughed as the rain drenched him. Quicksilver stayed dry in her cloak.

Some other travelers in the area, gazed at the rain as it came down. This had not happened in this area for nearly eighteen years. They wondered what had changed, and how this had happened. Had someone found a way to lift the curse?

They saw two figures coming towards them, through the mists. One was on a horse and the other walked, as there were no horses big enough for him. He did not mind the rain, and his companion wore a cloak, so it was hard to tell anything about her.

The agonor smiled and greeted them warmly. He looked around at their soggy clothes and shook his head.

"The rain is lovely, but it is very wet. Still, it is a nice reprieve from the dry heat of this time of year."

All they could do was nod. They did not have any tents, as they were local people, and had not needed a tent for years. The rain was wet, and cold, as it came down as it had not done so in years. But they closed their eyes though and smiled. It was a pleasant change from the dry heat that had been all they had known for eighteen years.

Quicksilver smiled as she turned her face into the rain, and felt it fall down her face. Cold did not bother her, and she did not mind being a little wet. It was nice to be able to help her people find peace after all these years. And she was helping others too, by ending the curses that they brought about by killing her people.

She could have hated the humans for what they took from her. She could have wanted them all to die as her people had. But Quicksilver was not the kind to hate an entire race for the mistakes of a few. She did not like the fact that she had grown up an orphan, but she had learned by the examples of others that all hate did was harm you, not anyone else.

Quicksilver did not know how to hate someone. She had been loved all her life, and no one had ever hated her. She had never been in a fight with anyone, had never argued with anyone, because no one had ever given her a reason to do so. She was gentle and caring and wanted to help others.

Even though she had grown up without her people she was still an Undarai. She was still one of her people. And she was going to show this world the power of forgiveness, and strength of love. She would teach the humans, elves, and dwarves who lived here that one person could change everything.

After the storm ended, the lake was filled with water once more. It would take time to recover, but animals and fish would return to the lake. The clean waters sparkled in the sunlight, and tiny waves crinkled the surface.

Quicksilver smiled at it. It was beautiful, and peaceful after the storm. The air smelled fresh and clean, and warm. The humans gazed in wonder at the lake, and hoped that maybe other problems would go away, if the curses were lifted.

CHAPTER TWENTY

As they parted ways, the humans looked at the silver haired maiden, and they realized that she was not human. She was far too beautiful to be human, and her ears were pointed. Maybe she did have something to do with the lifting of the curse.

Theac smiled and knew that he was lucky to have run into her. Maybe she could help his own people, who were having trouble. Not because of the horns, but because they were not human. Elves lived the forests, and avoided the humans if they could, and so did the dwarves. Humans seemed to have trouble accepting anyone who was different from themselves.

Quicksilver and Theac made camp near the new lake. The breeze off it was cool, and some birds had landed on the water. There was no food in it, but it was cool, and restful. Quicksilver fell asleep listening to the water as it lapped the shore. Theac gazed at her and felt hopeful for the first time in a long time. He knew who and what she was, and he was glad that at least one of them had survived the greed of the humans, though he was curious as to how she had escaped.

In the morning, as they made ready to leave, she noticed something. Some more diamonds rested on the pillow she had been using. She scooped them up and placed them in a pocket. She did not understand where the diamonds were coming from, but she could give them to people, so she kept them.

Theac's ears twitched, and he looked around. He noticed some dust along the road, indicating that someone was coming. He pointed out the dust to Quicksilver, and she studied it. She had not been on this planet long enough to be noticed. But something told her that these people were looking for her.

The riders numbered three, and they spotted Theac before they saw her. Theac was very tall after all. They came over, and then noticed Quicksilver. She was watching them cautiously, her pale eyes studying them intently.

The three riders were experienced travelers. They all bore weapons and packs, and they were all women. They dismounted and gazed at Quicksilver. Quicksilver gazed back at them and wondered about them. They were all tall and graceful, and each had a scar in the same place, over their right eye. As one, they bowed to her, and the middle one, with black hair, spoke.

"Greetings, holy one. We have been looking for you. We are the Scarred Ones. We carry these scars as a sign of penance for the murder of your people. Just three days ago, we all had the same dream, and were told, in this dream, to come to the lake that was not, and we would find the one who could undo the curses that have befallen this world, and we were to help her in her journey."

Quicksilver closed her eyes. She was not frail and did not need to be protected. She could fight, with her sword or her magic. But she also knew that it was not Rose who had sent these women. The Ultimate Mother had sent them. She sighed and accepted their offer.

"Do you know where some of my people's horns might be found? I can feel them if I get close, but I really do not know much about this place, or where the horns might be found." The leader of the women nodded.

"There is one only a few days away from here. It lies in a canyon that swallowed a city when it was brought there. Getting to the horn might not be easy, but I am sure that you can do it." Quicksilver nodded, and then asked them their names. The leader smiled and responded.

"I am called Cat, this is Talon," she gestured to the woman on her right, who had blonde hair, "and this is Fang." She pointed at the woman on her left, who had brown hair.

Quicksilver smiled at them and told them they could call her Quicksilver, and then she introduced Theac. He nodded at them and smiled.

Quicksilver mounted her horse, and with her companions, she made her way towards the next horn. She asked them many questions about the lands they were in, such as what were the customs and what did most of the people do.

They told her, that since the deaths of her people, a lot had changed. Many places that had once been prosperous had fallen into ruin. The curses that had befallen the ones that had killed her people were many and varied.

Some had died violently, like in the castle she had found the first one in, and others had had natural disasters happen, like at the lake. Some places had been burned, and in other places, there had been plagues. Instead of the power they thought they would gain, all they had found was destruction and death.

Quicksilver lowered her eyes. She did not think that the humans had deserved the curses. Instead, she found herself filled with sorrow, that this had had to happen at all. If the humans could have learned to live with what they were given, and not seek more, maybe things like this would not happen.

They passed through a small patch of forest, and Quicksilver smiled at the sounds of the birds in the trees. Squirrels chattered as they jumped through the branches, and a few chipmunks could also be seen. All around them were the sounds of life. Cat studied Quicksilver and found that she was a little sad.

"Why are you sad, Lady Quicksilver?" Quicksilver sighed.

"I am sad that all this had to happen. I am sad about my people, and I am sad about the people who suffered because of ignorance. If the humans could have known what would happen, none of them would have died. If they had tried to be more understanding, maybe they would have found more happiness in their own lives. Their lives are so short compared to the other races. But they have so much potential for greatness." Cat nodded and found that she agreed.

When they finally arrived at the canyon, they found the way blocked, by a pile of huge stones. It was obvious that the stones had been moved recently, as they could see the trails left by the ones that had blocked it. The foliage along the edge of the canyon was torn up, evidence of recent activity.

Quicksilver wondered if everyone on the planet knew about her. She had not been trying to attract attention, but this was only the third horn she would find. She could feel it, behind the wall of stones. Cat and her companions frowned at the pile of stones, and Theac shook his head.

"Who could have done this, and why?" Theac asked, studying the stones. Cat shook her head, and Quicksilver went over to the stones. She touched them and closed her eyes. She could feel the ones who had done this, and they were close.

"Bandits moved the stones. They were paid to do so, by someone they did not know. They are close by, watching us." Quicksilver looked over at some trees, and then she turned to the stones in her way. She drew three runes upon the stones and stepped back.

The runes flared and the stones began to fall apart. They crumbled into piles of sand, years of erosion happening in moments. The way was suddenly clear. And then the bandits made their move.

Quicksilver turned, drawing her crystal blade, and it gleamed in the sunlight, as she faced them. Her face was cold, and she seemed to make the very air around her grow cold. The three women urged their horses forward, and the bandits suddenly found themselves facing the Scarred Ones, and they could not match these women in combat.

When the fight was over, one of the bandits was still alive, and he was taken over to Quicksilver. She had not had to use her sword, as the Scarred Ones had done all the fighting, but she kept it out. The bandit stared at her, as she gazed at him.

"Who told you to put the boulders in front of the canyon?" She asked. He looked down and did not answer. Quicksilver closed her eyes, and then knelt in front of him. She took a breath and touched his face. This startled him, and he looked into her pale eyes.

There is no anger, not anymore, as she studied him. There was sorrow, and disappointment. He could not face what he saw for in those eyes he found not anger but acceptance as if she understood him better than he understood himself, and he looked down, feeling tears in his eyes. Then she spoke.

"I know you are scared. You do not understand why you were paid to block this canyon, and now all your friends are dead. You feel alone, and you do not know what to do. Just tell me, why did you and your friends block the canyon, and who told you to do it?"

He shuddered. Yelling and threats were what he had expected, not this. Not understanding and sympathy. Not acceptance and sorrow. So, he told her.

"A man came about a week ago and told us he would pay us a bag of gold to block the canyon. We thought it was a strange request, as no one goes into the canyon anyway, but we wanted the gold. So, he paid us, and we put the stones in the way. Then he told us that if we killed the one who came to the canyon he would return and pay us more gold."

Quicksilver studied the man. She knew he was telling the truth. Who was this man, and how did he know of her? She had only been on this world for a few weeks, and she had taken steps to prevent anyone from finding her. So, who was he? And how did he know that she was looking for the horns of the Undarai?

She shook her head, she would investigate it later, for right now, she needed to go into the canyon and retrieve the next horn. Quicksilver looked over at the Scarred Ones and told them to let the man go. He did not know who the man was, nor could he find him. If this mystery man wanted to try to stop her, he would not succeed. She would do what she had come to do, and no one would stop her.

Cat nodded and released the bandit. He stood up and studied Quicksilver. Then he shook his own head and refused to leave.

As a bandit, he did not really have anywhere to go. He would stay and help her. Quicksilver sighed and nodded. If he wanted to stay, she would not stop him. But she would go into the canyon on her own and get the horn.

So, she walked into the cool canyon, pulling her cloak around her. She could feel the horn, as she drew close to the city that had been swallowed by the canyon. She could feel sorrow here, in the city. Those that had survived had left, though only a few had survived. Here and there, amid the broken buildings, skeletons could be seen, mutely asking for help that had not come.

As she entered the area in the center of the city, she could see a skeleton of a man, holding the horn. She moved over to him, and shook her head, and whispered.

"You did not find the power you were hoping for, did you?" With those words, she reached up and took the horn. As she pulled it way, like in the castle, all the skeletons collapsed into dust. She sighed, and made her way out of the city, and back to where her companions were waiting.

Now she had three horns, and only needed to find nine hundred and ninety-seven more. She knew that she could do this, and she would do this. She would find all her people's horns and end the curses that had befallen those who had taken them.

She would find them, and she would not be stopped. She did not know who the mystery man was, but she would not let him get in her way. This was her journey, and she would not fail, neither her people nor herself. So, with her companions, she traveled to many places, and claimed the horns of her people. It was not easy, but she did not give up. And she found that there were many people, elves, dwarves, and humans who wanted to follow her.

These people had no formal leadership anymore. The curses had destroyed many kingdoms. Not just the human ones, but elven and dwarven lands had been destroyed as well. As she traveled around, ending the curses, the people chose to uproot themselves and follow the one who set them free.

They did tell her of a sorcerer who had been trying to gain control of the lands and the people. He was the one who put obstacles in her way, trying to stop her from gathering the Undarai horns. He wanted to rule, and she was in the way. But she would not stop what she was doing, for she would not give in to fear. She was made of stronger stuff than some thought she was.

CHAPTER TWENTY ONE

The sorcerer, Gavin, glowered at his men. She had found many of the horns now, and her followers were growing in number. She was different from what he had expected, and he did not understand why she could not be stopped. She was only a girl, albeit an extraordinary one. She could not be an Undarai, but he knew that only an Undarai could claim the horns and end the curses. And she did not look like an Undarai. But no matter what he put in her way, she prevailed.

He had to find a way to stop her. He did not want the curses to end. He wanted the power for himself. He wanted to become the only one with power. He wanted to overthrow the gods themselves and claim this world for himself. And no little girl was going to stop him.

He had tried to put a spy in her growing camp, but that had not lasted long. The spy had been converted over to her side. He needed to find a way to stop her. He slammed his fist on the table in front of him and told his men to leave him.

As he turned to the window, he heard a noise behind him, and turned to face an extraordinarily beautiful woman, with sapphire eyes, and full red lips. She gazed at him and shook her head.

"So, you are the one that had been trying to stop Quicksilver. You will not succeed. Now that people know that an Undarai still exists, they will do anything to end the curses. They want her to succeed. Already many places are doing better, and she will continue to claim the horns. You cannot stop her, and if you keep trying, you will most likely end up dying." He glowered at her and responded.

"She is no Undarai, they are all dead. I will defeat her because she is just a girl. I do not care how many people follow her, and I do not care how many horns she has claimed. I am the one who will claim the power of the horns and I will overthrow even the gods." Rose shook her head. This man was completely delusional.

"No one can claim the power of the horns, without causing a curse to fall. You seem to have a lack of intelligence, as you are unable to understand that those horns were never meant to give anyone power. The power of the Undarai was never just in their horns. Their magic was never meant for anyone to control. I think I will enjoy watching you fail, as you will if you continue to stand in her way."

Before the sorcerer could respond to that, Rose was gone. He shook his head and turned to the table. On it was a map that documented the places of the horns. He had tried to claim the horns but had been unable to even touch them. If he could get the ones she had, maybe he could claim them. He smiled, and thought, maybe if he let her get all the horns, then he could take them from her.

Quicksilver looked out over the encampment. It had grown, as she had collected the horns. She did not want to be a leader but found herself thrown into the role of one. She had only come here to get the horns of her people, not gather a following. But they followed her, and she saw to it that everyone was taken care of. She made sure that there was enough food and shelter to go around.

They were approaching a desert. Somewhere in the desert, there were a few horns. She knew that there had once been a race of nomads in the desert, but there was not anymore. There was no water in the oases, as they had all dried up. Without water, there could be no life.

There were wagons now, and the wagons could carry some water. Quicksilver did not know how this all got started, or why they wanted to follow her, but she felt responsible for them. So, she made sure that there was plenty of food, and she could use her magic on the water barrels. There was a rune that would replicate the water, and food, so they did not need to worry so much about running out. They would still be careful, though, so she would not need to use the rune very much.

CHAPTER TWENTY TWO

Rose had spoken to Kit about the situation with Quicksilver, and she would talk to Quicksilver too, so she would know that it was ok for her to love Kit. He wanted to make a home for her, and on the very planet that she was on, he had found a place where the mountains met the sea. In this place, Rose's architects and workers had begun to build a tower, that Kit had designed for Quicksilver.

A low wall would surround the grounds, and trees would be planted, as well as gardens. The tower would be made of white marble, and it would rise above the trees, tall and graceful. A harbor could be made, as the mountains falling into the sea formed a natural barrier and produced a cove. The cove was protected by the mountains, as they joined the sea.

The base of the tower would be broad, and hold kitchens, dining halls, and rooms for bathing in. The second story would have rooms, along with flushing toilets, for people to live in, and there would be infirmaries for those who were sick. The rooms would be able to accommodate single people, or families. On the third story would be the library, and classrooms for the children to learn, and for the people who wanted to learn about healing.

The fourth story would be for Quicksilver to live, with rooms just for her. She would love plenty of windows, so she could look in any direction, and see the mountains or the sea. She would also like to be able to have her own study, with books, for just her. And they would put in a room for the horns of her people, so she would be able to keep them safe.

Each floor would be slightly smaller than the one below, so that the top floor would the top of the tower. Because of the skill of the High Fairies, there would be room for a lot of people, without compromising the strength of the tower, or the gracefulness.

Careful landscaping would provide gardens and groves with benches, and picnic tables, without harming the land around it. Kit wanted to create an environment of peace, and happiness, a place where one could heal, not only the body, but also the mind and spirit. He wanted to make a place for Quicksilver, which encompassed all of who she was.

He knew that there might be some people who would try to attack the tower, at least at first, but he knew that Quicksilver would be able to manage such times with skill, and she would be able to protect this place. She was very good at averting hostility, as anyone who spent time with her would know.

So as Quicksilver journeyed, finding the horns of her people, Kit and Rose's people worked on the tower, so when he was ready to ask her for her hand in marriage, they would have a place to call home. And Quicksilver would be able to grow her healing herbs, as the land here was very fertile.

Rose was sitting in Quicksilver's tent when the slender girl finally entered it. Quicksilver smiled and went and gave Rose a hug. Rose returned the embrace and stepped back. She smiled and spoke.

"You are looking well, and healthy. But you need to delegate a little better. You do not need to manage everything by yourself. And I have a message, for you, concerning the problem with your feelings towards Kit. The Ultimate Mother has stated that Kit is compatible with you, as he has tasted of your blood. All children you might have with him will be Undarai. So, it is ok for you to love him, and for him to love you."

Quicksilver was overjoyed at this news. She was incredibly happy that she did not have to hide how she felt about Kit anymore. She had been worried about that for a while and had asked Rose to investigate it. Now she had an answer, and it was a good one.

"I am glad that I can love him, and I know he is glad too. I hope to join up with him soon, and be able to talk to him, about this and other things. Through our connection, I know he already knows." Rose smiled and nodded.

"He is looking forward to seeing you, after you have finished what you are doing. And he is making a surprise for you, but I will not tell you what it is. He wants to be able to have it finished by the time you are done with your journey, and I must say, he is making timely progress, with the help of my people. It will be unbelievably beautiful when it is done."

Quicksilver was startled, though she had already felt Kit on the planet, though she was too far away to read his thoughts clearly. But she knew that anything Kit made would be perfect, though she did not know what he was making. She looked forward to seeing it when it was done.

Rose had to leave, as she was busy, but she promised to stop by again as soon as she could. Quicksilver nodded, and got ready for bed, thinking that maybe she should delegate, so she did not feel so overwhelmed. She thought about who she could appoint to take care of different things around the camp and fell asleep making a list in her head.

CHAPTER TWENTY THREE

In the morning, she called the ones she had thought about, and talked to them about delegation, and asked them to help take care of helping her with the camp. She asked Cat to see to the patrols, and scouts, to make sure that there was no danger to the camp, and she asked Fang to make sure that the animals were cared for properly. She asked Talon to make sure that everyone got something to eat, and she asked Theac to see to the other types of supplies.

These four she asked, because they had been with her the longest, and she trusted them. They were qualified to do the tasks she had asked of them, and she made sure that everyone in the camp knew she was the one who had told them to do these things. Thus, things went a little smoother, as these four stepped up into the roles she had given them, and made sure that everything was taken care of, so all she had to do was make sure that they moved off in a timely fashion.

Quicksilver was glad that she had delegated, as everything in the camp was done within an hour, as after everyone ate, they went and packed their gear, in preparation for moving out. The camp was able to move off in an orderly fashion, and they made better time than they had been.

The reason she was able to have so many people and not cause a stir in any kingdom, was because there were not any kingdoms anymore. Most of the kingdoms had been destroyed by the curses of the horns. There were a few city-states, but no real kingdoms. So, this substantial number of people were able to move without causing trouble.

She had picked up some elves and dwarves as well as humans. She had passed through their lands, and they had attached themselves to her, as the elves felt they had failed in their alliance with her people, and the dwarves just had nowhere else to be.

They all moved out into the desert, as twilight was falling. It would be nearly impossible to get anywhere in a desert, moving about in the day. Though the night was dark, there was enough light to see with, so they moved out into the desert, moving towards the horns that rested in the sands.

CHAPTER TWENTY THREE

Kit looked up, as some of Rose's men came over, dragging a human along with them. He was dressed in fancy clothes and looked like he was a noble. He was shouting at the men holding him, demanding that they let him go. Kit put down his chisel and went over to the group.

"What is going on over here?" The High Fairies looked over at him and responded.

"This human was lurking over by the wall. He is a magic user, as he tried to put an enchantment on us, but human magic does not work on us. He is not very friendly and does not have very good manners. We believe he is working with the sorcerer that has been causing trouble for Quicksilver, as she looks for the horns of her people. Rose told us about him and told us to keep an eye out for him."

Kit studied the man, who stood glaring around him. Kit did not like anyone who tried to hurt Quicksilver, and he did not like people interfering with her either. He frowned at the man, and then asked.

"Why would anyone want to stop Quicksilver? She is helping people by collecting the horns, and ending the curses that they brought upon themselves, because of what they did to her people. I do not know why anyone would want the curses to stay."

The man glowered and did not say anything. Kit shook his head. Humans were confusing to him. He did not understand why they did some of the things that they did. He sighed, and looked over at the High Fairies, and asked if they had some place where they could put the man and keep him from bothering Quicksilver.

They had put up some sheds and decided to put the man in one of them. They could place wards around the shed to prevent the man from getting out. The magic user, whose name was Yetis, fought them, but they were stronger than he was, and forced him into the shed, and put up the wards that would keep him in it.

Yetis yelled through the walls, demanding that they let him go, but everyone ignored him. They all went back to work, determined to get the tower and its grounds finished before Quicksilver finished finding all the horns. They were making timely progress, and the foundations of the tower were laid, along with the first two floors.

Kit worked hard, to make his vision of the tower into reality, so that Quicksilver would have a strong home, a place where she could live and work, a place of rest and peace. He wanted to make it perfect and make it last.

Quicksilver did not think she would ever get the sand out her clothes. They had just gone through a sandstorm, and while she had been able to keep most of the sand mostly at bay, some of it had dumped on her. She shook herself, trying to get some of the sand out of her hair.

Everyone else had fared better, though there was a lot of sand, none of it had gotten into the food or water, so that was a good thing. Theac had made sure that the horses were all right, and the Scarred Ones had made sure that everyone else was fine as well.

She had found one horn already and was close the next one. Already the desert was beginning to recover, as they had found an oasis, filled with water, though there were no plants yet. Then the storm had hit, and Quicksilver had drawn a rune of shielding around the camp.

The storm had lasted a few hours, and Quicksilver had

found herself getting some sand on her. Now the storm was over, and she found that the sand seemed to be everywhere. It was uncomfortable, and itchy. She closed her eyes and concentrated, using her magic to get rid of the sand. It fell away from her, and she felt a lot of relief.

As she opened her eyes, she found Theac watching her, and she asked what was wrong. He shook his big head, and sand fell from him.

"One of the horses got hurt, and the owner wants to know if you could do something, or if the horse will need to be killed." Quicksilver shook her head. No horse was going to die, so she made her way over to it, with Theac following her. The horse was on its side, one of its legs broken. Quicksilver knelt next to it and drew a rune of healing on the injury.

The rune flared and surrounded the injury. Quicksilver held the horse, as the bone set, and the horse struggled with pain. Then it was over, and Quicksilver helped the horse up. The owner was overjoyed, as he had had the horse since it was a foal. Quicksilver smiled at him and told him to take it easy on the horse for a few days, so it could fully recover from the injury. He nodded and took the horse over to one of the wagons.

Quicksilver took care of a few more injuries, not always using the runes. Most of the injuries were minor and did not need it. She always had some bandages and herbs ready for use and had begun to teach some of the humans how to heal. She was a good teacher, as she was very patient, and kind.

A few days later, she had the second horn, and they moved out of the desert, and towards some mountains. There was a horn in the mountains, where the dwarves lived, though the dwarves were not the one who had killed the Undarai. Only the humans had done so.

As they reached the city, Quicksilver gazed at it. It had once been a lively place, and wealth had flowed into it. This city, or its ruins now, had once been a center of trade, but now it was silent, with only the wind blowing through it. It stood as a monument to human nature, as if it showed what could have been, if the humans had not gotten jealous of the Undarai and had not gotten greedy for more than they had.

She entered the city and walked its empty streets. There were no signs of life, anymore. There was nothing but emptiness, and sorrow. Her pale eyes took in the stores, once so full of life, now there was nothing. She sighed and wondered why the humans were never content with what they had, why they always felt as they would never have enough.

She went into the palace, and found the horn resting above the throne, and was surprised to see that someone was on the throne and was still alive. There was an old man covered in masses of unkept hair, his fingernails long and twisted. His clothes, once fine and clean, were now rotting and falling off. He looked up as she approached and frowned at her.

"Your kind have all been dead for years. Do you come to haunt me, Undarai? Or do you come to mock me? There is nothing left, as you can see, because of your people." Quicksilver studied him and then spoke, her voice gentle.

"My people did not go around killing humans for no reason. My people wanted to help the races learn and grow. The humans became jealous, and they started the killing. My people wanted nothing to do with violence, and murder, but that is all in the past. What has been done, cannot be undone. I could hate the humans for what they took from me, but I do not. I have forgiven the humans for taking my people, as hating them serves no purpose.

My people did not want to die, but they did not want to kill either. They never fought back, only fled from the humans. I am an Undarai, and I am the last one. With each horn that I claim, I can feel my people, and their sorrow. I can see their memories through my connection with the horns. And all of them are sad that the humans could not see the damage they were causing to themselves. Look around you, and you will realize that if you had tried to be patient, things would never have gotten this bad. All you needed to do was be content with what you had and learned from my people."

The old man looked down at his hands. He closed his eyes, and thought, that if their places had been reversed, he would not have been so kind. The horn that he had so sought, to try and bring back his son, had only cost him everything. He had not found what he had been seeking, which was the power of the Undarai. All he had found was sorrow and pain, and now the forgiveness of the last of the Undarai.

He began to weep, and the young Undarai stepped forward, and embraced him. He cried into her shoulder, as she held him as a mother would hold a weeping child. Finally, he pulled back and gazed at her, finding only love in her eyes. He reached up, and took the horn, and thrust it into her hands. She took it and gazed at him. He leaned back in the throne and sighed. And he closed his eyes and went still. For the first time in a long time, an expression of peace touched his face.

Quicksilver left the city, her eyes filled with sadness. She gripped the horn tightly and went to her tent. She found herself weeping, thinking of the price that had been paid for each horn. She thought of the lives that had been lost, and she thought about the old king sitting on his throne, all alone.

She went to her tent, to be alone, and found herself thinking of what she had lost, and all the things she would never be able to do because of what had been done. She felt lost and alone, and she found that she did hate the humans for what they had taken from her, but she did not want to feel hate. It was an ugly emotion, and she did not want it.

As she sat there, she found herself facing a being of rainbow light. There was no clear outline, just a presence. It enveloped her, and she found a sense of peace. Like Rose before her, Quicksilver found herself in the presence of the Ultimate Mother, the very essence of the universe. She was given a choice, like Rose, between what she wanted the most, and a more difficult path.

She could have her people back, and grow up among them, but in doing so, more lives would be lost, that she could save if she became a High Priestess of the Stars, like Rose, a guardian of the mortal races. She could have her heart's desire or choose a path that would take her far from any home, but she would be saving people without number.

Like Rose before her, Quicksilver chose the harder path, and sacrificed her ability to hate. She hated the humans for what they had done, and she did not like the feeling. So, she gave it up, and took the oath of the High Priestess of the Stars and became the Guardian of Peace.

A sense of peace permeated the entire encampment. A quiet evening passed, with everyone feeling peace and contentment for the first time in a long time. Quicksilver was with them and there was nothing that could harm them.

CHAPTER TWENTY FOUR

Yetis glared at Kit, who came in with some food and water. Kit set it on top of an empty box and studied the man. The man really wanted to just throw the food at him, but he knew that Kit was faster than him, and could dodge the food, and slam him into the wall. Kit did not have much patience with this man, who had tried to hurt Quicksilver. The only reason Yetis was still alive was because Kit was not a murderer.

Kit, like Quicksilver, believed that all life mattered. He did not eat meat, though he knew that others did. He did not really care about this man, but he would not let him starve either. He knew that the man would eat the food after he had left. Kit did not talk to the man, though he knew that some of Rose's people had tried. The man was stubborn, though, and would not talk to anyone.

"She will succeed, and he will become nothing." Kit paused and looked over his shoulder. The sorcerer was sitting down, looking melancholy.

"I do not know about that, or why you seem so set in hating her, when I know that she does not hate you. That is one of reasons I love her so much. Because she knows how show you how valuable you are to her. She is everything that I am not. For I hate you and would see you dead. Only knowing that she would be disappointed in me keeps me from killing you."

"You would be doing me a favor in killing me. I have worked for the most powerful man on this world, until she came and started ending the curses. Now everyone knows that an

THE FOUR GUARDIANS

Undarai still lives and is helping to end what the humans have done. We wanted their power, and all we got was death and destruction. We did not understand why, until later.

We killed beings of power, yes, but they did not fight back. They did not kill us, though they had just cause to want to. They just tried to hide, and they tried to make us listen. They valued our lives, but we did not care about theirs. We just killed and killed, until there was none left, or so we thought.

Now she has come, and gathered a following, and ends the curses that we brought upon ourselves. She shows us mercy, though we did not deserve it. She shows us kindness, when all we showed her people was hate, and death. And I do not understand why."

Kit gazed at him and responded.

"She is just that way. She knows what you did to her people, but she also knows that humans sometimes have trouble accepting those that are different. She accepts people as they are, and just loves everyone. She understands people and wants to help. She just wants people to find a way to be happy and accept themselves. Quicksilver has always been able to see the best in people. And she finds ways to help them see the best in themselves. I grew up with her, and I know her better than anyone else, and I know that all she wants is to help people find happiness. That is why I am building this tower for her. I am making sure that she will always have a place to find some peace and help people. I am doing my part to help her, as sometimes she forgets to take care of herself."

Yetis studied Kit and sighed and looked down. Kit shrugged and left. He had work to get done. They were getting ready to start on the top of tower, and he wanted to make sure that everything went well, and no one got hurt. Putting in the windows was going to be interesting, as there were so many. But Rose's people had made sure that these windows were unbreakable and would allow Quicksilver to see all around the tower.

Theac studied Quicksilver. Ever since she had come out of

the city, she had been different, calmer, and more peaceful. She was more mature, in a way. The change was in her eyes, and the way she held herself. Noticing him watching her, she smiled at him, and he found himself smiling back at her.

Theac moved closer to her and asked her how she was doing. Quicksilver smiled and told him that she was fine. He nodded, and she studied him, and asked.

"Why are you suddenly concerned? You know that I am doing well, as you are near me often. Are you feeling, ok?" Theac nodded.

"It just seems like something has changed, about you. You seem a little different, ever since we left that city behind. You are calmer and seem to be more in control. You seem to have matured somewhat."

She smiled and looked into the distance. After a moment she spoke.

"I experienced something, for which I was not completely ready. In the city, the king was still alive, and he told me why he had wanted the horn. He had taken the horn, to bring his son back from the dead. Even the greatest of my people could not do this. No one can raise the dead. It is forbidden to do that. A necromancer can only give a semblance of life, not restore it.

The humans thought much about my people that was false. Our horns, when we are in our true forms, is just a channel for our magic, it was never magical in and of itself. They believed that our horns would give them power over death, even though they had killed us. If our horns could bring back the dead, then why did my people not use them to bring back those who had been slain.

I realize that many things were believed about my people were just misunderstandings, and much that I thought about humans was false. For a long time, after Rose told me about what had happened to my people, all the humans were monsters. That all they wanted to do was just destroy my people because we were different. I hated them for what they had taken from me, but I realize now that some of them did what they did because of loss, that they wanted to do good things, they were just misguided."

Theac studied her, as she fell silent, and then he became aware of others, who had drawn close. Quicksilver did not seem to see them as she thought about what she had said, and she looked up, and gazed at Theac, and began to speak again.

"I have come to understand much, and I realized that hating the humans only harmed me. I looked at myself, and I did not like what I found. Hate is a poison, that if you let it fester inside of you, you are the only one who is harmed. Most of the humans that had a hand in the killing of my people are dead. It is not productive to hate dead people. Why should I hate them if I only harm myself? So, I gave up my hate towards the humans. I surrendered it and have chosen to just be happy with what I have and help others to be happy."

Theac studied her and nodded. Then she became aware of the others who had gathered close. She blinked in surprise, and then blushed softly. She had not expected others to hear her. They all gazed at her, and Theac knew that they would follow her, no matter what, because she loved them. And they loved her.

Through many terrains, and many places, Quicksilver gathered the last of the horns. Now she had all of them, and the curses that had plagued this world were over. It would take time to fully heal, but now they could. Quicksilver sighed, as she gazed at the people that followed her. Now she had to find a place for them to live and grow.

Rose showed up the day after she had found the last horn. Quicksilver smiled and embraced her. Rose laughed and looked around at the encampment.

"It seems you have a few people to find a home for. I think I can help if you want me too. Kit is ready to show you something. It is finally done, and he is excited that you are done as well. He has a whole party planned for showing you. So, let us get everyone together, and I will open a portal, to take you all to Kit's surprise."

Quicksilver nodded and called everyone together, and introduced them to Rose, who smiled and told them that she was going to open a portal to a place that had been made for Quicksilver but would be big enough for all of them as well. They were very excited about this, and they all got ready. Rose looked over at Theac and smiled.

"Some of your people are already there. They were living near where Kit had chosen to build his gift for Quicksilver. They were invited to help and moved in." Theac smiled. It had been a long time since he had met any of his own kind. It had taken Quicksilver a few years to track down all the horns.

When everyone was ready, Rose raised her hands and a portal opened, near the sea. They all filed in, and found themselves on a beach, where some mountains met the sea, forming a cove. A harbor had been built, with a shipyard, for building boats. Some were already being built.

But all eyes went up on the hill, and they gasped. The tower of white marble stood there, gleaming in the sunlight. The top of the tower looked like it was built of glass, and the sunlight reflected off it. It was graceful, and beautiful and everything that Kit had wanted it to be.

Quicksilver gazed at the white tower, her eyes wide with wonder. Rose smiled and touched her arm. Kit was approaching, walking through the sand, watching her. She ran to him and threw her arms around him and kissed him. He wrapped his arms around her and held her tightly.

Rose studied them both and smiled. It was about time, she thought, for these two to be together. Rose knew that they would happy together. Kit was overprotective, sometimes, and could get jealous, but he loved Quicksilver with all his heart, and he would do anything for her. And Quicksilver loved him, more than she could say, and was grateful for him and his support.

As the two lovers pulled apart, Rose laughed, and Quicksilver and Kit both blushed. Everyone smiled and they cheered, to see a home that would be theirs. Kit led the way to the tower and showed them around. He showed them the kitchens, and the kitchen gardens, and the dining halls, and the bathing rooms, the toilets, which were a big hit with people who had never seen a flushing toilet.

Then he showed them the apartments, where they would live, all with toilets. And the infirmaries, nurseries, and rooms for if quarantine was needed. There were electric lights, in all the rooms, and even classrooms, not just for little ones, but also for those who wanted to learn about healing.

And he showed her the top of tower, which was just for her. All the walls were glass, so she could in every direction, the mountains, and the sea. She had a private bathing room, and toilet. She also had a personal kitchen, with a refrigerator,

And he showed her the garden room. Here, flowers would bloom anytime of the year, and there was a large variety of flowers. And there were shrubs, and small trees, and a watering system, so she would not need to worry about watering the plants.

Even the gardens for the kitchen had a sprinkler system, as did all the landscaping and lawns. They were all on automatic timers, so no one would have to worry about watering. As for mowing the grass, and trimming the trees, Theac and his people would take care of that. They were very good at it and enjoyed it.

Everything was made to make sure that everyone would have a job and help take care of the tower. And to make sure that this was a place of peace and rest. Everyone would be able to pursue whatever they wanted to. There was space for farms to grow food, outside the tower grounds. Farms inside the tower grounds would interfere with the whole peace vibe.

They did not want the farm animals to be noisy, and messy in the grounds, so a space for farmers was set up outside the grounds. There were already farm buildings and farm animals on the farms, so any of Quicksilver's followers who were farmers could move in immediately.

There was also a marketplace set up, outside the grounds,

with stalls, and stores, waiting to be filled with products. There was everything that was needed to start a land of peace, and plenty. Rose's people had put in stores that would carry paints and canvases for artists, and thread and needles for sewers. There was a blacksmith shop, and a carpenter store.

Rose's people would trade with Quicksilver's followers and had made sure that this place was ready for growth, and prosperity. There was everything that they needed to start with, and they were happy for a place to call their own.

Kit told Quicksilver of Yetis the spy, and told her that he had escaped, and rumor was that he was coming with his master, and they were bringing an army to conquer this place. He was only a few days away from the tower. The people who were there with Quicksilver were saddened to hear this, but they would fight if they needed too.

Quicksilver shook her head. No one would need to fight. She was an Undarai, and she could do things that no one else could. She would not let this man destroy what Kit had built. She would use her magic and defend the people and the tower.

The sorcerer looked up, as his scouts told him that they had seen a girl with silver hair waiting for them. She was alone, on a pale horse, and just waiting. He nodded, and rode with his men, to the hill she was on.

"Come no closer, sorcerer. You will not conquer any place today, nor will you harm anyone." He shook his head.

"You should never have come to this place, girl." She studied him.

"You are not welcome here, as I will not let you hurt anyone under my protection. Turn around and go away. Be happy with what you have and leave my people and my home alone." He shook his head. And kept on coming.

Quicksilver raised her hand and drew five runs in the air. They glowed and then expanded and then the dragons came. These were Undarai Dragons, and they were unlike any dragons that had ever been. They roared and not just fire came out, but ice, acid, stones, and lightening. The sorcerer could only stare, as the dragons unleashed upon his men complete devastation.

His men broke and began to flee, unable to defeat these dragons. He yelled and threatened, but to no avail. He turned to face her, and she gazed at him. Her face was calm as she studied him.

"I told you; I am like no other Undarai. I am a Priestess of the Stars, and I am the Guardian of these people. No one shall harm them. No one will ever harm these people." He launched an attack on her, but a white dragon got in the way, and breathed ice upon him until he was frozen solid.

Quicksilver studied him and shook her head. She lowered her head, and tears filled her eyes. The dragon, whose name was Snow, nuzzled her gently. Quicksilver wiped the tears away and turned her horse. The dragon stayed with her, though all the others had returned to the realm where they would stay until she called them forth again.

Quicksilver returned to the tower, where Kit and the others were waiting. Kit could feel her distress at what had happened and went to her. He held her close and comforted her. She looked up at him and smiled. He looked down at her and asked.

"Will you marry me, Quicksilver Undarai?" Her eyes widened for a moment and then she smiled and spoke a single word.

"Yes." Everyone cheered as he kissed her, and she kissed him back. They were married in front of the tower, with Rose officially binding them, and everyone cheered, throwing flower petals into the air. And thus, the second Guardian began her own journey into the future, helping to keep the balance of the universe.

BOOK THREE

Chapter one

Blackbird

The young Spirit wolf did not understand why this human had put her into a cage. He would feed her on scraps, but only if she begged good enough. She could only get water by licking the snow off her cage. He had found a way to steal her magic, and he used it to control his tribe. She would recover, slowly, and he would take it again.

She hated him, but she had not the strength to break free. She was starving, and cold, and she was helpless. She prayed to the Great Ones for death, but it did not come. She did not know why this was happening to her, but she wanted to die.

Then one day, she heard a commotion, among the tents. A young warrior from another tribe had come, to ask for help. His tribe was plagued by a mysterious illness, and he had heard of the shaman of this tribe. But the shaman was evil and would not help. The young warrior walked away, frustrated, and angry when he heard a sound.

Stepping around tent, he found a wooden cage, with a beautiful young woman in it. She looked ill, and thin, and she looked at him, with pleading eyes. He drew his bone knife and cut through the strips of frozen leather holding the cage together. As soon as he cut a big enough hole, he reached in and helped her get out.

He was very quiet, and holding her in his arms, they slipped away to the river where his raft was. She seemed to barely weigh anything. He placed her on some hides and pushed away from the bank. He could hear a commotion in the tents he had just left, but it was getting dark, and he was careful to get into the middle of river.

She watched him, as he skillfully maneuvered the raft. He had not told the shaman where his tribe was, and he had gone into the village of tents by a different way, not by the direction of the river. The shaman could not find the tracks of the young warrior, as so many tracks covered the ground. And a wind came up, blowing the snow everywhere.

He cursed the young warrior. Without the spirit wolf he could not maintain his hold on the tribe. His rivals would take advantage of his weakness. He would not likely survive the week. But he did not know where she had gone, and he could not find her in the dark. And as he stood there, cursing, a knife found its way into his back.

After a while, the young warrior, looking over at her, could see that she had fallen asleep. The steady rise and fall of her chest announced this. He turned back to the paddle and made sure that they did not get snagged on anything in the river.

He was the son of the chief of his tribe. He had come to find a way to save his people. Something told him, that this woman was the answer. There was something about her. He wondered why she had been in a cage. Probably the shaman was responsible. She was most likely the shaman's woman, but he was so wicked that he treated her poorly.

The young warrior, whose name was Beartooth, sighed, and shook his head. He had come looking for help, but all he had was a woman. Finally, as he began to get tired, he could see, through the light of the moon, a place to pull up on the bank of the river. The woman stirred, as the raft stopped, but she was so tired that she did not wake up. He laid down next to her, on the furs, and fell asleep.

In the morning, as the sunlight touched her face, the spirit wolf panicked for a moment, until a strong, but gentle hand touched her shoulder. She looked over at the young warrior from the day before and remembered what had happened.

He smiled at her and handed her some meat and berries. She stared at the food for a moment, before taking it and eating. She watched him warily, as if afraid he would take the food. Then he dipped a wooden cup in the river and handed it to her. She took it and drank deeply.

"I am Beartooth, of the moose tribe. I went to your village to get help in healing my people, but the shaman would not help. I suppose in taking you, I have angered him, but I could not just leave you there. What are you called?"

She gazed at him for a moment, and then replied softly.

"I am called Tarina. And I thank you for rescuing me. The shaman is a wicked man and was using me. I can help your people, as I know some healing. And I want to help you, as a way to say thank you for getting me away from him."

Beartooth smiled and handed her some more meat. She took it, and watched him as he stood up, and pushed the raft back into the river.

"We will get to my tribe in a few days, down the river. My father will be grateful for any help that you can give us. My mother was the first to die, from this illness, and she was our healer. I hope that you can help us." Tarina nodded and watched him. She was still weak from her imprisonment but knew that she was safe with this man.

She watched the riverbank and watched Beartooth. He was different from the humans she had met before. He was tall and strong, and gentle. He made sure that she was warm and gave her food. He watched the riverbank, making sure that they were not being followed. He did not know that the shaman was dead, nor would he have cared. He liked Tarina and hoped that she could help his people.

Tarina knew that her kind were forbidden to mate with humans, but she found herself attracted to this young human. He was funny and made her laugh and made sure that she was safe. He was special. And in just the few days that she spent with him; she knew that she wanted to be with him for the rest of her life.

When they arrived at his village, the people greeted him, and told him that his father had fallen ill. Tarina hurried to the tent of Beartooth's father and knelt next to him. He was pale, and wane, but she took a breath and used her magic to save him.

After she had healed the chief, she went to the others who were ill, and healed them all. The chief gazed her and saw the way his son looked at her. He smiled and nodded. He liked this woman, with her magic, and his son did need a wife. She was obviously sent by the Great Ones to help the tribe. He spoke to her, and his son, and she shyly agreed to be wed to him.

Beartooth could not have happier. The ceremony was held a week after she arrived, and they moved into their own tent. She knew she should not have done this, but she loved this human, and wanted to be with him. She was not thinking of any consequences, as she laid with him.

A year later, she bore him a daughter. The tiny being came on a clear night, the moon bright in the sky. Beartooth held the small infant and smiled at his wife. She smiled wearily back at him. She knew that this child was special. A great destiny awaited this tiny crying being that she had given birth to.

They would not name the child, until it had lived for a least a year. But the small being did not need a name. Tarina nursed the baby, and Beartooth played with her. Beartooth's father also adored the baby and would often carry her around.

They moved around, following the herds they needed for food. Tarina would care for the baby, as her husband and the other hunters went out to get food, though the herds were smaller than they had been. And wolves hunted the herds as well. But Tarina could not feel any of her people nearby and was saddened by this.

It had been a long time since Tarina had encountered one of her kind. The shaman had trapped her for about two years, and now she had been among the moose tribe for a time. She missed her people, but she was happy, as she carried the baby, and held her husband.

Other tribes also followed the herds, and as the herds had not been as prosperous as they should have been it was hard sometimes, with the hunters from other tribes competing with them. They were having a hard time hunting enough food for the whole tribe. But the Moose tribe was surviving, and the child was growing.

At six months, the baby spoke for the first time. And her first words were mommy, and daddy. She smiled and gurgled, and laughed, as her father tickled her toes, in the warm tent at night. Tarina smiled, as she watched her special child play with her father.

She was soon walking, though her mother still carried her as they travelled, and she would talk. The tiny child learned quickly and enjoyed listening to the others of the tribe. None of the other children learned this quickly, but Tarina knew that it was because of who the child's mother was. Usually, children of the spirit animals were fast learners.

As medicine woman of the moose tribe, Tarina had a special staff. It was tall and perfectly straight, worn smooth, and decorated with feathers on the top. This was a symbol of her standing in the tribe. She carried it with her in pride, knowing that she was important to these people.

But as the time of her daughter's naming ceremony drew close, she knew that something was wrong. Not with her daughter, but something had changed, something in the air, subtle, in the behavior of the tribe. And the behavior of the animals. A raven had been seen, a bad omen. It had been seen in the trees near a kill. The raven had been watching the tribe for a while, and everyone knew that the black birds were never seen unless death was near.

On the eve of her daughter's naming ceremony, the child disappeared. Tarina could not find her, and a storm was brewing. The winds picked up, howling around the tents. Beartooth went outside to look, as Tarina made sure that the child was not hiding somewhere in the tent.

They did not know that the child had wandered off, following a raven. She had never seen one and was curious about it. But it was dark, and the small child could not find her way back to the warm tent. She found some shelter in a bush, and huddled there, as the wind howled, and the snow began to fall.

Then she heard her mother and father, and called to them, but the wind stole her voice. She climbed out of the bush and crawled in the direction of her parents' voices. She tried to find them, but she could not see. Finally, she fell into the snow, and something soft and warm wrapped around her. She did not know what it was, but she was cold and tired. She fell asleep, wrapped in warmth.

When the sun rose, the small child woke up, and looked around. The sun blinded her, as it reflected off the snow. Then she saw something nearby. Her mother's staff. She waddled over to it, and found her mother, and father, frozen to death in the snow.

They had fallen, trying to get to her. She had only been about five feet away, when they had succumbed to the cold. The child did not understand this, as she knelt next to her mother, and shook her cold shoulder. In the end, Tarina's magic had been overcome, as she had sent as much of it out as she could to save her daughter. It had been Tarina's magic that had saved the child, but in saving her daughter, she had sacrificed her own life.

Beartooth had only been human, so he had not had protection from the cold, and had died next to his wife, believing that both his wife and daughter had perished with him. Their frozen forms clung to each other, as even in death they held on to one another.

The child looked up at the sound of voices calling to her parents. She raised her tiny voice, and the people came over to find her kneeling in the snow next to the still forms. She looked up these people, who had helped take of her, and pleaded with them to wake up her parents.

Beartooth's father looked at this child, and then looked at his son. He lowered his eyes. The times were tough, and he could not take the child into his home. He was not married and had to lead the people. The others could not take her, as they had to care for their own families.

So, one by one, her people turned away. They left the child in the snow, kneeling and pleading with them for help. But they left and did not look back. She did not understand, could they not wake up her parents? Why would they not help her?

CHAPTER TWO

She tightened her hands around her mother's staff, and it came out of her mother's hand. She sat there, tears in her eyes, and suddenly looked up. A raven, like the one she had followed was sitting the trees nearby. It cocked its head at her.

"Why do you sit there, little one?" It asked her. She wiped her eyes and looked up at it.

"Mommy and daddy will not wake up. And no one will help me." The bird looked at her and spoke softly.

"They will not wake up. They have gone to a place where you cannot go. You need to leave them and find your own path. I can take you to a place where you will safe. Just follow me."

Holding onto the staff, the small child walked away from her parents, and followed the raven as it led her south, out of the cold north, to the warmer lands where she would find a place to be safe. He took her to a monastery, where they took in children, both boys and girls.

The monk looked at the small girl, as she stumbled down the road. She did not know how long she had been travelling, but she was tired. The monk stepped forward, and caught her, as she fell. He could tell that she was a barbarian from the north, though her clothes were tattered, and her feet bleeding.

Her hair was black, and tangled, her skin a light brown. She was small, maybe two years old. She was also thin, as if she had not eaten in a while. She looked up at him, and he gazed back at her.

"What is your name, little one, and where are you from?" He wondered, but she had passed out. He carried her easily, and looked up, as he heard something in the trees, and he saw a raven watching him. The monk shook his head, and carried the small figure, who still held onto the staff. She would not let go of it.

The father abbot looked at the barbarian girl. He did not really know what to do. Brother Gabriel had brought her into the infirmary. She was resting now, her feet wrapped in bandages. She was so small and seemed so vulnerable. They did not know anything about her, but he knew that they could not turn her away. He would put her with the sisters of the order. They would look after her.

All the girls were looked after by the sisters, and the boys were watched over by the brothers of the order of Theros, God of the arts. This monastery was dedicated to helping those who needed it and of course the arts, such as painting and sculpture.

She did not speak, as she was so young, and did not understand their language. But she clung to the staff and refused to let it go. The staff was three times her height, but she would not let it go from her sight. It must be special to her. The father abbot sighed, and called the mother superior, who oversaw the girls, and told her that they would take the barbarian girl into the school. She would stay in the infirmary until she was better, and then she would be taken to the girls' dormitory.

So, about a week after she was brought into the monastery, the small girl found herself in a smock, her feet covered in shoes, and her own small room. She only had her own room because none of the others wanted to share with her. It was a small room, only big enough to hold a bed, and a chest for her clothes.

The small girl was called Blackbird, because of a raven that was seen frequently near her. She was quiet, as she did not know the language, but she was a fast learner. She was too young for learning how to read and other things that they instructed the children, but she was not the only little one here.

She stayed mostly in the nursery, with the other children her age. She played by herself, and was alone a lot, though they would take the small children out into the woods nearby to gather berries, and to play in the small stream. She liked being away from the confining walls of the monastery, as she was not used to being confined.

All the children here were orphans, or unwanted by anyone else. She was an orphan, as she knew that her parents were dead. So, she learned to be a southerner, who knew many things that her people did not know, but also many things that they did.

The one thing she did not like was the shoes. They pinched her toes, and she could not feel the ground. But if she took the shoes off, she got in trouble. She did tell the sisters that the shoes pinched her toes, but they just told her not to whine.

She recovered from her ordeal quickly, and she thought that she would be able to leave, but no one would let her. She was told she was to stay here, until she was old enough to be considered an adult. She did know how old she had to be, but she did not want to stay. But the raven told her she would need to stay, until she had learned things from these people that she would need to know.

So, she stayed, and she began to learn how to read and write. She also learned her numbers, and how to tell time, with the sundial. She took on more duties, as she grew older, and learned to wash the clothes, and bedding, along with some cooking.

She was still taken, with the other children, into the woods, where she found an injured wolf pup. Pets were not allowed, but she smuggled him into her room. No one knew he was there because she did not share her room. She cleaned up the messes and made sure that he was cared for.

She also came across a young eagle, who was hurt, and she cared for him as well. The bear, though, she could not smuggle into the monastery, but she visited the bear as often as she could. She could talk to these animals and understand them.

She knew that if the sisters at the monastery discovered this, they would probably burn her as a witch.

Witchcraft was denounced often, in the sermons. Magic was the realm of the gods. Only the gods could use it, and anyone who dared to use magic was evil, and served demons. Only bad things could come from using magic.

CHAPTER THREE

By the time she was ten, though, something bad happened. A plague came through the land and destroyed the people. Blackbird did not get sick, as she had never been sick, but the monastery was hit hard. Their prayers went unanswered, and all the monks and the nuns died, along with many of the children. Those children who survived, all but Blackbird, left the monastery to find homes elsewhere.

Blackbird did not get sick, but she stayed at the monastery, even though she was now the only human there. The raven who had brought her here, whom she called Blackie, did not leave, and the wolf pup, Midnight, now grown, stayed, along with the bear, whose name was Goldie, and the eagle, whom she called Sunbird.

There was food here, in the orchard and fields. She read all the scrolls and books and played with the animals. She did not know how long she was alone there, with the animals, as time did not seem to matter. She knew that the monastery was getting old, as the weeds and plants were getting wild. She could not keep up with the repairs that the buildings needed.

Then one day, as she rested beneath some trees, Blackbird heard a sound, the sound of human voices. They were laughing and singing. Blackie lifted off the branch of the tree and flew high, looking for the source of the sounds.

It was a troop of traveling performers. Their brightly colored wagons were in a circle, and they were practicing their acts. Some were juggling and others playing instruments. Some were dancing, and others knife throwing.

Blackie returned to the monastery and told Blackbird what

he had seen. She did not know what to do, as she had not seen another human for a while. She climbed up onto Goldie's back, and the bear took her closer, to see the humans. Midnight stayed close, and the two birds wheeled overhead.

Blackbird looked only ten, though she had been at the monastery for ten years, before the plague, and she had lived here on her own, with the animals for many years. She had been here for about fifteen years since the plague. She did not know how things had changed in the world.

Someone among the traveling troop spotted the young girl sitting on the back of a large golden-brown bear. She was watching him getting some water from the stream. Her clothes were nearly worn out, and she had no shoes on. She looked a little wild, as she gazed him.

"Who are you, and what are you doing in this area?" She asked him. "I have not seen anyone around here in a long time. It has only been me, Blackie, Sunbird, Goldie, and Midnight for a while."

The man smiled at her and responded.

"I belong to the Traveling Edwards Troop of Entertainment. We do not really come here very often, but I do wonder where you came from, little one. Where are your parents?" She shook her head and replied.

"My parents have been dead for a long time. I was staying at the monastery, but the plague came through and killed everyone, except me. I do not know why I did not get sick. But I have my animal friends, and we take care of each other." He nodded and studied the staff she carried. It was worn smooth, and was decorated with feathers, in the fashion of the northern barbarians.

The plague had been over for fifteen years, and she had been alone all this time, but she did not look like she was old enough to have been around for the plague. He thought about it and decided that it was not important. He asked her if she had eaten that day, and she told him she was hungry, and so were her friends.

He looked at the animals and could see that they were just as special as she was. The animals all had intelligent eyes and a protectiveness as they stood close to the girl. They obviously cared about this girl. He gestured for her to follow him, and the bear moved off, followed by the others, as they made their way to the encampment.

The man took her to the one who oversaw the troop. Michael Edwards studied the girl and asked her what her name was. She looked at him and spoke.

"I am called Blackbird. I was born in the north, but after my parents died, I came south. I was living in the monastery, but then the plague came, and I was the only one who lived. My animals have been taking care of me since then."

Michael gazed the animals and smiled. He was already thinking about how to put them in his show. She was very pretty, with a promise of great beauty when she was grown. She was a northerner, but that did not bother him. Everyone knew that the barbarians were spirited.

"Well, Blackbird, why don't you and your animals stay with us? We travel a lot, and you would be able to see a lot of different places. We would be happy to teach you our ways, and to include you in our shows. Your animals would be able to perform as well if they want."

She looked at the animals, and Blackie clacked his beak. She nodded and looked at Michael.

"We will stay with you if you do not treat my animals as pets. They do not like being petted and have baby talk and such things." Michael nodded and called his wife, Margaret, over, and introduced her to Blackbird.

Margaret studied Blackbird, and the state of her clothes, and immediately went into the wagon, and emerge with various articles of clothing. She had Blackbird try some of them on, and then when Blackbird found a dress that fit her, Margaret took her measurements, and told her that she would sew her some performer's clothing for the shows.

Blackbird nodded and she looked around. The animals

settled in near Michael's wagon and watched her. She found these people to be the opposite of the monks and nuns. The monks and nuns had believed in discipline, and quiet. These people were loud and raucous.

The clothing that the monks and nuns had worn were sober robes of brown, with white belts. These people wore a riot of colors, blues, reds, and green. There were a few children her own age, and unlike the children at the monastery, who had not wanted to be near her, these children invited her to join in their games.

Until dinner time, she found herself playing with the other children. She found it fun and liked these children. She had never actually been allowed to play noisy games. Dinner was a stew, and she ate all of what was placed before her. There was some food for her animals, and she made sure that they were fed.

Blackbird liked these people and was glad that they had come along. She was excited to go to new places and see new things. But she also knew that she was different from these people. She had been educated at the monastery, and most of these people did not know how to read. She had read all the books and scrolls at the monastery, and she remembered everything she had read.

The next day, as they made ready to leave, Blackbird was called over by Michael. He smiled at her and told her that he was going to teach her how to juggle. It was easy once you got the hang of it. He handed her two balls, one red and one green, and showed her how to juggle them. It took her some time to get the hang of it, but she was a fast learner.

So, as she traveled with her newfound friends, she learned how to entertain. She started with juggling two balls, and then three and then four. Goldie and the animals were willing to help, though it did take the horses a while to get used to Midnight. They kept shying away from him. But he ignored them. They were not what he would have wanted to hunt anyway.

The animals did help with the shows. Whenever they came to a village or town, they were included in the entertainment. Goldie would dance, without help, and Midnight would jump through hoops that were on fire. The two birds would perform tricks and catch things that were thrown at them.

And Blackbird also learned how to be thief. That was something else that these people were. They only stole from rich people, who would invite them into their houses for entertainment at parties. Blackbird had been reluctant to steal at first, as the sisters at the monastery had frowned upon this behavior.

But she was good at it. And she was a very good distraction. She learned how to use her staff in her act. She could hit the balls with her staff and make sure that they did not land on the floor. And by doing this, she could make the balls look like they were disappearing at times.

Something was beginning to awaken with Blackbird. She was reaching the age where her magic was beginning to come out. It manifested in little ways, at first. She began to be able to heal, with a touch, and she could make the balls do things that should have been impossible. Like figure eights, or even triangles. She did not understand how she could do these things, but she could.

Blackbird was special, and Michael and the others knew this. She was growing, and her power was too. Michael watched the crowds and was careful to only let her perform a few times. If she did have magic, there were those would want to take her. For magic was mistrusted, and there was group of people, who called themselves the Hunters, who would do anything to get rid of it.

Michael's troop became well known, and they were finally invited into the castle of the king. They were one of several troops brought in, as it was the king's birthday. They also knew of a treasure that they wanted that was within his walls. They could not have known that this performance would change Blackbird's life.

As the others entertained the crowds, Michael, and a few others, along with Blackbird, went looking for the Gem of Dragons. It was said to hold great power and could grant the wishes of those who held it. Michael wanted it, he knew that Blackbird was small enough to get into the treasure room, through an air duct, built to keep the air flowing. She would get inside, and then open a small door, that, with the festivities upstairs had been left unguarded.

Blackbird squeezed through, holding onto her staff, as she would need it to open the door. As she dropped out of the shaft, she could not see anything, as there was no light in the treasure room. She crouched down, and looked around, and saw a light glimmering on the bottom of the door. She made her way over to the door and used her staff to push it open.

Michael and the others came in, with torches, and she waited by the door, to keep watch. One of the men called to Michael, and they went over to the Gem. It was carved in the shape of a dragon and was one of the most beautiful gemstones Michael and the others had seen. They wrapped it up in a bag and hurried off. Blackbird followed them and moved quietly down the hallway.

Then someone called out to them, and as they turned, they could see some soldiers. The game was up! The captain of the guard had noticed that some of the entertainers were missing. He had sent some soldiers to find them, and now they spotted the entertainers coming from the direction of the treasure room. They yelled and started running after the thieves. Blackbird found herself lifted in Michael's arms, and he carried her, as they ran.

Michael put the bag into her arms and looked at her. She was frightened, as she studied him. He kissed her and looked back. A shout told him that one of the others had been caught. He looked around and spotted a window. It was over a pond, and he kissed her again, and as she tried to hold onto him, he threw her out of the window. She screamed, as she went flying, and landed in the pond. She looked up, just in time to see Michael go down to the soldiers.

Her heart stopped, as she watched the man who had become as a father to her fall out of the window. Anger, fear, and grief flooded through her, and her magic exploded. The staff she held lit up with a rainbow of colors, and fire flooded her vision.

CHAPTER FOUR

When she woke up, she found herself in a forest. Blackie, Goldie, Sunbird, and Midnight were all there. In her arms she held the bag that contained the Gem. She did not want the Gem, as it had cost her a family. She threw it, into the bushes, and began to cry.

Goldie went over to her and pulled her close. They did not have to tell her, that all the members of the troop were dead. She already knew that all the troop would have been executed. She had found a place to belong, and now it was gone, just like her parents, and the monastery. Everything was gone, except the four animals who stayed close to her.

She did not know what had happened after the fire had exploded out of her. She did not know how she gotten here, and she did not care. She did not understand what was happening to her, and she did not know how to find the answers. She looked up finally, at Goldie, and asked.

"What is happening to me? Why am I able to do all these things?" Blackie clacked his beak and spoke.

"You are growing. Your mother was not human, and her magic is your heritage. You do not need training to access the magic that is your birthright. You do need to learn to control it, and that will take time. But you need to be careful. You could hurt yourself if you are not."

Blackbird nodded. She sighed and snuggled against Goldie's soft fur. She fell asleep, tired emotionally and physically. Goldie looked over at Blackie, and he nodded. They knew where they needed to take her. She needed to learn control, but they could only teach her so much.

As they sat in the forest, a sound caught their attention. They all turned and looked up as a wolf entered the clearing. Her fur was silver, and her eyes were deep blue. She trotted up and sat on her haunches. Then she spoke.

"I am here because of the child you are caring for. She is summoned to the Council of Spirits. I am to take you to them. We will leave in the morning." The others looked at each other and nodded. That was where they had been going to take her anyway.

When Blackbird woke up in the morning, she was hungry. Midnight had gone hunting and brought her a rabbit. She started a fire, and cooked it, then ate it. She sighed sadly and looked over at the bag that held the Gem. She went over to it and picked it up. Though the wolf escort did not like to be delayed, she waited until Blackbird was ready.

She gazed at the Gem and closed the bag. It was hers by right of blood. It had cost her family, and she would keep it. Blackbird looked over the animals, who were watching her. She closed her eyes for a moment and shook herself.

Then she went over to Goldie and climbed up on the bear's back. Blackie cawed loudly and took off from the branch he had perched on. Sunbird followed him, and both birds wheeled overhead, and Goldie and Midnight followed them from the ground. The guide led the way as they traveled.

It would take a while to reach the Council. They traveled west, through the forest, and would stop only to rest and eat. Blackbird held on tightly to her mother's staff and wished that she knew more about her. The young girl tried to stop thinking about what had happened at the castle, but she found her mind would not let her forget.

The animals found food for her, from berries to fish. She learned a lot about what was safe to eat and what was not. She was glad that she was not alone, and the animals were glad they could help her. They did not know what the Council would do, as Blackbird was part human, but they knew that they had to take her there.

It was several days before they reached the edge of the forest. They looked out at the empty lands and moved forward carefully. Blackbird was uncertain about this place. She did not entirely like it. But the rocks were still, and there were no sounds other than them. Their feet crunched on the loose rocks of the soil, and their breathing seemed unnaturally loud.

Finally, they came to a place where the rocks formed a gate. They could see the land on the other side of the gate, but the animals knew that to pass through here was to enter the Council's chamber. They each took a breath and plunged inside.

Blackbird blinked, as they did not come out on the lands, but into a cave. Every animal was represented here, from the smallest to biggest. She had not seen some of these animals before. She looked around with wide eyes, and the four animals with her gazed at the council.

There was a lot of noise, until the newcomers were noticed. Then every member of the Council fell silent. Blackie landed on a perch and spread his wings. But before he could say anything, a big owl came forward, and spoke.

"So, you are here, with the half breed. She should have been brought here sooner. I do not understand why you took her to the humans in the stone building." There was suddenly a lot of noise, as some protested, and others agreed. Sunbird let out a loud screech and called for order.

Half breed she might be, but she shares our magic. It runs strongly in her, and we have come seeking help, she needs guidance from us. As for why we did not bring her sooner, we did not know how strong she would be, and a power greater than any of us told me to take her to the stone building." Again, noise filled the room, as voices overlapped.

Suddenly a big animal, an elephant, raised his trunk and trumpeted. Silence fell. The elephant looked at the trembling girl, and he could see what some of the others had missed. She was strong in magic, stronger than any of them. It pulsed within her, wild and uncontrolled.

He stepped forward and faced her. She looked up at him, and he touched her face. After a moment, he stepped back and faced the others.

"She is chosen, by the mother of us all. She carries within her the mark of destiny. She must be trained and taught about who she is. We cannot ignore her, and we dare not let her run wild. If she is not trained, she could wreak terrible destruction. We must give her enough training so she can control what she has."

This brought more debate. Some were agreeable to let her be trained, but others still did not believe that she should be trained. Blackie looked over at his companions. The Council was divided into factions, and without all in agreement, she could not be trained. Everyone had to agree.

Blackbird looked around at all the creatures that were here and thought that it seemed as if some were missing. She dug out the Gem and as the light of a nearby torch glinted off it, all went silent. Blackbird gazed at the shimmering Gem and wished that someone would come to help her.

The Gem in her hands shook and trembled, and she dropped it. It did not hit the ground, but instead floated above the stone floor. Then it grew and a dragon appeared in the chamber. It stretched and roared, as it faced the Council.

"Since when did the Council of Spirits squabble as children? You have before you a child of magic, and you bicker as if you were fighting over a bone. She comes before you to get help, and all you do is shout like spoiled children. Where is the vaunted wisdom of the spirits? Have you been in such close contact with humans, that they have rubbed off on you? Look at the child in front of you and see her as she could be."

As the Council looked at her, she changed in their eyes, and became something more than what she had first appeared. Standing before them now, was a woman dressed in black, holding a staff, and standing tall. She gazed at them, with black eyes, and a stern demeanor. The image held for a few moments, and then faded, leaving behind the child, who was watching these beings, who were deciding her fate. The animals of the Council looked at each other and knew that they could not deny her. She was to be trained, as they would train any of their young ones.

The dragon turned to face her, and reaching down, he touched her face with his.

"You have a great destiny before you. You will grow in power, and you will be able to do great things. Be cautious, though, as there will be those who will want to use you for their own ends. Do not trust blindly, but never lose your faith in yourself or your friends." She nodded, and the dragon looked at the Council one more time, before fading back into the Gem.

So, Blackbird was taken to the Training Grounds, where all young spirit animals are trained, on how to use their magic. She was not certain about this, but she knew that she needed to learn to control the power that was her birthright.

Blackie, Goldie, Sunbird, and Midnight were all allowed to stay with her, during this time. She was given a cave, to dwell in. It was cozy, and warm. There was a place for a fire, and a room for sleeping, and a kitchen. She went to the training grounds every morning after breakfast and began to learn how to control her magic.

CHAPTER FIVE

Her magic, though, seemed to defy control. It would run wild, and cause problems on the grounds. She did not understand why it was so hard for her, to control it. It seemed so easy for everyone else. She tried everything they told her to do, and it still ran away with her.

Finally, though she managed to gain some control over it. She learned that she could channel some of the magic into her staff, which helped keep it under control for longer. The staff could act like a siphon, and would take some of the magic away, so it would not overwhelm her.

With this knowledge, she got better at control the magic. It would still run wild, just not as much. She learned about her mother, as well. And she learned that by marrying her father, her mother had done something that was forbidden among the spirits. Something bad could happen when a spirit animal mated with a human. It would affect any offspring of hers, though it would not happen until her grandchildren were born.

But for now, she did not worry about it. She had enough to be doing without worrying about any future children. She was not thinking about anything like that. She just wanted to learn to control the magic. And using the staff helped a great deal. Then something happened, that would change the course of her life, again.

As she was preparing to cast a healing spell, a spirit bear came up. It was not Goldie, but a male, and he called to all the spirit creatures, even those still in training. Something had happened in the human world, which affected the spirits.

An elven sorcerer had found out how to control the magic of spirit animals and had captured some of them. This had happened before, as with Blackbird's mother, but this was more serious. The elven sorcerer was using the magic of the spirits to affect the mortal realm. He had started a war.

Not just any war, but a war between the spirits and the mortals. The gods had withdrawn, not wanting to get involved, meaning that the spirits were on their own. The gods would not get involved unless there was no other way of preserving the world.

All spirit animals were called to the war. Even the young ones, not yet fully trained. All of them were needed to fight this war. Blackbird did not want to fight in a war, as she was part human. But what could she do? She was still young and did not have complete control over her magic.

Her animal friends did not want her to get involved with this either. She was far too young to be a warrior. She could not transform all the way, between a wolf, and human, as her mother had been a spirit wolf. She did not have enough training for this,

The animals knew though, that Blackbird could be important to this war. She was strong in magic, and in spirit. She was also wise for her age. She had after all read an entire library. Maybe she could do something. If the spirit animals that the elf had could be freed, maybe the war would end.

So, with her four animal friends, Blackbird set out to find a different way to end this war, other than a lot of death. She went to the battlefield, though no real fighting had happened yet. She looked over at the elf's army, across the way.

She waited for night fall, as she could move about in the dark and not be seen. Midnight would go with her, as his black fur was suited to the dark of night. So, they waited, as the sun sank down on the horizon, and they then began their work.

She, along with Midnight, crossed the field, between the two armies. She asked silently for some help, as she knew that this was dangerous. But Blackbird knew how to be stealthy, as thieves had trained her. She held her staff tightly, as they made their way through the camp, to where the animals were.

The cages were heavily guarded. There were two guards on each cage. As Blackbird studied the cages, she could see the misery of the animals, and the fact that they were not doing well. The spirits relied on their magic; it was a part of them. And for it to be stolen, was killing them.

Blackbird knew that a diversion was needed, so she could get close to the cages. Midnight took a breath, and then ran out, barking and growling. He attacked one of the guards, and the others ran to his aid. Blackbird used her magic to undo the locks on the cages and open the doors.

As soon as the doors were opened, the animals trapped in the cages came out, and chaos broke out. Shrieking and roaring, the animals began to attack their captors. The elven sorcerer came running out of his tent and launched a counterattack.

But he faced Blackbird. She gazed at him, her staff dancing with light, and she closed her eyes. The magic tore through her and exploded outwards. The elven sorcerer did have magical shields, but they did not last long before that raw power. It was like a pillar of fire lit up the night, consuming everything in its path.

But there was something about this fire. It did not harm the spirits, just passed through them. The only ones affected by it were those who were allied with elf. They were sent spinning through the air, to crash into the ground.

Blackbird sagged against her staff. She felt cold, and tired. Her legs were heavy with weariness, and she could not stay standing, even with the staff. So, she sank to the ground, and knelt there. Her long black hair fell around her face; her black eyes were closed.

Blackie found her and called to the others. They came quickly and found her asleep. She used up much of her energy. But the magic was still within her, just a soft glow now. She would recover, and the magic would be restored. But she had stopped a war, by unleashing her power, and letting it go.

Blackbird slept for three days. Her body needed the rest, as she was still young. As she grew, using her magic would not be so hard on her. She would grow stronger and stronger. She would be able use her magic more and more, without getting tired.

CHAPTER SIX

As she slept, someone arrived. Rose stood over the young girl and gazed at her. She knew of Blackbird and had been watching her. Rose had come to have a talk with the girl, and to help her. Rose knew what it was like to be different. She understood Blackbird and knew what she was going through. Rose had some similar problems when her magic was first appearing.

And when Blackbird was older, she would be able to make the choice that Rose, and Quicksilver had already made. She had the potential to become the next of the four guardians of the universe. She needed help and guidance, and Rose and Quicksilver could both give it to her.

When Blackbird woke up, she found a fire, and some food. She was starving, and ate the soft bread, and scooped out some of the warm stew. She did not know who had made the food, but she was grateful for it. After she had eaten her fill, she looked around. Goldie was sitting nearby, with Midnight, and the two birds were perched above.

She looked over at the sound of footsteps in the forest floor. A young woman approached, holding more firewood. She smiled at Blackbird and placed the firewood on the ground. Blackbird gazed at the woman, who was extraordinarily beautiful. Rose smiled and spoke.

"Hello, Blackbird. My name is Rose, and I am here to help you. I can help you gain control of your power and learn to keep it under control. You do not need to be afraid. I have been watching you for a while, and I know that I can help you, if you let me."

Blackbird studied this woman, curiously. Who was she, and how could she help? Rose smiled and waved her hand, and the fire changed color. It turned blue. Blackbird blinked and looked at Rose.

"Who are you, and how did you change the fire that color?" Rose sat down and gazed at the girl.

"As I said, my name is Rose. I have magic, like you, and it took me a while to learn how to control it. Our magic is similar, and I can show you how I learned to control it. I can teach you a lot, and I know someone else who can teach you as well. Her name is Quicksilver, and she can teach you about a different type of magic."

Blackbird sat quietly, thinking. She did need to learn about magic, of any kind. She needed to learn how to control it, and how to use it. She gazed at Rose, who watched her. Despite the fact they had just met, there was something about Rose, that was almost familiar. Like they had met before.

Blackbird looked over at her animal friends. They all agreed that Rose was here to help her, and they knew that Rose could teach her. So, Blackbird looked at Rose, and nodded.

"I will go with you, so I can learn about my magic. I need to learn to control it, so I will come with you, and you can teach me." Rose nodded. She knew that Blackbird was still tired from what had happened. But Rose could take them both to Jewel City, where she could teach Blackbird, and when she was done, Quicksilver would take over.

So, Rose stood up, and opened a portal in the air, and she made sure the four animals came as well. Blackbird found going through the portal to be strange, but her eyes widened as she saw the city. Rose had made sure that they were not directly in the city, so Blackbird would be able to see it properly. Rose was not above making sure that people admired her city.

Jewel City gleamed in the morning light. The walls shimmered, each a distinct color, and the trees and plants danced in a breeze. Sweet flowers sent perfume into the air, and Blackbird could see animals moving around among the people.

Most of the animals were of course, dogs and cats, with birds singing in the trees. There were horses, too, along with the vehicles that needed no gas. There were no messes, no sewage in the streets, not at all like what Blackbird was used to. The animals moved among the people, free to come and go as they wanted.

The streets were broad, and well maintained, with room for everyone to move without feeling crowded. The vehicles moved quietly, without any loud sounds to interrupt the sounds of the people. There were cafes, where you could sit and enjoy drinks, and lunch, and talk without feeling like you must shout to be heard.

And it seemed that everyone knew Rose and greeted her warmly. She smiled and nodded in response. Rose took Blackbird and her animals to the palace at the center of the city. Here they were greeted by the biggest man Blackbird had ever seen, and he smiled down at her.

"My name is Ox, and you do not need to be afraid of me. I am Rose's husband, and I was just going to check on the horses." Blackbird nodded and watched him leave. On the top of the stairs leading into the palace, they were greeted by a man with black hair, and almost serpentine features.

"I have a bath ready for both you, and a change of clothes. If the animals wish to bath, they can use the ponds in the gardens. No one will mind if they do. And I have a room ready, with a door that leads into a garden, so the animals will be more comfortable." Rose nodded and turned to Blackbird.

"This is Shadow, my butler, you could say. He takes care of making sure that the palace is run well, so I do not have to worry about it. He takes care of tiny details, so I can focus on other things, like training you. So, let us go take a bath, and get a change of clothes."

Blackbird nodded and followed her into the palace halls. Rose knew where they were going and led Blackbird down the hall to the bathing rooms. Blackbird slipped out of her dirty clothes and slipped into the bathtub. She sighed as the warm water soothed her tired body, and she found some soap to scrub off the dirt from her skin.

After she was clean, she stayed in the water for a while, and the water stayed warm. After a while, Rose climbed out of her tub, and came over to Blackbird's. Blackbird was falling asleep in the tub. Rose woke her up, and helped her out of the tub, and helped her dry off.

Clothes had been brought, and Blackbird slipped into a dress, which was a little fancier than she was used too, but she did not mind. Rose smiled, and they left, and went to the dining hall, where a feast had been laid out, and Rose sat at the head of the table, with Ox on one side, and Blackbird on the other.

It was then that some things clicked for Blackbird. Obviously, Rose was a particularly important person, as she was honored with the seat usually reserved for the king, so she had to the ruler of this place. Blackbird had not thought about that, until she found herself sitting next to her.

Blackbird's animal friends had not been forgotten. Room at the table had been left for them, so they could stay close to the girl. Food was placed in front of them, and they ate with gusto. After a while, Blackbird began to feel sleepy, so Rose stood up and took her hand. She smiled at the others and led Blackbird to her room.

Blackbird snuggled down into the soft blankets. Midnight jumped up and curled up at her feet. Goldie slept next to the bed, and the two birds perched on the trees just outside. The girl fell asleep, warm, and comfortable.

CHAPTER SEVEN

The next morning, breakfast was brought to her, on a tray, in bed. Food was also brought for the animals, a lot of it for Goldie. She was a bear after all. After they had all finished, the servant took the tray away, and told her if she needed to relieve herself, that the red door would take her to a room for that.

Blackbird had never used this type of toilet before, and was startled when it flushed, after she was done. She stared at it for a moment, watching the swirling water. Then she turned away and gazed at herself in the mirror. A girl of twelve looked back at her, with black eyes, and black hair, and light brown skin.

She felt mostly recovered from the attack on the elven sorcerer. She looked around the room, and found a wardrobe filled with dresses. She tried some of them on and settled on a dark red dress. She brushed her hair and braided it.

A knock came on the door, and Rose entered the room. She smiled at Blackbird and asked.

"Do you feel up to training today? I know you used up a lot of energy, and I want to know if you feel ready to begin." Blackbird thought about it and decided that she was ready. So, she told Rose that she felt ready to begin. Rose nodded. She led Blackbird to a clear space outside the city.

Rose turned to face Blackbird and asked.

"What is magic?" Blackbird thought about it and responded.

"Magic is doing things with energy, that you cannot do with your hands."

"That is a good explanation, but it is not entirely correct. Magic is manipulating universal energy, that everything and everyone generates. Magic is a force that connects everything together. Those who can feel it, can use it to do things that would otherwise be impossible.

Most people who can use magic, are limited by their bodies. They can only do so much with it, before they get tired, and must rest. This is because they can only use the magic that they feel. And it is dangerous to try to exceed what your body can manage. Elves are stronger in magic, because unlike the humans, they are connected to the magic, in a way that the humans are not. Magic is energy, and elves are strong, because they can feel it more strongly. This is also what makes them live longer and can help them when they are facing other magic users. Humans sometimes struggle with magic because they have a limited view of what it is.

Most magic is based in the elements, fire, earth, air, water, and spirit. But each of the elements depends on the others, a balance if you want. Fire cannot exist without air, and air needs water. Earth needs both fire, and water. And each depends on spirit to bind them together. Now, we will start with fire. It is considered by many to be the most powerful element, but both water and earth can put it out. And if you take away air, fire goes out."

Blackbird listened carefully to what Rose was saying. She wanted to learn control of her magic, and Rose was making more sense than the spirit animal teachers she had had. Rose turned and made a gesture, and targets appeared.

"I want you to concentrate on fire, on its properties. Heat, light, and energy. Fire is all of these, and if you can feel it, you can use it, to hit each of the targets. When you think you are ready, go for it?"

Blackbird gripped her staff and closed her eyes. She filled her mind with thoughts of fire and raised her hand. A ball of fire formed on her fingers, and she released it. It hit one of the targets, dead center, but the other balls she released went off mark.

Rose put out the fires, and turned to Blackbird, who was looking nervous. Rose smiled and looked out at the targets.

One was blackened, but the others were untouched. She turned back to Blackbird and told her to do it again. Blackbird nodded and raised her hand.

Her concentration slipped, though, and she ended up releasing a fireball into the sky. Rose put it out and studied her.

"You need to focus a little more, and not worry so much. You are doing fine; you just need some practice. After we are done here, I think I will take you to my meditation garden. Meditation is good for learning how to focus on just one thing. Now try again."

Blackbird nodded and she raised her hand once more. Her staff lit up, as she unleashed the fire. She hit almost all the targets but missed the last two. Rose smiled and nodded and told her to do it again. Repeatedly, she fired off fireballs, until she could hit all the targets.

Rose nodded and smiled.

"Let us head back now, so we can get something to eat. And then we will go to my meditation garden, and I will teach you how to meditate, though I am sure the monks helped with that, at least a little." Blackbird nodded and followed Rose back to the palace.

After lunch, they went to Rose's Garden. It was peaceful, with a stream gurgling through it, and a soft breeze caused the branches to sigh softly. It was a quiet place, and Rose took her to the center, where a small hill was set. The grass was soft, as they sat facing each other. Rose closed her eyes and tilted her head back.

Blackbird watched her for a moment, and then she too closed her eyes. She let the sounds of the garden relax her mind, and she found herself walking through the monastery again. It was silent, but not sad. She had many fond memories of the monastery, even though they had been strict. She missed the monks and sisters and wished that they had lived.

After about an hour, Rose touched her, and she opened her eyes. She sniffled a little, and Rose held her for a moment. Then they left the garden and went to the library. Blackbird had never seen so many books. Her eyes widen, as she gazed upon row after row of books, and scrolls.

Rose led her to an area of the library that dealt with magic. She pulled out a couple of books on magical theory, and on the element of fire. She then led Blackbird over to a table and had her sit down.

"I want you to read these books. You can read for as long as you want. I will send someone to get you for dinner. After dinner, I want to take you to the theater, and show you something you have never seen." Blackbird nodded and turned to the books.

Rose left and went to take care of some things she needed to do. The books would keep Blackbird occupied for a while, as they were thick. Blackbird liked reading, and she dove into the books with gusto. And because of how special she was, she remembered everything that she read.

When dinner time came, someone came to get her, and she was led to the dining hall. Rose smiled as she sat down, and Rose asked her how the books were. Blackbird enthusiastically began to talk about what she had read. Rose listened and made comments every now and then. Blackbird was happy, and she was glad that she had come here.

After dinner, Rose took her to the theater, which was a gigantic round building. It had many different rooms, each for showing a different thing. Some played movies, others were for plays. Some were for children, and others for grown-ups. Some were historical and others made up. Blackbird had never seen anything like this, and she gazed around in awe at all different things that you could hear.

Rose took her to a movie and smiled as the girl stared in awe at the screen. Rose knew that education of any kind would be good for her, and she would make sure that Blackbird learned as much as she could. Blackbird could be if she chose to be, the next guardian, like Rose and Quicksilver. So, Rose would make sure that this special girl knew as much as she could teach.

A routine was soon established. Every morning, Rose would

take her out to the practice field, where she would practice fire magic. After fireballs, came other ways of manipulating fire, such as spinning disks of flames. There was also flaming whips, and small balls of fire that could be juggled. Rose taught her many ways to control fire, and how to use her staff to siphon off excess energy, so she would not be overwhelmed by the magic.

After she had mastered fire, they moved onto air, which was quite different. Air was movement, but it also took the path of least resistance. If something got in its way, it just went around. Air could be gentle, but it could also be strong. Tornadoes were air, and they could be very destructive. Each element had two sides, a gentle side, and a dangerous side.

Using air, you could create a disc of air on which you could ride. Or you could create balls of air that were hard and could cause damage if thrown. You could also harden the air around you to create a shield that would protect you from any attack.

Blackbird learned about other things, other than just magic. She went to the theater and learned about how they created the movies and how hard they worked on the plays. She learned how court worked, and how politics worked, and she learned about different things, through the books in the library and through all the things she saw in the city.

As she progressed through each of the magics, she grew more confident. She had had trouble with confidence, as she had always been a little afraid of her magic, but Rose taught her how to not be afraid, and how special she really was.

After air, she went onto earth, which was not just rocks. Earth was growing things, plants, and animals. Earth was steady, and immovable. It was the element of stubbornness, and power. Blackbird learned to move stones, and how to get something to grow. She learned how to use vines to trap or climb something.

After earth came water. Water was known as the element of healing. It was gentle and soothing, or it could cause a flood. Like all the elements, water had two sides. It was gentle and calm, or it was a raging torrent crashing through the canyons.

After water came spirit, the element of binding. You could do many things with spirit, like bind the other elements in many ways. If you bound fire and water, you got steam or fog. If you bound earth and water, you got a mudslide. If you bound water and air, you could make a hurricane or waterspout.

Each of the elements depended on a balance. If the balance was disrupted, bad things tended to happen. Too much water, and you had a flood, too much fire and you had a firestorm, too much air and you had a tornado, too much earth and you had a rockslide.

Too much spirit, and you could lose yourself. The balance that existed between each element was what was needed for life to exist. If the planet had too much fire, everything burned, if it had too much water, nothing could grow, if it had too much earth, there was no water, and if it had too much air, nothing could live.

Even science was based on the elements. In alchemy you used different parts of earth to create new things. In medicine you combined different plants to create something that would help someone. Everything could be traced back to the basic elements.

Everything was connected to each other. In a circle, never ending, life created life, and death was a constant. Though not everyone died, sometimes, not everyone truly lived. Some beings, like the elves, would let years pass by without really doing anything.

This is what set the humans and the dwarves apart. Even though the dwarves lived longer than the humans, the dwarves were industrious. They worked hard to create a legacy. The halls of the dwarves were legendary for the artwork and strength that they had.

Humans did as much as they could with the time that they had, or most did. They did not let years pass by, because they had so few compared to the other races. They lived, and loved, and worked. They did not always do good things, but they did things.

No race could compare with humans for prolific work. They were artists, and builders. They were poets and songwriters. They were explorers and discoverers. They lived as fully as they could, knowing that death could take them at any time. But they were not always the best at peace.

Humans had always been warlike. War was almost second nature to them. They wanted more, and they were willing to kill for it. Blackbird did not understand this, for if their lives were so short, why would they want to die faster?

Rose told her that humans were like this because they wanted to leave something behind, whether it was violence or peace. They just wanted to be remembered for anything. Some would leave behind such legacies of peace and joy that they were honored for millennia, and others would leave behind legacies of death and violence.

Humans wanted to be remembered. And their lives were so short, that sometimes they would go to extremes to be remembered. They were emotional and confusing. Many of the other races sometimes wondered how the humans had not wiped each other out with all their wars.

It was easy to feel despair when trying to read human histories. The victors wrote the history, and sometimes it was jaded in their favor. Blackbird wondered how she could find the truth, when it was hidden by all the lies the victors told.

Rose told her that truth was a dangerous thing. It could set you free, or it could bind you tighter than chains. Truth was a true double-edged blade. It was liberty or death. Truth was one of the most dangerous things to know. To know the truth was to see the world without all the illusions that we surrounded ourselves with.

Everyone lied to themselves, and everyone lied at one time or another to others. Truth was said to be in the eye of beholder. Many tried to see the world as it was, without lying to themselves, but it never worked. No one was ever completely honest all the time because many could not truly understand the truth that was revealed.

To see yourself without all the lies, was to see the darkness inside. Everyone had darkness, everyone could be selfish, and everyone could be cruel. Life was never what you wanted, and you surrounded yourself with lies to make the world more bearable. No one wanted to admit to being selfish or vain, but everyone wanted to be ok.

Blackbird wanted to see the truth, to see the world or universe, without lies, without hiding. Rose told her that many that did manage to do this had either died, or gone insane, unable to accept what they had found. For in the truth was hidden what and who we really are.

To know the truth, about herself was something that Blackbird was determined to find out how to find that truth. To truly know herself, and to find a way to accept that truth, Blackbird believed that would help her be more in control of herself and her magic. Rose agreed but told her to be careful.

CHAPTER EIGHT

Blackbird had been in the valley for about three years now. She had worked hard to learn about her magic, and how to control it. Rose told her that she had learned everything that Rose had to teach her, and now it was time to go to the White Lands and learn from Quicksilver. Blackbird had met Quicksilver a few times, and she was excited to go and learn from her.

Goldie, Blackie, Sunbird and Midnight would, of course, be going with her. They had watched over her for the last few years and were proud of her progress. She was stronger now than she had been, and more confident in herself. She now looked sixteen, with long raven hair, and black eyes. Her face had matured, and her form was growing.

Midnight was looking at her in a new way. She was beautiful, and he liked the way she smelled. He knew that if she were a wolf, he would bring her meat from his kills, and they would share it, and they would do this until they went off into the woods for about a week and would be a bonded pair when they came back. But she was part human, and though he accepted that fact, he knew that humans were a little more elaborate in their courtship. But he knew that he wanted to be with her, and he would do anything to be her mate.

So, Blackbird packed her stuff, and made ready to go to the White Lands. Her animal friends went with her to the place where the portal would be opened. This portal was different from others, as it was a permanent portal. It was used for trade between the White Lands and Rose's valley.

The White Lands were different now than they had been

when they were first founded. They now encompassed nearly the entire world. There were a few lands that were not a part of the White Lands, but that did not matter. All the elves, dwarves and other races that lived on this world followed the White Lady, who was Quicksilver.

Many of them were healers, and farmers. They did have an army, but it was small. The army was called the White Soldiers. They were always ready to fight for the White Lady, and to protect her people. In all the years that she had lived here, though, no one had challenged her, since that the sorcerer's failed attempt.

Now Blackbird would live in the White Tower, and learn from Quicksilver, who had mastered all her people's magic, and was ready to teach Blackbird. As the portal opened, Rose touched Blackbird's shoulder, and the girl looked at her.

"The White Lands are special. They have not had a war there in nearly twenty years. The people are dedicated to peace, and healing. They are not as my people. They are more concerned with taking care of others. They are a peculiar people, and they do not like to disagree with anyone. You will not need to be defensive there, as all the people are more concerned with your welfare then theirs. Have fun, and know I will visit, when I get the chance." Blackbird nodded and took a breath, and stepped through the portal, followed by her animals.

Stepping through the portal was like stepping through water. It was cold and seemed to seep into her very bones. She shuddered, but it only lasted a few moments, before she was on the other side, and gazed at the White Lands for the first time.

Everything was calm. The people did not hurry, nor was there any shouting. A tall young man, with green eyes came up to her. He smiled and introduced himself.

"I am Kit Nightstalker, Quicksilver's husband. I have come to take you to the tower. Quicksilver is heavy with child and cannot travel much right now. Rooms have been made ready for you. Just follow me." Blackbird nodded and looked around at the city. It had started out as just a village, but now had grown into a city. Elves moved about gracefully, greeting the others of different races gently.

There was noise, of course, but it seemed muffled. There were dwarven blacksmiths that pounded on anvils, and there were people talking, and buying and selling. But no one was in a hurry, and no one argued or raised their voices. There were street performers and laughter. But there was no trash, or messes.

Everything portrayed calm and happy. There was no noise that was not happy. There were children of every race playing together, and their laughter filled the air, but no one got hurt, and they were not afraid.

Here in the White Lands, crime was unheard of. There was no theft, no murder. Everyone cared about each other, and everyone knew that they were important. Quicksilver ruled here, and she loved everyone. She accepted them, as they were, and she knew that everyone could be happy.

They did not stagnate, as a society, though. She encouraged innovation and experimenting. They were passionate about things like learning and caring for the sick. They were the ones who you could call upon if you were troubled, or sick.

Many advanced societies had discovered the White Lands, and they found it to a good place if you stressed out or struggling. All were welcome here if you followed the rules. Some had tried to take advantage of the society and tried to convince people to follow them.

Some slavers had tried to take some of Quicksilver's people, and they learned that though she was normally gentle and calm, Quicksilver was not someone to cross. She had gone after them, in her own ship and had retrieved her people, and then destroyed the slaver's ship. She did not tolerate slavers, just as Rose did not.

Rose's empire had grown as well. She now ruled over five worlds, including the one she had faced Corwin on. The people of these planets were not all as advanced as the Valley, but Rose was helping them. She had brought in many reforms, like offering education to everyone. She made everyone equal in the eyes of the law. So, if a nobleman mistreated a servant, that servant could take the nobleman to court.

Rose did not tolerate mistreatment of any kind. She made sure that all were treated fairly. Though many nobles did not like this, they understood that Rose was not the kind of ruler you made angry. She made sure that the laws of the Valley were upheld in all worlds of her empire. She made sure that everyone had a chance to advance in life if they applied themselves.

The judges that upheld the laws were not noblemen. The people chose them. They could not buy their way into office or stay longer than two terms. They would be paid for their service, and when they were done, they did get an allowance, but it was only half of what they had been making.

Rose had found ways to eliminate corruption in her empire. She had made sure that everyone was treated fairly. She also made sure that the noblemen would take care of the people that they were responsible for. She made sure that the laws were followed, and she had established the Secret Police. No one knew who the Secret Police were, as they were secret. She also had a regular police force to make sure that everyone was safe. The Secret Police made sure to watch the people, and they would report to the regular police who would act on the information they were given.

Rose did not want people to become paranoid, but she wanted to make sure that her people were safe. The Secret Police worked regular jobs, and made friends, and acted normal. No one was arrested that spoke against Rose's reforms. Everyone could talk about what they wanted to. Everyone knew that they were free to speak and express themselves, and they were able to protect themselves if needed.

In the White Lands, though, everyone got along. There was no need for judges or police, or anything like that. There was no crime. Everyone knew the laws, but they never broke them. There was no need for police. If you needed to talk to someone, there were resources for that. If you needed a mediator, those were available.

The White Lands were peaceful, and easy going. Everyone was kind, and there were resources that that everyone could use if they needed them. Things like abuse were no longer tolerated, and everyone knew that Quicksilver would help if they needed her too. There was no violence, no theft, no poor. Everyone had a job, and they would do their job, and get compensation for their work. Just not money. Instead, they would receive food and clothing for their payments. Everyone had plenty to eat, and shelter, and clothing. No one was needy, or homeless.

Blackbird looked around at the White City. Everything was pale in coloring. There were no overly bright colors or dark ones. There was dark hair, or skin, but the clothing was all pastels. And all the animals seemed to be pale in color as well. There were no overly dark horses or dogs or cats. It did not look washed out, just pale.

Blackbird mentioned this to Kit, and he looked over at her, and smiled.

"It has something to do with Quicksilver's influence. Pale colors are calm, verses bright colors or dark colors. It started about two years after we moved into the Tower. Even the grass and the trees are paler than they are elsewhere. Quicksilver likes lighter colors, and it became reflected in her surroundings. You will get used to it." Blackbird nodded and followed him through the archway that led onto the Tower Grounds.

Kit was right. Even the grass was a light green instead of dark green. But it did not look unhealthy, simply different. Then Blackbird saw Theac and some of his kind. She had never seen anything like them before. They stood taller than even Goldie when she stood on her hind legs. They were trimming some of the trees and making sure that the plants were watered and cared for.

Kit greeted them, and they smiled and waved at him. He

introduced Blackbird, and they greeted her warmly. Theac's people were thriving here, taking care of the grounds of the White Tower. They enjoyed their work and made sure that every plant was tended to.

Blackbird watched them for a moment longer then hurried to catch up with Kit, who had not stopped. He looked back at her, and smiled, and slowed down. She then saw the Tower and her eyes widened.

The Tower, made of white marble, with the glass top, gleamed in the sunlight. It was a beacon of light and hope to the people of this world. A busy harbor lay nearby, and the ships were all white. Everything was light and white.

Quicksilver was waiting for them on the steps of the Tower. She was pregnant with twins, and she was due soon. She smiled and greeted Blackbird with a hug. She then led the way into the Tower, the animals following, and they made their way to the elevator. Quicksilver had trouble with the stairs. But they all fit into the elevator and went up to the second floor, where all the living quarters were.

Quicksilver took Blackbird to the room that had been prepared for her and her animals. It was spacious and had accommodations for the animals. There was even a small garden. Blackbird gazed around, and found the room was nice. It was comfortable, and peaceful. Quicksilver smiled and told her.

"I will give you a few days to settle in before we begin your lessons. You can wander around the Tower and its grounds freely. A list of the rules is posted on the refrigerator. We will try and make you as comfortable as we can. If you want to eat in the dining halls, you just go to the elevator, and go back to the first floor. Signs will guide you. But the fridge is full, so you can eat here also if you want. I will send someone to bring you to my rooms when I am ready to teach you." Blackbird nodded. She was getting tired, though it was not really time to eat.

It was nice to just rest in her room, after the long walk, and everything else. Quicksilver and Kit left, and she sat down on the couch, looking around. It was very calm and peaceful here. She was uncertain about being here though. It was not that she did not like it, it was just quite different from Rose's city.

CHAPTER NINE

The next day, Blackbird, with Midnight close by, explored the Tower, and its grounds. Everyone was nice and smiled at her. She would ask questions, and they were always ready to answer her. She was glad that they did not mind her animals. In fact, some of the children asked if they could play with Goldie. The big bear did not mind and spent some time with the little ones.

Midnight stayed close to her and wondered how to begin courting her. He did not want to frighten her off, but he did want her to be his mate. He was unsure how she felt about him and did not know how to find out how she felt for him.

Theirs was a peculiar relationship. She had found him when he was little and wounded. She had nursed him back to health in her room. Secretly, of course, as the nuns were very strict about pets. He was not a pet, but they would have viewed him as such. But no one had ever gone into her room, so she had been able to hide him.

The past several years, his feelings for her had changed. He had always been fond of her, but his feelings had grown and changed. He cared for her, but in a way that was different than before. Maybe he could ask Kit for advice. He knew if he asked Blackie or Goldie or Sunbird, they would probably tease him. He needed advice and hoped that Kit would be discreet about it.

It could not hurt to ask at least. He was willing to learn about courtship, or human courtship so he could tell if she liked him, or how to approach her. So, while she was in her lessons, he would find Kit and asked him about it.

The next day, Blackbird was not given any lessons, as Quicksilver had gone into labor. Rose was there, and her sister Dophina, who was the foremost healer in the Valley. Blackbird waited outside the door to the infirmary, listening to the sounds within. Kit paced back and forth and watched the door anxiously.

Finally, the sound of crying filled the air. The babies were born. Blackbird followed Kit into the room and gazed at Quicksilver. Even tired she was beautiful. Her silver hair was damp with sweat, and her eyes looked a little gray, but she held her twins, a look so tender upon her face, that Blackbird was touched by it.

The two babies, one a boy and one a girl nestled close to their mother. They were still now; Quicksilver having soothed them. They did not move much, as she held them against her. As they opened their eyes, though, everyone could see that the girl was blind. Her eyes were pure white and did not move as her brother's did.

"What are their names?" Rose asked, as she smiled down on them.

"The boy is to be called Storm, and the girl will be called Skye. They are the first Undarai to be born in a long time. I am now no longer the only one of my kind." Quicksilver smiled and kissed her babies. She sighed and laid down against her pillows. She was tired but happy.

Kit smiled down at her and took the babies. They wiggled in their blankets, and he soothed them. Quicksilver smiled at him and sighed. Dophina smiled and told her to get some rest. Quicksilver nodded and closed her eyes. Her body was already beginning to heal, the bleeding slowing down, and her stomach showed no signs of stretching. As her blood could affect others, Rose gathered the bloodied sheets, and threw them into the fire.

Blackbird went to the infirmary the next day, as Quicksilver had asked her to come by. The twins were in a bassinet next to her bed. She had just finished feeding them. They were wide awake, and the boy was watching everything, as the girl just laid there, her tiny hands gripping the soft fabric of the blanket.

Blackbird sat down on the other side of Quicksilver and smiled at the babies. Quicksilver looked at her and smiled.

"I thought we could begin your lessons today. I will be in bed for a few days, but that does not mean I cannot teach you. We will begin with lessons on healing. There are many ways to heal, and I will teach you as many as I can. We will begin with herbs. I will ask questions from time to time, so pay attention to what I say."

Blackbird nodded, and Quicksilver took a breath and began to teach her about different herbs and for what they were used. Blackbird paid attention to her and would answer the questions correctly every time. After a few hours, they took a break, as Quicksilver needed to feed the babies again.

The babies were well behaved. They only fussed if they needed something. If they did not need anything they just lay quietly. Rose would come in, and help change them, and she would occasionally take them for a walk or something.

Blackbird knew something about healing already, but Quicksilver knew more. She had studied for years and had learned much. And she was patient with Blackbird. She would make sure that Blackbird did not get confused with all the different herbs, and she made sure that she did not use terms that Blackbird did not understand.

A few days after her babies were born, Quicksilver was able to go back to her rooms. Blackbird found Quicksilver's rooms to be interesting. They were not filled with luxury items, but quite simple things. All her furniture was simple and comfortable. There were plants everywhere.

Quicksilver took care of her babies even while teaching Blackbird, and while Blackbird was learning about herbs and other ways of healing, Midnight was seeking out Kit.

CHAPTER TEN

Midnight took on human form as he came up to Kit. He was a tall youth, with black hair, and golden eyes. His nose was hooked, and his mouth firm. He was well built and dressed in clothes like Kit. Kit looked at him and smiled.

"How can I help you, Midnight?" Midnight hesitated and took a breath and responded.

"I want to court Blackbird, but I do not know much about the courtship of humans. If she were a full-blooded wolf, I would take her a kill, and we would go into the woods for a week. But she is part human, and I do not know much about their courtship rituals."

Kit smiled. He knew about loving someone who was different. He could feel Quicksilver in the back of his mind. She was happy and was glad to be a mother. Kit gazed at the young man who was watching him and responded.

"I do not know much about Blackbird, but I do know that when I was courting Quicksilver, she liked to get surprises. It is difficult to surprise someone when you share thoughts, but I managed it. When you are courting someone, you need to find what they like and give them gifts. Take her on a picnic or a walk on the beach. Give her flowers or treats that she likes. And never be afraid to let her know how you feel."

Midnight thought about this. Blackbird was busy with her studies, but she was given time in the evenings for herself. She had always like watching the stars come out. So, Midnight went to the kitchens, and got some food together. He inquired around about a good place to watch the stars and made plans to take her out and watch the stars come out.

Goldie saw all this, and she smiled. Blackie found it amusing and Sunbird was confused. Sunbird did not understand when things had changed between Midnight and Blackbird. Blackie just told him that the two young ones were made for each other, and to leave them alone.

So, after her lessons, as she was leaving the top of the Tower, Blackbird found Midnight waiting for her. He seemed a little nervous, and she wondered if something was wrong. But he asked her to come with him, he had a surprise for her. She was tired and a little hungry, but she followed him, and found herself on a hill near the sea.

A blanket had been spread out, and food laid upon it. She looked at Midnight, curious now, and he smiled at her and helped her sit down. He took a breath and spoke up.

"I know the stars here are different than the ones at home, but I thought you would enjoy watching them come out. You used to watch the stars a lot, and I know you have been working hard, so I thought you would enjoy just watching the stars." She studied him and smiled. She did like watching the stars come out. So, she allowed him to prepare some food, and they watched the stars.

They stayed out for a while as the stars came out, and the moons came up. For this world had two moons, and they were two different colors. One was a pale pink, and the other a pale blue. Midnight glanced at her, as she watched the stars and moons.

The light from the moons tinted her skin, and her black eyes reflected their light. She was incredibly beautiful, and he wanted to say something, but could not find the words. So, he just watched her, until she looked over at him. He blushed and looked away. Blackbird studied him and wondered what was going on. But she did not say anything, as they watched the stars shine in the sky.

After a while, they packed everything up, and went back to the Tower. Midnight took on the form of a wolf, as they reached their rooms. He curled up on the floor near her bed, and she studied him for a few moments, until sleep took her.

The next day she was up early, and found Midnight in the kitchen unit, trying, and failing to cook breakfast. Goldie took on her human form and shooed him out of the kitchen. She shook her head, and threw the burned food into the trash unit, and cooked breakfast. Blackbird did not know what to say, but she did almost laugh at the sheepish expression on Midnight's face.

After breakfast, Midnight walked with her to the elevator, and told her he would see her later. Blackbird nodded, and the elevator door closed. Midnight stood there for a moment, and then went to the kitchens on the first floor and asked if he could learn to cook.

The head cook studied him for a moment and shrugged. She took him over to where some women were kneading some dough and showed him how to knead. It took him a few minutes to get used to the motion, but he did manage it. After that, he was taken over to the spits, for though Quicksilver did not eat meat, there were others that did. He was shown how to turn the spits, so the meat was evenly cooked.

All that day he spent in the kitchens, learning how to cook. He wanted to impress Blackbird with his skills, so he paid close attention to what the cooks showed him. He knew it would be some time before he was good at cooking, but he wanted to learn.

When Blackbird returned to the rooms that night, she found that Midnight had cooked some food for all of them. he smiled at her and told her that he had spent that day in the kitchens, learning. The food was quite good, and she told him so. The others looked at each other and nodded. They knew that Blackbird and Midnight would make a good couple, so they decided to encourage this

The next day, as Midnight walked down to the kitchens, he found himself intercepted by Kit. Kit studied him and asked if he knew anything about how to fight like a human. Midnight did not, as he could always change form and fight as a wolf.

Kit nodded and told him that learning how to fight as a human might help him if he was going to be going on adventures with Blackbird.

So, Kit took Midnight down to the training grounds of the White Soldiers and began to teach him how to fight as a human. Kit was quite a good fighter, and he was a good teacher. He taught Midnight how to fight with his bare hands, with a bow, and with swords. Kit preferred his hammers to a sword, but he knew how to use one, just in case.

So, Midnight learned how to be a human, how to fight with weapons, and how to cook. He was a good student, and practiced much, but always found time to spend with Blackbird. He would take her on picnics, or to the market, and watch her as she gazed at the various wares on display. She was learning about the languages of the people, elven and dwarven as well as the different human dialects.

She kept up her magic practice, though Quicksilver had told her she would be learning about the rune magic of Quicksilver's people. Blackbird was one of the few who would be able to learn about the runes and use them. Blackbird was excited about that. She wanted to learn as much as she could.

So, these two drew closer, as they each learned what their teachers taught them. Midnight grew stronger, and more adept at fighting, and Blackbird grew in wisdom and learning. And they grew closer to each other, their feelings deepening, and growing stronger.

Before she knew it, Blackbird had been in the White Lands for four years. She had learned about Quicksilver's peoples' magic, and Storm and Skye had grown much as well. Storm and Skye were never far from each other, as Storm was his sister's eyes. They were close and Storm, even though he was only four, was protective of his sister.

Skye was a quiet child, content to listen to the world, but her brother took her places, and let her touch things so she knew what they felt like. The people of the White Lands looked after the twins, helping their mother take care of them. Blackbird like to spend time with them as well. They were both very curious and liked to ask questions.

CHAPTER ELEVEN

Rose came one day, and spoke alone with Quicksilver for a time, and then Blackbird was summoned to Quicksilver's rooms. Blackbird entered, uncertainly, for she felt as though something bad had happened. Rose looked at her seriously and took a breath.

"The world you were born on is in trouble. War has broken out, between the races. The elves started it, and now the humans and dwarves are involved. The different tribes of the elves have always been separated, until someone came along and unified them, and then he declared war on the humans and dwarves. Now war threatens to consume the entire world unless someone can stop it. You are needed, as you can help stop this. The elves need to be stopped, and they still remember the girl who killed the elven sorcerer.

You are the only one who can end this. Your power is needed. This is your home world, and you have been chosen to save it. You are ready, as both I and Quicksilver agree. You have learned all that we can teach you, now it is time for you put your knowledge into practice."

Blackbird lowered her eyes. She was not sure if she was ready. She was afraid she would fail. But as she looked at these two women, she also knew that she did not want to disappoint them. They had both taught her about the Ultimate Mother, and she knew that this would be her trial of faith.

So, Blackbird took a breath and nodded. She would go to her home world, and she would find a way to stop this war. She did not know how, but she would find a way.

Rose helped her get ready to go. She packed traveling

clothes, a tent, and blankets into a special pack, which would hold as much as she could put into it without it getting heavy or too full. She also put food into it, though she did know how to survive off the land. Of course, her animals would be going with her, and she was glad for the company.

She tightened her belt, and looked over at Quicksilver, who came up to her and handed her a box, filled with healing herbs, and a special vial. The vial held the essence of the lily known as the Undarai Tears. This would heal anything short of death, with only a single drop. The vial would never run out, but she should use it only if she needed to.

Blackbird wrapped her hand around her staff. She had taken off the feathers and other decorations, and now it looked like just an ordinary wooden staff. But Blackbird knew how to fight with it, and how use it so her magic would not overwhelm her. She was strong now and determined to do what she could for her home world.

Midnight gazed her and noted how much she had changed. She looked eighteen now, her heart shaped face a light brown. Her raven hair fell around her in a cascade of darkness, and her black eyes were calm and steady. Her hair was held out of her face with a band of gold ribbon he had given her for her last birthday.

She had matured much since she had left her home world. She had grown much, and she was beautiful. He loved her, and admitted that he would do anything for her, even die for her, if that was his destiny. He shook himself and changed into his wolf form. He could change in an instant if he needed to.

Finally, they were ready to go, and Blackbird looked at Rose and Quicksilver. They both smiled at her, and Rose told her to concentrate on her destination, and open a portal to the place she wanted to go. Blackbird nodded and closed her eyes. She thought of the monastery where she had grown up and raised her hand. With a slashing motion, she opened the portal and followed by her animal friends she stepped through.

CHAPTER TWELVE

The monastery was even more overgrown then when she had left it. Some of the walls had fallen over, and the roof had collapsed. The trees and plants once so carefully tended had become overgrown and wild. Weeds now dominated the monastery, and the well had fallen in.

Blackbird gazed around, sadness in her eyes. She had fond memories of this place, and to see it now, in ruins, made her sad. She did not know how to stop this war, but she knew that she would find a way to do it. Goldie snuffed and Blackbird looked over at her.

"I know we cannot linger here, but it was my home. I am sad that it has fallen into ruin. But where are we supposed to go? I have no idea how to stop a war. No one here knows me, as I have never walked in circles with the rich and noble."

Goldie regarded her and spoke softly.

"You do not need to be rich or noble to get people's attention. You know more magic than any of those who live on this world, and you can do things that they cannot. Use what you have learned to your advantage. No one can beat you in a sorcerer's duel." Blackbird agreed and she looked around at what was left of the monastery.

Midnight nuzzled her hand, and she smiled. They still had plenty of daylight to travel with. So, they left the buildings behind, and Blackbird used her abilities with the element of air to find the nearest group of people. She turned to the southeast, where she got the strongest response, and they began to walk. Blackbird would ride on Goldie sometimes, or she would just walk.

It took a few days to reach the group she had felt. They were refugees, looking for sanctuary from the armies that walked the lands. Blackbird gazed at them, thin and worn, and helped them. She had food, and healing herbs that she gave them, and treated their wounds.

They told her that the war had forced them from their homes. They were looking for a place to hide, and she told them of the monastery, which though it was in ruins, would shelter them for a while. They asked her who she was, and she told them her name. They thanked her for the directions to the monastery.

She asked if they knew where the closest army was, and they were told two days away in the mountain pass of Kilai. They were curious about why she wanted to know but did not press her. It was a dwarven army, which was fighting an elven force. The elves used magic, but the dwarves were strong. They needed help but no one would come.

Blackbird would. She knew that she could help, and so she turned towards the mountains and made her way to the pass. Since her animals did not need to rest as often as she needed to, Goldie carried her when she needed to rest, so they got to the pass only a day after leaving the refugees instead of two.

She came upon them from the opposite side than the elves. She waited with her friends until some dwarves came to see what she wanted. As they approached, the big wolf let out a snort, and Blackbird looked up at the dwarves.

"Who be you?" One of the dwarves asked her. She smiled at him and spoke.

"My name is Blackbird, and I am here to help end the war. I am a magic user, and I can use my power to end this war, if you let me help. These are my companions, Blackie the raven, Goldie the bear, Sunbird the eagle and Midnight the wolf." The dwarves looked at each other and wondered how this young girl was going to help end the war. She watched them and knew what they were thinking.

"Please let me come into your camp, and I will see what I can do for you." The dwarves gazed at her and sighed. She was just one human; she could not do much damage to an army their size. So, they brought her and her animals into the camp.

She went to the healers' tent and helped tend the wounded. She was very good at this, and the healers were grateful for some help. Then an attack came, and Blackbird went out to the front lines. They were barely holding.

Blackbird could sense someone getting ready to use magic, and she stepped forward. Her black eyes swept the crowd of elves before her, and she spotted the magic user. She brought her staff up and concentrated on him. He was going to throw a fireball, so she raised her hand, and solidified the air in front of the dwarves. The fireball hit her barrier and dissipated before it touched the dwarves. The elven magic user blinked and gazed at the dwarves. He then saw a young girl holding a glowing staff, and he frowned. She was very young, but he could feel great power within her.

The dwarves gazed at her, as she prepared to protect them. With the failure of the fireball, the elven attack had faltered. The dwarves took advantage of this hesitation and pushed the elves back. The elven magic user prepared another attack, only to be thwarted again by the girl.

He attacked her directly then, and the fight was on. The elven soldiers fell back, as did the dwarves. It was extremely dangerous to be caught in the middle of a fight between magic users. The elven magic user did everything he knew how to do, and she stopped him every time.

Finally, he threw a lightening attack at her, and it hit her shield, and bounced back. His eyes widened as his own attack hit him and broke through his shield and he fell to the ground, burnt to a crisp. The elves fell back even more, and the dwarves gazed at the young girl who was staring in shock at the burned body of her opponent.

She had never seen anyone die like that before. He had managed to utter one short scream before his lungs had evaporated. The dwarves shouted and attacked, driving the elves back and the elves retreated. They did not stop to pick up their dead or wounded, they just fled.

After the elves had fled the dwarven king found the girl. She was tending to the wounded on the battlefield, not caring if they were elves or dwarves. She knelt next to an elf and bound his wounds with compresses and bandages.

The dwarven king studied her. She was crying, as she tended to the wounds. The animals who had come with her were close by watching over her.

"That magic user be one of their stronger ones. He been killing many of my people." She looked over at him, and nodded, but did not speak.

"I never seen anyone be fighting like you. You be a good magic user, but you also be human, so I be wondering why you be helping us. The scouts who brought you in, be saying you said you are stopping the war. I wonder how you be doing that."

She shrugged. She did not know herself. As she gazed at the fallen warriors, she wondered how one person could stop this. How did you stop something that someone wanted to happen? She needed to know more about the ones who started this.

She looked down at the elf she had just helped and asked him softly.

"Why did the elves start this war? It seems so out of character for your people." The elf looked up at her and responded.

"The elven tribes are contentious, and we never got along. But then one wizard stepped forward and proposed that we unite, as we had once long ago, and conquer the other races. We are the Elder Race; he said and did this not give us the right to rule? He was incredibly good at persuading the leaders to join and declare war on the other races. We have conquered much, now only a handful of places continue to resist us, but we do not want to continue fighting. We are the Elder Race, but we do not reproduce like the other races. For every human or dwarf that dies others are born to take their place. But we elves do not reproduce at the same rate. For every elf that falls, there are none born. Every five elves are replaced with one.

If this war continues, we will vanish. We are losing even as we are winning. But no one can stop the wizard. He is relentless and holds the hearts of our leaders. They will not listen to us anymore, only to him. He must be stopped before he destroys our people."

Blackbird gazed at the elf. She lowered her eyes. Once before she had faced an elven sorcerer, and she had won, through luck mostly. But she was not a child anymore, and she was stronger than she had been. But to get the wizard's attention, she needed to stop the elves. Her eyes went down to the elven camp. And then she asked the elf.

"Is one of the wizard's lackeys here?" The elf nodded and told her that the leader of the army here was controlled by the wizard. Determination touched her face, and she stood up. This war would end, no matter what it took.

With her animal companions, Blackbird made her way down to the elven camp. She would not wait to stop this. As she approached, the scouts called at her to stop. She looked at them and raised her hand. Vines burst from the logs they had surrounded their camp with, wrapping tightly around them.

The logs held the elves tightly, and then a space opened in front of her. She strode into the camp, followed by her animals, and everyone who tried to stop her found themselves wrapped tightly in vines. Blackbird made her way to the center of the camp, where the commander was standing in front of his tent.

He frowned at her, as she approached. She faced him squarely and raised her hand.

"This war will end, one way or another. The killing will stop, and the innocent will no longer be afraid. The elves will not win, and they will not die out either. I will not allow this to continue."

"And who are you to make these statements? A barbarian from the north is all you are, and you cannot stop this war with vines and words."

She gazed at him and closed her eyes. She opened herself to the magic that was around her, to the power that was hers.

"I am Blackbird, daughter of the north. I am Blackbird, child of magic, and I have come to stop you and yours from destroying this world. I am Blackbird, keeper of the balance, and sister to Rose and Quicksilver. I am Blackbird, and I am a priestess of the Stars, and I will not allow you to destroy this world."

The elven commander looked into those black eyes and saw something he had not seen before. This child before him was power incarnate, and her staff flared as she faced him. The spell that surrounded him broke, and he found himself suddenly aware of the mistake that he had made in helping with the war.

He trembled and found himself on his knees. He stared around and horror rose in his eyes. How could he have listened to the magic user? This was madness, and only destruction would come from this course.

"What have we done?" He cried. He gazed up at the girl, who studied him. There was an aura of power around her, as her black eyes gazed at him.

"I have set you free, and I want to help your people. And all those who are suffering because of this wizard. I will need your help, and I know you will help me." He nodded. Of course, he would help, help undo the damage that he had done.

She released all the elves that she bound with vines and asked someone to ask the dwarven king if he would join them. She would need his help too, in ending this war.

CHAPTER THIRTEEN

The wizard, whose name was Torin, did not feel it when the spell was broken. He was busy with his conquests, and with his concubines. So, he did not know that someone had come to stop him, and she was more powerful than he would ever be. He did not know that Blackbird was coming for him, and she would come with an army at her back.

The dwarven king studied the young girl. She was standing at the elven commander's table where all the maps were laid out. She was studying them and thinking about how to stop the wizard. The elves were relieved that they were not going to fight the dwarves anymore, but they wanted to help the rest of their people. This army was not big, even with the dwarves, but they had Blackbird, and they were willing to follow her, as she had set them free from the wizard.

"So, the wizard is here, at the city of Newtonia, and is directing the armies through that city. He is holding the main elven leaders with him, so he can control the rest of the elven peoples. He is in a strongly defended place. But there are several armies between us and that city, and if I can release them from his grip, we would come to city with a goodly sized army.

We will need everyone we can get to help get us to that city and face him. But it will come down to me and him in the end. I will face him in a duel, and I will stop him. The work will not end there, however. Much damage has been done to the places he has conquered, and that damage must be repaired. We will need to work together, even after he is beaten, so we can fix what he has broken."

The dwarven king, Theros Firebeard, nodded. He knew that it would take time to heal the wounds of this war, and he was willing to work towards fixing what had been done. He would send word to the other dwarven rulers and let them know that they had finally found someone strong enough to challenge Torin.

Blackbird talked with the leaders, and decided to take a few days rest here, to help the wounded, and make ready to march. She knew that it was not going to be easy for the dwarves and elves to work together, but she also knew that they would try. They all wanted this war to end, and she had given them hope that it could. That put a lot of pressure on her, to keep her end of the bargain, but she would do it. She was not going to disappoint anyone.

Blackbird slept in a tent that the elves set up for her. She was tired from everything that had happened, and she was glad she had made some progress. That night, she had a dream about a building that was like her monastery home but was different as well.

The building was massive, and it had walls around it. The grounds were well groomed, and there were orchards, fields, and gardens. As she walked down the path, she could see the building was special. It rose from the ground, imposing and strong. She reached the door, and pushed it opened, and she looked around.

Two big doors faced her leading into a room filled with books. Books of every kind, from the ceiling to the floor. And there were rooms leading off this main room. They were filled with books as well, and she could tell that each room represented a world and all the books in that room belonged to the ones who lived there.

As she realized this, she found herself facing a being of rainbow light. The light pulsed, and shimmered, and she heard a voice inside her head.

"This is the Ultimate Library, where all the knowledge of the Universe is written down. You face the choice of your sisters, the choice between what you want most in your life, or the choice to follow the harder path. You can have your parents back, live with them and eventually die, or you can choose to become the Guardian of Magic and Keeper of the Library.

If you chose the library, you will be connected to everything and everyone. You will feel the knowledge of this place in your mind, and you will know everything, about everything, and everyone. You will share their burdens, even as I do. And you never again be truly alone. You will know the truth, without all the lies that people tell themselves. You will know their darkest secrets and their greatest joys.

Or you can give it all up and your parents will live again, and you will go back to them, as their child, and you will grow up without knowing all the things you know now. You will be a mortal, and you will live and die as a mortal, and no one will ever know you, except your family. But in doing so, you will cause the deaths of uncounted peoples, who, without you, will not stand a chance of survival. It is your choice, my daughter, your happiness, or the lives of those you can save. What would you sacrifice for your choice if you so choose to assume this burden?"

Blackbird lowered her eyes. It was a choice between what she had wanted all her life, and the lives of others. As she stood there, she thought about her parents, and she knew what she would choose. She looked up at the light and said firmly.

"I choose to follow Rose and Quicksilver. I will give up my fear, of myself and the power I hold, so that I can help others, for even without my memories I know I would live a mortal life feeling like I had betrayed those I care about. I will choose the harder path."

"DONE." The voice echoed through the air. Blackbird shuddered as her mind opened, and a thousand upon a thousand voices began to whisper in her ears.

"The change will come gradually, so you can adjust to the changes. Be careful, for knowledge is to be given when it is earned, not just because you can. You will find many changes now, that you have made this choice. Awaken now, Guardian of Magic, and Keeper of the Library."

Blackbird shuddered as she woke to find herself still in the tent. Voices filled the air around her. Whispers surrounded her, but she was able to ignore them. she rose to her feet, and went to the basin that had been left, and splashed some water on her face.

Midnight, in his human form, entered the tent and studied her.

"Are you all, right? I thought I felt something happening in here." She looked up at him, and she could almost see his thoughts, which were mostly of her. She blushed at some of the thoughts he was having, but she shook her head.

"I just have a headache. I did not sleep very well. And you should try to control your thoughts, as I would not want you to get distracted while we are travelling." He blinked, and then he blushed slightly.

"So, you made the choice, last night, then? I am sorry about my thoughts, but when I am around you, I cannot help it. I love you and want to be with you. And maybe when this is over, we can be together." She gazed at him. She loved him too, and did want to be with him, but a lot was going on right now.

She went out of the tent and talked again with the leaders of the armies. The dwarves were getting ready to march and making sure that they had everything they needed. The elves were tending to their wounded and getting ready to move out.

Midnight stayed close to her, and she tried to ignore the thoughts of those around her. She would need to get a grip on this, and all the discipline that Rose and Quicksilver had taught her was helping. She just needed to get used to it.

The next day, all was in readiness for them to leave. Blackbird settled onto Goldie's back, and at the head of the army of elves and dwarves, she led the way. Two birds wheeled overhead, calling to her, as they scouted ahead. Midnight, in his wolf form, followed her closely.

She would not hide her coming. She knew that would be

nearly impossible anyway. She would just not let anyone know that she stood against the wizard. They would tell anyone who asked that they were done with their tasks and were heading to the city to find out where he wanted them next. It would be a journey of several weeks, maybe longer, depending on terrain and obstacles in the way. And of course, the weather, as it was getting late in the year.

They would be traveling through lands he had already conquered, so they did not need to be afraid of being attacked by anyone who followed him, just the rebels that were lurking about. The dwarven king had sent word to the other dwarven armies, letting them know that there was hope for ending the war, and they were to go if they could to the city where the wizard was.

The first few days of the journey were uneventful. The sun was warm but not too hot, and they stopped frequently to rest the horses and the men. Blackbird continued to learn how to control what she could do. She would be distracted easily by stray thoughts of others if she did not concentrate on blocking them.

On the fifth day of leaving the mountain pass, Sunbird called down to her, and let her know that trouble was ahead. Another army was coming, with the wizard's flag at its head. Blackbird called to the leaders of the elves and dwarves and told them about the army in their way. They wanted to avoid fighting if they could.

They made camp next to the road and waited for the other army. They did not want to be recruited for another campaign, but maybe Blackbird could persuade them to come to the city with them. Maybe she could set them free from the influence of the wizard just as she had before.

As they waited, Blackbird could feel the thoughts of the army pressing down on her. It felt like she was being smothered with a pillow. She closed her eyes and shut down her own emotions, closing herself off from the emotions of others. In doing this, she found that she could tolerate the thoughts of the others. Her emotions were affected by the thoughts and emotions of all the others. But if she shut down her own emotions, she could control the flow of thoughts better.

This revelation was startling, but helpful. Now all she needed to do was learn to control her own emotions, and thus control the ability she now had. It would not be easy, but she could do it, and was determined to learn how to control this.

The leader of the other army approached the tent of the leaders. He did not understand why the dwarves were not in chains, until he entered the tent.

An extraordinarily beautiful young woman was sitting at the table, which was strewn with maps, and letters. Her raven hair fell around her, held back from her face with a golden band. Her black eyes looked over at him and he could feel the power she held.

"I did not know that a woman had been put in charge of this army, though I must wonder why one such as you would be here, and not in a palace." She frowned at him, and a young man, standing nearby, glowered at him.

"I am not an ordinary woman, if that is what you are implying. I am a mage, and I serve as he commands. The dwarves are under my spell, and they are eager to do whatever I ask of them. I doubt you can say the same." He studied her. Even if she were a mage, with her beauty, Torin would never have let her leave the city.

"Maybe not, but I still wonder why you would be in charge here. Emperor Torin has decreed that all women of any significance are to go the capital city so he can choose his bride. All single women of age are to report there for his choosing. He would not let someone like you get away, as you are quite possibly the most beautiful woman I have ever seen." He leered a little with these words, and Midnight gripped his sword.

Those intense black eyes gazed at the general. Her mouth twisted slightly, and he found himself suddenly sinking into the ground.

"Tell me, general, do you think if I plant you, you will grow more intelligent? I am heading to the city anyway, so your words are empty. I know what I am doing here, and I do not like to be treated like I am an idiot. And if I, was you, I would not squirm too much. The worms might get ideas." She looked away and studied the maps on the table.

"From where we are, we will need several weeks to reach the city, where Torin is. By then he will likely have already chosen someone. Even if we travel hard, it will still take time. We need that time, to gather more people. I think we will cut some time, if we travel west, and then take to the river. We need to go in that direction, anyway, so we can find someone important." The general stared at her, and Midnight went over to her.

"If we take this man's army with us, but it will take a lot of boats to carry these people to the point here in the river that is closest to the city. I do not know if we can find that many." She looked up at him and pointed to a place on the river.

"This town makes boats. They are making several that will be big enough for our purposes, and the dwarves will not get on boats, as they cannot swim. We can get wagons for the dwarves. But we do not need to hurry. We need to be at this town here, before winter sets in. And I can take care of food and other things, so we do not have to worry about starving through the winter. But we do need to be at this town before we can go to the city where Torin is."

Midnight studied the map. He nodded and went to get the leaders of the dwarves and elves, so Blackbird could tell them what they needed to know. As for the general, he was pulled out of the ground, and she studied him.

"I will be needing your army so you might as well resign yourself to my command, or I could just replace you. You can send word ahead if you want, but I would not give to many details. He might misunderstand what you trying to tell him. If all goes well, then you will not have to worry about him anyway."

The elven and dwarven leaders came into the tent, and eyed

the general, who was studying Blackbird. She explained to the leaders that the general, Taylor, was coming with them, and they needed to change directions. She told them that they would need to be in the town of Bayou, by winter. They still had a few weeks before winter would start, but they did want to know why they needed to go to Bayou, and she had to explain that someone important was there, and they would need this person for their mission to be successful.

Though they did not understand fully, they decided to trust Blackbird, and go with her. Taylor did not like the idea, but he reasoned that if he could bring a woman who was as beautiful as Blackbird, Torin would reward him.

So, Taylor announced to his men that they would be traveling with Lady Blackbird, as she journeyed to Torin's city of Newtonia. They were going to make sure that she made it to the city, for the choosing of the emperor's bride. But winter might start before they made it that far so they would be going to the town of Bayou, to winter there.

Blackbird was getting more used to the thoughts and feelings of others, as she traveled with the army. She learned to shut down her own feelings, so she would not be overwhelmed by others. Midnight was never far from her, not because he was jealous, but to keep her safe. She was incredibly beautiful, after all, and she could not keep herself safe all the time.

By the time they reached Bayou, winter was setting in. The first snows had come, and they were bogged down. They would not be able to go any further until spring. So, they set up camp around the town, and Blackbird made sure that everyone had shelter and food.

The armies did set up some defenses. They were in an area that had trouble with rebels. Some humans in the area would probably want to attack them, even though their numbers were great. Blackbird watched over them, and even Taylor found himself more willing to listen to her. As time went on, the leaders found that Blackbird was wise for her age, and she managed to address all their concerns. They did not know how she seemed to know what they were thinking, but they came to trust her.

CHAPTER FOURTEEN

All through the winter, the armies waited, and then Blackbird found herself being awoken in the middle of the night by noises outside her tent. She threw on a robe and stepped outside. The guards had someone who was trying to get away.

"What is going on, out here?" She asked.

"This man was trying to get into your tent, My Lady. Midnight was watching and alerted us to his presence." The man glowered at her, and she raised her hand, bringing to life a light which illuminated the man's face. She studied him and then smiled slightly.

"So, you are the one for whom we have been waiting. Let him go, and I will talk to him in my tent." The man frowned and the men released him. Midnight stood up and grabbed the man's arm and propelled him forward into the tent.

Blackbird settled onto her chair and gazed at the man. He studied her and looked around.

"I came here to kill you, and you let me into your tent? Just who are you, and why would you be waiting for me?" Midnight frowned at the man, but Blackbird just shrugged.

"You are the leader of the rebels. I have come here to end the war and make sure that everything goes back to the way it is supposed to be. I do not intend to take the throne once Torin is overthrown. I have other things I need to do. You have chosen to take the throne of the humans. The elves and dwarves still have their own leaders, but the humans do not. They need you."

The man frowned at her, studying her face. Who was she

to decide such a thing, and why did she sound so confident about this? This did not make any sense to him. She was flying the flag of the usurper, and she was making decisions for the humans.

Blackbird gazed at him and sighed. She did not know how to explain this to him, but after she had helped overthrow Torin, she was going to be looking for the Ultimate Library, as that was where she would reside, unless she was needed. She had no intention of taking over the rulership of the human lands.

This man, Borthin, was the heir of the throne of the human lands. He was going to take over when Torin was overthrown. He did not understand that now, but he would later. As he stood there staring at her, she closed her eyes, and took a breath.

"All members of the royal families of the humans have been slain. There is no one else who can take the throne. You have been chosen by fate, to take the throne. You are the one who will be king, and I will help you get there. Go, and gather all your followers, and bring them here. In a few days, the snow will be melted enough for us to continue to our destination. We are going to the riverside town of Goyin, where we will take boats and wagons, and get to the city of Newtonia, and there we will end this war, and you will take the throne."

Borthin gazed at her, and then looked over at Midnight, and asked.

"Does she always just assume that she will be obeyed?" Midnight studied him and responded.

"You may not understand, but you will do what she tells you. She is more than what you would think. You might as well just do what she tells you, because you end up doing it anyway, and it is less embarrassing if you do not argue with her." Borthin studied Midnight. With her new abilities, Blackbird knew what someone was going to say, so she knew how to respond to what they would say. She took a breath and continued to speak.

"I know that you do not understand completely. You only

want to free your people from the tyrant who has taken over. The elves are just as tired of this war as you are, but their leaders are basically being held hostage. They need help just as much as anyone else. All they want is to go back into their forests and live in peace.

I am offering you a chance to make a difference for these lands, and to help people heal. You are a natural leader, and you would be able to help a lot of people by helping us end this war. You are needed."

Borthin lowered his eyes and thought about what she said. It was something that he had been thinking about. But it would take some talking to get his men to join with these armies, but he thought he could talk them into it. He looked up at her, took a breath, and nodded. So, he slipped away and went to where his men were. They were close by, so he did not have to go far.

It took until almost sunrise for him to convince them he was not enchanted, and that he was serious about this plan. They came up to the camp, and Borthin led them to where Blackbird was standing. She looked over at them and smiled. She knew that it would take time for them to understand, but they would. Now that they had Borthin, they only had to wait for a few days to move out.

Taylor had sent word to Torin about Blackbird, and Torin was extremely interested in her. He wondered where she had come from, and where she had learned about magic. If she was as strong as Taylor said, then she would make a good empress. He was very eager to meet her, and he was unaware of any trouble connected to her. He did not know that she knew what he was thinking, and she would face him, with that advantage.

After a few days, the camp gathered up their supplies, bought as many wagons as they could, and marched to Goyin. They arrived within four days of leaving the town of Bayou, and they found several large river vessels resting in the water. They purchased more wagons, and the dwarves settled into them, as everyone else climbed into the boats.

The journey was faster now, than walking. The river would take them within a few days of Newtonia, and they would be ready for the fight when it came. The river flowed quickly past its banks, as the smell of fresh flowers filled the air. All was calm and peaceful, as they made their way down the river. They had been joined by more dwarves during the winter, and others who had found their way to the camp, ready to stop the war.

Blackbird made sure that Borthin was prominent in the meetings of the leaders. She would ask for his advice and give him some in return. He was wise and knew how to get people to follow him. He still was not sure if he wanted the throne, but as with the others, the more time he spent around Blackbird, the more he came to trust her.

CHAPTER FIFTEEN

Blackbird watched the wagons on the bank of the river. The creaking of the boats filled the air around her, as did the smell of fresh tar. She liked the sway of the boats, as she found the motion relaxing. She knew that Torin did not know her true agenda in going to his city. He thought she was coming, called by the allure of power, to be his bride. She would prove to him and others, that she was not one to trifle with, and his city would fall, and the war would be over. She would make sure that Borthin was crowned, and that the elves would be set free, to return to their forests.

Torin felt secure in his power. He had enchanted elves and others and made sure that they would not betray him. He did not believe a woman was any threat to him, as women were inferior to him. He did not know that the woman he would be facing was one that knew his innermost secrets, and she would use those to end his reign, and stop the war, and make sure that peace was established.

Just killing him would be just the start. That was not the end of what she needed to do. She would need to get Borthin on the throne, and make sure that peace was established. She would need to undo the spells that Torin had woven, and make sure that the people understood that the war was over, and they were free.

When they arrived at the town that they would be leaving the river in, Blackbird found an escort waiting. Torin had been told of her arrival, and he wanted to make sure that she reached the city. She smiled at Midnight, knowing that Torin would not view her arrival with an army as a threat to him. He did not think that a woman was capable of being a threat.

They made their way across the land, and were joined by others, who knew the true nature of this army. They all wanted the fighting to end, and unlike Torin, they believed that this young woman could do that.

Her arrival in the city was heralded by rose petals and cheering. People lined the streets hoping to get a glimpse of this woman who had made such a stir in the land. Her army marched right into the city, and they looked at each other, as they made their way through the streets.

Blackbird could only shake her head. It was almost overwhelming to be around so many people, but she managed to keep her thoughts ordered, and focused on the task at hand. She did wonder if the people would cheer if they knew the real reason she was here. She gazed at the grand palace, where Torin would greet her, and he would gaze for the first time upon her.

As she entered the plaza in front of the palace, she could see him. He was watching with eagerness. He was already planning the wedding, and how to make her his. Midnight leaned close to her and whispered.

"Are you sure about this plan? The others are all watching, and they know that you are here to dethrone him. Challenging him now might not be the best thing to do." She looked over at him and responded just as quietly.

"The plan has been made not just by me, but all those who are here. I will not back down from this, as it is the only way to end the fighting. You know that, so just trust me, ok." Midnight nodded and dismounted. He helped her down, his hand lingering on hers.

Blackbird gripped her staff, and she gazed at Midnight. He stepped back and nodded at the people with her. The dwarves, humans, and elves all moved to form a semi-circle around Blackbird and Torin. He frowned at this movement, but he looked at the woman.

Her black eyes gazed at him, a touch of melancholy in them.

Her long black hair flowed around her, as she stood there holding onto her staff. She looked at him, her heart shaped face smooth and unreadable. She was firm and balanced on her feet and she was ready for the challenge.

"What is this, my Lady? Are you going to challenge me? You are but a child, and a woman, so how do you hope to defeat me?" Torin inquired. Her dark eyes gazed at him, and she responded.

"Appearances can be deceiving. I am here to end the war that you have started, and make sure that peace comes to this world. You have enchanted the elves against their will and nature, and you are killing them. The elven numbers have dropped since this war began and they do not have enough children to replenish their race.

You have waged war on the innocent and have torn this world apart. Hate grows every day for you, and you have disrupted the balance. I am here to stop you, and I will. For I know what you fear the most and I am not afraid to do what must be done."

Torin gazed at her, wondering how she could know anything about him. He was afraid of something, but she could not possibly know what it was. He was afraid of losing his power, of losing his magic. He stood forward and faced her and spoke firmly.

"You will regret challenging me, girl."

Blackbird placed her staff in the ground and drew a circle around herself. Torin did the same. As they stood there, Torin made the first move. He sent a fireball at her which hit the circle and was deflected. She just stood there, taunting him by not moving, just smiling.

He growled and threw lightening at her, and again it was deflected. Blackbird watched him, and then raised her hand. He poured more strength into his shield, preparing for a fireball or something similar. But her attack was not physical. Blackbird attacked his mind. He flinched as her mind wrapped around his. He held his ground, gritting his teeth, pushing back against her mind, but she was stronger.

His greatest fear was losing his magic, for without it he felt that he was nothing. Blackbird pushed against his mental barriers, and then she found a weakness in his mind, and pushed into it. His body trembled as she forced her way into his mind, and found his connection to the magic, and blocked him.

"NO!!" Torin screamed, as his magic slipped away. He fell to his knees clutching at his head. He could feel the magic flowing around him, but he could not touch it. His head came up and focused on the girl in front of him. He rose to his feet and grabbed his sword and lunged at her.

But her barrier was still up, and as his sword struck it, a force was unleashed, and everyone was knocked flat. They could not see or hear or even smell anything. Finally, everything cleared up, and everyone looked around.

All the windows in the city were shattered. All the people were panicking, as they did not know what had just happened. Screams rent the air, and the smell of fires began to fill the air. Smoke began to choke those who were in city.

Blackbird was unconscious. Midnight, his ears ringing, scrambled over to her, and knelt next to her. He tried to shake her, but she would not wake up. He looked around, and could see others were beginning to get up, staggering to their feet.

He knew that they could not stay here. The buildings were cracked, and there was glass everywhere. As people began to recover, they too knew that they could not stay here. Midnight gathered Blackbird into his arms and made his way to the streets, knowing that it was dangerous to go out there, but also dangerous to stay put.

Some of the others spotted him and began to follow. Borthin staggered in his direction, and Midnight was glad he was still alive. They moved carefully through the streets, which were filled with panicking people. He had to step aside into alleys frequently, to avoid be trampled to death.

Suddenly, Midnight heard a noise, and he looked up. One of

the buildings was falling over. People pushed others out of the way as the stone tower began to fall into the street below. The sound was deafening as the stones hit the other buildings and came crashing down.

Midnight stared at it for a moment. Then he looked down at Blackbird. He would not let her get trapped here, so he began to climb over the rubble. Borthin followed him and stayed close. The noise of falling stones was echoed in other parts of the city, as the towers fell over.

Dust joined the smoke, which grew thicker, and Midnight choked on it. Above the city, two birds wheeled, and Midnight heard them. They called to him and guided him and Borthin out of the dust and smoke-filled city.

When they finally reached the land beyond the city, Midnight looked back, and stared at the city. It was burning and collapsing all at the same time. Huge dust clouds rose from the towers as they fell over, and smoke from the burning buildings rose in spirals over the broken city.

"What happened?" Borthin asked, staring at the city. People who broke free also stopped to watch the city burn and fall apart. Wind picked up, blowing the smoke and dust higher into the air. Midnight looked at it and held Blackbird closer to him.

"Blackbird cut Torin off from his magic, and in rage he attacked Blackbird, but her barrier took the blow. His sword was enchanted, and as it contacted her barrier, it exploded, and the backlash swept through the city. All the energy from her barrier and his sword was released all at once. That was what caused all this damage."

Goldie, in her human form came up. She was followed by elves and dwarves who had managed to get out of the city. They gathered around Blackbird, and Midnight. The two birds landed, and took on their human forms, as they moved closer to Blackbird.

She was beginning to stir, and slowly opened her eyes. She did not have any strength and was glad that Midnight was holding her. She turned her head and gazed at the city. Her eyes were sad, as she saw all the destruction of city, brought about by Torin and herself.

Without Torin, she knew that the fighting would stop. But first people needed to know that Torin was dead. Blackbird did not have the strength to send a magical message to let people know that the war was over. But Torin's spells that he had woven around the elven leaders was gone. Without him to keep the spells going, they simply ended.

Through this means, they realized that Torin had been killed, and that they were free. All around the empire that Torin had built, the fighting was ending. All the elves looked in the direction of Newtonia and raised their voices in joy that they were free. The dwarves cheered, and the humans threw down their weapons.

But near the city, there was no rejoicing. Many innocent people had perished within the walls. The war was over, and now the rebuilding would begin. But they would mourn those who died in the city, as the pride of Torin had been brought low. Borthin moved among the survivors, comforting them as best he could. Blackbird was placed underneath a canvas on some blankets that were found.

It would some time before she regained her strength. The fight itself had taken a lot out of her, and having her barrier broken in that manner, was draining. She would need time to recover. In the meantime, the survivors worked to help those who needed help.

Midnight stayed close to her, as she rested. Borthin took charge of the people, and he made sure that shelters were built for everyone. As he gazed at the city, he knew that no one would ever go there again, and cleaning up and repairing the city would be impossible.

As he thought about it, he had a dream, of a city that could be built from the stones of Newtonia. It was a new city, filled with people of every race, beautiful fountains, and gardens. Wide streets and new buildings sparkled in the sunlight.

Instead of repairing the old city, he would use its stones to build a new one.

After he had the dream, he went to talk with Blackbird, and the leaders of the elves and dwarves, about the city he had envisioned. The dwarves were experts on stone building, and the elves knew how to build gardens. So, as Blackbird rested, work began on the new city.

Blackbird knew that Borthin was going to be good king. He did not overwork anyone and made sure that everyone had their needs taken care of. The survivors needed something to do, to take their minds off their sorrows, and the elves were glad to find a way to make up for some of things that had happened during the war.

Blackbird watched, as the foundations of the new city were being laid. She could stand now, though not for very long. She was getting better, slowly. Some of the people, elves, and dwarves along with humans, had all decided that they would serve her. She did not know how to take this, as she had never intended to be a leader, but she could not deny them either.

She thought about the monastery and wondered if she could find a way to make the Ultimate Library appear there. It would be nice to be able to go home after all this time. But she knew that the library would appear where it was supposed to be, not where she wanted it to.

CHAPTER SIXTEEN

As the city began to rise, one day, as Borthin went to visit her, he found her gone, along with all those who wanted to follow her. They had left, as the time had come for Borthin to trust himself, and not rely on her so much. She would always be found when she was needed, and Borthin knew that he had not seen the last of that remarkable young woman.

They made their way towards the mountains, moving slowly, knowing that what they were looking for would only be found when they were ready. Blackbird was drawn to the mountains, and she taught the people who had chosen to come with her about her religion, and they all wanted to follow it. She knew that it would take time to get used to having these people with her, but she was glad that she could help them find something to believe in.

Finally, after many days of travel, they found themselves winding through a pass, narrow and straight. They made their way through it and found themselves looking down on a valley.

Blackbird gazed down into the valley, and she could see the Ultimate Library rising through the trees. Walls surrounded it, as it was a sacred place, and not just anyone could enter it. For here rested all the knowledge of the Universe. There were those with dark dispositions who would try to use the knowledge here for their own ends if they could enter.

The group was weary, as they made their way down to the valley floor, and through the trees. The smell of pine sap filled the air, and birds could be heard singing in the trees. A brook bubbled merrily through the forest, and the smells of summer were everywhere.

Blackbird led the way, as she moved through the trees. She was eager to get to the library and find rest there. The forest gave way to clear ground, and the walls loomed overhead. She led the way around the walls, to the gate, and here she stopped.

There was no sound, now, not even their breathing could be heard. Blackbird reached up and knocked on the door. The sound echoed through the air, and everyone trembled. Then a sound of creaking was heard, and door opened, revealing an incredibly old man, who gazed out at them, and his rheumy eyes found Blackbird.

"So, you have come at last, Guardian of Magic, to claim the library as your home. Well, it took you long enough. But your companions should know that if they enter here, they will not be allowed to leave. Only you and a select chosen few can come go as you please. For the knowledge that is contained here in this building would be tempting to use for the benefit of personal advancement. Only certain people can enter here and leave. All others will not be able to leave.

Blackbird looked at the people with her and studied each of them. All of them were willing to do this, but she still asked if they wanted to do this. They all agreed to the terms and conditions, and the old man nodded, and opened the door.

They all walked in and gazed around. It was like a monastery. An orchard and some fields were prepared, along with herb gardens, and everything that was needed for life to exist here. Even berry patches and grape vines. There were even a few wells. Blackbird smiled as she looked around, and listened to sounds of birds, and insects, and running water.

The building itself was massive. It needed to be, to house all the knowledge of the universe. There were bedrooms, and even suites for families. There were kitchens and dining halls, and everything that was needed. Bathing rooms with large tubs and soap. All their needs were taken care of here.

And so, Blackbird became the Guardian of Magic, and keeper of the library, and she would leave it when she was needed.

Otherwise, she would stay here, and take care of the books that recorded all the knowledge was known.

Midnight gazed at her, and then asked her if she would marry him, and she smiled and said yes. He took her hand, and she called out to Rose and Quicksilver about her and Midnight, and they rejoiced with her. She and Midnight were joined together on the grounds of the Ultimate Library, and they began their lives as husband and wife, bound for all time.

BOOK FOUR

chapter one

Elizabeth

The city was falling. The sounds of crashing stones and screams filled the air. The smell of dust and blood was everywhere. Then the people looked up, as a shadow filled the sky. An earth elemental rose and swung his fist into the buildings, knocking more of them down onto the people.

In the harbor a few ships could be seen. They were far out from the shore, and all the people upon them gazed at the falling city. These people had listened to the king's brother, who held a book against his chest as he watched the city crumbling into the ground. The city was doomed, because the king had not listened to his brother, Cormorai, and had unleashed the elementals upon the city, because the people had rebelled against him.

These three ships held now all that would remain of Atlantis. They pushed their vessels with magic, leaving behind their homes and families who had not listened to Cormorai. A few books, and weapons along with food and clothing were all that was left.

Cormorai gazed at the city, as it fell into the sea, the land upon which it was built crumbling underneath the sea, and he bowed his head. He had warned his brother not to do it, not to unleash the elementals, but the king had not listened, and had tried to kill Cormorai.

As Cormorai stood there on the ship, he spoke softly, a

prophesy coming into his mind.

"From that which is barren will the child come. Earth daughter, the elements will be hers to command.

Wolf Born, the animals will come to her call. She will lead her people, and all who stand against her will fall."

He shook himself then and turned away from the city that was no more. The three ships turned to the sea and left behind all that they had known to search of a new home and find a way to survive. The sea could be dangerous, and they knew that all the known lands would not welcome them. So, they made their way to a land that was not known, where no one would find them, and where they could begin anew.

They found a land several months after they began their journey. The ships were destroyed, in a storm, and they floundered onto the land, and they made their way along the coast. They did not hurry, as they knew that they would have time to find what they were looking for in a home. But with the destruction of the city of Atlantis, their magic had waned, and their life spans were shortened. They were no longer as long lived as they had been, and their children no longer had magic.

Atlantis had been built on what was called a Well of Magic. As long as the city had stood, the people had been connected to the Well and had enjoyed long life and powerful magics. But with the city gone, the Well was plugged, and they were no longer connected to it, so they began to age, and change into mortals.

As the people made their way down the coast, they were bent on survival. So, they did not teach their children how to read the language of the ancients. They passed down knowledge through stories, and they kept their advanced way of fighting, but much of the knowledge was lost, and no one could read the books anymore. Though they kept these books, no one could read them.

A few centuries had now passed, as the remnant of the people of Atlantis made their way down the coast, they found a child, near death, whose skin was paler than theirs, and whose hair was lighter. They did not know where this child had come from, but they took him in, and saved him. They did not know that this child was king Arthur's son, sent into exile to save him from the enemies of his father.

They did not know any of this, as they took in the child, and made him one of them. They did not understand that through this child the one of their prophesies spoke of would be born, and she would be someone that would shape the world.

CHAPTER TWO

Merlin knelt next to his fallen king. King Arthur lay upon the battlefield, bloodied and beaten. Merlin closed his eyes and thought about how this had happened. He knew that he would be the one to tell Queen Guinevere, and she would not take this well.

Ever since Arthur had sent her son into exile, Guinevere had taken refuge in a nunnery. She had never forgiven Arthur, and though she loved him, she had not wanted to stay with him. Before this battle, Arthur had gone to her, and asked for her forgiveness. She had not given it to him, and so, Arthur had gone into battle without her favor, and this had led to his death,

Merlin was the son of a high fairy, and a human. Usually, children of this kind of union went insane, as the human half could not manage the power of the High Fairy blood, but Merlin was special. He had been bound to the isles of Avalon, and through that connection, he had managed to survive the madness and become who he was now.

The sounds of battle had ended, and now there was only the moaning of the injured. A frigid wind seemed to fill the air with the coldness of the grave, as it wound through the fallen soldiers and knights. All of King Arthur's knights had fallen upon the field, defending their king. There would never be such a group again. Twelve knights of the Round Table, and all of them had fallen defending the one they all loved.

Merlin closed his eyes, as tears fell. He had served his king all the years of his reign, and now he did not know what to do. Then a sound reached his ears, the sound of walking feet, crunching on the ground of the battlefield. Merlin, anger rising in him, gripped his staff and stood up, determined to do what he needed to protect his fallen king.

But as he turned, he found himself facing a young woman whom he had met before. Her sapphire eyes glazed around her sadly, even though she held a burning sword in her hands. She had fought in the battle, as was evidenced by the blood on her armor. She raised her head and gazed at Merlin; her lips parted slightly.

"I had hoped to find him before his death. I had some news that would have brought him comfort. I came to tell him that his son lives and has been taken in by the descendants of the Atlantis survivors. Arthur's bloodline will survive.

Now, a decision must be made. The bloodline of Arthur will be joined with the royal bloodline of Atlantis and through that union a child will be born. This child will be special in many ways, and she will go through many trials. Her destiny will be to claim the throne of Avalon, and if she chooses to, she can join me and my two sisters as a guardian of the universe.

But she will need a name, and I leave that to you. What will you call a child of Atlantis and of Avalon? And I also wish to join her with my son, who will be born sometime before her. He is already in me. An arranged marriage between my son and heir, and the house of Pendragon, with the child of Arthur's. but she still needs a name."

Merlin gazed at Arthur, and knew what he would name a girl child, and so, Merlin looked up at Rose, and his response was firm.

"She will be called Guinevere, after the Queen." Rose nodded. It was a good name. Merlin studied Rose as she looked around the battlefield. She sighed, and then looked back at Merlin.

"Camelot will be placed on the main island of Avalon, and Arthur and his knights will be buried there. Guinevere will also be buried there when she dies. And all the tribes of Avalon will be told of the child, who will come when she is ready. The heir of Arthur will come to the isles of Avalon, and she will claim her throne, when she is ready to do so."

Merlin nodded, and then looked up, as some centaurs appeared. They came to the place where the knights of the Round Table had fallen, and they bore them all away. Even Arthur was taken, so he could be placed with honor on the isles of Avalon, where all the non-human races lived, so that the humans would not slay them.

For this was Arthur's true legacy. He had believed that all the non-human races were equal to the humans, that they were important to the earth, and so he had, with help from Merlin, made a pact with the guardians of Avalon. He brought the non-human races to the isles, to protect them from the persecution of the humans, and they protected the isles from intrusion by the humans. No human could enter the isles, except a few of those who took care of the Rocs, those massive birds of legend.

The four islands of Avalon each had some races upon them. There was minotaur along the coast, centaur in the forests, griffons, and hippogriffs, harpies, and dragons, along with fauns and satyrs, and nymphs. There were elves, and leprechauns, fairies, and giants. There were even dwarves and trolls, goblins, and other kinds of creatures, all from the myths and legends of the humans.

All were equal in the eyes of Arthur, whom they named their king. Though they had not fought with him, in this last battle, they had not done so because of his human subjects. The knights agreed with Arthur, but the common soldiers would not fight alongside monsters.

So, Arthur had gone into battle with inferior numbers, knowing that he would die for his people, and hoping that he had made a difference. He now lay in state on the main island of Avalon, a large stone placed upon his grave. Arranged in a circle around him were his loyal knights. Each with a stone of their own. Their names were carved upon the stones, and the symbol of the Round Table underneath.

The castle of Camelot moved in the night and disappeared

from the human lands. It rose now through the mists of Avalon, its towers reflecting the moonlight. Guinevere hung herself, and her body was taken to Avalon to be buried with her husband.

No one among the humans could find Arthur's grave, and along with the races he had taken to the isles, and the isles themselves faded into myth and legend. Many began to doubt their existence and believed that they were just stories told to children and no longer important.

As the centuries turned, the humans could not have guessed that the bloodline of Arthur survived in a place that they did not know existed, and would not for a long time, but the descendants of Atlantis now had a bloodline that would change the world when the child was born.

CHAPTER THREE

The man paced through the rain. The screaming of the woman could be heard even through the falling water, and the thunder that crashed through the night. She should not have been pregnant. The healers had declared her barren. His first wife had died in childbirth, and he taken this woman because she was the fairest in the tribe. His son, three years old, was in their tent with an old woman who would keep him out of the way.

Bear knew that this could be the child of destiny. The prophesy had spoken of the child coming from that which was barren. The screaming in the tent rose to a crescendo, and then the sound of a child crying in the stormy night.

Though it was forbidden for a man to enter the birthing tent, Bear did it anyway. He was the war chief of his people, and he was not one known for his patience. The women in the tent glowered at him, and he ignored them. He knelt next to the woman and asked to see the child.

It was a girl, her tiny face perfect, as she gazed up at him with solemn eyes, as golden as wolf's. He wiped some blood off her tiny wrist and studied the image there. On her skin was what looked like a tattoo of a wolf, howling at the moon. He nodded and placed the child into her mother's arms.

"When she is ready to begin her training, I will come and take her." He said in his deep voice, and with that he stood and left the tent. The woman gazed down at the tiny infant in her arms and held her close. The midwife looked at her and asked if she would name the child. The woman gazed into those golden eyes and said softly.

"Her name will be Wolfheart. For her eyes are the eyes of a wolf. And she will need all her strength to survive her father's training." The midwife looked at her companions. If Bear had his way, the child would not be allowed to be a child for long.

Bear was not a good man. Flora had accepted his hand in marriage because she had believed that no one else would. It had been declared that she was barren by the healers after her first marriage had ended with no children. They had done everything they could think of to evaluate her, and she could not have children. But she was the most beautiful woman in the tribe, and her father was the chief.

Bear was war chief. Though much had been lost to them over the centuries since their people had come to this wild land, their fighting style had not. They had ways of fighting that no one else in these lands did. They were a strong tribe, and they had prospered over the years.

All that they had now was because of Bear. He was the best fighter, and the best hunter. No one could beat him. And now that the child of the prophesy had been born to him, he would be even more arrogant. He would be puffed up in importance at the fact that he had brought the Earth Daughter into this world.

Bear was a descendant of Arthur, and Flora was a descendant of Cormorai. Through this union the child that Cormorai had prophesied would come to his people had arrived. And Bear would teach her how to fight, and how be a leader. He would not be gentle, as he believed that she would need to be stronger than even him, and he would do whatever it took to make her a perfect warrior.

Wolfheart did not leave the tent for the first year of her life. Their people were only semi-nomadic. They had certain places they would go at certain times of the year. Now was the time of year when they traveled to the canyon edge, where they would remain until she was old enough to lead them.

The river ran strong, and they set up next to it. They had been here before, and they knew the best places to set up, for protection from rival tribes and the elements. Bear did set up the tent with Flora, and she would take care of the children, including his son, as she was the woman.

Bear's son, whose name was Soaring Eagle, though most just called him Eagle, was three when Wolfheart was born, and he was spoiled by his father. He was very curious about the child he now shared the tent with, as he had not seen a baby before.

Wolfheart was exceptional. By the end of her first year, she was walking, and could talk a little. Her mind was developing faster than her body, but that was expected with the child of prophesy. She did not understand why she was different, but that difference would make her life difficult.

By the time Wolfheart was two, her father decided to begin her training. Though she was small, she could learn somethings that he could teach her, and he took her away from her mother. Throughout her life, Wolfheart would hold onto the tiny innocent child her mother had taken care of, but this child would be buried underneath layers of anger and discipline.

Bear took the child and began to train her, and he was not gentle. He demanded perfection, and if she could not achieve that with the first try, she was punished. She learned the hard way not to disappoint him. She did not understand why he did the things he did, but she learned not to show weakness.

Every morning she was to run to the river, and spend twenty minutes standing in it, resisting the currents. She was to walk until only her head was out of the water, and not get pushed by the water. One day, she did not do this, and thought her father was not watching. But he asked her if she had stood in the water, and she told him she had.

Bear had watched her, as he always did, and was furious that she had lied to him. As punishment, she was to lay on a bed of hot coals for three days. Because of this, the girl never lied again. Pain was an effective way to stop a bad habit. For the rest of her life, she could not lie without pain shooting through her.

Once, when she was five, Bear took her to the base of the

cliff in the canyon and told her to climb it. It was close to five hundred feet high. Wolfheart was afraid to climb the cliff, as she did not like heights. When she told her father this, he grabbed her, tied her to a tree, and grabbed a slender branch. He pulled off her shirt, and whipped her, repeatedly, and spoke these words repeatedly as he did.

"A true warrior is never afraid. A true warrior never backs down. A true warrior does what others cannot. A true warrior does not feel pain." Every inch of skin was whipped from her back. Bleeding, and in pain, but not showing it, the girl climbed the cliff, her hands and feet getting cut on the sharp rocks. When she reached the bottom of the cliff, Bear told her to go to the tent, so she could get cleaned up.

She did not limp, though her feet were bleeding. Her back stiff, the small child walked back to the encampment, and went to her mother. Wolfheart did not cry, as she lay on the furs, and her mother placed a cool hide on the wounds. Never had this happened, and the person does not bleed to death. But Wolfheart did not die, she merely rested, and listened.

This would the first and only time that someone stood up to Bear. Flora looked over at him as he entered the tent and gazed at the child. Wolfheart did not look at him, her eyes focused on the hide in front of her, and Flora demanded to know what he thought he was doing. Bear looked over at her and frowned.

"I am teaching her to be strong. If she is to lead our people, she must be strong, and be a true warrior." Flora shook her head and responded.

"You will kill her if you keep this up. She is just a child, and she is going to die if you do not let her recover from this. She will need weeks to recover..." Flora did not get to finish, as Bear raised his fist and hit her. He beat her severely, but not fatally and then knelt, and looked at her.

"Never question what I do again, woman, or I will kill you. She has one day of rest, and then she will continue her training. She is the child of prophesy, and I will make sure that she is unstoppable. No one will be able to stand in her way when I am done."

Flora crawled over to her child, and even with her own injuries, she tended her daughter. She placed compresses of herbs onto the child's back, and she wrapped her in soft hides. Her brother stood close by and wondered why his father had done this.

Eagle was also training now, just not as intense as his sister. She would practice for hours, shooting her bow, practicing with knives, and doing things that no one else did. Bear was determined to make her the perfect warrior, and she learned to do things perfectly on the first try or suffer pain.

She no longer showed any emotions on her face. Emotions were for the weak. The only emotion her father ever showed her was anger, and she learned to hide her anger, and all her other emotions, for if they showed it meant she was weak.

Wolfheart became unbeatable. She learned to take down opponents that were bigger than she was, and she learned to hunt without making sound. She could get all the way up to the deer without startling them. She could stand still for hours, without moving until the moment was right to strike. She learned to be faster than the striking snake, and to stronger than the bear.

By the time she was ten, the only one who was better than her, was her father, and he was the only one of which she was afraid. At ten, she was slender but strong, and her father believed she was ready to go hunting without him, but her brother asked to go with her.

So, they packed their gear, and made ready. Neither of them knew that today would change everything. As they made their way into the forest, their father went in a different direction with many of the other hunters. They did not know that a rival tribe was nearby, watching.

CHAPTER FOUR

Wolfheart and Eagle made their way north, along the cliffs of the canyon, their father made his way south, along the river. They had made it about an hour from camp when they felt something. All the noise of the forest was gone. On instinct they looked up, to see if there was a storm coming. That was when they saw the smoke, thick and black, coming from the direction of the camp of their people.

The two young ones looked at each other, and then dropped their gear, everything except their weapons and made their way back to their people. On the way, Eagle injured his foot, twisting it on the rocks. Wolfheart, though smaller than he was, helped him along as they made their way back.

When they reached the camp, they both stopped. Nearly all the tents were on fire, and the bodies of their people lay scattered on the ground. It was obvious that they had put up a fight, as there were several bodies of their enemies, but the people had been caught off guard, and most of the hunters, the fighters, were with Bear, hunting along the river.

Wolfheart looked around, at the devastation, and found that she could not cry. The last time she had cried had been when she was five, when her father had whipped every inch of skin from her back. She helped her brother toward their tent and found their mother.

She had been raped repeatably, and then her throat had been cut. Her glassy eyes stared unseeingly at the blue sky. Flora had died in pain, and torment, her face still twisted in fear. But still Wolfheart could not cry. No tears came, as she knelt next to her mother's body.

She heard a noise behind her, and turned, just as an enemy warrior came into view, his stone knife raised. Eagle leapt up and the knife meant for Wolfheart entered his chest. A scream of rage was torn from her lips, as she watched her brother fall, but the man turned towards her, and found her knifes burying themselves in his chest, piercing his heart.

She turned to her brother, who was gasping as his lifeblood spilled over his hands. She knelt and gazed at him, and he looked up at her.

"I wish I could have gone hunting with you." Were the last words from him that she would ever hear. His eyes closed, and he died in her arms. She held him for a long moment, ignoring the blood now covering her. Then she looked around and wondered if anyone had survived. She knew that her father and the other hunters had gone south, but she did not know if she wanted to find them.

She wondered briefly about the enemy warrior who had killed her brother and believed that he was just one who had stayed behind to loot the bodies of the dead. She would track this tribe of murderers and kill them all for taking her people from her.

As she knelt there, covered in her brother's blood, the young girl threw back her head and screamed into the sky. She was alone, as she knelt there, and she knew that the traditions of her people needed to be upheld. That meant that she had to burn the bodies of her people, so that their souls would be able to join their ancestors.

So, she placed her brother gently on the ground, and began to gather all the bodies of her people. It took a while, as they were numerous, but she managed to drag them all into the cave near the village, and there she burned them.

She watched for a moment, and then turned her attention to the fallen enemy warriors. These she would throw into the river, to trap their souls and stop them from reaching the ancient ones. She threw many bodies into the river, as her people had fought back.

Her work done, she gathered some supplies and set off after the hunters and her father. They would be able to hunt down any who had survived the attack on the village and kill them for what they had done. It took her most of the day to find the hunters.

They had been ambushed and killed. They lay as they had fallen, trying to fight back, but even the greatest warrior can be killed by a well-aimed arrow. She stood over her father's still form and felt nothing. She was neither glad nor sad that he was dead. She had no emotions for him, not even relief that he could no longer torment her. There was simply nothing.

She gathered the fallen hunters, and as she had in the village, she burned their bodies. Wolfheart watched the flames claim her father, and knew that she was alone, truly alone. She was the last of her tribe, and now all that was left for her was to avenge her people.

The young girl, only ten, began to track the ones who had ambushed the hunters. She found traces of them in the forest and followed them. they had not made any attempt to hide their trail. They did not think that anyone would follow them, as they thought the tribe was wiped out. They did not know that they were followed by a young girl, who wanted to kill them.

It was sunset now, and she would have to wait until day to continue her hunt. She found a hollow tree and climbed inside of it. All around her the sounds of the night filled the air. She could smell the smoke from her people's burning bodies, and the scent of burning flesh lingered in her nose. She did not sleep so much as rest, until the first light of dawn broke the sky.

She ate some meat from her supplies and began to follow the trail once more. She did not stop, as she followed the trail of the murderers. She walked and walked, seemingly unaware of the blood on her feet. What was pain to her? She did not stop all that day, and finally at sunset she came upon the warriors who had survived and listened for only a moment to their bragging about what they had done. She gripped the metal knives she had taken from her father. They were of Atlantean design and had never rusted or shown any sign of age. There were four in all, and she held two in her hands as she charged forward.

Blinded by rage and a grief she could not express, Wolfheart was unstoppable. They fought back against this child, but she was beyond them. Her golden eyes were filled with fire, and she moved like the wind. They could not catch her, and her knives sang their death song.

There had been twelve of them, fully grown men, and they all died at the hands of a ten-year-old girl. She stood in the center of their encampment covered in their blood and screamed into the darkening night. It began to rain, as if the earth cried for her, as she could not.

Throughout the rest of her life, she would never forget that night, when she had avenged the deaths of her people, and trembling with rage, she ran into the forest. She went deeper into the forest than most ever had, for this forest was filled with dark things, things you could not see until the moment they had you in their grasp.

This forest she entered was a realm where evil things had been confined separated form the realms of the humans. The separation between this forest and the human realms were thin here and because she was magical she was able to enter here. She would live in this realm of darkness for many years. For this was the year 1492, when the white man would find the lands of her people and begin a time of change.

CHAPTER FIVE

Very few people went deep into the forest of Shadows. Unseen creatures lurked there, waiting to kill the unwary. No one who knew what the creatures looked like or could tell anyone what they had seen. Only the dead could tell. And the dead did not speak.

But into the forest she went, cleansed by the rain, and holding knives in her hands. She could survive even here for she would learn the ways of the forest of Shadows, and she would live where no one else could. She was not afraid of anything, not even death. Her father was gone, and he was the only thing she had truly feared.

Into the forest, the Earth daughter went, to live and survive in a place no one else could. She would become a creature of the forest, living by instinct, and learning about the dangers, for in this forest even the plants were dangerous.

She lost much of her humanity, becoming like an animal, living on instinct alone. She hunted and ate and rested in the forest. She learned that the scent of blood attracted the shadow walkers, and she would wash herself after every meal. She learned that some berries were good to eat, and others made you sick.

She learned not to sleep, for if you slept you were vulnerable to the creatures of the darkness. She would rest, in meditation, and so be aware of what was happening around her. She always kept her knives nearby. She never let her guard down, as that would lead to death.

Sometimes she would go days without eating and she learned to be wary of the water, for there were creatures in the water that would grab you if you let them. She was always on the alert. Her long hair, black as night, grew tangled and wild, and her eyes gleamed in the dark, a fire burning in them that would not go out.

She moved unpredictably. She never stayed long in one place. She always made sure that she was alone when she left the thickets and moved into the clearings. She did not trust anything, for trust was a good way to get killed.

How long she was alone in the forest she did not know. The days blurred into nights, and she did not keep track of time. For time was not important, only survival was. She did not care how long she had been here, only that she still lived. Then one day something happened that would change the course of her life.

The sunlight sparkled on the pool. She was washing off the blood of her latest kill when she suddenly stiffened. She could feel someone watching her. It was strange though, as she felt no threat coming from the watcher.

Slowly the girl turned and saw someone on the edge of the clearing. The woman watching her was beautiful, with chestnut hair and sapphire eyes. Her full lips were upturned at the corners, and she cocked her head at the girl kneeling by the water.

Rose studied the girl and could see curiosity in those burning eyes. But as Rose stepped closer to her, the girl took off into the forest. Rose sighed and stood there for a moment and knew that she could find the girl anytime now, and she would earn the girl's trust.

The girl did not think like a human anymore. She was fully an animal. But Rose knew that the human part of her was just buried beneath all the layers of survival instincts. Wolfheart was still there, just buried. And Rose would help her find herself again.

The next day, the girl found the woman again, as Rose was talking aloud. It had been a long time since she had heard a human voice. She crouched down in some bushes, fully hidden, and peered out into the clearing. It was the woman she had seen the day before. She was sitting on a stump, and just talking to herself.

It was dangerous to do this. The forest was full of creatures that would be attracted to the sound, but for some reason, no beasts came. But it was as if no one could hear the woman except her. The woman did not move as the girl crept a little closer. The woman smiled slightly but sat quite still. She continued to talk, telling the girl that her name was Rose, and she was a friend, and other things.

A sudden sound on the edge of the clearing though sent Wolfheart back into the trees. Rose sighed and stood up. She seemed to twist slightly and vanished. The shadow-walker growled in frustration that its prey had heard it and slunk off to look for more.

Wolfheart stayed in the bushes, not even breathing, until the shadow-walker was gone. She wondered about this woman called Rose, and who she was and why she was in the forest. Wolfheart had not heard a human like voice in so long, it was like rain on a parched land.

Slowly, as Rose came every day, Wolfheart would stay a little longer every time. Rose began to walk when she visited with the girl, and the girl began to follow. Wolfheart would not be able to find her way out of the forest on her own.

So, every day for an entire year, Rose led Wolfheart farther and farther through the forest, until they finally reached the end. They walked slowly, as Rose was in no hurry. Rose also talked about the Ultimate Mother, and taught Wolfheart about the others, Quicksilver and Blackbird. And as they traveled, the Shadow Forest was left behind, and Wolfheart found herself at the edge of an ordinary forest, filled with trees that had no menace.

Rose had led the girl through the barrier that kept the dark things out of the human realm. Hers in this forest in the Americas, the girl had found her way to the edge of the white mans territory near the sea that is known as Florida. Here she would find the first people other than Rose and her brother

RACHEL HARWOOD

that would show her kindness.

CHAPTER SEVEN

The forest had changed here, not so wild, and dangerous. Here birds were singing, and squirrels moved through the trees. Wolfheart sat on a tree stump and listened to the sounds around her. This place was far different from the deep woods, for here there was a sense of peace and security. There were no dangerous creatures here, no threats. So, the girl was content to just sit and listen to the sounds of life.

Suddenly, a crash sounded through the trees. Wolfheart looked up, as the animals scattered. She frowned and made her way towards the sound. Another crash came, and she peered around a tree to see a man cutting a tree down.

The man was different from her people, in that his hair was lighter, and his skin was paler. He chopped at a tree, and it soon came down. Then he tied the tree to a four-legged animal she had never seen before, and he hauled the tree away.

Curious about this man and what he was doing, she followed him. He was not aware of her, as she knew how to walk without a sound. He soon came to a place that he had already cleared of trees, and a woman was washing her clothes in the stream that ran by their home.

A short way from the stream, the man placed the log on a wooden contraption, and began to strip the bark from it. A pile of logs already prepared lay next to the foundation of a log cabin. Wolfheart had never seen people like this, and she wondered who they were and where they were from.

The man worked hard to strip the tree and prepare it for it place on the cabin. He had the walls waist high already and wanted to have the cabin ready before the winter. He already had a place for the animals, a corral for them and a shelter.

The girl listened to the sounds of the animals as they lowed and neighed in the corral. She had never seen animals like this and wondered what they were called. The people had two more of the animals he had used for moving the tree, and a two more that she did not know what they were for.

The cows chewed the tender young grass, and lowed. They had already been milked, and now they just ate. They had a trough for water, and it was full, as they were not thirsty right now. The horses drank deeply, and ate some grass, waiting for their turn to taken out of the corral for work.

Wolfheart watched the man and woman, hidden by the trees and bushes. She could hear them talking, but she did not understand what they were saying. They were both young, with no gray in their hair, and no wrinkles. They were dressed in clothes she did not recognize and wondered what type of animal would have that kind of hide.

The man, whose name was Tayler, was a young farmer in the new world. He had come to this place with his wife, Elizabeth, and they were going to make a home for themselves away from all the bustle of the big cities. Tayler had grown up in a rich home, but he wanted to make a living for himself by the sweat of his brow. Elizabeth had wanted to be with him, and she had followed him down to the south, where they had bought some land and animals, and now were learning how to care for them.

Neither of these two knew much about farming or anything like that, but they were learning. There was a village nearby, where they would go for help, and to sell a few things now and then or buy something. Sometimes some of the villagers would come out and help them on their house.

Today though, they were alone, or so they thought, as they did not know that Wolfheart was watching them. She was like a shadow, just standing still, watching and learning. She listened to their voices and by watching and listening to them she began to learn about them and their language.

For several days, Wolfheart watched them. She did not approach them, just stayed hidden and watched and listened. Then, one day, as Taylor came into the woods to get some more trees, he spotted her, standing next to a tree, and watching him.

She was not wearing clothes, as she had not needed too for a long time, but her thick and tangled hair fell around her. She was a native, he could tell by her coloring. But she was alone and had obviously been that way for a while. He could tell she was very thin, as if she had not eaten in a while, and she was wary of him, as she stood there.

He did not make any sudden movements, as he studied her. Instead, very slowly he reached into the basket Elizabeth had given him and pulled out some bread. The girl watched him, her body tense, as he moved. He reached out and placed the bread on stone, and then stepped back. Her strange golden eyes studied him for a moment, before she slipped forward, and took the bread.

She gazed at it, uncertainly, as if she did not know what to do with it. She looked at him, and he took some more bread out of the basket, and took a bite. She studied him and then took a bite out of her bread. It was soft and good. She had never tasted bread before and decided that she like it.

Taylor smiled and began to cut down a tree. The girl sat down and watched him. She was quite beautiful for a twelve-year-old girl, though she did not smile. She was much older than twelve, she just looked that old. She watched Taylor, until he hitched the trees to the horse and went back to his homestead. She followed him.

Elizabeth was startled when her husband came home, followed by the girl. She noticed the knives resting in makeshift slings on the girl's hips and around her feet. And she noticed that the girl was naked. Taylor looked at his wife, and then at the girl who was watching them both.

"She came up to me today, and I gave her some bread. I think she liked it. I do not know what to do about her not having clothes. But she is alone. I have not heard of any natives in the area, so she is probably an orphan. I know she is a little wild, but maybe we could help her out. She looks very thin."

Elizabeth nodded and gazed the girl. She just stood there watching them. She did not move, as Elizabeth came over to her, walking slowly. The girl did grow tense, as the woman approached her, but she held very still. Elizabeth looked into the golden eyes and smiled.

"Why don't we do something with your hair? I bet I can get it cleaned up and untangled. I have some soap, and a good solid brush, which should help." The girl studied her, and then reached up and touched Elizabeth's hair. It was soft and clean. Wolfheart allowed the woman to take her over to the stream, and Elizabeth began to wash her hair.

Elizabeth could feel the girl's tenseness, as if she did not want to be touched, but she also did not fight what was happening. Elizabeth had never met anyone who could sit as still as a stone, as her tangled hair was washed and then brushed. The tangles were very stubborn, and Elizabeth knew that she was hurting the girl, but the girl did not move.

Finally, after many struggles to get the tangles out of her hair, the girl was finally tangle free. Her long hair, reaching her waist, was now soft and fell about her in curls. Elizabeth studied the black hair, and then she began to braid it. This would keep the hair out of the girl's face and allow her to manage it better.

Then of course, they needed to find some clothes for her, so Elizabeth went into the tent they were using until the house was finished and brought out some dresses. All of them were too big. Taylor found some old pants of his and had the girl try them on. The pants were big but were easier to hem for her slender form. An old shirt of his completed the ensemble, and the girl seemed to like it.

As she touched the cloth, she spoke softly.

"Soft." Both Taylor and Elizabeth were startled, and then Taylor smiled, and responded.

"Yes, cotton is soft, and it is good for clothes. Wool makes warm clothes, and cotton makes soft clothes." The girl cocked her head and asked.

"What is cotton?" Taylor smiled and told her that cotton was a type of plant that when it was ready to harvest, you could collect a part of it, and take that part to a weaver who would turn the cotton into cloth, and you could make clothes from the cloth.

Wolfheart thought about this and nodded. Then she heard the cows in the corral and looked over at them. She looked back at Taylor and asked.

"What are those?" Taylor smiled and told her that they were called cows. You could milk the cows and drink the milk or make cheese and other things with it. He told her that cows were also able to provide meat, when they could not give milk anymore, and you could tan their hides and make leather for saddles and boots.

It was now late, the sun getting low in the sky, and Elizabeth began to cook dinner. Wolfheart watched her for a moment, and then asked what she was doing. Elizabeth smiled and told her that she was cooking. The girl had not eaten cooked food for a long time, as fire could attract dangerous creatures.

At least in the deep woods it would have, but here there were no dangerous creatures, and the fire was warm and bright. The girl looked up at the sky, watching it change colors as the sun got ready to set. When the food was done, Elizabeth put some a plate, and handed it to the girl.

Wolfheart did not have manners, as she ate as fast as she could. Eating slow could get you killed. After she was done, though, she went to the stream and washed the plate, and herself. Wolfheart did not follow them into the tent, as she like to see what her was around, so nothing could sneak up on her.

The next day, she was still there when they got up. She was standing by the fire, which she had kept going through the night. She was standing very still and did not move as they emerged. Her golden eyes watched them, as they came over,

RACHEL HARWOOD

and Elizabeth began to cook breakfast.

CHAPTER EIGHT

All through the day, the girl watched them, and would ask questions about things. Taylor and his wife were very patient and answered her as best they could. She was very curious and seemed to want to know everything.

For a few days, she watched them, and learned more about them, and their culture. Then, Taylor needed to go into town to get some things, and Elizabeth would go with him. The girl climbed into the wagon and sat perfectly still. Taylor looked over at his wife, and simply smiled.

Down the road they made their way, the horses pulling the wagon, which creaked. Every so often the horse would snort, and huff. The birds filled the air with their songs, and some insects could be heard chirping in the bushes.

After about an hour, they came to the town. Wolfheart had never seen houses like these, or so many people. She did not know if she liked it here, but she did not say anything. She had no interest in any trouble, she just wanted to watch and learn. They pulled up in front of the general store, and the girl followed them inside.

Some of the people had had trouble with natives, and they frowned at her, dressed like a man. She ignored them. She did not care if they liked her or not, but their animosity did make her tense. She placed a hand on the hilt of one of her daggers and stayed close to Elizabeth.

Finally, one of men came forward, as Elizabeth began to make her way over to the counter to pay. She looked over at the men and knew that there might be trouble. Taylor had gone to the blacksmith to get some things, so he was not here to help.

The girl watched the man, as he came over, and he looked at her, and said very slowly.

"We don't want your kind here, go back to where you belong." Elizabeth frowned at him, and looked over at the girl, who studied him. Her golden eyes were filled with fire, as she gazed at him without fear.

"Your breath smells like you eat rotten food." She told him. Her nose wrinkled, and she continued. "You should also take a bath, as you can kill a bear with your smell." Everyone stared at her. What she said was true, but no one had ever spoken to old Gus like that.

"Why, you little brat. I will teach you some manners." He lunged at her, only to nearly fall over as she moved out of his way. She did not know what a brat was, but she did not like to be touched. This kind of behavior she was more familiar with, as she had been trained by someone who had a temper. But she did not know if these people would like it if she did something like kill the man. Killing was only to be done if there was no other choice. This man was just a blowhard and a bully. He was not worth killing.

The man stumbled, and managed to catch himself before he fell over, and turned to face her. She did not move or show any emotion on her face. She gazed at him, and he could tell that the others were laughing at him. He did not like to be laughed at, and so he lunged again.

She moved in the opposite direction than he was expecting her too, and he fell into a barrel of apples. The apples fell out of the knocked over barrel, and the storekeeper called out, telling them not to hurt his produce. Wolfheart looked over at him and shrugged. She had not done anything. Gus climbed to his feet, his face as red as the apples, and he faced her squarely.

"You should be more careful, you do not want to do any more damage to anything in here." He glowered at her and turned to walk away. He stopped for a moment and looked back at her.

"This is not over, savage; you will pay for embarrassing me."

With those words he left the store. Elizabeth came over and asked her if she was all right. Wolfheart nodded. He had not touched her, so she was fine.

They hurried out of the store and caught up with Taylor, who looked over at them, and asked if they were all right, as he had heard of trouble in the store. Elizabeth told him about Gus, and what he had tried to do. He looked over at Wolfheart, who shrugged. He was glad too, that she was not hurt.

But Taylor knew that there would be trouble. Gus was a proud man, and he would not let the embarrassment of the store go for long without doing something. They hurried home, and Taylor watched the girl. She did not seem to be afraid of anything that Gus or his friends might try. In fact, she had completely put the incident out of her mind.

Over the next few days, the girl learned more about the pale strangers, and Elizabeth began to teach her how to read. They had a few books, and the girl was intelligent and caught on quickly. Taylor continued to build up the house. The house was now tall enough that he needed a ladder and some help to get the logs in place.

The girl did not understand though, why Taylor and his wife seemed to be uneasy. They both knew that Gus was capable of great mischief, and they were worried about what he might do. They did not know that the girl did not sleep.

CHAPTER NINE

Gus looked over his friends. He knew that she was just a girl, but that made the embarrassment all the worse. He would teach her to mess with him, and he would teach Taylor and his wife to take in a savage.

They did not know that the girl was sitting in a tree, watching them. She did not move, as she watched these men. She did not know what they were doing, but she felt like they meant trouble. She shifted on her feet, without a sound, and watched.

Gus lit a torch, and he moved closer to the house, and threw it. The torch did not make to the house. Wolfheart leapt out of the trees and caught it. She gazed at the fire for a moment and threw it back at the Gus. He dodged it, and it fell against a tree, one of Gus's friends kept the fire from spreading. Gus glowered at the girl and charged at her.

This would not be like the other fight. There was no one around to get hurt, and she was mad that he would try to harm Taylor and Elizabeth. She faced him and beat him. But she did not kill him. She looked down at the semi-conscious man, leaned down, and whispered.

"You should have left well enough alone." Then her golden eyes went to the men who had watched her take down Gus. She stepped away from him and studied them, seeing the fear in their eyes. No one had ever been able to take down Gus. And she looked just twelve.

The men came over and picked up Gus and took him back to their horses. They would not face her in the dark, nor would they want to. She watched them, as they left, and then she went back into the trees.

The next day, as Taylor and his wife woke up, they found the girl washing in the stream. She was washing her clothes too. She had gotten some blood on them. The smell of blood was dangerous. She would wash until there was no trace of blood anywhere.

Then, they heard a sound of horses, and looked up, as some soldiers who oversaw keeping the peace, came into view. They rode in, and looked over at the girl, who ignored them, and continued to wash her clothes.

The leader of the soldiers, whose name was Victor, dismounted, and gazed at Taylor, who frowned at him. The leader took a breath and spoke.

"We need to talk about the girl, you have taken in. She attacked Gus last night, and the healer does not know if he will live. His friends claim that she came out of nowhere, and nearly killed him. We need to take her in and question her." Taylor frowned at him and asked.

"How could she have hurt Gus? He is twice her size. Gus was the one who started the trouble yesterday in the store. She never touched him, and I doubt she could take him down."

The girl looked up and gazed at the leader. Her golden eyes burned fiercely, and she stood up and went over to him. She looked at him and spoke firmly.

"That man came here last night and tried to burn Taylor's home down. I stopped him and taught him a lesson about attacking people who did nothing to deserve it. Come over here, and I will show you." She led them over to the sight of the fire, and the torches that still lay scattered around the ground. The fire had been put out, and the torches had been used.

She pointed out shoe prints from several men, and held up a tooth, that she had knocked out of Gus's mouth. She faced the soldiers and spoke again.

"I did not touch that man in the store, for there were others who would have gotten hurt, but I will not tolerate an attack on Taylor or Elizabeth. Neither of them did anything, and I did what I could to protect them."

Victor studied the ground. He looked over at the girl, who gazed at him, without expression. Her eyes were filled with fire, and as he looked at her, he knew that she was telling the truth. He did not know what to do, now. But beating Gus as badly as she did was not ok.

Taylor looked at Victor and shook his head. Elizabeth went over to the girl and stood next to her. The soldiers looked at each other. They did not believe that the girl was capable of the kind of violence that Gus had endured, though she was obviously strong willed. She was just a girl, and a young one at that.

Victor sighed. Then he looked over at the girl and said firmly.

"You will need to come with us and tell the magistrate your side of the story. He will decide what will happen. You may have been justified in your actions, but we do have laws. I will escort you to the courthouse, and you can tell the magistrate about what happened." Her golden eyes studied him. And then she nodded.

"Just do not touch me. I will come and tell this magistrate what happened." Victor nodded, and Taylor and Elizabeth decided to come as well. Taylor got the wagon out and they all went into town. The people looked over at them and wondered why Taylor and his wife had taken in this girl, though no one believed that she could have hurt Gus as badly as she did.

They all got out in front of the courthouse, and then they went in. The magistrate looked up as they entered the room. He studied the girl, who was dressed in men clothes. Her long black hair, done in a braid, was draped over her shoulder, and he could see daggers in the belt on her waist, and sticking up from her boots.

But if she was armed with knives, why did she not use them on Gus? She did not seem like she could beat a man like Gus, as she was small and slender. There was something about her though, that seemed to set her apart from other girls of her age.

She stood forward and gazed at the magistrate and told him what had happened the night before. She repeated what she had told Victor, and Victor told him what they had found at the farm. The magistrate, Harold, listened to what they said, and leaned back.

If what she said was true, then Gus was in the wrong, but if he died, then she would be in trouble. It would be murder if he died. Gazing at this girl, though, Harold could not believe that she could beat a man as big as Gus.

She was slender, and only twelve, as far as they knew. There was no way she could beat up someone like Gus, so Harold dismissed the matter. He believed that maybe some of Gus's friends had just gotten tired of Gus and tried to blame the girl.

Gus would live, though he would never be the same. He would be quite different, because he believed that the girl would come and finish the job, if he ever tried to hurt someone again. He would never raise his voice or cause trouble again. And he stopped drinking.

As for the girl, she had dismissed the matter already. She had made sure that Taylor and Elizabeth were safe, and that was all that mattered. She did not care one way or another about Gus or his friends. They did not matter, so she did not think of them.

Rose learned of the matter, shook her head, and smiled. The man was lucky, and she did not care about him. She was concerned about Wolfheart's behavior but knew that the girl just needed some time to adjust to being around humans again. She would learn how to behave, and she would be all right.

Taylor and his wife knew that the girl needed a name, one that would be acceptable by others, but she did not seem to like any of the names they tried. Finally, Taylor asked her if she would like to be called Elizabeth, like his wife. She thought about it and decided that that was a good name.

CHAPTER TEN

They could not know that something was going to happen, and they would not live much longer. For a plague of yellow fever came through the town, and both Taylor and his wife fell ill. Taylor told the girl, now called Elizabeth, about his family up north. He told her that if he and his wife died of the fever that she should seek out his father.

Elizabeth tried her hardest to keep them alive. She tried many herbs that she knew, but to no avail. A week after falling ill, Taylor and his wife died of yellow fever. Elizabeth sighed, and packed some things in the wagon, and hitched up two horses to it, tying the other horse and the two cows to the back of the wagon.

She burned the cabin, barely finished, with the two people inside. She watched the fire for a little while, and then climbed up onto the wagon and took the wagon into town. No one wanted to buy the cows, as they were all suffering from the yellow fever plague as well. But she knew that there were other towns, and someone along the way would buy the cows.

Taylor had told her that his family lived in a city called New York. So, she would find her way there, and let his family know what had happened. Then she would go from there. She did not know what would happen to her now, but she had been raised to be a leader, and she would find a way to be one.

Two towns later, she found a buyer for the cows, and she watched as they were lead away. The spare horse she kept, as she would need him to take over for one of the others from time to time, so they would not get overly tired.

She wound her way north, looking for the city of New York,

to find Taylor's family. She passed through many small towns, and then finally she reached a city. But it was not New York. She sighed, as she asked which city this was and was told it was Boston. She pulled up in front of an inn and parked the wagon. A man came out to help her with the horses, taking them into the stable to be fed and watered. She entered the inn, and sought out the innkeeper, who looked at the young woman, and frowned.

She was a native by her coloring, but her English was perfect. She was dressed as a man, and her knives were prominent. Her golden eyes made him think of a wolf, and her demeanor spoke of confidence and danger. He learned to not underestimate her, when a drunk man reached out and touched her.

The reaction was instant and bloody. She grabbed the drunken man's arm and planted her knife in an extremely sensitive spot. He doubled over, holding himself, as the blood spread. She did not blink or show any kind of emotion, as she gazed at the innkeeper.

He told her to take the room at the end of hallway and told one of the barmaids to show where it was. He was now pale, and little shaky, as he watched her walk away with no expression on her face. She could have just swatted a bug for all the emotion she showed. She found some water in the room and washed the blood from her hands.

The next morning, breakfast was brought to her in her room. She was already up when the knock came on the door. She answered it, and watched the maid place the tray on the small table. She then asked how much she owed for the room and everything and the maid looked at her.

"No charge, miss. That man you managed yesterday was an old lecher, he was always grabbing us, and touching us. None of us would have had the courage to do what you did. This is our way of thanking you." Elizabeth nodded and told her thank you. The maid smiled and stepped back.

Elizabeth ate the food, and found her horses already hooked

up to the wagon when she came out. The man had gone to a healer, and though he would not die, he would talk soprano from now on. Elizabeth left the city and continued her way.

When she finally reached New York, she gazed at the large city. She would ask around for the family of Taylor and find them soon. She did not know that entering the city would change the course of her life, and the lives of many others.

For as she entered, she noticed a man being beaten, and no one was doing anything. She stopped her wagon and went over. As the one who was beating the man raised his hand, he found it caught in a grip of iron. He turned to looked and blinked.

The one holding his hand was a twelve-year-old girl, with black hair and light brown skin. She gazed at him, her face showing nothing, as she stood there, holding his hand from striking at the other man.

"This is none of your business, girl. My slave was disobedient and needs to be punished." Her golden eyes gazed at him, and she shook her head.

"You have no right to strike a defenseless man. I do not care if he is a slave. You need to be punished for your actions." She released his hand and struck him hard. He went down, and she kicked him, causing him to curl up.

With the man down, she looked over at the slave who had being beaten and spoke firmly.

"You are no longer a slave to this man or anyone. You are free to go as you will." He stood up and gazed at her. She did not understand how this worked, but he was grateful for her help. He took a breath and asked her what she was doing in New York, and she told him that she was looking for someone. A man by the name of Obadiah Yorin.

The slave nodded. He knew where to find Obadiah and told her he would take her to him. Obadiah was a prominent merchant, and his former master had done business with him before. She climbed up onto her wagon, and the slave whose name was Noric, followed her up.

He led her through the streets to the place where Obadiah lived. She gazed at the fine house, and walked up to it, followed by Noric. She knocked on the door and a man in the uniform of a servant answered the door.

She told him she was looking for Obadiah, as she had news of his son Taylor. The servant gazed her for a moment and told her to wait. She nodded and stayed on the stairs. After a few moments, the servant returned and told her to follow him. Noric stayed close to her and gazed around.

He had never been inside the house of a rich man before. All the dealings his former master had had with Obadiah had been at the waterfront. The floor had rich carpets, and perfume fill the air. The paintings were all by masters, and each one was worth a fortune. The furniture was all red maple, and polished until it gleamed.

If she was impressed by the richness, she did not show it. She did not gawk at anything, and she did not even seem to blink. Her face was expressionless. The servant led them up into the top floor, and down a long hallway, to a polished door. He then knocked and opened it.

The furnishings in here were just as luxurious as the ones in the hallway. Two men were in the room, both elderlies, though one was more robust than the other. Obadiah was on the bed, as he was ill. The other man stood by the window. This man was different. she could feel something about him, though she was not quite sure what it was.

Obadiah gazed at her and asked her what news about his son. She gazed at him for a moment and responded.

"Your son has died. A plague of yellow fever came through the area he and his wife were, and they both got sick. They took me in, and helped me, as I was wild when they found me. I am sorry that I bear this type of news, but I was under honor to come and let you know."

Obadiah closed his eyes. He had been afraid of this. He had loved his son and would miss him. As he studied the girl, he felt impressed by her willingness to come all this way to tell him the news. He looked over at the other man in the room and asked him to get his will.

The other man nodded, pulled out a parchment, and handed it to Obadiah. Obadiah looked through it, and then asked the man to cross out Taylor's name and put Elizabeth. She would inherit what Taylor would have.

Taylor would have inherited half of his father's business. Now Elizabeth would. It would include two ships, and a lot of money, and the house she was standing in. Taylor had a sister who would inherit the rest. There was another house, that Taylor's sister would get when her father died, as well as the rest of the company. She would not be happy about Elizabeth, as she knew that in the event of her brother's death, she would get everything. But Elizabeth's arrival disrupted that plan.

The man, who was Obadiah's lawyer, nodded, and made the changes. His name was Merlin, as in The Merlin. He had attached himself to this man because he was able to distribute some of the products of Avalon through Obadiah's company. Now he would work with this girl, whom he knew was Arthur's heir.

He knew who she was the instant she had entered the room. She looked exactly like Guinevere, except her coloring. She was dark, where Guinevere had been pale. But she was just as beautiful. She did not react to the knowledge of her sudden inheritance, other than a slight frown on her face that faded fast.

Obadiah smiled at her and told her that a room would be made ready for her, and he would teach her what he could about business before his death. He wanted her to succeed. She thought about this and nodded. She would use this as a first step toward her own goals.

She talked with him for a while, as Noric went to make sure that the room was made ready. She listened as he told her about the business, and the laws that governed it. She asked questions from time to time, and he answered them.

Merlin watched her, as she learned about the business she

had inherited. She was intelligent, and quick on the uptake. She would make a good merchant. But she was destined for more. She was the last heir of Arthur, King of Avalon.

After a while, as the sun began to go down, Noric came to take her to the room. She followed him and asked why he had stayed after she had told him he was free. He looked over at her and spoke.

"No one has ever cared enough to stop that man from beating me. I feel like I owe you my life, and I will repay you." She studied him and seemed to sigh. She did not want a slave, as she viewed slavery poorly. She did not know why it even existed.

As she stood in the room, alone, she thought about what had occurred. And she wondered about this Merlin, and why he seemed to be familiar even though she had never seen him. Suddenly she looked up, and found Rose sitting on one of chairs, along with two other women.

"I am glad that you made it here with little trouble. We need to talk to you. These two women with me are Quicksilver and Blackbird. We belong to a small group of people that follow the one we call the Ultimate Mother. I told you about her while we walked in the forest. We want you to join us, and help keep the balance of light and dark, of life and death, of good and evil.

We have each faced a choice, and we each chose the harder path. We have become Guardians of the universe. I am Guardian of Destiny, Quicksilver is Guardian of Peace, and Blackbird is Guardian of Magic. We want you to join us and become the Guardian of Justice. Together, the four of us will help keep the balance, and make sure that the universe stays in balance." And then in the center of the room, the rainbow hued being of light appeared, and spoke to Elizabeth alone. The others could not hear what she said.

"You are different from the others, in your suffering and hardships. These have taught you how to be strong and firm. You have faced many trials that no one else has. Now you face the choice of your sisters. Your choice is to have your family back, and grow up with them, leading them for many years, or the harder path, of forsaking what you want most, for the sake of others. You are capable of great things, if you chose to follow the path that all these women have. The choice is yours.

Elizabeth studied her and thought about what she had been told in forest. She never forgot anything, and she looked down. As a leader she could help people and she could use her talents, and abilities to make sure that everyone was treated fairly.

Slowly the girl looked up and gazed at these women. Then she nodded. The past was done, and could not be changed, so she would help build a better future, and help those she could. Elizabeth did not hesitate to take the oath that would bind her forever on the course she had chosen.

Elizebth was still young by the standards of the other guardians. Though the other were all married Elizabeth had yet to meet her destined companion, if she chose to get married at all. She was different from the others and always would be. No matter how old she gets this girl will always sand out.

Now Rose stood up and smiled at her. The circle was complete. All four of the Guardians stood together and would always be joined in the purpose of keeping the balance of the universe and helping those who needed them.

This was just the beginning of their journeys and adventures. United in their cause, the Four Guardians of the universe would traverse the universe and all its dimensions. They would keep the balance and make sure that the universe stayed on the course of its creation, and that all the destinies of all those who lived within the universe would be fulfilled.

ABOUT THE AUTHOR

Rachel Harwood

this author is a single mom with one son, and has wanted to share her stories with the world. these stories are a lifetime in the making and the author hopes that those who read them find the enjoyment in reading that she has had in writing

Made in the USA
Middletown, DE
30 April 2023